# BlueS

TATIANA STRAUSS

Camilla sweet love.
So lovely to know
you. A joy!
Love,
Tatiana
X

*Other Books By The Author*

DogRose

PussyWillow

Copyright © Tatiana Strauss 2021
Tatiana Strauss has asserted her right to be identified as the author
of this work under the Copyright, Design and Patents Act 1988
This book is sold subject to the condition that it shall not,
by way of trade or otherwise, be lent, resold, hired out, or otherwise
circulated without the publisher's prior consent in any
form of binding or cover other than that in which
it is published and without a similar condition,
including this condition, being imposed
on the subsequent purchaser

This book is a work of fiction. Any resemblance to persons, living or dead,
events or locales is entirely coincidental

All rights reserved. No part of this publication may be reproduced,
distributed, or transmitted in any form or by any means, including
photocopying, recording, or other electronic or mechanical methods, or
by any information storage and retrieval system without the prior written
permission of the publisher, except in the case of very brief quotations
embodied in critical reviews and certain other non-commercial uses
permitted by copyright law. Any person who does any unauthorised
act in relation to the publication may be liable to criminal
prosecution and civil claims for damages

Cover photograph by Maria Matheou


Visit www.tatianastrauss.com to find out more about the
author. You will also find news of any author
events and you can sign up for e-newsletters so that
you are always first to hear about new releases

Follow Tatiana on Instagram: tatiana_strauss_author

*Acknowledgments*

My loving appreciation and thanks to Sarah for your eternal friendship, play, belief in my human expression and your limitless love. So many thank yous, Maria, for your love, your contributions, for your constancy, fun and so much more. To Mandi, to GlenRay, to Amelia, thank you for being all that you are in my life. To Katharine, and Nicci too, you who came along later to walk the walk with me. To every friend who cheered and supported me and read me along the way, my heartfelt thank you. Thank you dearly to Barry, who saluted me in everything I am, who was here from the beginning of my path as a writer—and so many more beginnings—you mysteriously took off—god, that hurt—and god, I've grown—but you're always here and your mark is forever in my life and in my work. Thank you to my mama, who was the maker of my own human beginning. To my papa. And my siblings—to Vanessa in particular, for you know why. My thanks to Jean McNeal and Giles Foden for encouraging me in the early days of the novel which was to become this series. To UEA. To John Boyne and Henry Sutton. To Ivan Mulcahy. To Broo Doherty. Thank you to Kosta Ouzas, Tamsyn Bester, Alex and the team at SPH. Thanks to Henry Glover. To Grace Mattingly. To Dani Zargel. A huge thank you for the teachings and inspirations of the Buddha and the many teachers thereof; to Abraham Hicks for inspiring me via your extensive YouTube presence and teachings, also for your book, *Ask and it is Given*; to Eckhart Tolle for *The Power of Now*; to Anita Moorjani for sharing your NDE in interviews about your book, *Dying to be Me*. Thank you to Aaron Abke for your extraordinary gift of articulating a myriad spiritual teachings, and for resonating into my life in the last moments of my final edit of this book. Thank you to all and everyone who inspired me—on purpose or otherwise—who supported me; who led me to grow by shadow or by light; to all those I have loved, still love, and those who loved me or love me still...appreciation lives in me for you all.

BlueSpeedwell

When I run after what I think I want,
my days are a furnace of stress and anxiety;
if I sit in my own place of patience,
what I need flows to me, and without pain.
From this I understand that what I want also wants me,
is looking for me and attracting me.
There is a great secret here
for anyone who can grasp it.

*—Rumi*

*Episode One: Blue Speedwell*

He was waiting for me down on the street, all lounging against his bike, which itself leaned up on its sturdy metal stand, the two at an angle more acute than seemed possible, for sure like the triangle they formed ought to collapse. The hot sun shined his dark shaggy hair a reddish tinge, made an aura around his head—whilst beyond him, all sort of growing out of the light around him, was the square, its central garden and abundant flora crowned by the skyward branches of the vast London plane trees.

His attention was full-on into the paperback resting in his hand, and I felt the pull, my face all burning up in a kind of dumb protest. Those yellowed pages were a part of me; they were mine; they were *my* musty whiff, my ache, my pleasure. *Shhh!* The faded orange spine was all broken, had that floppy way of staying open, and I was trying not to wait for it to fall to bits at any moment. It still blew my head off—though of course it had to be, see—that of all the books he might have chosen from my sagging shelves, this was the one he'd gone for.

I was like a scratch in a record where the needle got stuck, all kept repeating the wish I'd thought to hide it as soon as I'd met him three-four

1

weeks ago, before he had ever come over to mine; should have. But once he'd homed in on it, I didn't want to bring on any weirdness or questions or anything, so I sewed my mouth up, just let him borrow it.

About choking on the lump in my throat, I skipped down the bubbled asphalt steps. I felt their soft thaw underfoot, all like I was in a version of a hideous melting Dali painting—like for sure I must be melting too—this firing up some memory of a painting I'd done of a liquefying girl for an art project at school around the same time I was given that book. Just a bit before it, to be honest. Like it had been some kind of a premonition. The world felt sure-as unstable.

As my shadow crossed his page, he looked up, breaking into a terrific smile. I saw the way his eyes left my face, flicked over my bare brown legs, flew across my body on their way back to meet my own cloudy greys. I got the look of wanton heat he signalled, a shimmer rising up and running right through me, a crazy kind of a blue snow, all glittery bits of indigo, seeming to flurry around in my gut and all about us too, so I felt way dizzy and crushed-as, like a heady perfume was making me beyond drunk.

I came and leaned up against him, pretty much daring the intricate balance of the triangle to break; like I wanted the tangled mess of bike and man and woman out in the open, just sprawled on the road. Broken maybe. He'd flipped my book closed and it lay loose in his left hand, resting beside him on the long padded seat of the bike, his fantastic square-looking thumb crooked between the leaves.

As we kissed, my body went feral, all swelling and feeling to radiate out beyond its confines and into the sunlit air. His free hand scudded across my cheek, took a hold of my neck in a gesture which in that moment made me his; and his alone. I was glad. It simplified things—for a second or so at least.

'How was it?' he asked.

'Ridiculous. I had to be a dot.'

'A dot? What do you mean?'

'I mean they actually asked me to play a dot. A piece of static, like you see on TV when the picture goes.'

He let his fingers slide into my smooth dark hair, all staring at me with those eyes of his. 'Some dot. You think you got it?'

'You never can tell.' I wrinkled my nose. 'I don't know if I want it—pretty humiliating. But I swear I was the best dot possible.'

'What a perfect way to show off your talent,' he said. 'Reductive. Essential core—ha. Idiots. Come on. You ready?'

He unhooked my helmet from the handlebar of his oily black bike, passed it to me, bent and retrieved his own from where it was wedged between his boots. We slipped on our leather jackets, sticky-as from lying across the fibreglass top box like a couple of limp sunbathers the whole time I was in the casting—and I was hit by a kind of sweet gratitude, awed by the awareness of the thick skin they were made of, yielding yet hard, once living organs containing flesh and bones; now inanimate casings containing me and him; also flesh and bones.

He tucked my book inside his jacket, up against his heart so all my gratitude went dirty; I felt bad for him and I wanted to snatch it from him and sling it into the garden. Or lay it next to my own heart maybe. More like.

'You want to put on your jeans?' he asked me. 'You should. It's about forty-five minutes on the motorway.'

I shook my head. I was boiling, could feel the prickle of sweat in my hair where it was pressed against the foam of the helmet—while a fresh clamminess was causing my cotton vest to glue to my back already.

He got astride the bike, thrusting it forward so it flipped off of its stand, which flicked up, folded itself away with a fantastic snap. I stood watching him kick-start the engine. As it roared into life, a celebrated wildness ran through me, and he met my smile all pure, indicating with his head for me to jump up behind him.

My short black skirt stretched its ribbed fibres, its hem clipping the tops of my thighs, him between them. I wrapped my arms around his waist, tucked my face sideways against his back as we took off, and as we circumvented the square and smoothly came out into the flow of traffic on City Road without a pause in pace, I hollered out my delight over the drone of the motor. The sun flickered fast through spaces between the glittering cars, images passing into my retina relentless as fire down a fuel line.

He was well into me being a speed freak and he opened up the throttle, shooting past other vehicles, all weaving in and out of them. We came into our rhythm, playing with the soft sway of the bike, tilting this way then that, and by the time we took the sharp corner into the one-way system, we felt to be of one mind, one body.

Accelerating up the straight, I went flying all inward, backward and—*oh twisted joy!*—I was at one with the other. The streets about disappeared, came overlaid with countryside, and just like that I was in County Cork in Ireland, the threadlike road unspooling dark beneath us as if generated by the black tyres of his yellow dirt bike. Its high pitched whine rung out into the clear air, eating up all sound; I was tickled at how the open-mouthed sheep were made voiceless. Slipping my hand up under his denim jacket, I could feel his heart beating all steady, in contrast to my own rushing like crazy in my ears with the wind. His smell kept whisking into my breath so it seemed I could taste him. I couldn't separate him from the velocity. Each was equally fundamental.

I lay my head into his back, my long layered hair flicking and whipping right to the roots of my helmetless head. Clean out of the heathland rose myriad pointed rocks, some gargantuan, like the gods themselves, all full of approval it felt, with magnificent cloaks of lichen blooming on their great grey backs. He began to slow and then he was stopping and the road turned static, its rough surface and loose chippings coming into focus, no longer a running ribbon.

He twisted his body to look at me. 'I want to show you something,' he said, pale-blue all shining in his face, the black of his huge-as pupils asking me to fall right in. When he showed me a smile my heart bounced way up into my throat.

The dirt bike was still purring, its vibrations running through me, buzzing between my legs, all like he was touching me. I wondered if he wanted to; if he'd ever dare, and I just gazed into him, wishing he would do just that. I didn't care, didn't even think about how he might get into trouble if he did. I didn't think about what trouble I might get into either, it was totally irrelevant.

He turned away, cut the motor. My eyes scudded over the rolling moor, senses tuned into his warmth, his pulsing core energy, so he and the sunshine and the wide-open land felt to be kind of merged...

The greasy black bike drew to a stop at a traffic light, all hemmed in by great gleaming lumps of metal, red and black and blue cars and a screaming white transit van. People began to idle across the road. I watched a little girl hopping along by her mother's side, swinging herself from the tightly held grip on her hand, as he wove us through the vehicles, all using his feet to guide the front wheel onto the white stop-line. He put his hand on my knee, turned, smiling, to catch me in his periphery. Our helmets clashed when I tilted into him to hear what he was saying; faces forced by the law to be at a measured physical distance for our own safety, keeping us all kind of isolated, muffled in our padded orbs.

'I'm thinking we could carry on up to Mum's,' he was shouting. 'What do you reckon? You up for that?'

'What?' I said. 'Pardon?'

'I thought I could take you to meet Mum.'

I mashed a smile into my voice. 'It's a bit soon, isn't it?'

'I'm due a visit—' the lights were changing and he cut himself off '—tell you later,' voice all yelling over the guttural roar of the bike as he cranked the accelerator. I felt the force of our instant speed as we blasted off from the clutch of cars, and I couldn't help shrieking, all otherworldly, like I was at the fair, my body tensing, arms gripping his torso against the pull of motion.

We zigzagged from one road to another, passing Lord's cricket ground, in moments whizzing into Baker Street—there snarled in traffic. I clocked the long line of tourists waiting in a snake to enter the Sherlock Holmes museum, which was the house where Sherlock Holmes was supposed to have lived in the stories.

'What is it with that place?' I hollered.

'People like the line between dreams and reality,' he shouted back. 'That house doesn't exist—but it does, eh?'

I laughed, all so he could hear me, my stomach going tight-as.

Leading me on foot along a steep skinny sheep trail, he took long uneven strides, kind of rocking himself upward off of his thrusting foot. I threw myself into his rhythm, blotto on the feel of him all mimicked in my body. When we reached the top of the hill, the land fell away and I saw there was an impressive view of a valley, at the bottom of which glittered a lake. The pale-purple haze of heather made the whole thing look unreal.

He stood staring out at it and the peace was just hideous—then he looked at me, and I knew he wanted me to say something. But I didn't. I didn't give a flying pig about the view. I looked down at my feet, found them buried among clusters of heather bells, which were never going to ring, however much they tried.

I felt a stupid urge to weep, couldn't stop staring up at him, this mess of feeling all churning inside of me. He slid his gaze away.

'Get that ice cream then, shall we?' he said, all in his cracked-as Irish brogue, voice seeming to enter me and break me open.

'We should've ridden up here. That's what dirt bikes are for, isn't it?'

'I wanted you to feel the peace.'

But I was turning, ignoring the trail, letting the hill take me down itself, faster and faster, so I didn't have a choice. There was a joy to my thumping footfalls bruising the springy tufted grassland and all its glorious flowers.

I dumped myself on the slope above the bike, knees drawn up from my cut-offs, my back to him as he followed me down in a slow-mo kind of a way. I listened to his footsteps closing in on me, got to feel them through the peaty earth, braced my shoulders in the hope he would lay his hands on me.

He for sure avoided me, flung himself onto the dirt bike, all like he must be angry with me. I smirked, eyes hot, said, 'Beautiful view.'

And I just sat there as if I was carefree, the way adults seem to think you're supposed to be when you're fourteen—like they'd forgotten what it was like to be my age. But what I really wanted was for him to see I was older, much older, in my heart and in my mind, than he seemed to think; I wasn't just a kid you could palm off with an ice cream cone. I wanted him to see I was a rapturous beast, with an appetite for a whole lot more than sweets. Because I was sick of kissing boys, sick of their fumbly petting.

I wanted to say something profound, grown up, so I rattled on about

6

the landscape, telling him words I'd read somewhere, how it echoed in my bones and how I was made up of the same stuff, I was all the elements of nature. But as he looked at me, listening in alert interest, I started to feel a bit of a prat. I shut myself up, making out like I was thinking intense-as, while all the while my mind was filled only with him: the image of him; the feel of him. His smell. I ran my fingers through my hair, dropped my hand to my thigh. I noticed he gave me a strange kind of a look.

'"Shall I compare thee to a summer's day?"' I murmured, even more twatish, letting my eyes skim over my legs before threading to his.

He gestured with his head, raising his eyebrows. 'Town?' He patted the seat of the yellow bike. And I got the sense he was nervous then, the thought all springing, maybe…maybe something was going on inside of him too. 'Hop up,' he said.

I stood real slow, showing him my animal nature, all struck myself by the sure lithe sway in the hips and limbs of my body, kind of like it wasn't even mine. My hand went and took a hold of his shoulder, used him as a lever, my leg all arching itself over the end of the yellow bike. I let my fingers graze his back, reach around to clutch at the fur-lined flesh of his belly. And I was settling myself behind him, pulling myself right up against him, all like we were spooned together in bed.

As the black motorbike raced us along the multi-laned Westway flyover, the tall inner-city buildings gave way to the spreading sprawl of what felt like a never-ending London. I began to realise the sting of the cold into my legs, our accelerated speed taking the heat out of the air in a way I maybe hadn't known before. Regret crept in at my not putting on my jeans. I looked over his shoulder and the speedometer showed seventy, way over the forty mile an hour limit. And suddenly it wasn't so fun: the wind whipped into my helmet, tugging at it, all trying to yank it off, the strap biting at my throat. My lips flailed out of control, rubbery-as, stretching and contorting into faces that had nothing to do with me, I swear. I gulped, working to breathe, lungs stoppered by the force of our generated gale—and punishing fingers raced into my eyes, poking under the visor with sharp little fingernails. I wore a half helmet, and it wasn't really mine; it was his spare, and now I really knew about that. It didn't fit me properly.

I pushed my face into the shield of his body, witnessed the cityscape slip by in a watery blur. I felt very far away from it, something in me shrivelling—like the opposite of the Awareness or presence my uncle had always gone on about, taught me to feel—and it was almost a kind of a grief.

When we slowed all abruptly, relief streamed into my muscles, and as we sailed past a yellow speed camera, I realised he knew where they were on the road. In a bit we were pulling up at a red light. I couldn't believe we still had the motorway to come. I felt like turning back for home—but I was never going to tell him. Instead I smiled when he asked was I having fun. As we shot off from the lights I braced myself, gripped him harder, felt the clench in my jaw as a raw kind of a pain. A huge billboard flashed down my visual cortex, for sure telling me to drown myself in Bushmills Irish whisky.

Parking up the skinny dirt bike in town, I told him I didn't want an ice cream and he made a kind of one-breath nod, took me wordlessly into a pub. We found an empty banquette and I sat myself in a splash of sunshine, all relishing the diffuse feel of it coming through the glass. The way it made me squint so I saw the edges of my dark lashes laced in gold. I fingered my hair, stared up at him when he asked me what'll it be.

I bit my lip.

'Shandy?' he suggested.

'I'll have a whisky,' I told him, thinking he'd refuse me.

He didn't blink. 'With ice? Water?'

'Neat. A double.'

I watched him as he ambled to the bar across the loud-patterned carpet. He moved without grace and I liked that. I stared at his bum in his jeans.

'Some crisps,' I yelled out, all laughing.

I called him Swan Neck. It seemed a cruelty because his neck was actually very short and solid—but it was an inverted kind of a compliment I was sure he would pick up on.

I was on holiday—along with my older sister and her dippy frizzy friend—staying with our uncle, see, who ran a super-prestigious racehorse stable for some wealthy French owners. It was a big fancy set-up in that small community in Ireland, was seen as a boon by some, as a blot by many. We were The English.

My uncle used to manage a stable in Suffolk, close to my home, so I had been working with racehorses all my life, had been in on the training and breaking from a young age, discovered a rare and powerful instinctive connection to them. I had been allowed on the training track for several years, at first with the assistance on an outrider on a pony, a kind of big brother to the racehorse, there as a safety measure, but later I was allowed to take the track on my own.

I had hoped to become a jockey, was discouraged. It was dangerous. But I was going to be anyway. And then I had grown too tall.

*He* lived there, with my uncle, in that ugly Seventies bungalow built on kind of stilts, way up high on the mountain above the stables. His bedroom was at the end of the hall, used to be the living room before he came, and we three girls got to watch telly there, sprawled on his striped Indian sheets. His mattress was on the floor. The room, the sheets, smelled of him, all like earth and something unfathomable.

He was a stocky man, his bulk definite, really there, like a rhino or a buffalo maybe—yes, a buffalo, all tightly-curled chest hair too—but with that yielding fleshy belly. His skin was a bit pock-marked, kind of lined, his thick dark stubble rising high on his tanned-as face all blurring into his black curls. Though they liked him well enough, my sister and her friend for sure thought him disgusting, would never imagine my contrary sentiments. They laughed at him, using the Swan Neck nickname I'd coined as if it were an insult.

After the whiskies we went down to the harbour and bought giant portions of chips, put loads of salt and vinegar on them, stuffing the hot floury potatoes into our warm mouths like we hadn't eaten in a week. We stood the whole time, leaning our forearms on a railing, elbows brushing each other. We looked out at the dark undulating water, never at each other, and I knew the energy between us wasn't just my imagination.

White slices of seagulls wheeled above us, their pink legs like rude slits. I took to chucking my chips into the sea, laughing as the birds plunged down, all fighting each other to get at them. I got to feel him looking at me and I took a chip in my fingers, rammed it suddenly into his mouth, met the wet warmth of him, the hard of his teeth. And I ran, screaming, dropping my newspaper bundle, feeling him after me. My heart raced. I felt super-shiny and alive-as. I slowed, let him grab a hold of me—no one had ever caught me at kiss chase unless I let them. He shoved a fistful of chips into my laughing mouth, mashing them into my lips and up my cheek when I refused entry.

He pulled away from me kind of snappish, like he realised what he was doing. But he was still grinning and his breath was coming hard. I saw how he glanced around to see if anyone was watching.

'It's fine,' I said. And I went serious, staring at him all intent. 'Shall we go for a ride? I mean, like, just ride. Go anywhere. Just ride forever maybe.'

He reached out his hand, fingertips resting in the crook of my jaw, brushed the mess off of my face with his thumb. And he swallowed all awkward, like there was something sticky stuck in his throat.

We were streaking down the motorway and I was freezing now. And getting stiff. My bum started to ache. The sun shone brightly as ever, and I knew it was hot, but I couldn't feel it—it was as if heat was an illusion, some distant impossible idea.

Clinging to him with my arms and thighs, my whole body clutched around him, I was wrapping him, wrapping him. The sun seared into the naked soles of my feet, all into my nude breasts. Burned his opiate scent right into me. His mouth did things no boy ever could. I was thrown wide open. Eyes open. Cunt open. Self open. Then a sharp stab of pain. The grass soft and prickly beneath, he hard within me, and he was soft and prickly above. His stubble sheared the skin of my face, his tongue hard and soft, the skin of his body soft. We kind of flip-flopped over, so he lay beneath me and I rose up like his cock into the soft summer air, into the blue shimmering sky, my knees crushing the tiny indigo-blue flowers that abundantly inhabited the grass. Blue speedwell, they were, those flowers; tattooed into my memory with his scent. I saw it all, felt it all—every detail—all like time was slowed down and I looked through a kaleidoscope, everything heightened and multiplied.

I felt wild and natural, as if I'd spent my life making love and fucking, licking and sucking. It was the easiest thing in the world. He made me come, with his thumb this time, as I rode him, and I cried out onto the breeze, giving voice to all the silent heather bells, collapsing into laughter as the sheep got back their baas and answered, sober-as.

And on the greasy black bike, I wondered what in hell I was doing, all cleaving to this him that could only give me a shadow of the first. We were slicing through greenbelt countryside, passing hundreds of trees: old ones and saplings and tiny pathetic sticks in plastic tubes, their few leaves just about spelling life.

At last we reached the slip road to Windsor and the way became smaller and slower and bendy. I began to relax, letting my body get into the slanting rhythms of the bike, phewed-as to be led once more in the dance. I was still cold but the warmth of the sun shone into my left leg when we slowed to take a sharp bend. And the glint of it was warm through my visor. Tall grasses swayed in the verge.

We came to the wide gateway of Windsor Great Park and he slowed down, stopped, turning to me in profile. 'We're not supposed to drive in but I've done it before. Do you want to risk it? I know where I'm going.'

'Sure.'

It was so quiet and still in that moment, just the low hum of the resting engine, I could even hear birdsong, and I kind of wanted to get off right there. Just to feel the still sunshine. I wanted to take the helmet off that wasn't mine anyway.

'Is it far?' I asked.

'Nah. It'll take a few minutes.'

I smiled so my voice showed it. 'I'm starving.'

'I got us a bloody great picnic. Champagne and all. And fancy flutes. In the top box.' He slapped his palm against my knee, cupped it. 'You're icy,' he said.

I shrugged. 'I'm cool.'

We cruised down a wide avenue flanked by perfectly groomed grass run lengthways with five or six even stripes; beyond them, regimented mature trees, three-four deep, that went on as far as the eye could see, all the way to the castle way off in the distance. I kept waiting for the blue flashing lights to come but they didn't, just like he'd said, and pretty soon we veered off across the immaculate green, snuck through the trees, and came to rest in a wide-open vista. He parked the bike among the trunks, threw a red tartan rug out on the sward.

I slipped off my jacket, let it fall away from me, flung myself back onto the warm woollen fibres, crooking one arm up under my head. As I chewed on a long-tasselled grass stem, I stared into the vibrant blue of the sky, thinking about what an out-there colour it was. I thought of the posters I used to have on my wall of the Earth from outer space. We live on a blue planet, I wanted to say. And I thought of David Attenborough nature programmes and all the animals eating each other to survive; the males fighting each other to mate the females, killing each other even.

I felt a little flush of love for David Attenborough, just for his passion and continued wide-eyed awe. I wondered how he could get to be his age and express such innocence—and he wasn't even that old then.

'Don't you think they've got CCTV?' I asked.

'Course. But, I don't know, maybe they look the other way. Maybe there's a biker on watch who thinks this is what the avenues are for. They haven't bothered me before.'

'Done this with other girls, have you?'

He had the bottle of champagne in his hand. It wore a silver cooler round its fat middle, like an over-tight tutu. He peeled off the gold foil top, untwisted the bottom of the wire cage. It was Perrier Jouet, very expensive. I had never tried it but I'd told him it was my favourite, just because my friend had said it was hers. It had white flowers on the bottle, traced in gold. Anemones they were.

I sat up. 'Pass me a glass then.'

The cork popped, rocketing into the air, and I laughed, made a little scream. As the liquid came bubbling out of the spout, I caught the frothy fountain in my long-stemmed glass, held his out for the same.

We clinked and I gave him a crinkly look. 'Doesn't matter,' I said. 'About other girls.' And he leaned in, kissed me in a lingering kind of a way, so I felt myself go wavy, broke off, lobbing myself backwards onto the rug. I licked the champagne splashes off of my hand, balanced my flute on my belly. That sparkling blue of the sky, it could have been anywhere; any time. It could have been in Ireland; it could have been eight years ago. I closed my eyes against it.

Sleeping in that ugly Seventies newbuild, bedclothes directly on the tobacco-brown carpet of the tiniest room, the three of us, we were like a clutch of animals in a nest. All hot sleepy breath and bodies. My sister and her friend had no idea I had beaten them to it and become, I supposed actually, what they liked to call a slag at school. I knew they would be horrified. I didn't think about the thing they might call him. That he could go to prison. It wasn't like it is now.

I heard it first: the door being inched open, all whispering *shhhhh!* against the density of carpet. I turned onto my back, languorous-as, stretched out my legs under the covers, an invitation coming with a spread of joy inside of me. I was already smiling and planning my sneaky exit, readying to slither into my shorts and vest and hare out of there on the yellow dirt bike.

But it was some grey-haired friend of my uncle all peering round the door. I saw how his eyes scanned our teenage heap, now beginning to shift and stir, to yawn. My sister sat herself up on one elbow, face a puffy blear, fingers smoothing her bed-y black bob behind her ears.

He was staring at me, said, 'Ello.' And I got the hideous sense he *knew*.

'Alan?' my sister said.

I felt the wrench within him as he tore his eyes off me to look at her. 'Um…tea?' he asked. 'You want tea in bed?'

'Actually no. No thanks.'

Her friend went to say she did but my sister silenced her with a look.

The man smiled, more of a leer really, as he slid his gaze back to me. I writhed in the blankets, nestled my head into my pillow, pretended I was only semi-conscious.

'You…little se—kitten,' he said to me.

I screwed up my eyes against him, heard the door snap shut.

'What was that?' my sister said. 'Did he call you a—a *sex* kitten? He did, didn't he? That's disgusting. You're only a kid. Filthy bastard.'

He threw himself next to me on the red tartan rug, and I shot up, necked my champagne, all chucking the glass beside me, into the shorn grass. He had his eyes closed. I scanned his features, just for a change looking for signs. His nose was similar, but smaller; his lips fuller. He was actually better looking but I didn't care about that. For me his eyes made him, because they were that exact same pale-blue, all with the big pupils and everything.

He had taken his t-shirt off. I reached out and stroked his slim chest, fingers rippling the fine hairs there. They were sparse and sort of innocent, not like the matted shag I couldn't let go of, and his body was still boyish, even at twenty-four.

He got a hold of my hand, pulled at me. 'Come 'ere, you,' he said.

I dropped into him, nestling my face right into his armpit. I felt myself loosening, all that tension uncoiling. I breathed him in, let the scent of him fill me, so I got to feel myself going all out-of-bodied and elsewhere, expanding into the trees and sky, soaking into the earth beneath me, all filtering into the daisies too. I fell right into his fragrance—which was everything I knew and didn't know and wanted to know. And didn't want to know.

'You smell so good,' I said. 'I think it's my favourite thing about you. I think I'm your body odour junkie.'

He held my head in a tight clutch, made me feel sort of safe. 'Hey,' he said. 'Funny thing. You know that inscription in your book? I just saw it today when you were being a dot.'

My eyes came open, staring into the soft blur of his underarm. 'Hmm?'

'"Swan Neck." "To my little Angel Face." You know it kind of reminds me of my dad's handwriting—from the old postcards he used to send me when I was kid every now and then. Isn't that funny? I wonder where the old bastard is.'

'Yeh,' I said. 'I-I wonder…'

'Where did you get that book?'

'Some car boot sale I think.'

'So you weren't Angel Face? Doesn't it make you want to know who they were, though? "I'll always love you. Your blood runs in my veins." This long-necked man with a beautiful girl? It would be a good name for you: Angel Face.'

'Don't know about that,' I said.

14

And I saw the flecks of my blood, glistening all beautiful red against the green of the grass and the searing blue flowers of the speedwell.

*Episode Two: Cow Parsley*

Great hulks of pulley-type junk, all blobby yellows and blues, came riding high on the bow of the ship, sheeny-as and showing off—for sure giving me the Vs. They were like dumb outsized toys, like those fancy Lego pieces you get to add reality to your brick-made rockets and shit. I wished I could smash them to bits, kick them off the deck, couldn't stand they were nicking my right to be wedged at the water-slicing prow. Not that I wanted to be one of those figurehead girls, nothing stupid like that. I just wanted to be lost in the atmosphere, to be absorbed into the elements of wind and sea. I wanted to be outside of myself, see. And bigger. Bigger than my life and all the messed-up stuff of it. To get away from being told what to do and where to go and who I could be with.

And I realised right then all that rubbish I'd rabbited at him, about being made up of the same atoms as nature and everything, that day on the moor, it was true. A pang darted me down a metal walkway, a million nipples of non-grip grippy-bumps digging into my white plimsolls, making me slip all over the place. I leaned over the guardrail. Everything was freezing to the touch. On tiptoe, I extended my vision across the dark curve of the hull, relieved to meet my need to be forging into open water.

We rose up and plunged down. A fine drizzle came at me, smacking at my face in irregular rhythms. I let it soak into my every pore, right through my vest and my cut-offs, all puddling in my canvas shoes; felt myself gasping at the sting and the cold, pushed myself further into it, hair sticking to my face and throat, plastered to my scalp. I peered down, right into the frothing surging sea, saw a wide arc of white droplets rise up, come crashing into me with a rushing sound. Breaking and coming together again. The way I was having to do. I just about followed my urge to jump when—*whaaa!*—a poke made my heart go frog-hopping out of my chest, body all swivelling.

I found my sister, face crunched, full-on eyeballing me. Mental laughter leaped out of me, short and shrill. And then I fell hellish serious, staring at her through a salt-blear. I couldn't make out what she was saying. But it was clear she resented the pummelling cold and having to come and find me and I realised she was insisting I come inside. I just stood there.

And then she was shouting, going all pointy and reddening. I nodded quick-as, and when she got a hold of my arm, I didn't resist, just let her tug me along the dicey deck. We stepped over the sheet metal of the raised doorway, passed through the rubber-edged hole. The oval door was held open by a large rust-laced clip, so beautiful it hurt, its peeling paint covered in a patina of moisture. I wanted to be that clip.

'What the hell's the matter with you?' my sister was saying, as the air went still around us. 'You're such a brat sometimes. Just because you're going home early. You had a good time, didn't you? Can't that be enough?'

I gaped down at the blue-and-red swirly carpet, felt myself leeching into it as we trudged up the stairs to the upper deck and into the canteen.

'You should be glad to get away from all that weird talk.'

Her dinky-nosed frizzy friend was waiting at a table, all minding our bags. 'What were you doing?' she said. 'You look like a drowned rat.'

'Original,' I said.

'She was hanging over the side of the ship,' my sister told her. And to me, she said, 'Idiot.' But she gave me a smile that showed she cared, her eyes going soft. 'Didn't want to leave the horses, huh?' She was unzipping her purple nylon sausage bag, extracting a grubby pink towel. 'Here,' she said, passing it to me. 'Dry your hair for a start. Why didn't you wear your coat?' She turned to her friend, said, so I could hear, 'She always does things for attention. Likes danger, huh? Don't you? Idiot?' I tipped my head over, rubbed at my hair and scalp. 'Don't you?' she said again, sort of snorting.

I wheeled round with the stinky towel draping me, hands reaching out like monster claws, made some kind of guttural groan. I glimpsed her browned knees sticking out of her flowery skirt and I lurched into her. She shrieked. Her friend burst out laughing and then we were all laughing and it was nice.

'I got you a cake,' my sister said, sliding herself along the black vinyl banquette. I slipped in beside her, my skin dragging on the plastic. 'A Chelsea bun. Your favourite.' She passed it to me on a scratched-up industrial plate. 'Here,' she said, delivering a squat cup and saucer which chattered with the spoon, all splashing as I took it and put it in front of me.

'Oh,' I said, of the milky brew.

'What?'

I thought better of it, smiled. 'Nothing. Thank you.' I had just last week given up milk in my tea, and I supposed she'd forgotten. I knew my sister was looking after me, had been told to keep an eye. I took up the soft spool of dough, stared at its sticky bronze-glazed coat. I picked at a current, chewed on it, began to peel off the outer coil.

Gazing through the ancient window glass of the village café, all lost in the tufted green quilt slung over the Irish land, I was rushed with lush blue memories. It made me want to be out there really badly—it sort of stabbed me I couldn't—and I shifted my focus to the warm and hard of the mug of black tea clutched between my hands, there greeted by my distorted reflection. My neck went light-as—and I knew he was coming back with our second helping of spun buns. I let myself gaze up, watch him, smiled without showing my teeth, made like I was easy inside as I ate up all his burly maleness.

18

When he handed me my Chelsea bun, I brushed his fingers, the energy of his touch travelling all the way down to the place between my legs. I let him see the spark in my eye.

'Shhh,' he said.

'What?' I saw he looked kind of nervous and the smile I gave him was a play on innocence.

'You're too much,' he told me in a whisper. 'But for sure, what an angel face.' As he sat down, he flicked his sights over the room, the people. 'Now stop it.'

'Stop what?' I said, and laughed, cupping my chin as I leaned my elbow onto the red Formica tabletop. I watched his large square hands, loving the wiry black hairs that sprang from the first phalange of each finger. I liked that word. Phalange. It could be anything, I thought. Phalange. Phalange. Phalange. It could be rude. It could be a water bird. A wildflower. It was a kind of poetry, like us.

He took up his bun and tore off a strip. How I wished for his hands to be on me. I felt him lying below me, my knees all crushing blue petals into death, his nails tearing into the flesh of me. He put the piece of dough into his mouth and I imagined putting my tongue there, in his mouth, and my lips.

'I want to go,' I said.

'I know. Eat your bun.'

'Can't we take them away, our tea and cakes?'

He indicated the landscape through the wavy old glass with his head. 'Still raining.'

There was an elastic band in my pocket, I was absently fiddling with it, and I drew it out, strained the flesh-coloured fibre between my forefingers, aiming it at him. He watched me. I flicked it. It hit him in the face. He didn't flinch.

'You're such a kid,' I told him.

He shrugged, picked up the elastic band, caught an edge of it in his mouth, under an eyetooth, kept pinging it against his lip. My sights grazed his furrowed brow, refused his pale-as blue eyes. He put the rubber band in his pocket, took a sip of my black tea; black like his, but mine; he took a sip.

19

'Hey,' he murmured, leaning forward. 'You…you know what you are, is—don't you know? You're everything. And when I'm with you—I don't know—I feel like I'm everything too—I mean really *everything*. A part of it all.'

I could smell him. I could taste him. And I flinched.

The ferry lurched, all like it was hit by a huge wave at a bad angle. My tea slopped over the side of my cup, spilled over the saucer and onto my bare leg. It was tepid and rather pleasant, like warm fingers. I was eating the bun right up to my mouth, nuzzling at its entrails in one continuous consummation.

'You're disgusting,' my sister said. 'Anyone would think you were five, eating like that.'

I grinned, still with the bun in my face. I said, 'No one thinks I'm five.'

'You know what I mean.'

'I don't actually.'

'I think you were put on this earth especially to get on my nerves, that's what.'

'No, to teach you,' I told her, as I stuffed in the last bit of bun. I tried not to think of his fingers mashing chips into my mouth down on the quay that first day.

My sister gasped, all theatrical, and was laughing and saying something about how it was her job to teach me, older is wiser, experience is knowledge, something like that. I wondered what she would think if she realised just how experienced I was. I wondered if she would hate me for lying to her. And for getting there before she did.

And then I swear I smelled him, like he was right there. My head was swivelling, all manic. I thought I heard the scream of a seagull, eyes darting back to the spray-spattered windows and—*oh no!*—the chips were making a show of themselves—in my mouth, in the water—gulls diving in and fighting each other for them.

'Was that a gull?' I said.

'Not a *sea*gull!' the friend squawked.

My sister lost it, and her friend too, the two of them wrapping their arms around themselves, clutching their sides. Some kind of groundswell surged through me, all twisted and hurting. I wanted to howl, tears just came spilling right out of me, so I aped their laughter, bent over double, held myself, made out like it was funny.

Waiting in the tiny furnitureless room I shared with the girls on that holiday, I watched him dismount his yellow dirt bike, propping it on its stand next to my uncle's battered blue Land Rover. My feet were buried in our boiling sea of bedless bedding; the softness of a brushed-cotton sheet, a muck-yellow bobbly thing, all fingering one shin, the prickle of a woollen blanket up against the other. The room had a sweet-sour smell of youth. Of neglect maybe. And some kind of ecstasy, all those endorphins.

There were some dying wildflowers in a vase on the window sill, their tail-like tassels shedding bright pink seeds like some sort of hundreds and thousands you sprinkled on a cake. I realised the plants had drunk up all their water.

He rubbed at his thick stubble, unaware of me. I thought he was like a cowboy, his black curls swept back in a tangle from riding without a helmet. At that distance, you couldn't see his hair was finely threaded with shining silver, but he looked kind of silvery all the same.

I made like I just happened to be there, like it was chance I was opening the window to air out the room, but really I'd been looking out for him to get back from the stables. Us girls had been hanging about in his bedroom and I knew he would seek us out and take us all down to the harbour, but I wanted him to myself, so I'd left my sister and her friend lounging on his mattress, all soft skin against his rough Indian hippy bedspread. They were watching a film on video.

'Hello,' I called, waving.

He turned his head at the sound of my voice, changed direction. I leaned my crossed arms onto the window's edge, elbows jutting out into the balmy air, rested my chin on them, liking the feel of my hair all tumbling into my eyes.

'Long time no see, lass,' he called, crunching over on the gravel. 'How are you?'

'I wanted to help out with training today but I couldn't get a lift down. Do you fancy going back? Can I get up on one of the horses?' I felt like we were performing for the outside world, although I really had wanted to train too. He was the best trainer, my uncle's number one. He was at my window but keeping his distance. 'Can I?' I said. 'I mean, really, I'd like to race down at the practice strip. Maybe on Clean Slate?' Truth was, since he and I had crossed over into the light-side dark-side, I hadn't got up on a horse more than once. I wondered if I was growing out of it, like most girls did. But I knew I wasn't—it had only been a week and it for sure felt an age.

He did that squinty sidelong thing as he checked around the place, all crushed eyelashes and glinty blue. He inclined his body toward me, whispered, 'I've been thinking about you all day. What happened this morning? Why didn't you get up and come down with me?'

I blinked, didn't answer.

'You want to go horse-riding?' he asked. 'Or bike-riding? Angel Face?'

'Both,' I said. 'And…' I made a bawdy kind of a face. 'You-riding. How about that?'

He stepped away, raising his arm, just about yelled, 'I'll see you in fifteen minutes then,' and continued on to the office at the side of the house, me watching that graceless gait of his thickset body I liked so much; all that bulk pressing against his dark blue jeans and old suede waistcoat, just a black t-shirt underneath. The fleece on his arms caught the evening sun, looked all blurry and golden.

A veil of sunlight reflected off the sea, suffusing the upper deck of the ferry in a dream. My sister was a faded photocopy as she went off to get us a second round of tea and some chocolate bars—my uncle had given her a glut of spending money for the journey. She did her best not to stagger as she wove between the tables up to the counter, got in a queue behind a couple of old people and a woman with a drifting toddler.

'Pity we had to leave early, hey?' her friend said to me. 'I didn't quite get it, what the problem was with us being there? Just because the owner was suddenly coming from France.'

'I know,' I said. 'I don't see they'd have minded us.'

'Surely it's up to your uncle who stays at the house?'

'Hmm…' I said. 'I suppose he didn't want to be distracted with

22

looking after us.'

'We pretty much looked after ourselves anyway,' she said.

'I know. Really annoying, isn't it?' I looked down at my fingers. They were kind of knotted together, grippy-as. 'I think he wanted to be…what's it? You know, professional. You know, look responsible only to the stables and the racehorses and training and that. I suppose we can't really blame him.'

'Yeah…'

We zoned out into silence and I tried not to feel sick staring at the sparkling infinity of the sea. The horizon looked like it was swaying up and down; but it wasn't the horizon that made me nauseous.

Hanging out washing in the back garden, I was up to my knees in wild grasses, the busting scent of nature all wrapping me in rapture. A red admiral butterfly landed on a peg and I was speaking to it in a friendly kind of a way when the thud of fast footsteps came up behind me. I felt the thrill, braced myself—but it was my sister who rolled up close into my back, breath hot, voice a hiss.

'I have to talk to you.'

I turned. Her eyes were wild, she looked frightened.

'What's happened?' I said, nerves spiralling up from my gut. She shook her head. I could see it was hard for her to swallow. 'Is it Mum? No? What—is it Dad? You're scaring me.'

'Come on,' she said. 'Not here. Let's go for a walk.'

I saw she looked kind of furious too, indignant. 'What's wrong?' I said. 'What is it? Just tell me.'

She grabbed my hand and we left the bungalow by the driveway, sort of scuttling into the narrow country lane. The fragrance of cow parsley teased me, rich and musky, from the hedgerow, whilst she pulled me up the road a few hundred yards to where there was a wooden gate leading onto a field. She made me climb the gate and tugged me along inside the hazel hedge, as if we were on some crazy great escape mission. She yanked me down into a squat, shushed me when I went to say something. '*Listen*. I was in the house. Coming out of our room—and I heard them—I could *see* them, right, in the kitchen, the blurry shapes of them—all distorted through that mottled glass-stuff along the corridor, see—everything all fracturing, the colours of them broken and merging, all li-like a *horror film*—that horror—and I could see they were sitting at the table, two of them, and that *hor—*' her voice went all scratchy like a dirty needle on black vinyl. She tried to swallow, coughed '—that *horrible* Alan, it was, and some other old guy from the yard, that baldy one, his head all—*ugh*—through the glass and I *heard* them. They were saying—saying *stuff*—about *you*.'

'Stuff? About me? How—what do you mean, stuff?'

'I can hardly—they were saying stuff—*disgusting* stuff, I tell you—that you… you…oh god, they sai—they said you were *fucking—him*—our frie—you were fucking—'

'—wha—'

'—*fucking*—Swan Neck and—'

'—*what*?' I said. 'You what?'

Wet trails shone on her cheeks. 'Listen, there was other stuff too, but I can hardly remember, I couldn't—I just couldn't take it in, I was so *fucking* shocked. It was all I could hear: *fucking*.' She pressed her lips hard with the flat of her fingers. 'This is really messed up, it's twisted. I-I—*why* does this always happen to you—I don't understand, why would they say such a thing about you?'

I stared at her, my heart so loud she was a whisper. I shook my head.

'They said—*Alan*, he said—yes, that's it, something about you weren't a virgin and the other one was saying something about you—you being, I don't know, a-a precocious little—a sexy—and that Swan Neck wa—I mean, they didn't call him Swan Ne—they said you were—he was—they said *fucking*. You.'

'That's insane,' I muttered, my eyes all blurring up. 'Insane.'

'You're young,' she said. 'How could they think that? How could they even use those words about you—*at all*? I was stood there, and my heart went mental so I couldn't hardly think. It went so loud. I didn't know what to do. I wanted to go in there and—and *shout* at them but I-I couldn't—I couldn't…'

I looked at the ground and couldn't stop my blood beating too fast, all like it was echoing her. Every blade of grass was trembling. But I wouldn't let myself burst. I shot up, began pacing, gesturing at the sky

24

and the hills. 'Why would they say that? Who would ever make up such a thing about me? And *him*? I mean, why would they—?'

'—I don't know, but I really want to *fucking* scream at them. It's so disgusting. You're my little sister, for crying out loud. They're using you to—what?—letch at?—and be just *dis*gusting.'

'Hey but—hey but maybe—maybe it wasn't *me* they were talking about.'

Her head wobbled. 'They said your name, I heard your name.'

'It's some fantasy they're—hey, maybe someone else has got my name?' She shook her head, eyes hollow. 'But maybe they're jealous of him and trying to find a way to get rid of him—to discredit him. Because he's the best trainer. You think? What do you think?'

'Using you as a—'

'—*yeah*.'

'This is serious.' She reached out and grabbed my shoulders, hooked my eyes to hers. I could feel her shaking. 'The way Alan looked at you yesterday when he came in and we were all in bed. He's sick. Do you remember? Pretending to offer us tea? He called you a sex kitten, right out loud.'

'He did?'

'And he looked at you like he wanted—I thought he was disgusting then. Don't you remember? I mean, how *old* is that guy?'

'Oh god,' I rasped. '*What* is going on? What am I going to—what are we going to do?' I was so hot and pounding, the thought she might see the truth, like somehow I might be transparent, all coming in little explosions in my brain. I couldn't stand for her to look at me, threw myself into her hug, my head shuffling the same thoughts around and around like a nightmare deck of cards: what had he said? was he a liar? had he betrayed me, used me, showed off about me to these other men? who *was* he?

'It's okay, it's okay,' she kept saying, all stroking my hair. 'We'll sort it out. Somehow. We'll sort it out.'

'But I *am* a virgin. I am.'

'Of course. I know. I know.'

And then I couldn't stop it anymore and the tears came hot and wet, with all that mess of snot you never knew you had inside of you until it spilled out. I worried my sister would think I was over-reacting but she was snivelling hard too and we held onto each other.

She told me she wanted to talk to our uncle about it but I begged her not to. It was too horrible I said. And she agreed. As long as none of them tried anything. If any of them approached me I was to make a fuss, a really big fuss, and we would get them sacked and thrown off the place.

That night, when we were bundled on the brown carpet of our bed in the dappled half-light, she said to me, right in front of her friend too, 'I've been thinking, you know. About why they may have said that.'

'Oh?'

'I don't think you realise, but the way you behave with…you flirt. I know you're only playing, but… And I think actually he kind of flirts back too. Maybe that's what's given them some impression.'

'I don't really get what you're saying,' I said.

'It's a kind of energy. That you give out. Sexual. You've always done it. Look what happened at school last year? Why did everyone actually believe you'd *done it* with that Robin Remick git, huh? Everyone belie—'

'—energy I give out?' I produced a laugh. 'Sexual? That's horrible.'

'Unconscious,' she said. 'Just sort of natural, I suppose. You even had it as a little kid. It was kind of okay when you were little but now—well, it looks like you're asking for it. You know, you are quite developed—I mean physically. You don't seem to realise.'

'Developed?'

'You look older than you are. Older than me maybe. You have quite an effect. Men find you attractive. I've seen it. Lots of times.'

'But—what?—you think he does it too?' I asked.

'Kind of. I think so. It's making me kind of pissed off with him. I think he likes it. *Men* like it. People respond to flirting. And they forget how young you are, I suppose. I think those lechers have gone and made assumptions. I'm not saying that's okay, but I'm saying you might have to think about how you behave.'

'But you don't think he's, like lied, telling them we did it, do you?' I wiped my nose, all furtive, with the edge of the yellow sheet.

She touched my arm. 'Are you crying?'

'No.'

'I don't think he's that kind of man,' she said. 'It's them, not him. He's still our friend. But I think maybe we should talk to him about it.'

My voice was a thread. 'No. Please. Let's not.'

I clung to the sodden handrail, all tilting into the furious sea, my eyes stinging with salt and wretched tears, stomach retching, retching with nothing more to give. The boat would not stop rocking, just kept right on bashing into the waves, smashing them up into foam. And my hair whipped into my cheeks and mouth, punishing me, cat-o-nine-tails—at least nine tails; maybe ten tails, eleven, twenty.

Those foxtail flowers dying on my windowsill in Ireland, he had picked them for me, given them to me in a red tumbly bunch, blooms dripping over his hands, then mine, as I took them.

'Love-lies-bleeding,' he had said.

'What?'

'That's what they're called. Love-lies-bleeding. I'm giving you my bleeding love after you gave me yours. It's mutual.' He eyed me, colour coming high in his cheeks. 'We bleed for each other.'

The flowers were kind of scentless. I wished he'd given me cow parsley. I dropped my hand, held the plants limply at my side. 'We do. I'll put them in a jar.'

The ferry dived and flew through the waves. I was all-through soaked again but my stomach had stopped its spewing. I stood staring into the strange light, at the gossamer web of cloud that hinted at blue, and the forever glinting sea.

I turned to go back in. A tall foppy man was stepping from the door and I watched as he slipped, saving himself just in time, by way of that neglected door-lock. I felt the raw coldness of that handle, the crisp crunch of the peeling paint giving way all as if the hard lace of it was under my own palm. I felt the sheath of my body yield with his, his long form seeming to stretch and blow for a long moment, like washing in the wind. As he righted himself on his plush black shoes, he looked down, saw the vomit he'd skidded on.

He caught my eye, smiled in an angry kind of a way, said, 'Some people.'

The flush of acid felt like fluorescent moss in my mouth, like a neon sign, saying, this one, this one. I thought he was going to yell at me. Make me clear it up maybe.

'Some people,' he repeated.

I made my face at once empathetic and disapproving. 'Yes,' I said. 'Some people, huh?'

And I saw how he felt met for a second, understood. He just saw me as a sweet young girl who cared he had slipped in sick. I was so relieved, I felt instantly a whole lot better.

'Careful as you go in,' he told me.

'Thank you.' I made a thing of grimacing, stepping around my own puke.

Mucking out the stables, I was sifting through the straw, forking the dirty strands and horse dung into a large rusting barrow. The pungent smell was so familiar I liked it; it made me feel safe in the simplest way. And the action, the fluid ease in my muscles, was a kind of soother. I was whistling tunelessly, pretending to be a bird, bright and clear, when my uncle appeared at the door. I expected him to give me some instruction or something but he just stood there, staring at me. And the look on his face told me he had come about the talk my sister had heard the day before.

A sunburn of heat hit my cheeks. I stepped toward the wheelbarrow, let the muck slide off the fork and thump onto the growing heap within. I watched the way it broke up, bits taking themselves down the hillock in a mini landslide. I watched the way they crashed and settled. My uncle cleared his throat, made me look at him. He gave a stark jerk of his head, turned, walked across the yard in the direction of his sky-blue Land Rover.

I rested the fork handle against the wall, adjusted the waistband of my jodhpurs, everything too clear and detailed: the bumpy mottled surface of the wall; the soft swish of my black riding boots in the straw; even the memory of my recent ride came thrumming through my body. I wiped the prickle of sweat from my brow, ambled after my uncle, watched him getting into the vehicle, all slamming the door.

I came round to the passenger side. The leather creaked as I settled myself. My heart was trembling. I stared at my hands, examining the unique whorls of my fingerprints.

'I don't know what to say to you,' my uncle said, after a never-ending silence in which birds sang so sweetly.

He started the engine, twisting his body my direction, craned to look behind us. He reversed in a speedy arc before jolting to a stop, scraping the gears into first, then accelerated fast out the driveway. Without a seatbelt, my body was thrown forwards, hands pushing against the muddy dashboard, then backwards into the seat, me all clinging to it. I felt in the movements the force of his anger.

'Where are we going?'

'Your mother's going to kill me,' he said, almost under his breath.

I watched the bendy lane coming at us too fast.

'I'm sending you home.'

'What?' I said. 'No.'

'We're going to the house and you're going to pick up your bags and I'm taking you all into Cork immediately, to catch the twelve o'clock ferry. The girls already know and they're getting ready. They're packing your bag, I told them to.'

'Oh, but…I don't wa—'

'—you're *going*. No argument. No negotiation.'

'But I want to stay here. Please. Can't I just live here, with you and—and work with the horses?'

'You're a schoolgirl.'

We sped around a tight corner, the side of the Land Rover scraping against the hedgerow. Brambles lurched in and out of my open window scratching the bare skin of my shoulder. I didn't make a sound despite the lash of pain.

I wanted to ask him about *him,* about what was going to happen, but I knew it best to keep my mouth shut. I didn't know how much my uncle knew. I felt panic mounting as I began to realise I may not see him before I left. I wondered how I could work it, where I could find him. I was ready to run the moment we arrived at the bungalow.

'Don't expect to see that filthy bastard ever again,' he said, as if answering my thoughts. 'I've told him to get the fuck out of here and get the fuck out of Ireland. And he won't be coming to England either. You understand?'

We hit a straight bit of road and he slowed, took a sidelong look at me, but I couldn't even nod.

'Haven't you got anything to say?'

All I wanted was to beg him to let me stay. And let me be with *him*. I saw everything falling away from me, like the muck off the fork. I found myself saying, 'Don't—please don't tell Mum.'

He made a kind of nod. I think. I don't quite know what he did or what he meant. I didn't even know if I cared that much if my mum found out. I wanted to stay; to be with *him*. That was all I cared about.

'Please,' I said, kind of filling space.

I wondered what sort of reception I was going to get from my sister and her friend. I wondered if they knew. And that, I did care about. Would he have told them? I didn't dare ask. I didn't want to have to say it, what I'd done or anything. So I said a whole lot of nothing. I knew I would find out soon enough.

'Before you get any ideas,' he said. 'He's not at the house. He's gone already.'

'What—what do you mean "gone"?'

'I mean gone. He's left.'

'But he can't have.'

'What, you mean he can't have left without saying goodbye? Well he has, because I was going to kill him if he didn't.'

We were pulling into the gravel forecourt of the bungalow. I saw my sister's face peering out of our bedroom window. She smiled. She waved. She didn't know.

As I put my hand on the door handle, my uncle grabbed a hold of my near arm. He made me look at him. 'So no running off, you hear? You won't find him. I'm serious.'

I looked down.

'If you try anything stupid,' he said. And he sighed. I saw he was very upset. 'Just don't. I don't want any more trouble.'

My chest felt tight. I nodded. 'Okay. Neither do I.'

'That's rich.' He let go of me and I felt my body as a heavy weight and I let go of myself, slumping back into the seat. He sat regarding me for a while, I could feel it, then sighed again, muttered, 'I'm sorry. This is a terrible situation. It should never have happened. I'm a fool.'

I looked at him. I saw he wasn't blaming me. And I suddenly felt like crying.

'You know I love you,' he said. 'But I can't be responsible for you. Now go and grab your stuff and tell the girls we've got to get going. We'll grab some snacks on the way.'

That morning I had stolen out of the room at five o'clock, quiet as a cockroach, in my green nylon nightie, a horrid thing my mother had bought me the day before we left. My sister had a pink version, exactly the same, and she was wearing it too, next to me in bed. I preferred my big t-shirt to sleep in but it had rained and, what with all the stress, I'd forgotten to save my washing from the line. I snatched up yesterday's vest and my cut-offs and crept down the hallway barefoot to his room.

I had never done this before, it was too risky, but I slipped in, found him lying asleep in the curtained light, with his striped sheets and bedspread thrown half-off his shaggy body. I stood gazing down at him, the smell of him whispering into me, causing me to feel I was bigger than myself, as if I was expanding into the air, all out of control. That pack of cards shuffled inside my head, threw up the same questions. Does love lie? I wondered to myself. I thought about how I could stab him in his sleep and he'd wake up bleeding, like he told me he did. Bleed for me. Blood pouring over his hand, like those flowers he gave me.

I saw he was hard under the covers. And I felt so much love and need for him, all the way into the pulse between my legs. I was peeling off my nightie over my head, and I was naked and crouching against the mattress on the floor. I reached one arm over him, and then a leg, so my body was poised above him, knees into the lumpy mattress, then gently lowered myself into his deep sleep warmth, his furry chest greeting my boobs, soft and prickly at once. He woke with a start and I giggled in a whisper, covered his mouth with my hand. He rolled me off of him, shot up into sitting, rasped, 'What are you doing? Are you mad?'

'Yes,' I said. 'I'm mad. About you.'

His back propped against the scuffed wall, he rubbed at his stubble, blinked hard. 'We can't do this here.'

'Why?' I said. 'In case they all find out?'

He nodded, just once, sharp.

I gazed up at him. 'They already know.'

'What? Who knows? What are you talking about?'

I shrugged, reaching for his leg. 'No one, I guess.'

'What the fuck are you saying? You haven't told your sister?'

'Of course not.'

'I told you, this is not to be talked about, right?'

I smiled. 'Right.'

He shook his head. 'You're dangerous, you know that, Angel Face? Definitely a devil. I don't know what to do with you.'

I bit his thigh. 'I do.'

'Be quiet,' he said. And he was grabbing me, lifting me by my shoulders, pulling me up and onto him, kissing me, hands in my hair.

After all the vomiting right outside the porthole door, right on the deck, before I made it to throw up some more over the side of the hull, afterwards I was starving. And my sister bought us chips. I ate them, smothered in salt and vinegar. Without talking. Thinking of him.

'Are you alright?' my sister asked.

'You look better,' said her friend.

I nodded, smiled. I thought about how I'd pressed my fingers into his skin, leaving invisible impressions; my trace. And how I had padded all nude around his room, before we rode down to the stables on his yellow dirt bike, no one the wiser to our activities in his bed, and touched everything there was to touch with splayed fingertips. The walls, the chest-of-drawers, his keys, his wallet. The TV, the video, everything.

'I. Was. Here,' I kept whispering. I came and touched my fingers to his face, to his mouth, to his cock. He put his pointing fingertip against my heart, slid it down my body, let it rest at the exact point my flesh first parted its petals, where it was almost innocent. He told me he loved me.

Staring out the window as we tore down the motorway I tried my hardest to be a part of the blurry fly-by landscape. I tried to join with the hurtling trees, with the wild tumbles of cow parsley, the dashing ox-eye daisies, then just with all the rushing green, but I somehow didn't seem to be able to enter it, any of it, or feel it within me. I just seemed to be a human body stuck in itself, crammed in the back with my sister and her friend, my boxer dog all panting and stinky at my feet. In the fast lane, we raced past cars and lorries, their colours all flashing, and it felt like they were trying to get inside of me, big lumps of speeding metal hijacking the space I was making for the flora, all strangling me with the wrong kind of energy. I sucked in air, craned my neck to watch the pink-smudged blue, like maybe the sky would take me into its fold, like, please sky, take me into you, make me big again, let me break up in your atoms, no divide, and take me, take me back to him.

I strained to capture the last blinking beats of low-slung sun in my wet lashes as it broke through trees and vehicles. It came and went, shining, not shining, shining, gone, all so fast, glittering up my tears then not, as I tried to be back in the pub and all its loud ugly carpet, drinking peaty double whiskies with him in diffuse sunshine.

Every moment, each turn of the humming wheels beneath me, was taking me further away from him. I didn't even know where he was any more. I couldn't believe I would never see him again. I felt my dog sit up, swaying against my shins in the rattling car as she licked at my knees, the sound of her tongue rhythmic, thick, the heat of it humid. I let my hands find her smooth head, her nose all tipping up, wet against my palms, her tongue lacing itself through my open fingers. I tore my eyes from the sky that didn't want me anyway and met those of my dog, muttering little sweetnesses to her. She whimpered, trembling, and tried to climb up on the seat, her nails scratching in the nylon.

'Birdie, get off,' my sister said, pushing her down. She jabbed her elbow into my ribs. 'You know she's not allowed.'

I gave it back to her. 'Get off.'

'Ow! That really hurt.'

She went to slap me but I caught a hold of her wrist, and then the other too, as it flew up. We grappled, the dog barking, my mum yelling, all twisting in her seat, while my dad hunched over the steering wheel and ol' frizz-head cowered against the passenger door. My mother had to yank herself onto her knees so she was going backwards and put her oar in between us to make us shut up.

'Terry,' she shrieked. 'Slow down. Get in the slow lane, you'll get us all killed.'

'Why did you have to bring Birdie anyway?' my sister whined, as my dad, slowing, slid the car into the middle lane.

'I couldn't leave her with Stuart yet, could I? He may not be responsible enough.'

'Who's Stuart?'

My mum puffed out a breath. 'I mean, it was too long to leave her on her own and Steph next door wasn't going to be in.'

'But who's Stuart?'

Our mother turned away, throwing her body hard into her seat. My sister and I looked at each other, all in accord.

Screwing up her face, she whispered, 'Oh no.'

'Who? Is? Stuart?' I said.

'Just give us some peace, girls. We'll talk about Stuart later. I'm feeling sick after you made me face the wrong way with all your nonsense.'

'Is that why you're annoyed we're home early?' my sister asked. 'Because Stuart, whoever he is, the idiot, is staying? I don't get why you came to meet us if you're so damned concerned about Stuart.'

'Watch your mouth.'

'He's one of your special needs kids, isn't he?'

'He's not special needs.'

'Whatever. Some saddo boy in your care at work, right? That you brought home.'

'You're not fostering him?' I asked. 'Who's room is he in? Mine, I bet.'

'Yes, he's in your room.'

I threw my eyes up to the sagging grey fabric of the car ceiling. 'Oh, great. Is that why you got us those extra weeks off school then? So you could adopt Stuart with us out of the way? Telling the headmaster that tall story about your mother like that. I thought you did it for us, so we could stay in Ireland for a longer time.'

My mum turned, her face red and closed. 'Right. Enough.'

'I think Birdie needs the toilet,' I said.

'Well, she'll have to wait.'

I closed my eyes, trying not to think of any of it, not wanting to know about stupid Stuart or anything, ever. I stroked the dog's ears, felt her relaxing, warm and heavy, letting herself go against my shins. I went all floppy, a bit like maybe the sky would take me after all.

Lounging in the long wispy grass, yellow buttercups shining all around as a million suns, I let the dense heat bake into my bare legs, felt it pushing on them and into my chest, pressing into me like a body. I gazed at the skin of my thighs, watched it redden under the brown, seeing the actual spread of colour moment by moment; and floating above that speckled-ing red, my tiny filaments of golden hairs, all glimmering and flattened, basking in the bright. I drew a breath, the potent scent of some wildflower licking into my lungs. It made me feel full up and kind of tipsy. I succumbed, dropped all the way backwards into the scratchy springy turf. 'Ahhh,' I said. I wriggled my body, negotiated the bumps and hollows in the ground, found the places where I fitted into it. I am the earth, I thought. I am. I felt myself dissolving into the grass roots and crumbly soil, no separation. The million small suns bent over me, casting yellow circles with their mirrors, while the big sun pushed at my chest.

And I spread open my legs: I feel like he's lying on top of me the weight of him the heat pressing me down his burly body pressing me down his breath all at my throat I throw my arms around him feel the breadth of him the hotness and he's kissing me searching for me finding me everything blurry slur-y melding and mashing no margins everything all me and him his hand all sliding over my skin the two of us silky-as with sweat and—

'—called him Swan Neck,' came my sister's voice.

My eyes flew open. My blood drummed all through my body. But my mum was repeating the name and laughing. It was obvious my sister had been yabbering on for a while, talking about *him,* and at last I knew for sure my uncle hadn't said anything to my mum. I realised I had drifted off. I wiped the sting of sweat from my brow.

My sister giggled, milking our mother's attention. 'Yeah, because he has this really thick, *really* short neck. And he was really brilliant because he just thought it was funny, like us, and he let us call him that.'

'He would take us for ice creams down at the harbour,' her friend piped. 'And lark about, make us laugh.'

'Kind of like Picasso,' my sister said. 'He looks like Picasso.'

'No he doesn't, stupid. He's got loads of hair and his eyes are not all bulgy and enormous. He has really nice blue eyes.'

My sister gave me a look of showy triumph. 'Nice blue eyes?'

I felt my chest harden. 'What?'

Under her breath, she said, 'I knew you liked him. I knew it.'

'Course I liked him. So did you—you just said.' I leaned forward to look past her at her friend. 'You too. We all liked him. He's our friend, right?'

'But nice blue eyes,' my sister said, so my mum could hear.

'How can you say that to me?' I hissed.

Her breath went hot into my ear. 'Dunno. I guess I started thinking more about all that flirting. And all that trouble you got yourself into at school too, huh? And they weren't talking about whether you liked him or not, were they? They were talking about him *doing it* with you.'

'How can you?' My eyes smarted, everything hot. 'I can't believe you—Mum, have we got something to drink?'

My mother extracted a bottle of lemonade from somewhere down by her feet. 'So he looks like Picasso or he doesn't? I think *I* would like him if he looked like Picasso.'

'Yes,' said my sister, her friend all agreeing—though I could bet the little creep couldn't tell Picasso from Snoopy.

I glugged a giant swig of the drink, let it come back up as a loud burp fizzing around my gills. 'So what about that stable boy?' I said, smiley-as.

'Who?'

'The one you were soft on?'

Her friend giggled. 'Sam.'

'What was he?' I said. '"A golden Greek god"?'

'So what?'

'I actually liked him too.'

'You said you didn't.'

'And he liked me.'

'No he didn't.'

'Well he must have—because he kissed me out on the moor.'

'What? I don't believe you.'

I shrugged. 'Your call.'

'You bitch.' She was welling up.

'Stop it, you two,' snapped our mother. 'I'll have no language.'

'He can't have.'

'Well, he did. *We* did.'

'You—I really liked him, you knew that.'

'Yes, well, he liked me, didn't he?' I said, my eyes turning into the whizzing green out the window.

'But you knew *I* liked him. You told me you wouldn't do anything with him. You told me you never would. You said he was a slimeball. Why are you such a deceitful underhand *fucking* bitch?'

'Language, you two, I told you. Stop bickering. It's giving me a headache. I thought you all had a good time?'

'What could I do?' I chirped. 'He started it and I couldn't stop my feelings, could I? I can't help it if we liked the same boy—and that he went for me over you.'

Walking back along the river, the compacted mud path crowded to a narrowed hentrack by the singing flowers and green, I let my head be a part of it all. A light rain was spitting, and every now and then there were fat black slugs, like glistening dog poos, sliding their way across the damp earth. I stepped over them in my smudged-up dusty plimsolls. And then there really was a poo, all fresh and soft-looking and I was about stepping in it, iridescent jewels flying up, buzzing into my face— catapulting myself forward—over it—the stink flaring into my nostrils— sickened sound lurching out of me—squally momentum pitching me into a drift of cow parsley—*oh!*—*ahhh!* its crisp stems snapping and breaking, making a bed of themselves, saving me, generous-as.

The whorls of lacy white flowers tickled my skin, smelled like a girl, like maybe I smelled like cow parsley. I let loose my arms, rolling onto my front in the sweet pungent scent of myself. 'Ow!' Pain grabbed a hold of my eyes and darted them downward, legs kicking up. 'Ow!' I had

37

forgotten the nettles—but they hadn't forgotten me. Their sharp points of leaves, those tiny filament hairs, just brushing me, they had all the power of tiny knives.

I leaped up and ran a little down the pathway, all flat-footed and slapping the drum-like earth, caught a hold of myself as I remembered I needed dock leaves. Scanning the foliage, I found them, dark-as with blurry red dots, plucked a couple before seeking a spot where the grass was shorn, chucked myself down. I examined my legs, found already myriad white welts risen on my shins and thighs.

I started to pretend I was a doctor in a film, like it was a matter of life and death. By screwing the leaves up in professional fingers, I purged the bitter juice from them, teeth all clenching. I got this idea I could be both doctor and patient (who I decided was a nun) in the movie and I was muttering stuff to myself, making up a conversation about a life-saving specialist serum and the nun getting a message from God. I had to imagine a snake had bitten me and I was wearing a long white habit, which the snake had slid up.

'Are you alright?'

'Argh!' I squinted up, blood sprinting to my cheeks. It was *him*. The dark-haired silvery man from the stables, his rough brown face creased up as he stared at me. There came a tug, right up between my legs, in my secret insides, where no one could see. It was a sweet sensation that made it hard to think. 'I'm fine,' I said. I hoped he hadn't heard me being a movie.

I became aware of my legs as foreign objects splayed out before us. And I got this view of myself from his eyes, as if I was looking down on me. I was fiddling with my top, slipping the white elasticated frill off my shoulders, the way it was supposed to be. My long hair fell into my face in dark straggly strings.

He crouched, stared at the mass of white lumps, which had joined up by now, all like handwriting, on my legs. 'Looks like stinging nettles,' he said. His Irish voice had a hairline crack in it. The sound of him cut me open somehow.

I started rubbing the blackened blood of the dock leaves into the swollen pads of my flesh. I wondered if he might see my knickers, lowered my legs.

'Pretty bad,' he said. 'What happened? You fall in?'

'I'm fine,' I insisted, not looking at him. 'How are you?'

He laughed through his nose. 'Yeah, I'm good. Come on.' He held out his hand to me. 'Here.' I just stared at it, at the dark hairs growing like grass, all wild, from his fingers. That glorious jolt inside of me happened again. 'Come on,' he repeated. 'Let's get you back to the house. I won't bite. Once bitten, twice shy, huh?'

I smiled, gave him my hand, met his unbelievable pale-blue eyes. 'I'm not shy.'

'It's a saying.'

'I know. But I'm not shy. And I wasn't bitten—I was stung.'

He pulled me to my feet. I tugged at the frayed edge of my denim skirt to make sure it covered my bum. I was already pretty tall and he wasn't so much taller than me, but his body was like a bull, solid and really there, his face broad on his short thick neck. I saw, up close, the fine threads of silver running in his hair.

'Float like a butterfly, sting like a bee,' I said.

He kicked his foot in the earth so you saw the dust underneath the thin layer of damp. 'Mohammad Ali. How d'you know that?'

'I'm into boxing.' I raised my hands in punches, like huge red leather gloves were on them. 'You wanna fight?'

'I think you'd beat me,' he said, his eyes all crinkly when he met mine. I made a fast jab, thrusting my fist into his almost ugly face, drew it sharply back a fraction before it hit him. He flinched, chuckled, stood his ground.

'Whoa,' he said. 'What's that for?'

'Would you rather I bit you?'

He held up his hands. 'You win. Stinging nettles sting. I get you.'

'Good.' I nodded all curt, like I was a teacher.

He looked at my legs again; my eyes copied his. The bumps had gone red around the white now and they were burning like crazy. There was really a lot of them. I still had the dock leaves crumpled up in my fist so I bent and polished the welts up to a sap-tinted shine, all feeling him watching.

'There's some on your shoulder,' he said, flicking his eyes to show me where.

We walked along in all the buzzing growth, the feel of him next to me a kind of heat, like a growing blister, hotter even than the burn of the stings. I got the feeling we were music together. We passed under the weeping boughs of a huge pink chestnut craning over the river like it thought it was a willow or something, its carpet of fallen blossoms on the bare rich earth a wanton reflection of my own inner pink reaches. I was taken by such a vivid feeling of wanting to grab him I went almost breathless. I wondered if he was thinking the same and then I started to feel like he wasn't, of course he wasn't, and I couldn't believe it, but the thought made my eyes prickle. I hung back, stared into the cool river to be sure he couldn't see. There were all these water weeds swaying with the current and they kind of took me to somewhere peaceful, like I was in all that crystal clear, caressed in their soothing embrace. I marvelled that they could live under water.

He came up behind me, stood with his breath brushing my shoulder each time he exhaled. I felt the bite of it on the stinging nettle welts as a sweet torture. 'There's otter in there, you know. If you come and sit very quietly for a good while you can get to see them.'

'I'd quite like to be an otter,' I said. 'Or an under-water plant, maybe. Know what I mean?' I turned to face him. 'Can we come and watch for otter together? Sometime?'

Speeding through the vast blackness, just the hard bright cones of the headlamps flaring out before us on the country road, I felt I may as well be dead. The light was picking up the hedgerows then throwing them fast aside then grabbing for another slice in a continuous hunger, light devouring life, as if all that was left behind us was a dark void, just nothing.

My sister and her friend were bunched together, cosy, nattering and giggling, thinking they were hurting me. I felt sorry for them. They didn't know yet life was a cage, just a dark vortex, and they were falling through the black. I was waiting to get back home where I could shut my bedroom door on them. And everyone else too.

'Mum,' I said, leaning in. 'Seriously, I need my room.'

'I know you do, love. But you'll just have to sleep in with your sister for a couple of nights until we finish sorting out the box room.'

'Is Stuart coming to live with us?'

'Yes.'

'Have I met him? Is he the skinny one with all that black hair?'

'Yes.'

'And he's going to act all difficult, isn't he? All hurt and rejected by his parents or something.'

She patted my hand, which was resting on the back of her seat by her shoulder. 'He wasn't rejected, they—he isn't difficult. But you're going to have to be nice to him, and very understanding. You're both going to have to think about what it felt like for him, living in care for the last three years and nobody wanting him.'

I nodded. 'How old is he?'

'Fifteen.'

'Does that mean he's allowed to boss me about? Couldn't you have gotten a younger boy?'

'No one's allowed to boss anyone about, okay? I just want you to be kind and compassionate. To extend yourself for a young lad who's had a very rough time of it, losing so much—everything, one extreme to another—his parents, you see, and his lifestyle, his very nice boarding school, just everything. Can you do that? Treat him like a brother? Look, we'll talk about it appropriately tomorrow, when we're all rested and settled at home and you get to meet him properly.'

'Did they die, his parents?'

'We'll talk about it tomorrow. Yes. It was a car crash.'

'Oh.' I sat clutching the seat, silent for a minute or so. I watched the world being consumed, disappearing. 'But Mum, please, I don't want to sleep in with *her*. That's all. She's been driving me nuts. Can't we make up the camp bed in the living room? Please? I'll take it down every morning, I promise.'

She took a deep breath, sighed. 'Okay. You see, this is why it's not the best timing, you coming home early and all of a sudden, like this.'

'You're not kidding,' I said. 'But it's not my fault.'

'Sure, I know, love.'

I went to sit back but she caught a hold of my hand, pressing into it, looking at me out the corner of her eye. 'But what was really going on there? In Ireland? I got a weird feeling talking to your uncle. He told me something about a big race meet they threw at him out of the blue. But…I don't know. I know that man inside-out and he sounded funny to me.'

I shrugged. 'The owner was coming over from France without warning and I guess he didn't want it to look like he was distracted or something.'

'He didn't tell me that. He just said about the race meet.'

'I suppose he forgot to. Or he thought it was obvious. He was kind of stressed, I think. Under pressure. And he felt bad about ruining our specially-long Easter holiday.'

'Doesn't sound like Gordon to feel bad about that. He's hardly got a conscience, that brother of mine.'

'I don't know, Mum. I can't really speak for him, can I?'

She squeezed my hand. 'Course you can't. Don't worry, love. But you had a good time, did you, with the horses and the training?'

'Yeah,' I said. 'You know how I love the horses.' I sighed. 'I just wish I could've stayed like we were supposed to, see.'

'Me too. Such a shame. You barely got to the end of your forth week; he promised me five, huh? I really feel your uncle let you down. I'm sure he could have arranged for you to stay with a friend—or even a B and B for a few days. It would have been less hassle for him than getting you on the ferry out of nowhere. But we'll try and do something this next week. Go to the seaside, all of us, yes?'

'I don't really care.'

'Oh love…' She sighed, curling her hand up to cup my face. 'Tell you what, we'll arrange for you to go back for a month in the summer holidays. I'll make my bad little brother pay for his misdeeds. I'm certain he was up to something. Was it a woman, do you think?'

Rubbing down Delicious Punk I was all crooning some love song that was in the charts. I wasn't singing it to anyone, the song, it was just singing, but it grew a swollen red rosebud my chest, made me feel the love it went on about. Fistfuls of bright prickly straw came apart like strands of gold from the gelding's damp neck, tumbled free in the air. I took his head in my hands, kissed his velvet nose, gave him the song.

'Good boy,' I told him, feeling the tickle of his inside-ear-fur against my lips. 'Are you mine? Yes. Yes, you are.' I breathed in the smell of him, all real and nature. 'We had a good time, huh? More whacky races tomorrow, you and me?'

As I came out of the stables and into the yard a whistle rang out to my left. It was some local boy, about my age, one of the ones who came to muck out the stables. I knew he'd spied me smiling to myself and it annoyed me.

'Hey,' he said, heading over. 'You coming out tonight?' I shook my head. His blonde hair and pouty mouth had no effect on me but I knew my sister was swooning over him.

'Why not?' He had some grassheads in his hand and he aimed one at me. They were those wheatsheaf kind, with wings and sharp points all like darts.

'Better things to do,' I said, picking the sheaf off my vest.

He pitched another. 'A bunch of us are going up the moor with some cider. Come on. Why not?' He leaned into me, kind of smelling me, I could tell. 'We've got some weed too.'

'Maybe,' I said, just to shut him up. I crumbled the first grasshead so into fell into seeds on the concrete. 'They'll never grow. It's a waste.'

'Too good for us, are you, you English?'

I looked him in the eye. He had quiet blooms of acne scattered on his forehead. I said, 'You think that's me? You're nuts.'

'We could go out, just you and me, if you like.'

I giggled, all like a stupid girl and I could see he thought it meant I liked him. A movement behind his shoulder drew my eye to a man crossing the yard. I recognised him as my uncle's lead trainer. I watched the way he moved, all kind of graceless but easy. I thought maybe he was looking at me.

'Sam,' he called out. The boy turned. 'Mickey J is waiting for you. Step on it, will you?'

'Okay, boss.'

I let my eyes linger on him as he strolled on. I was seized by the impression he was gilded in silver. The stable boy lurched toward me, like he might be trying to kiss me, and I swayed back on my hips, started to walk away.

'See you,' I said.

I sauntered tall and slinky, stole glances at the silvery man as I took myself at an angle designed to bring myself into his periphery. I willed him to look my way. All the love that had opened in my heart with Delicious Punk seemed to just keep growing out of me, like pollen, and swell and swirl around him. When he didn't seem to notice me even, I found myself wishing I could disappear into the spangly blue air, and without thinking, I wheeled round, yelled to the stable boy. 'Hey!' He turned. 'Okay. I'm there.'

He gave me the thumbs up, made a gesture like he was puffing on a joint. 'Excellent. We'll have us a laugh.'

Arriving that sun-splashed day on the ferry from Fishguard, I watched the land coming ever closer over the sparkling peaks of water, until we were gliding through it, making our way up the estuary that led to the port. I felt like I was being swallowed into Ireland, swimming right up its gullet. It was as if I knew something special was going to happen, was happening already, right there, showing up in my pulsing body. The wind fluttered about in my clothes.

'Hey,' I said, turning to my sister leaning next to me on the guardrail of the ship. But then I just stared at how she was all lit up in the sunshine, an aura around her, her dark bobbed hair looking way bigger than it really was.

She stared back at me. 'Yes?' When I didn't say anything, she said, 'You weirdo.'

'You look like a—you look all religious.'

'I look religious?' She put her hands together, pretending to look pious. 'What are you on about? You mean because I'm praying?'

Her friend, who was on her other side, and didn't know she looked all religious too, with her fuzzy fair hair fracturing up into an even bigger halo, laughed. 'You look like a saint,' she said.

'But don't you feel you belong here?' I asked.

'We haven't even got here.'

'Yes we have,' I said, unfurling my sights to the land. 'We're completely in Ireland.' I was hooked by a white lighthouse sprouting from the green, frills of froth crashing below it at the rock's craggy skirts; but it didn't stop me from feeling the look my sister gave her friend.

'Duh,' she said.

'We're still on the sea,' her friend intoned.

'It's not really the sea anymore,' I murmured, like I didn't quite want them to hear me. 'It's an estuary.' Then louder, 'It's Irish waters.'

A swift flew over and I went with it, my heart soaring, pink-as, all opening like a dog rose inside my ribcage, and I felt like sprinting along the exterior passenger walkway. My muscles just seemed to want me to move. Instead, I breathed deep, eyes consuming the sad beauty of the tufted moorland shimmering with a purple haze, a cluster of cows grazing away at it, all like plastic toys, way off.

'Smell,' I instructed them. 'Leprechauns, see? You can smell them.' I glanced my eyes over the girls, feeling the laugh in my chest. 'Four-leafed clovers. It's lucky.'

'What are you on about?' my sister asked, all smirky.

'It's lucky.'

'What's lucky? There are no four-leafed clovers.'

'Yes there are. I found one once, on the playing field at school.'

'Sure you did.'

'I did. Last year. I showed you. I pressed it.'

'Anyway,' she said. 'It's a shamrock—the Irish emblem. And it's only got three leaves.'

Her friend drew a big breath through her dinky pink nose. 'It smells nice,' she said. 'Sea air. Salty.'

'But not,' I said.

She caught my eye and smiled, eyed my sister. 'Shamrocks are the same thing as clover.'

'Oh,' my sister crowed. 'Just 'cos Sean O'Reilly is your boyfriend, you think you know everything Irish.'

'He's not my boyfriend.'

'But you wish he was.'

And they went into some kind of mock-argument, laughing and crowding each other, all pally. I watched them, thinking how childish they were. And then my sister was taking out her Walkman from her jacket pocket, with it a crumpled white paper bag of lemon sherbets, feeding her friend and herself. She held one out to me, let it drop before my fingers reached it, both of them giggling and putting their black and blonde heads together to listen to their tinny music, a headphone each.

I picked up the yellow lozenge and tossed it into the water, watched it plop and sink, imagining how it would melt and make a sweet fizzy trail for the fish to follow. I tipped up my head, stared into the crazy-blue sky, in which the few clouds were transient thumb smudges of chalky-white. The air was sparkling and jumping around in the sunlight. I was going cross-eyed, all staring into the nothing of it.

'What are you doing?' my sister asked.

'You can see the atoms in the sky all vibrating,' I said.

'What's got into you? Can't you act normal?'

'If you like—oh, look at that pretty hamlet,' I said, putting on a posh voice. 'Isn't that interesting? Don't you just love the pastel-coloured houses? And notice that the lighthouse is, in fact—a penis.' The two of them broke into laughter while I stared at them, all like a disapproving grown-up. 'We shall take a trip over there with a guide, girls. And find out everything about the local history. I shall provide drawing materials for you to make sketches.' The sweet warm wind took a dive right up my canary-yellow rah-rah skirt and it flared up. I glanced down and it just stayed like that, all up and showing me off. I let it. 'The penis is one of the seven wonders of the world, girls.' My sister tutted, and I raised my eyebrows at her. 'Just like the cunt.' I gave it a beat, all relishing their startled in-breaths, the bashful giggle from ol' frizz-head—and the way it was obvious my sister was dying to give me a roasting but was struck speechless. I made a pop with my mouth. 'Which I'm sure you'll realise is number one. Of the wonders. Yes? Of course you must dress appropriately, like me, see. That way, you shall incur respect and admiration for your *inner* merits.'

I gave them a fake grin, fluttering my lashes.

My sister lurched forward and flicked down my skirt.

*Episode Three: Nettle Stings*

As ghostly light lit up the curtains, the living room grew all around me, too real and nasty-as. The dark blue ground of the drapes went glowy, the pink lilies heckling, as a sharp sliver of sunbeam poked through the gap between them, struck my eye. I tried to let it in, wanting to be burned to a frazzle, exploded maybe, spontaneously combusted, like people would talk about at school, my atoms dissipated into the nowhere I wanted and the nothing I was. I liked how no one would know where I'd gone; I didn't even have any shoes on to leave behind in the dust. Maybe my mother would find a melted bit of my hideous polyester nightie to wail over.

I vowed never to cry again—even as my eyes leached. It was the sunray did it. And twisting onto my side like a half-baked little foetus, I buried my head under the continental quilt, my flowery nightie snapping, making electricity with the hibiscus-patterned quilt cover—all like they were in love, making love, making their own sweet music. I sprung up, tore off the nightie, flung it across the room. It floated as if it were a bird and was always meant to fly, landed as a horrible elegant heap on the carpet.

It felt good to be nude, that sliver of sunshine slicing me in half. I tried to feel its warmth as I gazed at the knife-edge light dividing my pale breasts. But there was nothing in it.

'Shit,' I muttered. 'It's all shit.' And I let my body flop back into the emaciated foam of the mattress, into the mean creaky springs, felt like the camp bed was about to give way on me. I imagined getting folded up in it as it jumped back into its stowaway shape, my mum coming in, thinking I was gone out or something, and not getting found until I was wasted away into a paper-flat me. I would be one of those skinny cardboard dolls kiddie-you coloured in, cut out, and dressed in paper clothes with flaps to fold over the sides of the filament body.

The bed settled. I was not to be folded. I lay there, let my hands wander my boobs, fingers circling, tugging at my nipples. I craned my head, tried to reach my tongue to one—but no way. Putting a fingertip to the wetness of my mouth I trailed it down my body, pretending it was him all kissing me. But I couldn't really believe it, however much I tried. I felt an ache way up inside of me and it was too unbearable, I just couldn't stand it, so I stopped. I knew I could do it to myself and make the ache go away but I didn't want to. I just wanted it to be there for ever and ever, so I would never stop thinking of him and wanting him, never stop the hunger.

I drifted, the sound of my mum clattering around with dishes and talking in a continuous hum sifting into my brain, all commingling with images of flying fields as I took the hill-track in a canter. Delicious Punk was rippling beneath me, his breath tugging rhythmically. And then I was on a merry-go-round, the gelding turned into a stiff wooden swan in jeans, and I was clinging on, like I didn't know how to ride any more. There was shouting. They were shouting for me. And there was a loud bang and I was fallin—

—eyes jolted open, all rolling around in their sockets.

'What are you doing still in bed?' My mother was stood in the doorway. 'I've been calling you for breakfast.'

I felt chilly streams biting into my temples.

'Are you alright?'

'I'm fine.'

'What's this?' She was bending, picking up the nightie. 'What's it doing down here? Honestly, you don't look after anything. I just got it for you for your holiday. What've you got on, love?' Eyes dead-as, I flashed her my boobs. 'What do you think you're doing? You've got a brother now, you know. You can't run around naked anymore.'

I sniffed, wiped my palm upwards over my nostrils, smeared the wetness into the sheet. 'I never run around naked.'

'You know what I mean.'

'I've got a dad who can't be seeing my body already. And Stuart's not my brother. I only just met him two days ago.'

'You met him before, at the centre, you told me.'

'To say hello to, that's all. Anyway, why're we talking about Stuart again? He seems to be all you ever think about.' I aped a grin. 'Good morning, darling daughter! Good morning, dearest Mum.'

She chuckled, came and parked herself on the edge of my undernourished bed. Her hand rested on my quilt-padded hip bone.

'Careful,' I said. 'One false move and the whole bed'll blow.'

She reached up and smoothed the dark weeds from my face, stared into my eyes. I let them slide closed, hushed by her tenderness, let my breath go light, and I could remember being a baby it felt like. She had that pancakes-honey smell.

'You'll get your room back tomorrow, I think,' she said. 'Thank you for this. For being so good about Stuart and everything. He really needs this new home we're making for him.'

I just made a murmuring sound, hoping she wouldn't stop the stroking. I suddenly knew how the foal had felt when we imprinted it and I wondered, was she imprinting me so she could have me under her control? Whatever she was doing, it was working. I was lavender blooms giving out my sweetest aroma at the touch of her fingertips, all drifting into open sky.

She patted my side. 'Okay, love. Breakfast. Have you got your dressing gown?' I refused to open my eyes, felt a dark rush of grief, just a big gaping hole, as I pointed to where I knew the sofa to be. 'Ah.' I heard her move around the bed, heard the suck of the towelling robe as it released itself from the velour sofa, felt its weight drop onto my shins.

'Five minutes,' she told me. I listened to her scuff across the carpet, stopped myself from calling out to her, and the door clicked shut. There was the noise beyond of everyone gathering around the table. The smell of fresh coffee had licked into the room.

I rolled over under the covers, clenching my eyes shut, shutting out the light and my family and my newly fostered un-brother, all of them. I felt heavy in my body, as though poisoned. I tried to take myself back to Ireland, to the perfect dream of he and me, to him between my legs on his yellow dirt bike and the vibration from the motor which felt like he was touching me. To the waiting…the waiting…and then the getting. But all I got now was that deep reddish black behind my eyelids, and little black threads floating and tiny lights getting bigger and hurting when I squeezed my lids tighter together.

My mum was yelling for me. I dragged myself to a sitting position. She yelled again and I stood, all as though pulled by an invisible string, a reflex controlled by her. I wondered if maybe it was cruel to imprint a foal. That tiny newborn being manipulated into submission by human hands before it had even had a taste of its mother's milk. How beautiful it had been to feel the young life succumb. We had done it in tenderness. But it wasn't exactly for the foal, huh?

✿

I could tell they were my mum's footsteps treading up the stairs by the way they were light and measured. My sister's would be crashing and irregular, bounding steps at a time. Stuart's were laborious, weighty. And my dad's would be light and heavy at once, like he was trying not to be there but couldn't help it. But he was out anyway, on one of his marathon cycle rides he did just about every day after work in his stupid flashy racing gear.

She paused outside my room. I heard her draw breath like she was going to say something, then curtail herself so the breath was clipped to a sharp end. I could feel it in my own throat, as if it were mine. There came a light rap, with one knuckle, on my door.

50

'Sweetheart?' I just listened to our two breaths, until they joined up into one. 'Lovey? Are you asleep?' The doorknob slowly turned, creaking, and I watched as the door swung toward me, my mother's face in its wake. 'You're awake. Why didn't you answer?' I was lying on top of my green-and-pink bedspread, just lying there. 'What are you doing?' She came in, got up on my bed, kneeling next to my shoulder so I had to shift to make room for her.

'Nothing,' I said.

'What's got into you since you got back from your uncle's? I'm worried about you, love. You're moping about all over the place and it's not healthy. It's been over a week now—it's not like you. Are you going to tell me what's going on?' She stared at me, all earnest and big eyes and I could tell she really was troubled. I pressed my lips together, stared back. I hoped she wouldn't touch me. 'Listen, love, you know you can talk to me, don't you? You've always known that.'

'I don't really have anything to talk about, see.'

'Hmm.' I could tell she didn't believe me.

'It's just my age.'

My mother blew a laugh through her nose. It made me think of him and I looked sharply away, up into the shimmering blue sky through the window, and that made me think of Ireland and arriving on the ferry and more of him, so I stared up at the white ceiling and made my focus blur out.

'Maybe you're right,' she said. 'Maybe it's your hormones. But your sister was never like this.'

'Well, I'm not my sister am I?'

She smiled. 'No, that's for sure.'

'What does that mean?'

She sighed. 'Come on now, don't be twisting my words, you.' She paused, gazing at me, then reached out, took my hand. I cringed, but let her keep a hold of me. 'Is it that boy?'

'What boy?'

'You were talking about a boy—a stable boy I think—in the car, when we picked you up from the ferry. Sam, right? Your sister was very upset.'

51

'No,' I said.

She patted me. 'You'll get over it.'

'Yes.'

'Why don't you come downstairs? Watch a film with us, on the video?'

'Don't want to.'

'You don't even ask what we're watching? I happen to know you really want to see it.'

'Please, Mother. Can you go away?'

She sighed again, muttered, 'Hormones.'

'I heard you.'

'You said it first, love. Now listen, I think you should get yourself down to Dick and Estelle's yard. I've spoken to her and she says she'd love you to come take the younger ones out on treks.' She brightened. 'Wouldn't that be good? You can be with the horses and make yourself some pocket money too. Can you look at me, lovey, when I'm talking to you? I'm trying to help.'

I flicked my sights to hers. 'I think I might have outgrown all that actually.' She nodded, her eyes overcast. 'But thanks. I'm just going to read, okay?'

She looked about. There weren't any books out. 'What are you reading?'

'Oh. You know…'

My mother stood and went to my bookshelves. 'Want me to pick one out for you?'

'Mum.'

'Okay. But this won't do.'

She left the room at last and I drew myself to sitting, my bare legs all out like a doll. Slipping my hand under my pillow, I extracted the only book I cared about anymore. I opened the front cover and stared at the inscription there, at his scratchy words written out in blue ink. *To my little Angel Face. Your Swan Neck.* I ran my thumb over the words, had to brush away the splash of a tear that kamikazed nearly into them. I watched how the small splotch of damp, with a tail like a comet all crashing through space, wrinkled and swelled the paper. The old smell of the book rose from its rusty pages as a taste. My mouth and throat felt all thick and I shuttered my eyes, trying like crazy to remember his voice, to see his face. But all I got was some kind of jigsaw puzzle of forced ideas, things I could remember without them actually coming together as an image or his sound. I knew he had palest blue eyes with great big pupils that were always dilated, all like he was constantly interested in everything. I knew he was sun-browned and a bit craggy, had laugh-lines around his eyes and mouth and a frown cut into his forehead; that he was burly, with a bit of a belly even, furry and soft, and had a voice with a crack in it that just about killed me. But it was all I was left with, this empty kind of knowing in which he would not appear.

I went to the mirror, tried to see myself like he saw me, wiped at the black smudges below my eyes with the knuckles of my forefingers, hating the silvery bloating tears as they filled and spilled. All I could see was a very small stupid human being.

The crunch of a car drawing up in our driveway took me across my bed, all shuffly knees, so I could get to see who it was. So far as I knew we weren't expecting anybody, but it would be just like my mother to make some plan in which to try to involve me. Some friend sent over on a mission to get me out of my shell, as my mum would put it, or that what's-her-name from the riding school.

It was a close cloudy day out there, everything kind of faded to look at, all like my insides and my own blunted self. I didn't recognise the car and I watched from above as the door sprung open and a man's boot bit into the gravel, drawing him outward from the vehicle and into the open space of our front garden. It was when I saw his bald head I realised, with a skip and a stab, it was my uncle. My mother was coming out of the house, her dark hair pulled into a low ponytail, a thin pencil-line of grey glinting at her parting.

'Gordon,' she was saying. 'What are you doing here?'

He grinned. 'Surprise.'

'But why didn't you tell me you were coming?'

He was bending into the car, waving a bunch of flowers at her, those horrible kind you find at the garage that look fake, with too many bright clashing colours.

'How lovely,' she said, all quivery. 'No one ever buys me flowers. You are a dark horse. I wonder what you can want, turning up like this, all the way from Ireland like you still lived round the corner?'

And they were hugging each other, but all a bit stiff.

'Are you staying?' she said. 'Got a bag?'

'I'll deal with that later. I could do with a strong cup of coffee. I've been up all night.'

'I'm rather annoyed with you, to tell the truth, messing up the girls' holiday.'

'Straight to the jugular, eh sis? Never a simple glad to see you.'

She laughed. 'Oh, but I am glad to see you, Gordie, really I am. I just wish you'd let me know. I'll have to go shopping.'

'I've got supplies. A brace of pheasant and four fine bottles of Beaujolais.'

'Lovely. Always the hedonist, you. But maybe it'll do us good.'

'I went shooting especially—don't worry, all legal, from our land. Nabbed the wine from the Lutry's cellar.'

'*Our* land, huh? Legal pheasant with stolen wine. I love it.'

'It's not stolen. It's part of the deal.'

'You finally got the posh life you hankered after, Gordie. Living it up in Ireland at the Lutry's expense.'

'And I work hard for it.'

'You've done very well for yourself. I'm proud of you.'

He looked up at me the moment she turned her back on him to go inside, and I had the sense he had known I was there all along. He made a face, a sort of grimace and some kind of a shrug, with palms held out, like he was asking for supplication; sent my heart up into my mouth as I realised my worst fears were coming true.

I threw myself back from the window, all frozen on my hands and knees, trembling coming up through my arms until it was everywhere, in every cell, and even in the bed. I saw a silver cord of drool hanging from my mouth, felt it hit my cheek as I flipped my body onto its back, arms flopped out. I just stared up at the ceiling, waiting, the feel of the wet spit-string like a fine cut.

She was calling me and I was doing that thing, obeying her command like I had no will of my own anymore, had no survival instinct, was for sure imprinted, desensitised everywhere except where her heels met my sides and she was kicking me, her voice all kicking me, instructing me to scrape myself off the bed and follow my feet downstairs.

My mother smiled. 'Look who's here,' she said.

'Hello,' I said.

He came toward me. 'Aren't you going to give your old uncle a hug?'

'I don't know.'

'Lovey,' my mum said. And to him, 'She doesn't know what she's saying. She's been in a funk ever since she got back.'

Patting my shoulder, he said, 'That's okay. It was all a bit brutal, wasn't it?' I stared at him in a kind of terror. 'Leaving like that.'

'So what *was* going on?' my mother asked, like it was lines from a play or something.

'I explained on the telephone. The last-minute race meet.'

'And the owner coming from France,' I said.

'Ah. She has a voice,' she said to me, all smiling. 'I thought there was something else, though, didn't I, love? I asked her but she didn't seem to know. I thought maybe you had some kind of woman trouble or a new romance or something. Hmm? Wanted the girls out of your way, Gordie? For your womanising?'

'You will continue to have a bad impression of me,' he said.

She shrugged. 'Well you can't blame me. You were the one that—oh do let's not do this.'

'Quite,' he said. 'So I was a bit of a tearaway. And now I'm not. And there's nothing wrong with being a tearaway when you're young. It's natural, eh?' He looked at me, sucked on his lips. 'You can't punish a person forever.'

'I'm not talking about *that*,' my mother said.

'Oh, *that*,' he echoed. 'Drat. But I'm glad you agree.'

'Agree?' she said.

He looked at me. 'That teenage faux pas are not punishable forever.'

'For goodness sake, Gordon, what are you going on about?'

'You know I had a liaison with my history teacher?' he said to me. 'When I was fifteen.'

'Liaison. That's a laugh. How would she know that? What are you up to, Gordon? You can't just come here and start bringing your old troubles to my daughter. This is entirely inappropriate.'

My mouth was dry-as, like there was a cup of flour in it. Even though it came into my head, I felt no urge to say she'd told me herself about my uncle's misdeeds—more than once.

'It's true,' he said. 'I got in a lot of trouble. But it passed.'

She spun her eyes, all dark and turbulent, to me. 'Until he had it away with my best friend. And then, what—who? Just about any girl or woman or object that would let him.'

'It all passed.' He kept talking to me and it was as if everything about him was too sharp and in focus, almost unreal. I squeezed my eyes hard together, like looking at him was hurting them. 'You remember what the Buddha said? "This, too, will pass".'

'And you're still at it, as far as I can see.' My mother muttered. And to me, 'It's an addiction. It requires treatment.'

'You're still angry with me. But actually, I'm not still at it, as you say.'

'You created such a mess.'

'But it was a long time ago. I was a boy. I've let it go years ago—it's you keeps carrying it.'

'But my best friend, Gordon.'

'It took two.'

'I know, the little tart.'

My breath stopped. I stared at her, felt my eyes welling up through the pain in my chest.

'Don't say that,' he said, brow all furrowed. His eyes flicked to me for an instant. 'You shouldn't—she was never a tart. What we did was full of feeling. It didn't mean you had to turn against her.'

'Whatever you say.'

'She was very hurt. She never stopped loving you and hoping you'd make it up. You know, I'm still friends with her and she still—'

'—and you're kidding yourself saying you've got over it. You've still got a problem. You still let sex and women rule your life. Why else did you send the girls home early?'

'I'm dealing with the addiction. I go to meetings. I've changed.'

'Yeah, right.'

They were locked in their own stand-off and it was as if I could see a monster between them, a kind of energy all their making, which seemed to snap and flare in the air. He broke the contact with her, turned away with sagging shoulders, stepped across to the window.

My mother smoothed her palms over her shiny black hair, adjusted the band of her ponytail. 'Well, this is lovely, isn't it?'

'I'm sorry,' he said, his voice thick and fuzzy against the windowpane. I got the feeling he was speaking to me, saying sorry in advance for what he had come here to do. I saw he'd tried to pave the way but it felt like he'd made things worse.

She sighed. 'It's about time we stopped this. Perhaps we should do some conflict resolution. I could ask Val at work for a recommendation. You know you can't do it with someone that you know.'

He turned. 'Perhaps we should just sit down together and talk about it quietly like two adults, instead of from teenage reactivity.'

'You never want to do things my way, do you?'

'It's not that.'

'Then what?'

'Anyway, that's not what I'm here for.'

I felt the blood bleed from my face.

'Ah, so you're here for a reason. I knew it.'

His sights scudded to me. 'I'm going to the car to get my stuff. Want to come and give me a hand?'

I couldn't even nod, my whole body stiff as a dried out salted rabbit skin. I swallowed and my throat was spiky. And then he was going out the door, through the kitchen, heading into the rectangle of hazy light that was the hole into outside.

'Go on then,' my mum told me. 'Not that he deserves your help.'

And I stepped after him. As my feet ground against the gravel it felt to be sucking me down. I didn't want to think about *him* but his image finally came and fitted together, showed itself to me complete, running like a film. He was walking toward me, sun in his silvery hair, leading the keen three-day-old foal by a halter rope. He passed me the rope, our fingers brushing, lingering, full of love. In his fissured voice, he said, *In two years, you'll be up on him and he'll know you as his own kind.* And we were sat in a ditch on a prickly blanket, backs against dry crumbly earth, a bottle of cherry pop slumped beside us. I saw how his skin glistened with a light sweat, laugh lines all highlighted. He said, *You make me feel like a kid. I'm not a kid*, I said. He said, *More than a kid. Like life itself. You don't understand the delight of it. But you will. I'll make you.* And I told him, *Don't be an idiot. I do. I understand it all.*

I reached the car, stood by the open boot where my uncle was unloading his bags. I stared at his hands, all the time reading the raggy blue tattoos he'd etched into his fingers with a compass and ink when he was around my age.

L O V E

H A T E

I could feel my mother watching us through the window. I had thought I was going to beg him not to say anything but I just stood there, taking the plastic bags of wine he passed me. He must have thought he was going to say something too, because otherwise what was the point of getting me to help him? But we didn't even look at each other and I turned and went back into the house.

꽃

I scraped back my chair, excused myself and took myself up to my room as soon as the pudding had gone down. I'd hardly eaten anything and my mum had kept going on about it, so I'd taken a second helping of ice cream I didn't want and she'd gone on about how I couldn't just live on ice cream. I barely spoke a word, just watched the wine splashing into the goblet glasses and down their gizzards and the talk getting looser, louder—for sure kind of slur-y out of my mum. I glanced often at my uncle, caught his eye a couple of times. My sister and Stuart each accepted a little wine, and even I was offered some. I turned it down. She acted all grown-up but I could tell the alcohol hit her head by the way she went giggly for a while and then all glazed; whereas Stuart imbibed it with a definite assurance, poured himself a good finger more when the adults were in some passionate conversation. He grinned at me, reached for my tumbler, necked my lemonade and sloshed some red into my glass. We kept eye contact as he passed it to me and I swigged it in one. The speed of it down my throat, the warmth it created against my tissue felt luscious, relieving, and we took up a kind of game, the two of us, drinking illegally every time the opportunity arose. I felt all glowing, the tension subsiding in me, an acceptance of the inevitable emerging. Glancing again at my uncle, I saw he knew what we were doing and I nodded at him, gave him a phony smile, then kind of shrugged, tossed him visually away.

As I was on the staircase to go up, about to close the door behind me, I leaned back into the room, yelled out, 'Goodnight', and indicated to Stuart to follow. The grown-ups had their attention on me, saying sleep well kind of stuff, and I had to suppress my delight as he spilled a sizable snifter into his goblet, raised it to me, downed it. Glancing at my sister I saw she'd seen, was making clear her disapproval. I beckoned her to join us upstairs while he slopped some red into her glass.

He entered my room maybe ten minutes later, brandishing a bottle with quite a bit still in it. I gave him a look like my sister's, said, 'This is *not* a good start,' and swigged from the narrow neck.

He reflected my look, nodded all sardonic. 'I know.'

I drank again, smacked my lips together. 'Fucking nice Beaujolais. Just what I always wanted.' I swilled another mouthful. 'How did you manage to get it passed them?'

'It's just a matter of attention and angles.'

'So you're saying you're practiced?'

'It's what happens when you become a delinquent.'

'Is that what you are? Because of the home?' I glugged again.

He grabbed the bottle. 'No. But that's my best label. Special Reserve, like this plonk.'

'My mum thinks you're a little saint.'

'I am.'

We laughed, arranged ourselves top-to-toe on my bed. I chucked him a pillow and we propped ourselves up, all kind of slumpy at the same time.

'Hey,' I said. 'You wanna know? I'm in deep shit. Everything's about to go off.'

'You what?'

'My uncle's come to chuck me in the fire.'

'Your uncle? You seem to get on really good. Why would he do that? What about?'

I stretched out my hand, 'Pass it to me,' and let a quiet stream of warmth slide into me before resting the bottle in my hand on my chest. I stared up at the ceiling, felt the heat in my belly. 'See, I'm in love.'

'With your *uncle*?'

I kicked him. 'No.'

'Oh—*Oh* I see, you had sex when you were in Ireland—and he found out?'

'Something like that. How the hell do you know? You're good, huh? Actually, a wizard, you must be.'

'Just attention and angles.'

'Or a comedian.'

'Seriously, is that what it is?'

I nodded, took another slide of wine. 'Yup.'

'All the way?'

'Yup.'

He nodded, held out his hand for the bottle. '*Fuck.*'

'Why are grown-ups always—I don't know—I thought he wasn't going to tell them, the bastard.'

'He'll be thinking it's his duty maybe. But he seems a cooler kind of bloke than that.'

'Yeah.'

'Are you sure that's why he's here? I mean, obviously he hasn't said anything at this point.'

'Believe me, he's going to. Why do you think he brought four bottles of Beaujolais and opened every one before a drop was drunk?'

'Is he an alchy?'

'My mum reckons he's an addict. But I think it might be to sex. Can you be addicted to sex? Is that a thing?'

'I don't know.'

'He goes to meetings, one of those twelve step things.'

'A sex twelve step. Really? But he still drinks, which seems kind of weird—can you still drink on a twelve step thingy?'

'See, he's thirty-two—and that's the problem so far as my uncle's concerned. I reckon if it was with a boy he would've let it go. Or maybe even if he was just twenty or something.'

'Hang on. Who's thirty-two? Not…?'

'Oh,' I said, tension pricking through the hazy feeling as I eyeballed him. 'You too, huh?'

'You're telling me you're in love with a thirty-two-year-old man?'

'Yes.'

'And you—you had sex with him?'

'We made love. Yes, we fucked. Fuck you. It was great.'

'Heavy shit. This is serious. You really are going to be in trouble.'

'I told you.' I nodded at the bottle. 'Give.' As I raised it to my lips, I paused, gazing at him. 'Do you hate me now?'

He sat up, bowed toward me, all kind of attentive and soft. 'Look, it's going to be pretty shocking to most people but—well, put it this way, I've seen a lot, like *really* a lot, this too, a version of—and I'm not judging you, not a bit.'

'Great. I'm not just a version, you know—this is me, my life.'

'I didn't mean it like that.'

'For sure.'

'I'm just telling you I'm not green. I know about stuff. And I don't hate you a bit; in fact, I'm really glad you're here and I'm appreciating you telling me this shit.'

'Have *you* had sex?'

'Um…no.'

'Sorry.'

'It's okay. There was this girl I liked but…' He let himself drop back

61

into his pillow. We shared the last of the wine and he pretended to wring the bottle's neck over his mouth. A drop came out, all like a tear.

I jiggled his shin. 'I'm glad you're here too. Bro.'

He jiggled mine back. 'Sis.'

'Well, *our* mum will be please about *this*, at least. If she doesn't kill me.'

'Yeah…our mum. It's pretty cool to have a kind of mum and dad again. But it is pretty weird too.'

'Do you miss your parents?'

'Not so much. Anymore. But I wonder how this is going to pan out? Are they going to come screaming into the room?'

I snorted. 'What, like, all crazy and baying for blood?'

'Yeah. Wild fucking animal grown-ups.'

'You know what? I don't care. Let them. Let them be fucking wolves.'

'Ha—I reckon they're going to be very English and contain themselves down there—one bright noise of commotion, then hushed up voices—'

'—so as not to alert the *other* children—'

'—yeah, and then they'll come at you all quiet—'

'—my parents are going to *freak* out. I think she hates sex.'

A low laugh shook him, came tripping into me through the mattress, and I shoved my fist into my lips. We escalated into gagged hysteria, everything going slur-y and the room taking off around our shoulders, all kind of spinning and dancing like some kind of messed up celebration.

⁂

I stepped out of my knickers and laid them, splayed out, on top of the pile of my cast-off clothes. I liked those knickers; they were white with double red cherries on them. I'd made a neat pile, folded my skintight jeans, which I had taken in myself by hand, last summer, with a friend I didn't see any more, folded the dark blue denim legs over themselves into three, then folded my white off-the-shoulder top I was in love with, all like they do in a shop, from the front, with the edges of the elasticated Broderie Anglaise frill and the arm-holes tucked behind. My silky pink bra was spread out, its cups eyes, its back-strap running over the edge of the pile like a long thin tongue.

When my mother spoke, I just about leaped out of my skin, imagined my faded tan all rippling to the ground in a rumpled circle around raw bloody feet. 'What are you doing in there? Come on, there's people waiting.'

'Coming,' I said. 'I've just got to…'

'What? Do you need some help?' Her voice was coming toward me.

'No.'

'Want me to do you up?'

'No. Don't come in.'

'You know you have to—'

'—I *know*.'

I took up the gown they'd given me to put on. It was still folded and when I shook it out it ponged of something astringent, all prickly up my nose. It was old, the tiny-flowered print just about gone, was huge and shapeless. I did up the thin tie behind my neck, the bulge of the strip of white medical tape from the blood sample all inhibiting the bend in my elbow. I stepped out from behind the baby-blue screen, some kind of gathered rubbery fabric in a metal frame on big rubber wheels.

The nurse smiled, tugged on her cream latex gloves with a smack. Indicating the skinny trolley-bed, she said, 'Jump up.'

She had a big face. Big features. And wore red lipstick, her brown hair in a big top-knot with wisps coming out. I sat on the large strip of paper towel and watched her. The bed creaked, the paper snapped. Her wisps floated about as she moved. I tried to imagine her as a flower, one of those ones with lots of fine stamens.

'You need to lie down.' She came over to me as I attempted to settle myself, my two hands clinging on. 'Bring up your knees. Good girl. Now put your feet together and let your legs fall open.' She slapped at my thigh. 'All the way, that's it. Now relax.'

There was a metal thing in her hand and she squeezed some see-through jelly-stuff onto it, smeared it around. It looked like one of those things you put in your shoes to keep their shape. It looked big.

'Mum?' I said.

'It's alright, love. Want me to hold your hand?'

'No.' My hair was all in my face, snaking into my mouth. She swept it away, stayed standing close.

The nurse stood between my legs and spoke to my cunt. 'Okay, so I'm just going to pop this inside you and—'

'—is it going to hurt?' I asked. The metal thing had a long-levered handle and I saw it opened like a duck's bill.

'No, it won't hurt. It's just going to feel a bit cold and a little bit uncomfortable—'

'—you haven't warmed it up?' my mum barked. 'I think you should warm it up.'

'I've put the gel on it now. She'll be alright.'

'No. I want you to warm it. It's her first time. She's very young.'

'Not that young,' came the nurse.

'Okay. Close your legs,' my mother told me. I clamped them shut. 'I'm not sure this is necessary. It was over two weeks ago. I think the urine and blood tests are enough.'

'Well, I—'

'—get up, love.' My mother patted me. 'Go and get dressed. I don't see why she had to put on a gown anyway.'

'It was for her own modesty. She only had on that little top. I was trying to help.'

'Yes.'

'I'll have to talk to the doctor about this,' said the nurse.

'Fine. So will I. We'll both talk to Dr Mendleson and reassess. Good.'

'I shouldn't be doing this, anyway. I don't normally do these tests. We're already making special concessions for you. You should really be at the clinic.'

'I know. You're all being very kind and understanding.'

The nurse appeared uncertain, sort of hovering, wielding the metal shoe-thing, and I found myself lying there, staring. I couldn't believe she could put that thing inside anyone.

'Get up, lovey. Come on, you're done.'

All like I was stiff from too much riding after too long a break, I jimmied myself up, swung my legs over the side. They dangled and swayed and I felt about six.

'Are you alright?' my mother asked.

'I feel a bit funny.'

'She looks very pale,' said the nurse. She touched my forehead. 'She's hot. Sweating. Do you want some water?' I nodded. 'Shall I take her temperature again?'

'No, she'll be fine. I'll just get her home. Shall I help you get dressed?' I took the cool glass of water and gulped it down, shook my head. 'Go on, then.'

I slid myself off the trolley, the long paper towel sticking to my bare bum, all following me, until my mum flew forward and nipped it off. I heard the soft swishing protests it gave out when she crumpled it up, and as I adjusted the blue screen around me, I saw her hand it to the big-faced nurse who had to gather the bulky paper wad into her chest, all with the shiny shoe-thing in her hand.

'We're still going to need to take a swab, you'll find. It's the only way to discover some STDs.'

'She's fine. I know it. I'll keep an eye.'

'You can't be sure unless you test. Something like chlamydia won't show and could cause terrible problems later if we don't catch it now.'

I stepped back out of my knickers, wheeled open my makeshift door. 'Maybe we should do it now, then. I don't want to come back.'

'Yes,' said the nurse.

'No,' said my mother. 'Chlamydia requires only urine.'

'I really can't go through this again.'

My mum sighed and we all stood in the silence. The low hum of traffic entered the space. A black bird sang out its fluted whistle. 'Okay,' she said at last. 'But you must warm up the speculum and be extra gentle.'

We went through the whole procedure, me lying on my back, legs splayed open, nurse between them inserting the long metal implement. She facilitated its entry with latex-coated fingers, which parted and

65

adjusted my lips in a passionless technical exercise that made me feel like a piece of meat. I could never have known my anatomy could cause me to feel so frozen. She kept telling me to relax, kept tapping my thighs, getting me to tilt my bum up to her face. She opened up the foreign object inside of me and I felt it stretch me, went all kind of numbed out, and then she was leaning in, peering in and poking about, telling me, 'Just a little scraping feeling. Give me a cough. That's it. We're getting some of your cells'. I turned my head, stared into the soiled mushy pea-green wall for a countless amount of time. 'There,' she said. 'All done.' I found her fiddling with a little clear plastic pot and a cotton swab, realising it was the thing she had scoured about inside me. 'Everything looks fine,' she said. 'Lovely and rosy. Her hymen's broken, but that's to be expected.'

'I'm sure that happened before,' said my mum. 'What with all that horse riding. Don't you think?'

'It's possible, yes—likely. We'll get the results back in two weeks.'

'And the blood and urine samples?'

'Yes, those too.' The nurse turned to me, ripping off and passing me a strip of the paper towel I was lying on. 'Give yourself a wipe. That gel's a bit messy. I don't think there'll be any blood.'

I stuck the paper between my legs, slipped off the bed, bending to have a look at it as I pulled it away. The gunk was clear and shiny, like mucus that came out of your nose when you cried and didn't have a cold or anything.

'So you think you can manage to spend that penny now?' the nurse asked, all holding out two plastic pots with white screw-tops. 'One for the lab and one for me. We can do the pregnancy test right away.' She opened the door to her room. 'It's down the hall, on the right.'

'Wait a minute, sweetheart,' came my mother. She hared across to my makeshift changing room and emerged clutching the bunch of cherries that were my knickers. 'You'll want to stick these on first, no?'

The nurse closed the door and I saw her as one of those little tin women that come reeling out on the hour from a small door of an old-fashioned handmade Hungarian clock. I waited for her to chime, wondering what time it was. I felt like I'd been in that room, getting examined, for years.

'Lovey?' my mum said.

'Oh.' I took my pants, and we looked at one another, a kind of suspended animation between us, like we were both holding our breaths as one.

'You made a face,' she said. 'Your knickers were a smile.'

Her features sort of quivered. And then we were laughing in one big burst together, and tears were coming out of our eyes as we stared at each other and I was stepping into my knickers and the nurse even started to shake as she tried to stop herself from joining in.

'Come here,' my mum said, stepping over to me herself. She took me in her arms and I let her. 'Well done, you're a brave girl. Nearly there now. Just one last hurdle. It's quite a trial, isn't it? You're really doing very well.'

I scurried off to the toilet holding the back of my gown shut in the clamp of my fingers and came back to deliver my full warm pots into the nurse's hands. I could see the tension back in my mum's face as the nurse undertook the simple test. They told me I could go and get dressed but I stayed there, watching, waiting, not really feeling anything.

'It's negative,' the nurse said. A little dimple showed in her cheek as she looked first at my mother and then at me.

I nodded. 'I knew it,' I whispered.

'What?' said my mum.

'Nothing. Going to put my clothes on.'

Behind the screen, I shrugged off the gown, ran my hands over the flat of my belly. My head went empty. Then I put on my bra, my top and struggled into the legs of my jeans. 'Mum?'

'Yes, love?'

'Is there a coat hanger or something?'

'I don't know. Whatever for? Is there a coat hanger?' she asked the nurse.

'Um—no. What do you need a coat hanger for?'

'Never mind.'

'No,' said the nurse. Her big face poked round the screen. 'That's sounds dangerous, my dear. What are you thinking of? Are you alright?

You know the test is negative. You're not pregnant. And a coat hanger is not the way if you were. It can kill you.'

I stared at her. I indicated my open fly. 'What? It's to do up my zip. You pull with it, see.'

She was blank-as—until she got what I was on about. '*Oh*…my goodness…'

'So you don't have one?'

'Um—no. Do you want me to help you?'

'Okay. But it's easiest if I lay down.' I did so, right there on the lino floor, straining to draw the open fly as close together as possible with my fingers.

She kneeled next to me, bending over my pelvis, pulling on the zip tab, which didn't want to budge. Her fingers kept losing their grip. 'What do you do when you go to the toilet?'

'I don't.'

'That's very bad for you. Maybe you shouldn't wear your jeans so tight. But you must go eventually?'

'Course,' I said. 'I've got a coat hanger in the bathroom.' Feeling my mum watching, I craned my neck to look at her.

'Everything alright?' she asked.

'Breath in,' said the nurse.

And there was that lovely feeling when the zip locked into itself, sliding up with sudden ease and a soft purr, that lovely sucked-in holding feeling of the tightness of my jeans.

'Can you help me up?'

'But what do you do when you're out and you want to go?' She was levering me up to my feet.

'Oh…I just call a nurse to help me, of course.' She smiled and my mother shifted out of the way to let me through. Straight away I spotted a couple of wire coat hangers on a hook on the back of her door. 'You've got two coat hangers.'

'Oh. Yes.'

I turned to her. 'How did you think I was going to kill myself with a coat hanger?' They passed each other a look. 'What—you don't mean that old-fashioned abortion thing? Is that it? Is that what you thought I was talking about? You're nuts. I would never do that. And definitely not right here. I'd have to be off my rocker. And anyway, I know I'm not pregnant.'

My mother winced.

'What else could I think?' said big face. 'It was a strange thing to ask for, especially under the circumstances.'

'But I *knew* I wasn't. I'm not an idiot.'

'Hey, hey,' said my mother. 'Come on now, be reasonable. It *was* a strange request.'

The nurse's colour was up. She had gone all a bit wooden. 'Talking of which, we have to think about birth control. Do you think she might go on the Pill?'

'She's fourteen.'

'Yes, well—you don't want a repeat of this worry, do you?'

'There won't be a repeat,' said my mother.

The nurse looked at me. 'What do *you* think?'

❧

Feet buried in my pillow, head at a wonky angle, my face was drenched- as in the oblong of sunshine which crept across my bed in the late afternoons, warmth all amplified by the glass. I felt the forever-pleasure of the golden haze in my lashes, as if I didn't exist any other than that; felt myself unfurling every-which-way, yet in a state of utter inner stillness. The roar of a military plane ate up the silence, came out of nowhere in a second, like a bomb dropping, contracted the flesh at the base of my skull. My body went all alert, as if I was scared as hell and in danger. It made me think of that place in Japan where the giant mushroom cloud had erupted in the sky. They came often, those planes, that noise, because of the American base nearby, but you never could see them and you never got used to them. As the roar subsided, my muscles went limp in my legs, my bum. The telephone was ringing. I heard my sister answer it, heard her voice all tense and then she was yelling for me. I tried ignoring her but she came thumping up the stairs, banging on my

69

door.

'I know you're there. I'm not stupid, you know, you lying little slag. It's uncle Gordie. He wants to speak to you.'

'Tell him I'm out,' I said through the door.

'No way. Tell him yourself.'

She thudded to her room, slammed her door—and the silence afterward reverberated through the stillness, came all the way into my body, a kind of empty relief. I was tempted to leave my uncle at the end of the line, but heaving a breath, I got myself up and slipped downstairs.

The yellowed receiver was on the green carpet of the living room at the fullest possible distance from the phone without the force of someone pulling on it, its coiled wire retracting slow-as. I stood watching it, heard a tiny tinny voice calling out from it, went and picked it up.

'Hello?'

'Is that you?' said my uncle.

'No.'

'Your sister sounded cross.'

'She is cross. She hates me now.'

'I'm…sorry.'

'What do you care? She hates you too anyway.'

'I care very much. I'm calling because I'm concerned. I'm concerned for you.'

'Really? Then why did you tell? You took away—you *ruined*—you changed everything.'

'Okay,' he said. 'I'm not going to get into any kind of argument. I didn't want to tell your mother, you know that. And I nearly didn't. But I realised you could be—you know, I mean—what if you were pregnant? How irresponsible of me would that be?'

'Well I'm not. She took me to the doctor's, like the day after you left, and you wouldn't believe what I had to do.'

'I know. And I'm seriously relieved.'

'Lucky you. I don't really know how you think I can continue to even *like* you.'

'And how were they—the parents? I mean…'

'Stupid question.'

'Well, I—'

'—they didn't *kill* me, if that's what you wanted. Although maybe it would be better if they had. She was a bit fucking reasonable at first and I could see she'd been crying and hadn't had any sleep, and then she let rip at me, like really tried to provoke me it felt, my stupid ridiculous dad all trying to quiet her. But I just let her. I didn't tell her anything. She's being okay now. She feels bad for me, like she thinks I've been abused. I suppose I'm one of her cases now. And he just doesn't look at me the same anymore. So *whatever*, really.'

'I really am sorry, my lovely. They will get over it.'

'*Are* you? Where is he then?' He sighed. There was a long pause in which I heard his breath sticking in his throat at intervals, all like he was going to say something but couldn't. 'Can I come back?' I asked.

'Yes, of course. In the summer holidays. But I'll need to know you're not going to get up to anything like that again.'

'Why should I? I'm not a slag. I don't want anybody else. You should know that.'

'Hmm,' he said.

'You don't believe me.' My eyes burned. 'I'm not like you were, you know. Not everyone is like that—you made it worse, by the way, rousing her all up about the past—I love him, see, and he loves me. I'm not interested in anyone else.'

'I know.'

'Do you? Why would you say that? Did he tell you?'

'Look. I can't get into it. All I can say is, this hurts me too. I want you to know I'm here for you. I've been through stuff myself, you know that now. You will grow from this. Remember what I said: it will pass.'

There was a thickness in my voice and tears fell onto my hands. 'I don't want it to pass.'

'It's okay, sweetheart. It really will, I promise.'

'I'm going to stay with him in my mind—forever and ever. No one can stop me—and what's the *matter* with you? You didn't even say anything to me or say goodbye or anything.'

'Oh god. You're right. I'm sorry.'

'You ran away.' I smothered a sniff, wiped at my nose with my

71

sleeve.

'They were pretty furious with me. And very shocked.'

'Does Mum scare you?'

He chuckled. 'A bit. You?'

'Not really.'

'Good. She loves you, you know.'

'She loves you too.'

'Yeah, right.'

'Do you think she'll let me come though?'

Another pause. 'I hope so. Maybe not on your own.'

'Well, I'm not coming with—I'm not coming with anyone from this family. But maybe Stuart.'

'Let's just wait and see, hey? It's not for a few months yet.'

'I bet she won't let me. She'll probably make me wait till I'm sixteen.'

'We'll sort it out. But…you know, he—'

'—I *know*. He's gone. And you're going to make sure I never see him again.' I crashed the receiver into its cradle, spinning myself around to go back upst

am on that old bike i found in my uncle's shed all whizzing downhill to the stables down the twisting rolling lane cow parsley and brambles rushing by in my periphery my heart all coasting the rusty-red of the bike frame bearing me on its rotting nail-studded saddle the jolt of it hard into my gloriously bruised flesh riding the bumps in the road all sort of hurting and stirring at the same time sending tingles to my centre upward from the nub of my pink bright secret my hair makes fluttering wings like mercury and everything is laughing with me *oh no!* all tiny explosions in my face my arms some kind of swarm pummelling into my eyes mouth strangling spluttering blinding as i blink and squint and try my hardest to peddle backwards fighting the bike's natural downward velocity but the antiquated peddle-break system is inconsequential at this speed and trajector

going to crash everything in slow motio

not stoppi

shall i plunge myself into the hedg

eyes stinging burning as i cling to the handlebars in a blur *oh!* the road is slowing and i am taken up its sudden change of heart it's upward course it lets me stop i throw down the bike ripping at my eyes finding miniscule green bodies crumpled against my fingerti

he is crushing me in his arms i am aching and longing for his hands to love me his fingers with wiry hairs like seaweed hi

I ran through the living room door, out through the dining room, into the kitchen and out the back door. There was no place to be but in his arms. I ran across the tugging gravel into the village street, kept right on running until I reached the public footpath that ran around a field and led down to the river, which was more of a stream really, nothing like the river in County Cork where stinging nettles stung me, where he found me nursing myself, where we met and walked together under the canopy of pink chestnut spears and I dreamed to lay with him on their carpet of fallen flowers on the tamped damp ear

*there's otter in there you know* he says *if you come and sit very quietly for a good while you can get to see them i'd quite like to be an otter* i say *or an under-water plant maybe* i turn to face him *can we come and watch for otter together someti*

I was panting, bent over, leaning into my hands on my knees. I saw the inflamed white bumps, red all around, like they were still there on my legs. I knew they would be there forever. The stinging nettles had written his name in joined up handwriting on my legs even before we knew what that meant. He saw it and I saw it but to everyone else it was illegible, just a bunch of stings that made them feel sorry for me for about five seconds.

I uprighted myself and looked along the path. Nettles grew everywhere; it didn't matter where you were. They were dark now, and dusty-looking, with whitish tassels of tiny flowers. I walked right into them.

*Episode Four: Bindweed*

We stopped, Stuart and I, at the sound of a car at our backs, dug ourselves into the verge, all turning to tune into its red body looming toward us. We stuck out our thumbs. The hawthorn caught itself in my jacket, its tiny beginnings of green berries whispering at my shoulders. They made a scratchy song against his soft guitar case.

'Come on, come on,' I muttered. 'Please stop.'

The car rushed past and was gone. I tugged my hair out of the hedge, adjusted the bag on my shoulder, picked up my mother's fancy tapestry holdall from beside my feet. We trudged on along the country road under a dense sky, the prospect of rain growing in the air. My foster brother looked like he was made of string, that very white soft kind, all supple and willowy—a thread of a boy in a cream cambric shirt under Navaho poncho, guitar at his back. We'd been on the road for over an hour, had missed the main rush of traffic, having had to wait till my mum and dad were gone off to work before we could leave. We had chosen a day when my sister was staying with her frizzy friend.

'We're going to walk all the way to the motorway at this rate,' I said.

'We'll get a lift. Next one, I bet you.'

'How much you wanna bet?'

He elbowed me. 'A quid?'

'Two quid.'

'You're on. Want me to carry your bag?' He indicated the holdall straining in my grip.

'Don't be stupid. I'm not a *girl*, you know. I can carry my own bag.'

'True—you're an alien. It looks really heavy, is all. Why did you bring so much? I told you not to.'

'Because I need my things. I'm not leaving them for *her* to steal, am I?'

'Who cares what she does? You won't have to see your cow of a sister anymore or anything.'

'I just don't want her wearing my clothes. And you know she would. She'd wear my eyeliner and lipgloss too, if I left it. Just out of spite. And anyway, I might not be able to afford to buy any more for a while. No one's going to give me any pocket money. And what if I can't get a job?'

'True. It's a bummer you can't go on the dole 'til you're sixteen.'

'Yeh, six whole months and a half away. Flipping ages.' I butted my shoulder into him. 'But you're going to support me, remember? With *your* dole money, huh? You're not changing your mind? Until I find a job?'

'You know I will.' He put his arm around me, drew me into him. 'You know how much I love you.'

I dropped my bag, chucked my arms around him. 'I love you too. What would I do without you?'

'Stay at home. Go to school. Run away on your own maybe.'

'Imagine if she hadn't fostered you. The day you joined my family was a happy day, even though I didn't know it yet, thought having a new brother was a serious bore. An impingement.'

'Impingement?' He squeezed me tighter. 'Like this?'

'No,' I said. 'Like this. An im*pinch*ment.' And I nipped his skinny bum, hard-as.

'Oi. But mum's not going to think it was so happy anymore, is she?'

I pulled out of his embrace and we held each other at the elbows, staring into one another's eyes. He was smiling. And he nodded.

'She's going to be furious with you,' I said. 'I wonder if we'll ever see her again?'

'Of course we will.'

'After I'm sixteen.'

He shrugged. 'I guess.'

'You sure you want to do this? You like having a mum, don't you? Even though you're of age and can do what you like. Will I be enough for you?' He pinched my cheek and I yanked myself away. 'Ow. I hate when you do that.'

'I know you do.'

'I'll be enough? Family?'

I didn't notice a car was coming until he was sticking out his thumb and then the sound of it filled my head and I turned to see a small white van gaining on us. My heart leaped. I jutted out my own thumb next to his, all grinning. The van passed us and then it was slowing and stopping. The back windows had some sort of mirror stuff stuck to the inside so you couldn't see in. We ran the twenty feet or so down the road, me all shouting out, lamenting the loss of two pounds from my small pool of savings.

'We'll buy you a present with it,' he called, all jolty.

'I've already got the present.'

'You what?'

'The *now*, dummy,' I yelled.

Sort of skidding to a stop, he beamed at me. 'Now, now.' He was panting. 'I'll get you a lipgloss.'

'No, some paints—paints for sure—paints.'

He leaned into the ajar car door, pulled it wider. Soul music blared out. 'We need to get to the motorway. We're going to London.'

I joined him, smiling into the van. 'Hello. London. We're going to London.'

The driver was older than my bro, maybe eighteen or so, with a mop of curly hair cropped short at the sides, the top tumbling forward over greenish eyes. Something skipped inside of me when I saw him. 'Shame,' he said. 'I'm going to London on Sunday—to Brick Lane market. But I can take you as far as Bishop's Stortford today.'

'Great,' I said.

'How far's that?' asked Stuart.

'About an hour from London. You'll be well on your way. Do you know where you're going?'

'Got no idea,' I said, all blithe.

'Course,' said Stuart.

I nudged him, hissed under my breath, 'But we *don't*.'

He winked. 'I haven't said anything, have I?'

Since it was a van there was only a front seat, a sort of bench seat, so I slipped right in, Stuart after me, our stuff taking up most of the legroom. I put my feet up on the holdall, brown knees breaching the line of the windscreen like heather-hazed hills, the perspective all warped because they were in the foreground when they should have been way off behind the view of the rustling green wheat fields and hedgerows.

A crack opened up in my own hazy distance, deep inside, into which rushed Ireland, all those heather bells, my knees crushing tiny blue flowers, torso rising up into the fresh sky; it was an everlasting sharp unquenchable pain. I'll always love you. But then we were shooting off, as if we were at the start of a race, the black and white chequered flag flung downwards and my stomach flipping, all throwing excitement up into my throat. For a few seconds thought was guzzled, the void undetectable, and I felt elated. I wanted to laugh but I stopped myself. I knew the laughter connected to hysteria, was the same as crying, that tears would spring from it. It was too secret. I got a hold of Stuart's hand, squeezed it.

'So you're going for a visit, are you?' said the driver, glancing across my legs at our bags.

'We're moving there,' I told him.

'Groovy. Whereabouts?'

'Portland Square,' I said.

Stuart made a sharp in-breath.

'That's a bit posh,' the driver said.

'It's not. It's his old school friend's squat, see.' My brother jabbed me in the ribs. 'Only I didn't say that.'

'What's the biggy? Squatting's groovy.'

'Groovy,' I said, teasy-as.

He caught my eye, gave me a look that said he liked me. 'I'm Shirty.'

'James,' said Stuart.

I felt the gentle pressure of his elbow. 'Yes: Stella. Like in *A Streetcar Named Desire*—get it?' I pulled an agonised face, looked up at an imagined upper doorway, constricted my throat so my yell came out quiet, '*Stella…Stella…*' Stuart's elbow told me I was way out of hand. 'We're cousins, James and me.' He rubbernecked me, all glare—I could feel it, without even looking at him. I grinned. 'He hates when I say that.'

'Why, Jamie? What's wrong with cousins? Do you fancy her, is that it?'

'No, of course not,' Stuart said. 'What are you doing in Bishop's Stortford?'

'Picking up a delivery for my boss.'

'What kind of delivery?'

'I work on a market stall, selling household goods and toiletries and stuff. But I'm training to be a hairdresser.'

I felt Stuart hoot inside, all kind of mean and victorious—and I stifled my own gurgle. 'We're going to busk,' I said. 'In Piccadilly Circus. And at tube stations. You know?'

'No, *I'm* going to busk.'

'And sign on the dole,' I added.

'She can't sing to save her life. And she can't sign on. She's getting a paper round.'

'Bit old for a paper round, aren't you?' said Shirty.

'We're bohemians,' I said. 'Artists, potters, musicians. Doing a paper round is art in my world. My mother's a flower child from San Francisco.'

'Is that why you can't sign on? You're an American citizen?'

I nodded, mirth spilling out of me at the crazy image of my mum as an American hippy.

We hit the motorway and sped along in the fast lane, faster than anyone else, forcing everyone over, a whooshing crack jumping into me every time we passed another vehicle. The windows were wide open, my hair thrashing to the music, whipping me and Stuart and Shirty, the whole thing kicking life alive. The countryside flew by, the feel of summer in it, everything already turning heavy and darker green, though it was still only June. It looked like it wasn't going to rain after all, fine streaks of blue beginning to penetrate the clouds, all like pale-cerulean pencil marks. We yelled about London over the pumping funk and Shirty said he was planning to move there himself as soon as his hairdressing course was over.

'What's so funny, mister?' he said to Stuart.

'Nothing. I dunno. It's a bit woolly-woofter, isn't it?'

'Like fuck. I get to play with girls all day. There's money to be made in it. I'm setting up a shop in Kensington Market with a mate—he's forty-odd, been a hairdresser for fucking ever and is married, by the way, with three kids. We've already found a space and we're negotiating terms.'

'So you're going to be in London soon?' I asked. 'Don't mind him. His mother's a homophobic racist Neanderthal alcoholic.'

As Stuart drove his guitar-plucking nail into the flesh of my hip Shirty grinned, eyed me askance. 'In about five weeks. Hey, why don't you come and meet me on Sunday in Brick Lane?'

'Okay.

'I'll give you the details when I drop you off.'

'Stuart—*James*,' I barked. 'You're hurting me.' Turning to glare at him I saw how he was blinking a lot and looking fraught and I realised I was hurting him. I realised I had wanted to, but I couldn't see why. My eyes blistered, my own heart gripped tight, heat flaring into my cheeks. 'Oh,' I whispered. 'I'm sorry. I'm sorry. I didn't mean—'

'—who *are* you?' A bubble of spit blew from his mouth and popped as he spoke. 'I thought I knew you.'

'You do know me. I'm me. I didn't mean it—I don't know wha—'

'—maybe this isn't such a good idea. Maybe we should go back.'

79

He was bent over his guitar, his wavy hair falling in dark layers over his bony face, everyone gathered around, and in the candlelight, singing his own song, he glowed and became beautiful. I felt my heart plump up, all like it wanted to spill outside the reaches of my chest and hold me inside its pumping red ventricles; I felt a sort of sweetness I hadn't known in over a year. I understood right then I truly loved Stuart, who dared to be vulnerable and real, and it was so unexpected to realise the innocent depths love could take, it made me fly a little.

I gazed up at the high ceiling of the large living room. The wide architrave was all the more gorgeous for its crumbliness, and the old chandelier hanging from the central ceiling rose, which was a sunflower, shimmered, refracted yellow light around the room from its twenty or so dripping candles. In the daytime, sunlight hit the cut-glass teardrop crystals, scattered a hundred rainbows. Most of the wall space was crammed with drawings and paintings and large photographic prints, fashion images all deliberately scratched up, other shots ripped from magazines. There was a series of sculptures made from twisted metal, plaster, paint and paper; a projector running an art film on a loop, directly onto a section of scarred wall. Every piece of work was created by those who lived there or by close friends. The squat had been running around two years before my couple of months. I hadn't yet had the courage to stick up any of my own work, but the room I shared with Stuart was littered with drawings, all scribbly graphite with blue and green paint rushing across the paper. He'd put a load of them up, near our bed, each with a single thumb tack, and they were curling over, billowed in the breeze when it snuck through the open window whilst we slept.

Stuart's voice was plaintive, as was his song, and suddenly I needed to leave the room. I tried to be stealthy but I had to go part way round the circle of audience and he caught my eye. I saw a glint there, made some half-cocked gesture that tried to show him I was sorry; which I was, but somehow not enough, which didn't make sense—me needing to get away didn't make sense, none of it did. I couldn't even explain my feelings or actions to myself.

I was glad to shut the door behind me, absorbed into the deep darkness of the corridor. I just stood there, letting my eyes adjust. I rummaged in the pocket of my cut-off denim mini-skirt, fished out a few loose coins and started through the undulating shapes my eyes formed in the night-time air. My bare feet made a sticking sound as they peeled off of the cold stone, grit scratching into them and against the flags. I could just make out the high walls by now, bits of peeling paper making abstracted shapes the like of which I drew again and again, in a kind of compulsive lost state, up in my room. I felt how I was recording them for later. I reached the brown Bakelite light switch outside the kitchen, fingered it, but was reluctant to blow the dream of the dark in which I was merged.

And the thought of my dad came. I wondered what he was doing and whether he was missing me and did he, too, like the dark, where he could vanish, as he always seemed to want? I wondered if I'd inherited this wish from him.

The copper coins were sweating in my palm, chinking against each other. I could make out the old payphone on the wall but I didn't know if I wanted to call Shirty after all. He would only want me to hike it all the way to his flat in Kilburn. He never wanted to come to the squat, there were too many people, he said. Which didn't really wash because he liked people. I knew he was intimidated. He was from a different world—burgundy loafers, straight jeans, Camber Sands, that soul-boy hair. When I teased him, he complained we had no bed, even though Stuart went and slept on the sofa downstairs. Oh Shirty, I thought.

But I needed to feel his breath hot in my ear—I needed his crass *babe* to meet my hateful hunger. His tongue would follow the words, make a thick muffled wetness inside that little tunnel. I wanted the swooning, trembles deep within. The groans and the forgetting. For our bodies to form that fine sweat, skin against skin, hard and soft, shivering and shoving.

I lifted the heavy black receiver, put my ear to its bottomless purr, readied a coin in the notch of the slot. My forefinger worked the dial, the sound of its clunking return hypnotic-as. I listened as the number connected in small clicks, all going inside of me, felt the first rush of pleasure as if it were his fingers. The shrill ringing had just begun and my forehead was up against the wall, sticky, when the door to the living room sprung open, casting sharp rectangles of light into the hallway, a golden emanation, a kind of pain coming into my retracting pupils. I flicked my fingers into the hook, cut off the line.

There was a buzz of chatter, a gathered radiance, everyone moving and coming forward in the light. Stuart was among them, his tall skinny frame easy to spot. I could see his white skin shining from the slashes he'd cut in his t-shirt. He caught my eye and I looked away.

'Hey, you.' It was Eliot. Big man, big energy. His booming voice, all with its strange slothful drawl, sent nasty hot waves through my skin. 'What're you up to out here in the dark? You look flushed. Phone sex?' He carried on past me like he'd said nothing at all. He was *the* hippest, most artsy fashion photographer ever, was twenty-three going on fifty, scared the shit out of me. I routinely avoided him, felt we had nothing in common.

'Camomile tea?' asked Jessie, her long blonde dreadlocks matt as a cloudy sky. Her solid voluptuous body, with that hair, made me think of those woolly Highland cows. 'Or are you for more wine?'

Blinking, I turned with her into the kitchen, hung close to her floor-length gathered skirt, waited as she put the kettle on. I opened the door to the back garden for her.

'I'll help you,' I said.

'You like the garden, huh?' she said.

I took to plucking heads off the wild camomile flowers she cultivated among the many vegetables, crushing one between my fingers. Its scent was like the golden candlelight, rich, deeper than its colour. 'I like how you grow everything naturally.'

'It's the old way. Companion planting. Crop rotation, natural predators and all.'

'Ladybirds.'

'And mayflies. And even wasps eat greenfly.'

'I was wondering if I might help?''

'Of course. You don't need to ask. I'll be glad. Got green fingers, have you?'

'I don't know. But I just love plants. And watching them grow.'

'And eating them,' she said. 'Oh, look at the moon. You can really see his face.'

'His?' I looked up. It was full and bright and the face looked smeared with infinite tragic beauty. I was thinking of *his* face, something of his expression when he had made love to me. I tried to see his pale-blue eyes, huge pupils, the roughhewn skin. I could hardly remember him anymore, to actually see, the thoughts were all I had: words and blur. I put myself in Ireland to try and make him clearer. But it was no good. I stared up at the moon face.

'You think it's a woman?' Jessie was saying. 'That's very cool. Me too, from now on.'

We put the handfuls of flowers into a huge aluminium teapot. I stood right next to her as she poured boiling water over them, steam all rising, bringing the pungent essential oils out and up, the smell intensified, somehow ruddy. The brew was the colour of urine and tasted like earth, how I imagined Jessie might taste.

As I sipped the infusion, eyes into my flowered teacup, Eliot stepped toward me, forcing me to look up. I cowered inside, took a breath. He was towering and broad, not skinny, not fat, his fair hair quiffed to perfection. He wore a cornflower-blue silk cravat tied at his neck like a Forties film star, all tucked inside a white V-necked t-shirt. 'Hey you, we're starting an acting group. We're going to meet in the conservatory every Wednesday at five. You should join.'

'Okay.'

'You acted before?'

I shook my head.

'I think you'd be good. You need to start mucking in. Can't just be a recluse here, you know. It's a commune, yeh? Comm-unity?'

'I will.'

'So what are you doing, always up in your room? It's a good room, I know, but…'

'I draw. And paint.'

He nodded. 'Can I have a look?'

'Not yet.'

He nodded again, this time smiling. 'Cool. So you going to join?'

83

'Yeah, okay.'

'We'll do improvisation around a theme first time. Love, I reckon. And see what comes out of it. Thinking we might do a performance at a club for starters. Stir up the comfort zone. You up for it?'

'Yep.'

'You going to come out tonight?'

I hid in my teacup. 'Mmm,' I said, inhaling the chamomile. 'This is like the outside.'

'About time you came out. It's Lauren's night. She's got Tyrone DJ-ing, which is quite the coup, very cool. He's the best, always busy. It's—what, ten minutes' walk?'

'I know.' I glanced at Lauren. Her black-as skin all seemed to glitter like it was always slightly damp. Her hair was ironed, she called it.

She had turned to gaze up to me from her chair at the table. 'Come on, girlfriend,' she said in her American twang. 'You're gonna have a blast, for sure. I've got a great look for you, too. I found this wicked red catsuit just the other day, in some thrift store, way too small for my big ass. You're going to look great in it. We'll cut the neck. We can work it with this denim frill I've borrowed, this teensy skirt with built-in crotch—I just used it the other day on a shoot. Super cute.' My heart quivered as I nodded. 'Up in my room in say, forty-five? Maybe Karl will do your make-up, huh Karl, you reckon? Midnight-blue glitter all around her eyes?'

'Fabulous,' Karl said. He studied me from under his own dark eye-shadow and mascara-licked lashes. 'Maybe gold glitter, though. And loads of blue eyeliner.'

'Cu-ute,' said Lauren. 'And what about her lips?'

As they continued to discuss the look they were making for me, Eliot asked, 'So what's with you and Stu, then? You practising Sixties free love? Open relationship? Who's that other guy?' I shrugged, glanced around for Stuart, who wasn't there, felt a raw heat blush in my cheeks. 'It's a free country,' he said. 'Whatever it takes. I've got my vices.'

'Why would it be a vice?' I said.

He chuckled. 'You're right. I was well making a judgement—for all my bullshit about freedom. What a hypocrite.'

'Stuart and me are like brother and sister. We *are* brother and sister, see. That's it.'

'Ah. So the other one's your boyfriend.'

'I guess. If you want to label it.'

He laughed. And it was very loud, rumbled through me. I saw him like a mountain covered in yellow gorse; there was sunshine *and* thorns in him. A kind of exhilaration sparked up inside of me, all like I was up on Delicious Punk, racing on the final straight, my harlequined silks fluttering and snapping against my goose-bumped skin.

❧

Eliot was lounged in the deep buttoned sofa, its ripped brown hide revealing greyed-up calico underwear so—what with the scrapes and grazes criss-crossing its surface—it looked like some kind of intentionally worked canvas. He was pulling on a joint, his huge feet up, had commandeered the whole seat, was all filling the room with his massive slo-mo voice.

'Know yourself, that's what they're always saying. Like it's some sacred key. Like it has any meaning. *Know yourself?* I tell you, I'd believe it, if I hadn't been getting to know myself since I was ten years old, stuck in analysis, and yet right here, right now, I don't know who the hell I am. They say I'm like the sum total of my past, as if everything that happens to me defines me which, sure, maybe it does on a level but is that *really* me? The more I delve into it, the stronger all that shit becomes me, but this thing I think of as myself just *can't* be me. Otherwise I'd know myself, right? I don't know what I'm saying, but it's got to be making sense somehow.'

He tugged the longest drag, passed the spliff to pig-tailed Todd-baby, all sprawled in an armchair with brown-as Merl slung across his lap. As he resettled himself, Eliot scratched at his scalp and up under his t-shirt; you could hear the skin getting kind of torn up under his nails.

'Yeah well, the self is an illusion, isn't it?' I said, from my perch on two tatty gold-fringed cushions.

'Wow, man, yeah. I don't know. What the hell does *that* mean?'

'The self we *identify* with is an illusion, that's what I mean—my uncle calls it your "small self"—he goes on about it all the time—it's like we think we're our name, our sex, our nationality, our mind, our past even, like you said, but we're not—that's not the true Self—capital S, see?—is it?'

Todd-Baby's voice came strangled, all holding in smoke, his narrowed blue eyes flashing their electric spark. 'Course it is, baby.'

'No, all that stuff is just like the clothes we put on—they're not actually us, see. The inner or *actual* Self is, like, eternal. And you're not your body either—'

'—*course* I am my body,' came Todd-Baby, puffing up his wide chest.

'You're not. This is how my uncle would say it: you are Consciousness experiencing life *through* this body but you will never find your Self there. The Buddhists do this meditation thing, where they seek themselves in every part of their anatomy, like, Am I my big toe? Am I my nose? My liver?'

'Well, obviously, baby, I'm not just my big ol' bony nose, am I?'

'You know what I mean, Todd-baby.'

'Obviously, every bit of me is me. *Including* my nozzle, baby. And my liver.'

'*My* liver's fucked,' said Eliot. 'And it's definitely not me. Or maybe it is…hey, maybe I really am *actually* my liver. Fucked.'

'The liver is the one organ that can regenerate itself,' Merl said, his Edinburgh brogue butterfly-soft. 'So if you're your liver you're in luck, eh.'

'No, but see, your body does everything without you even directing it,' I said. 'It's its own intelligence. *You* are beyond it. See, it will just keep doing stuff for you—like making tea—like smoking your spliffy, huh, Todd-baby?—and heal itself even—without you needing to think about it. It's like, yes, you inhabit it, but it's not actually you.'

'I really kinda like being my body. Stop ruining it, baby. I don't see how I can't be my body *and* all that other consciousness rubbishio too—if you like.'

'See look, the body dies, but the eternal big Self is our fundamental life force, see? our Being—and it's all outside of space and time—it's this silent stillness inside of you. Everybody has it, see?—my uncle would make me feel it all the time—he'd make me go all still, just tune in, get my mind to stop thinking. Be Awareness, he'd say. Be Now. I swear to you, I really felt it.'

'What am I going to do with *that*, baby? I'm here on this Earth. *Human.* I'm actually living *now*—talking of "now". Right? Give me La Grand Illusion any day.'

'Ah but a human *being*,' Eliot quipped.

'And the illusion-self makes you suffer. See, your mind clings, obsesses about your pain—it just kind of magnifies it, continues it, the more you focus on it. Something like that. Cos you're not your mind either.'

'Now I really don't know what you're on about,' said Todd-Baby, taking a deep draw on the joint through his skinny lipstick-darkened lips.

'You don't want to, more like.'

'I mean, just *why*—why have this damned illusion self? that causes suffering? Seems messed up to me.'

'Um…I don't really know, see—sort of to help you see your *real* Self—something like that…'

'It's brilliant,' Eliot boomed. 'He'd say that shit to you when you were a kid? Pretty cool uncle.'

I shrugged. 'Kind of, I guess. He says we make ourselves suffer. But he did *actually* make me suffer…'

'Oh angel,' murmured Merl, his brown eyes all doe-ish. 'How?'

'Yeah, that's making sense,' said Eliot. 'We create our own suffering with our thinking—like, how we interpret a situation, I reckon he's saying—then drive ourselves mad obsessing about it. Yeah. I get it— have I loved clinging to the past, the pain. Still do. But why? So he's saying we're not our mind though? That's a head fuck. I'd like to meet him, talk this shit out. Let's do that.'

'But what happened when you were ten?' I asked. 'I mean, that made you go into analysis? Was that when your mother…?'

He shifted on the sofa, the leather creaked. He scratched at his cheek, an upward motion with the back of his fingernails. 'Yeah…' Scratched his arm, his skin rasping raw. '*That* suffering. I'm getting shunted about between my broken-down mother and my po-faced old man—who I can tell you, if he could've, would've given her a lobotomy. Thank God you can't operate on your own family. He probably would've liked to dig around in my brain too. It would've been cheaper than therapy. He would've liked to hollow it out, remake me the way he wanted. Still would.'

'So you don't get on?'

'Not since he left her, really. Maybe never. And when she killed herself, I refused to live with him. He sends me to boarding school—and that gets rough as hell. And then the therapy starts. I changed schools three times. The last one was in Suffolk. Good old Stu. He was only a little kid—I was sixteen by then, he must have been maybe nine—but for the first time I saw myself in someone else. I understood him; he understood me.'

Todd-baby was feeding Merl the joint, holding it up to his mouth, fingers all splayed. Merl took hungry drags, three in a row, all without releasing any in between.

'I see myself in Stuart sometimes too,' I said. 'I don't know if I like it.'

'I mean I saw myself in a *good* way.'

'Me too, but—'

'—he's done amazing, that kid. I wish you two would sort it out. I've seen the way you check each other out all the time. He'd be a killer boyfriend, couldn't do any better.'

'He's my brother.'

'Yeah. So what's with *that*? You guys don't even have anything to do with your—I mean *your*, not his, yeh—your parents.' I shrugged as he eyeballed me. 'You know, what they don't see, these therapist types—'

'—she's actually a counsellor—'

'—they don't see that it's all about creativity. Forget searching for the self in all your past trauma. All it takes to really connect to the *self*, the true essence, is allowing the free-flow of creativity. As soon as I became an artist, I became free. Even when I'm not free, I'm free.'

Out the corner of my eye, I saw Todd-baby and Merl each take another big puff, and finally the orange-tipped smoke came my way.

'Yeah freedom,' Eliot was saying, his eyes closing as he drifted in the freedom of his stone. His breath went heavy. He scratched at his cheek again, so the room just seemed to fill with the dry rasp.

Todd-baby and Merl were kissing, Merl curling into Todd-baby, knees all tucked up. Todd-baby's hand was cupping Merl's bum in his jeans, the other cupping his shorn head.

I took a sharp toke on the joint, watching the end flare redder as it crackled and fizzed. I held down the first draw, took another, saw the paper blacken and shrink from the tip. I leaned forward, all holding my breath in my chest, scraped the heavy glass ashtray toward me across the wooden floorboards and flicked the end of the spliff, ash falling away from it like black snow. I released a billowing cloud of smoke from my lips, watched it swirl in the air, took another drag, pulled it deep into my lungs.

'Oh,' said Eliot, gaping at me. 'Maybe don't…you don't wanna…' At his tone, the others turned their heads. They all three stared at me in a weird alert kind of a way, all like bullocks watching an animal that might attack. The dope was reaching into my brain.

'What?'

'It's…you shouldn't have…shit…'

Breath snagging, I realised the spliff must be laced with a chase, as they called it. 'Oh,' I said. 'Why didn't you say?'

'I tried,' said Eliot.

'Hardly. Is it going to hurt me? Will I get addicted? Am I going to be sick?' I felt the high go way into my body, opening up in my bloodstream. It was as if I could feel all my capillaries, everywhere, humming. 'Oh my God, it feels nice.'

'I doubt you'll puke,' said Eliot, levering himself up. I could see he was trying to be cool but I didn't care anymore. 'It's such a small amount. But if you do, we'll take care of you. Aw shit.'

'You won't get addicted,' said Merl, his voice coming as gentle arms wrapping around me. 'I only do it this way and I can control it completely, eh? The thing is never to inject.'

I went for another toke, the heat of the joint palpable against my skin as I inhaled, its moist cardboard roach warm between my lips.

'Stop,' cried Eliot, leaping up. He nipped the joint from between my fingers. I watched him in slow motion it seemed. 'She might be different than you, Merl. You never know a person's chemistry. Shit, I made it pretty fucking strong too.'

I felt my eyes closing, my body go floppy and heavy and heavenly. Everything was floating. I couldn't hardly sit up anymore. It was different to hash or grass. It just took me right over, made my mind feel blank and blissed-out. I felt a field of stillness growing within me, bleeding and connecting to an underlying silence, which was outside of me too, and everywhere, like this must be how you were really supposed to be, like actually this really was my *Self*. I had the feeling my body was disappearing. I heard a strange distant thud, felt a reverberation through my flesh, realising I had crashed onto my back. I didn't care, was totally settled in myself, everything inside still-as—and my body vanishing again, like this was my true state. The voices around me were fused into one, unintelligible, a wide breadth of sound, which I saw undulating in my head, like musical notes on a page, all beautiful. I was part of a daisy chain, everything, everyone, linked together.

I felt hands rummaging under me. I was lifted from the floor, opened my eyes to find my body in Eliot's arms, all up against his chest. He was warm and I was melting. 'Oh, this is everything, isn't it?' I murmured. 'Now I know why you…'

'No,' he said. 'It's nothing. Nothing at all, you hear?'

I wasn't sure if I actually nodded as I tucked my head into him. I might have said, I never felt so good, but I didn't know if the words, my voice, came out of my mouth or were in my head.

'I want you to promise you'll never do this again. Promise.'

*You* do it, I might have said—I wanted to say—but I don't think I could speak, nor cared to. I nodded, blurred sunshine in my being.

'I can't be responsible for—oh Christ,' he said.

Merl said, 'She can't take it on now, man. This is not the time, eh? You wanna get over yourself right now, big man.'

'I'm going to put you on the sofa, okay?' Eliot said. 'Merl is going to watch you. Won't you, Merl? Watch her, will you? I'm going to have to…'

I saw Eliot had the joint stuck between his lips, his left eye winking from the smoke. I was sure he was drawing on it. I wanted it. He lay me down, nestled my head into Merl's lap. I heard fantastic clacks as he took off across the vast room, the door slamming like it did at home when the wind caught in it. Home. I was glad I wasn't there. Where was Stuart again? Merl stroked my hair with too much tenderness. It was the nicest feeling I'd ever had, I thought. But I knew that wasn't true. It just felt like it, right now, under the influence of Eliot's horse. Why was it called horse? It was made from poppies. Poppies were beautiful. Boys crushed it under their feet in Afghanistan. I had the residue of boys' feet inside of me, felt them stomping and it was lovely. Merl's fingers were so gentle. I didn't need to look at him to know I liked the way everything about him was a soft kind of brown: brown hair, brown eyes, brown skin. Horse was brown too. Wasn't it? There was wet coming out of my eyes, purifying streams running down my temples and into his fingers. Resistance came into the way my cheek pressed into his warmth.

'Are you okay?' he said. 'You're crying.'

I nodded without opening my eyes. My face might have made a smile, I wasn't sure, but his belly softened.

'You've got the face of an angel,' he said.

Someone said that before, I wanted to say, feeling a delicate joy at the thought. My mouth made a clicking sound as it opened and shut, all like a baby bird.

'Can I use you in my new film, angel?'

I nodded. At least I think I did.

'You're a bit fucking good in those improvs, eh? Where'd you learn to act like that? You must have done it before, right? You haven't though, have you?'

I wanted to tell him I could be someone else when I acted, I didn't have to be me anymore, I could tap into and ride my feelings like they were ghosts of everyone, anyone, like all experience moved through me. When I acted, I seemed to have all of human nature inside of me. Nature itself. But my eyes just flickered, saw him gazing down at me. I wanted to tell him he looked like the Buddha. Then I wondered, why would I want to be someone else? I got the feeling that being me was the most magnificent permutation possible.

'Us lot can't act to save our lives, eh? None of us, really. Walter maybe. Henrietta's okay. But you have natural talent. You're something else, eh? Raw fucking beautiful fucking emotion. You *are* an angel, I reckon.'

And with closed eyes, right then, I saw *him*, like I was in Ireland right next to him and I knew this really was—he was—the nicest feeling I ever could have. I saw him. I felt him. He floated with me, fingers entwined. I saw his palest blue eyes, clear as the poppies growing in the back garden, clear as the sky. There were rushing images, a deep inner writhing, like we were making love and training the racehorses and imprinting the foal and I was leaning out the window having a coded conversation and we are in the café outside the café in the pub on the moor him shoving chips in my face fingers in my face playing kiss chase by the water fingers all over me and inside me everything all at onc

Jessie's large square room was all like an art gallery. She had filled the holes and cracks in the walls, painted them sparkly-white, framed up and hung her amazing collages around the whole space. She had moved all her stuff, including her bed, and put it in with Stuart and me, where she was staying for the two weeks her exhibition was going to be running. The first night party, the private view, as Jessie said, in a laughing ironic voice, was happening tonight.

I took myself from piece to piece, eyes running over the myriad images: cut-up photographs from her life, ripped bits of letters, diaries, postcards, words, countless scraps of anything all mashed together with a compelling aesthetic, her own artistic compulsion. I saw how they formed new forms from old forms, contained forms within, yet from a distance were abstracted; it was the rub between form and formlessness, I thought, feeling myself brainy and Shakespeare-as.

There were pieces made with her cat's whiskers, saved over the years as they'd moulted—which I didn't even know happened until then—all placed in rows under glass; as expressive as fine dancing pencil marks. And in slender glass vials were gathered hundreds of her minuscule fingernail slivers, like new moons, alongside her cat's claw clippings, which had earth all caught in them and appeared like tiny chips of mother-of-pearl. I wasn't sure how I felt about her trimming her cat's claws but I kept shtum.

She was fiddling at the trestle table she'd placed beneath her two large windows, was lining up rented wine glasses. The clear September sunlight caught on their rims, brought them together, like an infantry of soldiers on parade. Jessie had cut off her shine-defying dreadlocks, pruned them, she liked to say, with pinking shears, and Todd-baby had taken his scissors and his expert hand to the mess, turning her mop into a cool crop. Her dreads were encased in a perspex box, each one suspended from an invisible fishing line. They appeared to float in stillness, three-dimensional scribbles. She looked taller without them, leaner, like she was a lioness, all strong legs and arms, sensuous curves, and huge pools for eyes.

I scanned one of the collages, skimming from detail to detail, then stepped back to take in the shift of perspective, everything morphing into connective amorphous shapes. I felt Jessie had captured the kernel of joy. She made me want to see inside the picture, beyond its fibres, as well as every element of its nebulous whole.

I craned in close again. My heart made a skip. 'Wha—who's this?'

'Hang on.' She perfected the placement of a glass, then strode toward me, and I saw how her blonde hair shimmered as she moved through the throw of sunlight. 'Oh, no one. Just an old boyfriend.'

'But who is he?'

'Like I said, no one.'

'But he was your boyfriend.'

'He wasn't even a boyfriend—just some guy I went out with for about five minutes.'

'He doesn't have a name?'

She grinned, raised her eyebrows. 'What's in a name?'

'You don't see him anymore?'

'I don't see him anymore.' She shook her head. 'It was some years ago. I guess I was about your age, maybe a bit older. I think he might have been younger than me, I can't really remember.'

'And you don't remember his name?'

'You got it. Why, anyway?'

I gazed into the tiny image of a boy's face cut away from his body and any outward sign of his history. I felt strangely huge, in dispersion, all like time didn't exist. I was with him somehow, even as I was stood here. And I was with *him*, in Ireland. And maybe they were one. Him young; him not so young. They joined up in my mind, one person. There was gold thread spooled around the boy's head. It spiralled outward and took in a dried rose petal, a flat metal circle, then broke off into an area of painted black.

'Planets,' I said. 'It looks like he's the sun with planets encircling him. In Space. Eternity.'

'He's just a small part of the whole,' she said.

The moment hardened, my mind taking over, seeking answers. 'You really liked him, didn't you?'

She shrugged. 'I hardly knew him. Why the interest anyway?'

'I don't know. Maybe he looks like someone I know. But he can't be him because he's too young. And maybe better looking. He reminds me of him, see. He could actually *be* him if he wasn't so young and if he was, say, your mother's old flame, rather than yours. Or if he was sliding in time.'

'Funny. But you're right, there *was* a kind of flame there. Do *you* know his name?'

'Who's?'

She nodded at the little head. 'His.'

'His? How could I?'

'So what would it matter if I told you?'

'I don't know. Maybe they would have the same name and there would be some weird connection.'

She chuckled softly, her hand travelling to her heart. 'What was the other guy's name?'

'Like you said: zip.'

'Right.'

'Anyway, it's such a tiny photo, I can hardly tell. Do you have any more? Not cut up?'

'No. That was it.'

A tightness locked into my throat as a thought sprung. 'Where was it taken?'

'I can't remember.'

'Anything to do with horse racing?'

She made a grimace. 'Horse racing? No way.'

'What's wrong with horse racing?'

'Nothing, I guess. I think it's kind of cruel.' I held my breath, gazing at her. 'What?' she said. 'Are you into it? It's not a personal slight.'

My breath released in a long sigh, stomach all knotted. 'This work is really beautiful, you know. Really amazing. I'm going to carry on looking.'

She nodded, crossed back to her wine glasses. I watched her from behind as she took two more from a cardboard box and went to put them into military uniform. They clinked repeatedly against each other and I saw she couldn't align them, realised she was shaken too.

'I'm sorry,' I murmured, unsure whether I wanted her to hear.

She whirled round, the glasses held out like offerings. 'Oh me too. I'm being so stupid. Course I remember his name, it wa—'

My palm came up like a traffic policeman. '—no. Don't.' Her teeth were pressed lightly into her lower lip, upper lip lifted. She might have been forming an F. Or maybe a V. It could have meant nothing. 'I don't want to know,' I said.

I saw how her eyes expressed confusion, then a lightness, her lips tipping into a flashing smile. She let out a low laugh. 'I really liked him. He chucked me almost immediately. You really liked your one, huh? I can tell. Maybe it *is* him. You sure you don't—'

'—no way, mine is thirty-two—well, thirty-three by now. Actually.' She stared at me. I couldn't tell if she was shocked. I wasn't sure what I wanted from her. 'It was over a year ago,' I said. 'Nearly a year and a half. Last Spring. We were—*are* in love. We got separated. Forever, they

95

want it to be.'

She continued to stare at me for quite some time. 'That's radical.' She nodded, eyes warm, mouth held in like she got it and was sorry. She went and leaned into her collage, gazed at the boy's gold-wrapped head. 'Sometimes I wonder if I'll ever see him again. You don't have to be separated by grown-ups for that. I always got the feeling he'd become an artist, but it was probably just a projection. Because I wanted him to be like me. I was only sixteen but the feel of him has never left me. Stupid, really, he was such a lad, into motorbikes, but you know, sensitive at the same time. His father had left him when he was a kid, just ten or something, he was very hurt, I remember the whole thing. The one that got away.'

I could hardly swallow, my heart drumming, body aching like I was unwell all of a sudden. When my voice came, it splintered. 'What did his father do, do you know?'

'Oh God,' she said, head snapping to look at me. '*That's* what you were getting at. I didn't realise. It didn't occur to me. Yes...of course...his dad was a racehorse trai

all

rehearsing in a pub theatre, i'm this vulnerable little character frumped up in pop socks and way big synthetic skirt, waistband pulled in with a kilt-style safety pin. my-her mother made her think she's ugly. sweet seventeen, wearing old lady's shoes. i-she killed my mother. just this morning. didn't mean to. her mother. just happened while i was cutting the cake. i'm stacking supermarket shelves with an oddball of a guy, got the blooded little paring knife in my pocke

there comes

a flurry of movement somewhere behind me, the scuff of boots on the black-painted floor. i keep up my hell-bent verbal overflow, the strange strangled elatio

okay, calls

the director. hold up. we've got the bedroom props delivery. let's take a short brea

i hear

a faint dinging, all tinkle bells. she-i arrest her tremulous speech, fingers still fiddling with the hairgrips dug into her-my forehead.  all keeping the tension of my character high in my chest, my whole being shaky, i put my head down, go sit on a plastic chair at the foot of the black-painted cave of the stage.  rows of seating rise up behind me on a black plywood ra

i hear

his voice.  *wha—? his* voice.  my concentration pops.  i look up.  my heart about stops.  i see a tiny head rung in golden thread, see the same face, older now, all suspended in space above a corrugated-cardboard-wrapped louis XVI chair and a lamp and an olive-green trill telephone, all floating in the blackness of the thea

misfit i

am playing falls right out of me.  i am me, pure me, all my twenty-two years, looking at him.  i watch him cross the room, place the props where the director indicates, straighten himself, stretch.  such a warm feeling visiting me.  the director talks with him.  i listen to the tone of his voice, perceive his unblemished skin, the ease of his movements, the way his dark hair is all kind of shaggy.  and *he* comes and fills me.  i see how different this other he looks, but similar; uncannily more similar than he actually looks.  like maybe *he'd* looked like that, more than i could have known, when he was about twenty-four, and this guy was going to grow into looking more like him when he got to be thirty-two.  i find myself wondering: but what does *he* look like now, when he must be forty?  heat pulses through my blood.  this guy is taller, slenderer than him, a lot better looking even, in the conventional way, but his energy, the way he moves and holds himself, the particular shape and angle of his nose, which is smaller but the same, and his lips, which are fuller but match those in which i had discovered the sweetest hardest fullest kisses, these things tell me i was right, this young guy is *his* son.  it *was* his son in jessie's photograph, all those years ago; still is.  on the collage i own.  i feel the sting of tears.  his bo

walking down the hentrack pathway under the bluest sky *him* all sexy in jeans and t-shirt the smell of his sweat reaches for me wraps me infuses my pink crop top tiny yellow skirt my plimsolls plapping on the baked earth he grabs a hold of my hand pulls me up a grassy green tributary through a passageway of cow parsley white flowers brushing my bare midriff his big square hands they hold my slim sides hands on my skin pulling me down into a dried up ditch i see there's a grey-brown horse blanket spread out all covered in horse hairs and i'm laughing falling all into it with him his kisses blur me into the earth they suck me out of myself i am all lip i am nothing and everythi

his hands have a way of travelling everywhere each time knowing the exact right next place my hands clutch his shoulders in the dark under his t-shirt his warmth his furry belly against my exposed middle i see my reflection in the blue of his eyes in the black of the pupils miniscule a tiny me made knowable through him the way he looks at me i see right into him i see a pained ecstasy he trails his mouth down my body bites my breasts through my pink top blows hot breath into them as he holds his mouth over one then the other he trails downward sucks the flesh above my skirt hands working to bring up the cloth me wriggling raising my hips he kisses me all *there!* fingers too makes me co

our bodies calm i feel our slowing heartbeats his pressed against mine our arms wrapped around each other legs entwined bindwee

he cranes his head to look me in the eye kisses me on the mouth my own scent on his lips commingling with wafts of cow parsley all sort of floral and pungent and clean with the undertone of the earth we are lying in i pluck at the lacy flower heads dusting our shoulders our hai

we sit up side by side backs against the crumbly bank of swollen soil we suck on a bottle of cherry pop he takes my hand holds it in his lap his breath is the whole world his and mine togeth

you make me feel like a kid he sa

i'm not a ki

more than a kid he says like life itself you don't understand the delight of it but you will i'll make yo

don't be an idiot i do i understand it al

he goes quiet-as his breath coming hard i gaze at his profile something wounded he stares into my palm runs tender fingertips over the lines ther

i have a kid he says a bo

oh! my heart goes tens
i haven't seen him in quite a few yea
[i don't want there to be a ki ]
after a while he says it's really been too lo
my pulse thick in my ears i say wha
why haven't i seen him you mea
mmm
[what if he asks me to be a mu ]

his grip tightens on my hand hurting me his other hand travelling to his face fingers pinching the bridge of his no

you know he says all hoarse it's really hard being a parent a dad there are so many complications i never meant it to get like this it's just me and his mother we things got so rough we fell out really bad we were so young she didn't want me to see him and i just let that happen didn't fight for my rights or anything but it was so difficult i mean do you get it i wanted to see him but i didn't have it in me to you know what i mea

ye

i actually love that boy but i'm pathetic he pauses for a long time smears his fingers into his eyes i think about him all the time it's been six years since i had anything to do with him he's  nearly sixteen now i used to send him cards you know for a while there but i just in the end it was easier just to sto

he's sixteen i ask so he's not a ki

he looks surprised he'll always be my boy he sa

of course i mean i trail off try to think of something more to say i watch a green beetle struggling to get up the other bank of the ditch getting nowhere as bits of ditch keep taking it down i just want to laugh i'm so happy his kid's not a kid i lean over kiss his temple i get it  i tell hi

he grabs me and presses his face into the crook of my neck you're magnificent god you smell goo

y. his
boy! it really *is* his boy.  my face falls into my hands, the confusion welling up inside of me, blackening my blood so i get to feel i am all

99

merging with the black heart of the fringe theatre in which i am forging and creating another life, a made up life, from out of a floppy little manuscript come out of a playwrite's head…and i get to wonder what my own story will become, how will it shape? who will i love? and in all the darkness i discern a fine molten thread weaving from him to him to me to hi

{was a racehorse trai}ner,' Jessie was saying. 'Yes, a racehorse trainer—I remember distinctly.' Her eyes went all kind of strange, sort of filmy and like maybe she went off into her memory and everything was too real or something. 'My God, this means he's his *son*? Is he? Is that what we think? I mean, he has to be, doesn't he? This is too weird for words.'

I was biting on my lips, all nodding. 'Yes,' I said. 'I think so.'

'God, do you think we should track him down? He wanted to find his dad, I remember. Maybe we could help him.'

I shook my head. 'I don't know where he is.'

'But isn't this weird? Like it's meant to be or something. I mean, what are the chances?'

'It's the way life is,' I said. 'What do you call it—synchronicity. I guess. It's never what you expect. Or maybe completely what you expect. I don't know…'

'So maybe we can help him—with what you do know. I mean, that's going to be quite a bit of information.'

'No. It's not for me to do, for sure.'

'Well, I can do it. Maybe.'

'Maybe. But maybe he wants his dad to come find him. I know I would. He has to know his dad loves him…I don't know…fro-from the man himself. Don't you think? Maybe this moment is for—is about you and me, see.'

⚜

Jessie's show was a success. Most of her collages had red stickers next to them. The place was rammed with everyone I knew and maybe a

100

hundred others I didn't know. They spilled into the corridor and down the staircase, the noise of the chatter high up to the ceilings, like invisible birds buzzing above the coolest music pounding out of the gigantic speakers—it was a great cake of sound you could just about cut.

Tyrone and his decks were set up at the back of the room, opposite the windows, made it tricky to get to Jessie's two pieces of work there. The din danced in the density of my body, right to the core of me, almost hurting, giving me to feel I could fall apart, all like I might disperse right into another now. Be here. Not be here. My throat ached. I couldn't seem to recover from the sleep I'd crashed into that afternoon, felt I was treading water in a dream.

Moving through the crush all tugged by Stuart's bony hand, I recognised a couple of famous people I thought. I felt the heat of his sights on me. 'Are you okay?' he shouted over the ruckus. 'You seem a little—I dunno—hard to get to.'

I nodded, stupid tears springing as I glanced about the room to avoid his gaze. He pulled on my hand, pushed his face into mine.

'You're upset, I know it.'

I shrugged. 'You know, it's just Shirty—'

'—*don't* tell me it's Shirty. I know it isn't.'

'But Shirty shed me.'

'Yeah, like a week ago and you hardly cared then so…' He studied my face, hooked my eyes to his. 'You pretty much shed him yourself anyway. Ages ago. And you never loved him, did you? So what's going on?'

'Course not. But it's hardly cricket, is it?'

'There's something else, I know it. I know you.'

'Just a sticky wicket.'

'Come on, stop avoiding me with stupid stories that are *not* clever.'

I made a show of heaving my chest, relief all winding up from my heart. 'Okay. But I truly wish to God you wouldn't make me.'

The heavy beat merged into a new tune, cranked up, people whooping, throwing up their arms. I could see how Stuart was chuckling as he gazed at me, though I couldn't hear it. He yelled, 'I've got you by the throat, huh?' I wrapped my fingers around my own neck, made a face

101

like I couldn't breathe. 'Come on now, enough,' he said, taking hold of my shoulders. 'Shoot. No more delay tactics. Or else I'm going to have words with Shirty.' I couldn't help smiling, made an ooo-ing sing-songy sound. 'I mean it.'

'Okay, okay. You've got me terrified so… *O*kay, it's this: this photo I saw today. On Jessie's work.'

'You what?'

'A photograph. On a collage. It looks like…well, you know…like…'

'I know?'

I widened my eyes. 'You know…'

'What?'

'You know—*him*.'

'Who do I know?'

'*Him*, Stuart. The photo looks like *him*.'

'What? You—you don't mean—not…?'

'Yes, I do mean.'

'Swan Neck?'

I nodded as we stared at one another mute for a long second. 'Yes, and Jessie—'

'—there's a photo of Swan Neck on Jessie's work?'

'No. He isn't, it isn't, but—and he hasn't got a swan neck or any kind of neck—he's got no neck actually, and—'

Eliot, soaring above everyone, came pushing through the crowd, catching my eye, all beaming. I still found it difficult to see Eliot without a sliver of desire for an H-laced chase. But I never asked; he would never give it to me. He had a hold of a woman's arm. She was completely in black and very immaculate.

'—*no* neck?' Stuart was saying. 'You mean he's got a short fat neck? Like Swan Neck?'

'Not fat, you idiot—*thick*—he has a *thick* neck. No—no neck, I told you. No neck at all.'

'*This* is who I want you to meet,' Eliot boomed to his companion. He made a thing of introducing us. This is Carla. She was Italian, a major fashion editor, shook my hand and everything. 'This one's a brilliant actress,' Eliot continued. 'And a wicked little artist too. I want to shoot her for you.'

This was news to me. My cheeks prickled, a fluttering thrill arising in my chest.

Carla nodded, smiling. 'What are you proposing?'

'Show him to me,' said Stuart in my ear.

'I don't want to,' I hissed.

'I'm planning a collaboration with Jessie,' Eliot told Carla. He put his arm around me. 'Only she doesn't know it yet. Some sort of collage. Something very beautiful.'

'Of course. This sounds magnifica. But what about the looks, what are you thinking?'

He smiled. 'I'm talking with Lauren. Kind of sportswear meets wedding. Day-glo. With heavy eye makeup, fake lashes, the lot. Karl will do the makeup of course. Todd-baby the hair. I want to do something repetitive, like jump-frames in a movie—get Jessie to scratch up the negative, cut it up, splice it back together again. All direct. On the film. Collage-up the negative.'

'Hey,' said Stuart. 'Do you mind? If I steal her? I'm thinking of buying a piece and…'

'No problem,' said Eliot, releasing his hold from around me. 'Just needed Carla to meet her.'

'She's perfect,' said Carla. 'Bellissima.'

'I thought you'd like her,' Eliot said. 'Maybe you could do an article about her too?'

Carla was nodding in a contemplative way. 'Possible. She sounds interesting.'

'Who's her? This *she*?' I said. And they all laughed, Eliot looking at me with tremendous affection, like he was proud-as. The thrill in my breast burst its banks, flooded the whole of me, like a high, like riding, like sex. Stuart appeared excited, Carla amused. I stood there, felt in commune with them all—all back in the daisy chain. Who needed H?

Stuart yanked my arm, veered into my face. 'Come on. I need your advice.' As we cut away through the crush, he added, an edge coming into his voice, 'Eliot wants to make you famous.'

I leaned into his ear. 'You're *buying* one?'

'Yes. The one with the Swan Neck photo.'

'You can't.'

'For you. Now show it to me.'

'It's probably sold,' I said. But I knew it wasn't, had been keeping a jealous eye on it, where it hung, somewhat obscured, behind Tyrone.

'Take me to it, come on. Don't you want it?'

'You're mad. It's five hundred pounds. How can you afford it?'

'Trust me. I've been saving. Quite a lot of people have been buying my tapes when I'm busking and stuff. Plus I'm sure Jessie will work out instalments with me or something.'

'Why would you do this for me?'

'Because I love you.'

I stopped, looked at my feet in the old factory worker's boots I'd found on Portobello Market for just a few quid. My heart pumped louder than the music. 'Sorry Stuart, but you're...not getting ideas are you? Because of Eliot?'

He got a hold of my chin in pincer fingers, made me look at him, all the crowd pulsing around us. He shook his head, his angular face drawn. 'I never get ideas about you. Not everybody sees you like that, you know. Not everybody fancies you or wants you. You shouldn't be so vain. Some people just love you.'

'They do?'

'They do.'

'Oh God. I'm sorry. Sometimes I...'

'It's okay.'

'I don't know if I'm dependable...'

He laughed, hugged me, and I hugged him back. 'You don't know yourself. You're always there when I need you.'

And he got a hold of my hands, interlacing his fingers with mine, made me dance with him in the daft way we used to at home. He got all flushed in the face and his arms went pink. He was almost breathless when he said, 'Come on then, I'm going to buy you the picture. I need to see it.'

'Jessie will never let me have it. Not this one.' I took a shufti around the room, checking to make sure we weren't in her sights, then snuck behind the DJ table, tugging Stuart by his slashed t-shirt. 'Watch the wires,' I warned, as I stepped over the looping black snakes. We stood before the collage, each in our mutual awe.

'I hadn't seen this one,' Stuart said. 'I think it's my favourite for sure. I'm definitely buying it. Nowhere does it say it's not for sale.'

My blood was airborne. I pointed, without touching the surface.

Stuart leaned in. 'Wow, he's wrapped in gold. He's got no neck—you're right. But he's really good looking. Is that what Swan Neck looked like?'

'Not really. But yes. Sort of.'

❦

The rain ran down the windowpanes in swollen rivulets and it was as if the glass was in motion somehow, its surface volatile. It felt to be a portal to another world. The November light was falling fast, getting to that place where everything seems black and white—and I didn't want to break it by turning on a manmade light, not even a candle. I realised I had lost sense of time when the cold seeped into my flesh.

As I was laying the fire with scrunched up newspaper and the kindling twigs we gathered routinely from the nearby Regent's Park, Merl came in, striking the mains light. Something blew in my head, everything spangly.

'Ooch,' he crooned. 'I didn't realise you were here, eh? What are you doing in the dark, angel?'

'It wasn't dark. Yet.'

Todd-baby followed, carrying two cups of tea. He was wearing a fat cardigan tied at the waist, his blondie hair coming over his shoulders in two plaits. He grinned, sang out, 'Spliff time. You want a tea, baby? Merl baby, get her a tea.'

'Let's have candles, shall we?' I said, as Merl trotted back to the kitchen.

Through the open doorway, I could hear a rising hum of chatter, everyone gathering to get tea in the kitchen in readiment for our house meeting. I lit a match to my fire, watched the paper flare into the sticks, a crackling and a snapping, the fizz of the bigger hunks of wood all spreading as their splintered edges caught. When Merl came back, it was like he was the Pied Piper, the others lured after him, caught in the web of his magic. There was Karl, Stuart, Walter, Henrietta and Jessie, packets of biscuits and tea all floating through the air. I could hear Lauren singing in the kitchen in her huge voice. She was making us a stew for dinner.

'Where's Eliot?' I asked.

All I got was raised eyebrows, pursed lips; that look of inevitability.

'Is he alright?'

'Course he is,' said Merl, all soft. 'He's always alright. He can handle it, eh?'

I started to get up. 'He's in his room, is he? Shouldn't someone go and check on him?'

Merl put his arm on mine, the touch firm. 'No. No way. You're not going. Trust me, angel, he's fine. I saw him just now, just before he went to lie down. He's a big boy. He makes his own bed and he likes it that way.'

'Here, baby,' said Todd-baby, thrusting a mug into my hand. 'I'll make us up a spliffy.'

Merl kissed the side my temple. 'It's the good grass Jessie grew.'

'Eliot should be here for the meeting,' I said. 'He's the one understands all this legal stuff. We need to do this properly or we'll get chucked out.'

'Relax kid,' said Henrietta, waving a fat file in her fat fingers. 'He's not the one, actually. I've got it all here. I'm onto it. I do all the work. Eliot gets his facts from me.'

I widened my eyes. 'Okay lady.'

'The sun don't shine out of Eliot's arse,' she said.

I bit my lip, looked askance at Merl.

'You're a bitch, Henrietta,' he said.

'So they say, Merl. But face it, you all need me.' She grinned, all big red-painted lips and black hair nearly to her bum. She winked at me. 'Hey, and I need you, so let's say we're square. Let's party—the court date's in fourteen days.'

We went through the whole thing and Henrietta said we had enough of the law on our side to keep our commune going for at least two years, possibly more. She needed someone to attend the court alongside her and we all voted on Merl. The rest of us were going to go and sit in the public gallery for support. We talked about tactics and possible means of prolonging our rights and after a while the discussion dissolved and we broke off into cosy conversations.

It was a tainted sky beyond the uncurtained windows—streetlamps orbs of scratched-up light on the dirty glass, all shimmering like strange stars. Our candlelit room spawned its own unique romance, made me feel held, the warmth of the fire burning into my left side. I leaned against Merl, my legs up over Todd-baby on the giant settee and was puffing on a joint when Lauren called to me from the doorway. I looked up at her, loving the way her big body was bursting out of her barely buttoned silky brown shirt-dress, her glisteny skin, her breasts, darker, shinier, than the silk. She about took up the whole doorway.

'Someone here to see you,' she said.

'Who?'

'I don't know him. I didn't get his name. Some older guy. Bit weird. I left him outside, said maybe you were here, maybe not. You here?'

My heart seemed to stop. 'Older? How old? What does he look like?'

She pulled down the corners of her mouth. 'Thirty-something, I guess. Kinda thick set. Dark hair—a bit greying.'

I sat up, twisting my legs from Todd-baby's lap.

'You think you know who it is, baby?' he asked. 'Want me to go check for you?'

'He has your photo, cut from a magazine,' said Lauren. 'One of Eliot's. Says he knows you.'

'I'll go,' sparked Stuart, getting to his feet.

'No,' I said. 'It's okay. Wait, what colour are his eyes?'

'Hell, girlfriend, I don't know. Light, I think. You want me to let him in?'

'And his neck?' asked Stuart. 'Is it short and thick?'

'How the hell would I know? His *neck*.'

107

There was a fine trembling galloping through me. I stood up. My voice came breathy. I glanced at Jessie but she was absorbed in conversation. 'I'll go.'

As I staggered across the room, everything was sliding around, all like the world wasn't fixed any more. I could feel Stuart's sights on me. He was the only one who knew. Lauren glided out of the doorway, slipped back into the kitchen. It was a relief when I turned into the corridor and was out of Stuart's stare.

I reached the front door. Closed my eyes. Took a hollow breath. Smoothing my hair, I didn't know if I was petrified or ecstatic. My hand reached out, pressed the release button on the lock, drew the heavy door toward me. He had his back to me. He looked all wrong. His hair was short and he wore a tweedy jacket. Bile rose in my throat. He turned.

'Oh,' I said.

'You *are* here. Thank God, we've been worried sick—

'—who the fuck are you?' I said, bringing on an easy Edinburgh burr. I sank into a slouch, hardened my face.

He winced, leaned forward. 'It's-it's me—Simon. Mr Gatling.'

'I'm sorry,' I said. 'I don't know you.'

'Yes, you do. I'm Terry's mate. You grew up under my nose.'

My heart was going like the clappers, but it fed me, gave me into another life, like when I was acting. I made a derisive snort, 'What? What you on about, mister?'

'Come on now—'

'—I have no idea who you are.' I curled up my lip, squinted. 'Really, mister, you got the wrong girl. I've never heard of Terry and I've never seen you before in my life. Now if you don't mind…' I made to close the door but his arm flew out and held it.

'Come on now, love, I just want to take you back home. Your parents are—'

'—I *don't* know you, you hear me.' I kept my features tense, squinty. 'You've got the wrong girl.'

Something in his face went uncertain. 'But…'

'Are you going to let me shut the door—or do you want me to call my pals?'

'Listen, sweetheart,' he said softly. 'I know you know me and I know you.'

'Tell you what, you're freaking the fuck out of me. Now get your hand off of this door.'

'Is Stuart here?' He craned past me, yelled, 'Stuart? You little rat!' all like he was in *On The Waterfront* or something—and right through my scaredy-cat insides, I just about wanted to laugh.

Lauren's voice boomed out behind me. 'What's going on here? Are you alright, girlfriend?'

Without taking my eyes off my dad's friend, I said, still in the Scottish accent, 'This man thinks he knows me. I don't know him. He won't go.'

I felt the rush of her as she flew forward, all pushing me aside, her large form coming between us. Simon Gatling's ears seemed to fold back. 'Get the fuck out of here, you sick bastard,' she yelled. 'Chasing little girls from magazines. What's the matter with you?'

'But I know her. She's my friend's daughter. They're worried sick about her.'

'You know this guy?' she asked me.

I shook my head, keeping my lips tight and small.

'You hear that? Are you a perv, or what? Now get the fuck lost before we call the cops, you hear?'

He began to step back. 'She's underage.'

Lauren slammed the door on him, leaned on it. We stared at one another as we listened to his footsteps scraping down the stone steps.

'If this was back home you'd be on the side of milk carton, you know that? I guess we're going to have to find you somewhere else to stay for a while, girlfriend.'

'You think he'll come back?'

She nodded. 'For sure. Probably he'll bring your folks. Let's hope they don't bring the cops. I'm a sap, I should've realised the moment he showed me your photograph. I should've known. But what did you go to the door for, you dummy? Who did you think it was going to be?'

The moment I awoke I lurched to sitting, all like I was a wind-up toy on a spring. The cold hit my arms, my legs, feet shrinking as they came into contact with the wooden boards. I reached for my puny alarm clock, sure it had failed to go off. Stuart groaned, pulling the blankets up over his head. I struggled to focus

'I've got to go,' I said. 'We've got to get up.'

I rose, folded the hanging blanket back from the window, was cut by a draft as I tied the curtain back with hook and ribbon. There were crystal flowers blooming on the panes—I just had to run my thumb over them, feel their icy spikes. I saw how I left a trail of damage. I shimmied into my baggy jeans, pulling my bed t-shirt off over my head, fumbled into my bra and a sweatshirt.

'Stuart,' I said, lacing up my big boots. 'I've promised Lauren I'll be down by seven-fifteen. It's seven-thirteen.' He sat up, also on a spring, blinked hard, growled. I couldn't help smiling, even as I wanted to cry. 'You don't have to come,' I told him.

'I do,' he croaked. He stood, the covers pooling about his gnarly feet, wobbled in his granddad shirt and boxers across the mattress, which was straight on the floor. I watched as he sank back down on the bed, pulled on his black jeans, hair kinked every-which-way.

'You'll look after everything, right?'

'Course I will, I told you already.'

'My collage?'

'Stop it, will you. Trust me.'

I nodded. 'I was thinking, maybe you can bring it over after we've seen what kind of space I've got? I'll have my own room and everything.'

'If you like. But if you leave it here—'

'—I'm definitely coming back, don't worry. But I can't risk visiting, can I? Everyone said.'

'I didn't mean that. I just mean I'll look after it for you, I'll look after everything.' He stood, held out his arms and folded me into his bed warmth. 'You'll be sixteen in seven weeks and then you can come back and do what you like.'

'Seven weeks and one day. But what if they come after *you*?'

'There's nothing they can do. No one can make me say anything.'

'Mum and Dad will kill you. And the police might force you.'

'No one can force me. I'll tell them I don't know where you are.'

'Hey, but I was thinking in the night…what if they follow you when you come to see me? Like, get a secret detective even?'

'You really think your mum and dad would do that?'

'I don't know. But we should think about it. Be careful and that.'

'We'll think of every possibility and have some answers ready.'

'And be careful.'

'And be careful.'

'And what about the acting group?'

'We'll sort something out. Gather somewhere else. Eliot is bound to work it out. It's nothing without you.'

'We might not be able to—I might not be able to see any of you I'm thinking, until I'm—' There came a rap on the door. 'Coming,' I called. 'You've got all my drawings and paintings here too, all my art stuff.'

'I know. I already told you I'll bring over whatever you want.'

'But you might not be able to come.'

'I'm going to tell them you've gone to Greece.'

'To Greece? Why Greece?'

'Or somewhere. I'm going to come up with the perfect story—get Eliot and everyone to help devise something totally believable. You need to stop worrying. It's possible they won't even come.'

'They will.' I surveyed the big crumbly room as if for the last time, eyes all stinging. 'It was a good room.'

'It *is*. *Our* room.'

I slung my rucksack onto my shoulder, picked up my mum's tapestry holdall by its leather handles. We filtered out quite-as, so as not to awaken the rest of the house, descended the two flights of greasy stone steps.

I was surprised to find Merl and Todd-baby in the kitchen with

Lauren. They were puffy-eyed, sleep-smacked, dressing-gowned, Merl in paisley silk, Todd-baby in tartan wool. They came and hugged me and told me they would visit me all the time and we could meet in town and of course I was coming out with them dancing, I wouldn't miss a trick. Nothing was going to change, they said. When I told them there was sure to be another visit, there might be my parents, the police, a private detective, they just smiled a lot and said everything would work out, this wasn't a movie, it was real life and people could stay hidden if they really wanted to. It wasn't long til I was legal anyway. Stuart said they were going to work out every possibility and totally beat the system. Then Todd-baby gave me a little baggie of Jessie's grass, while Merl made me drink a tumbler of freezing cold water, clinking his own glass with mine. They loved me, they said.

Stuart took up my mother's posh bag from down by my feet, put his arm around me, drew me into him. 'People love you,' he murmured in my ear.

As the three of us left, I turned to look at the imposing old house, my heart tugging. I somehow didn't believe I would be going back. The once-cream paintwork was powdery, weathered away, and dirty yellow bricks showed where large fragments of render had broken off. The window frames were flaking, rotting. I had never realised just how disfigured the building was; I had only seen its magnificence. It was like maybe the house was dying. I felt its dying deep in my bones. But Merl, all tones of steady brown, and Todd-baby, electric blue eyes sharp-as, were standing on the timeworn doorstep, waving and smiling, all keeping the life in everything.

*Episode five: Grass Blades*

There were no windows in the back of the tour truck, just blind indented panels in the metal of the sliding door. The passenger area was built in a kind of pit, low down behind the driver, and I liked to sit in the smaller backwards-facing seat, feel the abstract sensation of velocity in my body without any relationship to the galloping landscape outside. I would lose myself in endless shadows rising and falling from the dim light, some kind of banshees, have brief awakenings in bright spears of sunlight as they glanced in and out of the window above.

My friends were parked on the forward-facing bench seat running the whole width of the van; behind them, a partition wall all separating us from the raw innards, in which was contained the theatrical magic, a break-apart world, the set.

I was hitting myself with rave music through my Walkman, in my heart a kind of pressure, an appalling sense of separateness. I encouraged myself to drown in this feeling as I watched my friends grappling together, overly big in their gestures, all obvious they really liked each other, whatever the complications she confided to me when we were alone in our constantly mutating shared bed-and-breakfast room, about

113

his uncertainty. They fought over some object hidden in his hand, she falling into him, all play protest. They were like children. But they were sexual.

The energy of Jessie's little boy visited me, the little pumping action in his pelvis as he snuggled into me, and I saw how sexuality was in a kid's DNA, even when they were small. Isn't that what my sister had gone on about with me? I almost relaxed, the innocent warmth of the boy rippling through me, but inner images surged: I was thirteen, all aiming a peanut into Robin Remick's mouth, the elaborate dance we devised so we could cop a feel, find that place of allowance where snogging could come about. Robin Remick…who I had been mad about, who had taken a girl the year below and flaunted her in my face, kissing her everywhere, in corridors and on the playing field, blighting her neck with love bites. I had heard they did all kinds of stuff in an empty classroom.

My friends had graduated to a banter. I could see they were really loud. It was one of their football pundit piss-takes, I could tell. *Titter-not*, she was sure to be saying. The way she pulled that face, I knew her voice went deep and haughty. *Hoist on his own petard*. I could never quite join in with them when they went into this one; I didn't know the lingo, and I wasn't interested in the game. But I'd laugh along when I wasn't enclosed in my music. Those strange phrases were to accompany me for years to come. They would sprout from my mind, out of the blue, no reason whatsoever, destined to become jokes I spilled nobody laughed at.

The two sort of settled, she leaning into him, his arm snaking around her, but some kind of tension still running through them. My music felt manic, the opposite of natural, actually aggressive. I ignored its prick, pretended to myself it was fun, rocked my body in my seat to the beat. The twisted feeling inside of me grew and blackened. I closed my eyes, slumped back, fake sheen all falling away.

A hand on my knee opened my eyes, made me jump. It was Vera, leaning into me, her mouth moving. I yanked an earphone out by its wire, felt the pop.

'What?'

'Are you up for a line run?'

I stared at her for some moments. 'Really?'

'It's been quite a few days,' she said.

'Later.' We had been on tour for nearly four months, after starting at Edinburgh Festival, had five months to go. 'We know the lines,' I said.

She sat back, glanced at Toby.

'Come on,' he said to me.

'I'm not in the mood.'

'We've got responsibilities,' she said. 'We haven't done the show for five nights. We need to make sure everything's fluid.'

I bristled. 'I know. I'll do it in a bit. I just need a bit of space right now. We'll do a speed-run right before anyway, won't we? Like always?'

They nodded, with a sort of judgement in it. 'Sure,' she said. 'But I need a run before we get there too. I'm feeling too detached from it.'

'Me too,' said Toby, squeezing her shoulder.

I saw how they had relaxed, interlaced their fingers, their unease in themselves, with each other, all transmuted into a bond in which I became the rub. Bully for them. They didn't realise it was me that had given them belonging. I went to stick my earphone back in.

'You alright?' she asked. 'How was your time off? Did you see Sunil?'

Yeah. Talk about it later.'

'Sorry,' she said.

'What for?'

'I don't know. You seem pissed off.'

'He's just a dick,' I said. 'He gave me five minutes. You would hardly know he lived with me. Always Paul this, Paul that. Paul always coming first and Sunil at his beck and call. He runs around doing everything for him. Thinks he owes him everything.'

'It sounds like he's in love with him,' said Toby.

'He is *not* in love with Paul.'

'Paul with Sunil, is what I'm saying, divvy. He's obviously into him from things you've said. And Sunil's living with you now, so speaks for itself: Paul needs to control him even more. He lived with him before, right? I mean, shared the flat? Was totally available?'

I sighed. 'Yeah…I reckon Paul would have liked something more to

115

happen there. Maybe he'd thought it was going to, in the early days, I mean, when he first took him on as part of the company. You know, when I met Sunil, when he was teaching us modern dance at Paul's dumb little academy, I thought maybe he was gay too. We all did. There is something kind of fey about him, I guess. But all us girls fancied him anyway. For sure Paul would have had high hopes.'

'I suppose Sunil feels he *does* owe him everything. I mean, without Paul, where would he be? He wouldn't even be a dancer by the sound of it, let alone in a company or whatever, with Paul. The guy made him, right?'

'Yeah—just about no one becomes a professional dancer when they start training at nineteen, huh? So…' I twisted my mouth, shrugged.

'So give the guy a break.'

'Fuck off.' I lashed out my foot, kicked him in the shin. 'Give *me* a break, I reckon. Who's friend are you?'

He yelped, laughing, pulled his legs out of my reach. 'That got ya, didn't it?'

'You drama school types are all the same,' I said, flicking my eyes over the both of them.

'Well, what about your foray into the Paul Blakeny place?'

'It's hardly in the system, is it? It's hardly drama school. No one in the business would give it a second glance. Besides, it was only three months. It was pathetic.'

'You shouldn't put yourself down like that,' said Vera. 'So what, you didn't get into drama school? If you'd gone to one instead of Paul's, you'd still be stuck there for another year. Instead, you're here, playing the lead role in this amazing new play, touring with one of the top companies in the country. We might even get a West End transfer. And you're a brilliant actress. Look at your reviews. You didn't need it. Why the hang up?'

'It's not a hang up.'

'Plus you wouldn't have—'

'—*don't* tell me I wouldn't have met Sunil if I hadn't done that stupid course. It might have—'

'—but you wouldn't have met Sunil if you hadn't done that stupid

116

course,' Toby said.

I barely knew what I was doing when I flew at him from my seat, the forward motion of the van getting hold of my body, making me light as air. I made some kind of a yell, all crashing myself into him, fists hammering into his ribs. He was laughing, shouting, entrapping me in his bent-up legs; made a vice of himself and straight-jacketed my arms around my waist. He held me tight until I went limp. I felt a rash of heat in my cheeks, tears mixed in with the tail-end of laughter.

'I told you not to,' I croaked. I could feel them looking at each other.

'I didn't mean anything bad,' he said, as he released me. 'It's obvious from when he came to see you that he's well into you. Being a dancer is a fuck of a commitment, all that practising every day shit, right? He just has other priorities.'

'I hate him.'

'I can feel it,' he said. 'In my ribs.'

'Come here,' Vera said. She patted the seat, drew me up against her, arm coming around my shoulders. 'You really had a crappy five days in London, didn't you?'

She smelled of a sweet perfume, lilies and violets, sort of tremendous and sickly all at the same time. I looked at her through smeared eyes. 'So shall we do the line run now, then?'

'Why do you stay with him?' she asked.

She was warm. I realised there was the sound of rain knocking against the van roof, looked up, way up it seemed, from the low angle down in the back seat, at the distant windscreen, saw the wipers sweeping water from the glass, gluey gullies falling down in arcs against a grey sky of spattering slanting lines. I became aware of the stage manager's thick left arm jutting from the steering wheel, his blockhead with his shorn hair that poked out all stupid. Next to him, his puerile little assistant. I felt the divide, the gulf between us and them.

'Huh? Really, why don't you finish it with him? Get him to move out?'

I sighed, let my sights drift out of focus, all into the rain. 'I don't know. When I'm in his arms, when he makes love to me, it all seems good. Why do we do anything? What about what you two are doing?'

'So it's sex—chemistry—that makes you stay?'

'Not *that* much chemistry.' I shrugged. 'He's got a nice cock.'

She chuckled. 'And that's a reason to stay with him?'

'Hey, you know the word cunt?'

She winced.

'He is one?' said Toby.

'No. I'm one.'

'Okay…'

'Cunt is a goddess. Cunti-Devi; a Hindu goddess.'

'You're saying you're a Hindu goddess?'

'I'm saying it's a great word that's been bastardised. And I've always liked the word, even before I knew it was sacred. All kinds of words derive from it, like kundalini and queen and cuneiform, see—and it's the gateway into life itself, isn't it? The cunt? So it's actually the biggest compliment you can give a woman. He calls me his little cunt.'

'So that's why you stay? Because you're a cunt—and he knows it?'

'Yes. And there's no one else. And maybe I love him.'

'So I can be calling you a cunt?' said Toby.

I smiled. 'If you like. But you should probably be calling Vera one.'

'No thanks,' said Vera. 'But there's loads of other men. Loads. And it's hardly a problem for you, you're a gorgeous young thing.'

'Not that young.'

'How young do you want to be? Twenty-one seems pretty good to me.'

I paused. I shrugged. 'I don't know…' I shrugged some more. 'Huh—hey but, when I was seven, there was this boy I liked, who used to catch me at kiss chase—well, he never caught me actually, I had to let him—I would always run in the same direction across the playing field and he would come after me and I would kind of stop and he would take me back to base, near the football goal, pull me down on the ground and get on top of me and do this thing, right?' I rolled onto my knees, energy into my pelvis. 'He would pump his hips, right? Like this, like he was doing it. He was only seven but he would pump his hips, all instinct, and me all instinct underneath. I would be saying, *Fuck, fuck*, like that. *Fucking hell.* Saying the words without realising what I was saying.

*Fuck*. I didn't swear at all, normally. It just came out of me. Saying the words of the act, even though I didn't know them then. Only later, I saw that. Then I would get all upset and push him off of me and be almost crying. But I kept letting him catch me. And he kept doing it. Until, in the end, I stopped playing, just refused to play anymore.'

'What a horrid thing—he can't have known what he was doing, huh?'

'No. But he did. Somewhere in him, he did. I knew, so he *had* to. And I kind of liked it too…'

'So that kid fucked you up, then?' said Toby.

'Are you saying I'm fucked up?'

'No, *you're* saying you're fucked up. Do you want another fight?'

I felt the tightness in my chest give way, a smile rising to my eyes. 'Bare knuckle?'

'Stop it, you two,' said Vera. I detected an irritation in her voice, her old tension returning.

'There's no *us two*,' I said. 'But did you know, I shouldn't say, but Stuart really likes you?'

'That's nice.' She eyed Toby, clearly goading him. 'Pity he's so young.'

'He's not young,' I said.

'Or I'm so old, then.'

'You're not old.'

Toby said, 'Yeah. You old slapper.'

Her face went stark, mouth pinched. 'That was unnecessary.'

'You're a sexist dick,' I said.

'Him—and all the rest of them,' Vera said. 'Why do we bother?'

'No,' said Toby. 'Why do you make yourselves victims?'

❧

It was a crappy club, like they all were outside of London and my intimate connections with cutting-edge cool, but I kind of liked it for that, liked the dirty black dance floor, the flashing traffic lights and the terrible outfits stalking across the scene on the heels of fluorescent flabby white girls with too much streaked hair. Young men, boys really, hung about the edges, casing the girls as they wandered about in bands, fluttering, giggling, all like street pigeons. It was pretty early for a club, eleven or so, and they were not yet drunk enough to be dancing, but I figured it would be a mess when they did.

Toby passed me and Vera each a long-necked bottle of beer, turned back to the bar, seized his own. We clacked our bottles together, the sound accessing our coiled energy, releasing a terrific surge between us.

'Really good one tonight,' he shouted over the scream of the charts music. 'Could you feel them? The audience? They were totally *there*.'

'They were like a single beast,' came Vera.

'A shoal of fish,' I said. 'Sardines, all like, glittering and swirling, no leader.'

'Exactly,' chimed Toby.

We three were our own bright cluster, heads coming together as we talked and swigged. 'It still gets to me how every audience is different,' I told them. 'They really do become one. You can feel the energy, huh?'

'I just love that feeling when you know everything's working,' said Vera.

'The performance, the audience, everything,' Toby said.

'And you can tell how good it is,' Vera was all staring into his eyes. 'But without any ego, just pure connectivity.'

'Yeah, and it gets a kind of momentum,' I said. 'Like you're more than the sum of your parts. But sometimes it's weird, isn't it? Like, you *know* it's good—more than good—sometimes it's the best—yet it makes no impact. They don't get it. What *is* that?'

'Ah, fuck knows—but irrelevant tonight,' Toby said. 'Tonight was a tight-skin moment, made the hairs stand on end.'

'But it does my head in, see. No one seems to get my best moments. You know the other night, when I cried in that scene with you, Toby? It felt the most real ever, yet the audience seemed dead.' I was glancing about the stinking room. 'It really pissed me off. Fuck. I hate it here. This is a dive. What are we doing?'

They both laughed, looked around with real affection.

'It's great,' said Vera.

'If you like a shit-hole.'

'Takes me back,' she said.

'It *is* pretty grim,' said Toby. He tipped up his bottle, his Adam's apple jumping as he necked it. 'Ahh. Who's for another?'

Vera, all chuckling, took a glug of hers. 'Yup.'

'I think I'm going to go,' I said.

'No.' She grabbed a hold of my arm, swung herself forward, taking me with her, called to Toby, 'Yeah, get us another—both of us.' My beer fizzed at the bottle mouth and bubbled down my hand as she pulled me. I felt the splashes catch my calf, felt them mark me. I imagined them picking up filth, black smudges on my skin, all like welcome bruises.

We reached the dance floor, coloured lights flashing and careening across us. The world was blue, was red, was orange, was green—each colour distinct yet overlapping. She snatched my beer from me, put it, along with hers, on a small round black table to the side. Everything was painted black, just like in a theatre; you could see the brush marks. She kept a hold of my hand, moving fast, dragged me after her, the tacky dance floor all sucking at my rubber soles. She turned suddenly, yanking me, and I let her fling me away then toward her, away and in again. I felt my pleated skirt kicking around my bum, glimpsed my legs, child-like, in white socks and trainers as if they were someone else's. I let my friend manipulate me, her face a glowing moon of slipping sliding smiles, her laughter all flaring over the music—but inside, my body was frozen, my mind running a stream of ugly thoughts. There had been so many times I'd watched her do this with Toby, the lance of envy, of craving, splicing through my happiness for them. It always looked so ultimate, so intimate, so alive; I would wish there was a man right there I could dance with like that, someone who would abandon I to me, just connect through movement that wasn't sex. The fury burned, I made a kind of yell, she lunged her smile right into my face and—*ah!*—*oh!*—something all broke in me, just like that, my mind leaching its contents into the gummy floor, where they stuck. I went light-as, empty, all letting the whole thing keep coming at me, escalating, me at the centre; I got to feel like we were moving in a body of bright water, felt the air almost viscous, myself borne in currents of elation.

After a time, which might have been short, or might have been long, I couldn't tell, nor cared, she pulled me over to our beers. The bitter-sweet liquid slipped down my throat, cool and secretly golden as I polished it off. It gave me its yeasty return.

Vera pointed. 'I'm going to the loo.'

'Me too.'

She took my hand as we sauntered across the spacious room, hardly anyone in it it seemed, the locals all clung to the sides, those little parties of girls clustered here and there. A strobe-light struck up and we were moving through a black and white blinking world, everything going faster than my still-sprinting heart. It was like being out of it, made me feel I could disappear. She pushed open the black-painted door with the symbol of a girl in a skirt on it. And all the colour came rushing back, thick yellow light over scratched blue floor tiles, blue walls. Sinks all abstract, like art objects.

The music went muffled when the door swung closed behind us.

'Phew,' she said, wiping her hand over her forehead. 'Lucky we're not reflex epileptic.'

'I think I might be,' I said.

Her eyes flew to me. 'Really? You shouldn't be in that light.'

'Not really. Metaphorically.' I could see she didn't know what I meant. 'Doesn't matter.'

'My brother's epileptic.'

'Oh. Sorry.'

'It's okay. It's very occasional.' She went over to a mirror, fingered her eyebrows into place, wiped at the corners of her mouth. 'He has it very mildly now. And it's non-convulsive, you'd hardly know. They call them absence seizures. He just has a kind of decreased level of consciousness for about fifteen seconds at a time—but it's not the reflex kind that gets triggered by outer stimuli—like that fucking light they shouldn't be using.'

I spoke to her reflection in the glass as she touched up her lips. 'I didn't know there any other kind. But what happens to his consciousness?'

'He just goes blank really. He looks weird—eyes go wide and

staring.'

'He doesn't get to feel like he's all connected, all everything? A sort of bliss?'

She turned, leaned her bum on the basin, pulled down her mouth. 'He usually doesn't even know he's having one. It doesn't happen so much now, but when he was a kid it was about fifty times a day. He used to get in trouble at school for being inattentive—until they diagnosed him.'

'Wow. Well I don't have that.'

'What *do* you have?'

'I don't.'

She stared at me, shook her head, smiling. 'Metaphorically? Come on, you can't say something like that and get away with it.'

'I just…' I shrugged, watched my foot tip onto its side. 'I don't know. It doesn't happen much anymore to me either. But I used to get this feeling—all like I was pulsing with the whole world inside of me type thing. Life would come so alive in me sometimes, it was—well, fucking beautiful. It happened a bit just now, when we were dancing.'

'Isn't that called drunk?' she laughed.

'I'm not drunk. Anyway, it's different. It's like I'm taken into another dimension, see—only it's real, like my body is vibrating too fast, possessed by its own atoms or something nuts. Full-on life. I used to like it, but now it seems to turn in on itself and sort of eat me up. I feel possessed and sort of angry.'

She was nodding. 'The word epilepsy comes from Ancient Greek, means to seize, possess. Or afflict. But maybe you are epileptic. Have you ever had a test, a scan?'

'I'm not epileptic. My mum knows all about that stuff. She would've spotted any signs. That's why I asked you about the lapse in consciousness—because maybe it's not that he goes blank—maybe he experiences a deep stillness inside, which is outside too, connects to the silence underneath all the noise and everything, a kind of essence which maybe is his real Self and—'

'—I don't know about all that.' She winced. 'Sorry, I've got to pee.'

'Me too.'

We went into adjacent cubicles of grey-speckled Formica. I slid the knob of the lock into its bracket, the click echoing Vera's, lifted my little red pleated skirt, sat, let my water stream out of me. My eyes went all hypnotised by the roll of toilet paper in the holder beside me, its tissue tongue waving to and fro in rhythm to my breath. My body was throbbing from the heat and the dancing.

The door to the disco opened, letting in a hard blare of music, the tick of a number of heels, like cat's claws, striking the tiles, all sharp, out of sync with the beat. There was hushed conversation, hissing cackles, footsteps clacking into loos, clattering all around me.

I snapped off a section of the tissue paper, wiped myself and was pulling up my lacy pink knickers when a cacophony of yells struck up. Stuff came flying over the cubicle doors, a rain of wet toilet paper splatting into the walls and the floor, big gobs slapping at my arm, skimming my cheek as I ducked, covered my head with my hands, my breath coming ragged and stuck in my breast.

'You fucking Southern slags.'

'You lesbos.'

'Get the fuck out of here, you lesbian slappers.'

'Oi you? Cunts. Who do you fucking think you are?'

I held my lips tight into themselves, a new cobweb of heat spreading through the surface of my skin, bringing it electric. The bombs kept dropping, mostly hitting the back of the wall on account of the force with which they were hurled, but splashes lashing out at me. One crashed into the umbrella of my interlaced fingers, the slop of it sliding down my forearm, warm drips into my face. There was continuous shouting echoing against the tiles. I got to realise the shells were drenched in pee, the smell high and ammoniacal. Sweat trickled down my back inside my cotton top. Or maybe it was their pee. Breath gathered inside of me as I hardly dared to breathe, sharp spikes spearing my throat, spikes that urged me to retaliate. Vera was silent in the cubicle next to me.

The missiles stopped, a dripping stillness sticking to the walls as I dared to raise my eyes, still the insults booming in the thin atmosphere, the clacking heels ringing off the ceramic floor. You could feel how the dogs in those shoes knotted together, the pack of voices commingling, bodies close. I got the sense they were shooting communications to each other, one of them every now and again barking at us to get the fuck off their turf. Then the outer door was opening, the scream of the music cutting through their flat vowels, their clicking footsteps swallowed and gone.

The door thudded shut, muted the four-on-the-floor, the shrill female singer. My mind reached out, a flat radar seeking sign of life beyond my cubicle. My breath released, heaved. All was still. I felt it as if the stillness originated inside of me and radiated outward, reflecting back.

'Vera?'

'Yes. Fuck.'

I stood, discovered my knickers at my ankles in all the splashed-up floor. I kicked them off. 'That was pee they soaked that toilet paper in.'

'No. Oh God, yes. Oh God, it's all over me.'

'Me too.'

I could hear she was wiping herself down, groaning. I wrapped a dry wad of tissue around my hand, used it as a buffer to pick up my pink pants, shoved them into the tampon dispenser. 'They were really nice too. Really expensive.'

'What? Nice?'

I went to the door, fingers on the lock. Hesitated. My heart started up again and I saw my hand was trembling. I squatted, holding back my long strands of hair as I craned my sights under the door, the reek of urine intensified. I could feel Vera waiting for me to be first, feel her tension and residual fear. I could taste her sweat; it wasn't mine.

The hyenas were gone. I stepped into the empty washroom, straight to a mirror, saw bits of wet tissue stuck to me. 'Disgusting,' I said. 'It's alright. You can come out.'

We splashed ourselves with water, straightened ourselves out and agreed to leave the club immediately. As we entered the strobing blackness, we found Toby outside the door, looking freaked-as.

'Where the hell have you been?' he said. 'We need to leave. I've been getting abuse from a pack of hardcore girls, one of them spat at me, then this huge fucking redneck lorry driver dickhead said he was going to nut me if I touched his woman again. I never touched anyone.' He clocked we were messed up, his eyes afraid. 'What happened?'

'We're going,' said Vera.

We took off toward the exit, the fire of many eyes upon us. My heart was up in my ears as a big bouncer drew the door open for us. I let Vera and Toby pass through.

'Run,' I said to them.

Toby rubbernecked me. 'What?'

I was biting my lip, felt the shimmer of a smile shaking there. 'Just run.' To the bouncer I said, 'You're going to give me a break, yeh? This is not my piss I stink of.'

'Yeh?' He looked surprised, shrugged. 'Okay.'

'Hold open that door for me. Promise?'

He raised his eyebrows, reflected my cheek, nodded.

'I'll be fucked if you don't.' I took a step back into the half-dead disco. Red. Blue. Yellow. In the black. White faces washed by the colour all staring at me across the room. I figured they probably wouldn't be able to hear my actual words over the blare of the music but I knew they'd know. 'You fucking wankers. You fucking tacky bitches. You're gonna fucking die in hell.' I turned and hurtled through the door, a scream coming out of me. 'Shut the door,' I shrieked to the bouncer as I ran off, everything mega-focus. I didn't need to see them coming after me, I could feel their energy, even while they were still in the club. Vera and Toby were not far down the street. I sped toward them, laughter coming, 'Run. Run.'

We ran, me gaining on them, catching them, passing them, our feet hard on the concrete paving stones. There came caterwauls from behind, but quite a ways off, and I dared to turn, saw the pack of bleached dogs strung outside the dive, the neon signage burning them alternately orange and red. My whole body was speeding, my energy bigger than its confines, seeming to radiate into the air. I was laughing, horrified at myself, glorying in my gall.

Our pub bed-and-breakfast was just down the road and I reached the door first. 'Quick. Hurry. Who's got the key?'

'You fucking idiot,' Toby rasped, panting. 'You're a nutter.' He struggled to get the key in the lock, half-laughing, half-riled. 'What the fuck did you do?'

'You could have got us killed,' Vera muttered, as we rammed into the hallway.

All of us were clamouring for breath. I slammed the door, leaned against it, bathing in the glow of some kind of rapture as I slid down the glossy paintwork onto the doormat, knees up and into my chin. 'They called us cunts. What a compliment. Goddesses, that's what we are—spiritually enlightened women. Yes.' Prickly coir dug into my bum.

'Shut up. You'll wake up the landlord. They'll have a fit. You're very, very stupid. What are you? A hooligan all of a sudden?'

'A fucking nutter,' Toby said again.

'A cunt,' I said.

'I'm serious,' Vera insisted. 'Those girls would have beaten us to a pulp. I grew up around girls like that. You do not mess with them. We were lucky as it was, in that loo.'

'And what about the guys?' Toby said.

'But we got away, didn't we?' I felt the shine in my eyes, my vision out on stalks. 'We're all good.'

'Like hell, we're all good,' Vera said. 'I'm covered in piss and I've strained my leg because of you.' She was turning away but reeled back, sort of gasping, eyes into my crotch. 'And talking of cunts, I can see right up your fanny, you're flashing all over the place, it's disgusting. What's the matter with you? I can't believe you go out without any knickers on. No wonder those girls attacked us, they must have seen when we were dancing.'

Toby's eyes flew down between my legs and I clamped them shut, dropped them fast-as, flat to the floor. The backs of my knees stung, coir spikes poking the delicate skin. I looked up at the two of them, one to the other. I felt defenceless, knew there was no point in trying to explain. I'm stupid, an idiot, like they said, I thought.

'I'm having the first shower,' Vera said, as she stalked off down the corridor.

My heart seemed to bottom out, tendrils of hate suffusing my blood, raising up onto my skin as those murky bruises I had just about asked for. Tears burned and I forced them away. But something in me was vindicated, wanted the pain, the dirt of it, everything, a little voice in my head saying, You deserve this. Of course you do. You're bad and you always have been.

☙

We were on our third curtain call, the three of us holding hands, me all in the middle, when I saw him. It was a large plush theatre, one of our best since the venue in Edinburgh, and out of the sea of unknown audience his face emerged above his clapping hands, bald head shining, the smile on him so huge I could taste the pride. My own smile, already focussed on the crowd in thanks, became specific, acknowledged him, my heart constricting as my eyes flitted to his sides, one to the other, ensuring my parents weren't there. How could he not tell me he was coming? I thought, sliding my vision away into the roaring throng. Little threads of annoyance smarted in my cheeks.

'My uncle's here,' I muttered to my friends. 'The wanker.'

We left the stage and the applause subsided, fragmented into chatter, the slap of the flip-up seats accompanying the drum of many footfalls. The others hoofed it to the dressing rooms, but I hung back, stuck my head out from the wings, scanned the swell of people. I spotted him descending the steps toward the exit. He didn't look my way and I watched him, affirmed he was alone. He looked content, at ease. A warm wave of affection took me by surprise.

I made a loop of my thumb and forefinger, stuck them to my lips and whistled, waving when his eyes flew to me. He raised his arm high, that huge grin overtaking his features. There was a flurry of smiles and acknowledgements from the surrounding spectators. I could see him all telling them something, like she's my niece or something, his face flushed, as I indicated, pointing upward, mouthing, The bar, the bar.

After having a couple of rounds, all on him, with Vera and Toby, where my uncle kept going on about how brilliant we all were and what an innovative take the play was, how everything really worked, the taboo subject, me as its figurehead, the challenging edges, him all quoting lines and mimicking us even, very funny and spot on, after that he gathered me into him and told them he was stealing me away. He hadn't mentioned a thing about not seeing me for nearly two years and how I kept avoiding him along with the rest of my family, treated him like he was one of them. He didn't seem to mind or blame me, was really *there*, and by the time it was just the two of us I was pretty relaxed, feeling a whole lot of love for him, recognising his own pure love for me. He took me to a restaurant he'd booked, quite the fancy joint, where we tucked into starters of local langoustine with frilly seaweed I wasn't going to eat. I told him about our adventures on tour, all kind of acting stuff out in a long energetic spiel.

'...and I was yelling, "You fucking filthy *dogs*!" all making them chase after us, see, really fucking insane, scary-as, but brilliant too because everything was warping and kind of altered state, you know? And these hideous tacky pigeons, they'd fucked themselves over in their dumb white stilettos—they thought *they* were tough but I showed them what tough was, huh? I showed them.'

He didn't laugh, the way I wished, just watched me with a slight smile and clear eyes. So I told him other stories, all the time swearing a lot, trying to get his energy up, trying to get him to see how fun I was, how alive and vital, what a rebel I was, all like him, see, trying to get him to keep on loving me—but my heart finally crested, went for a slow descent I pretended not to notice even as I was caught in its undertow.

'...so I told him, you're full of shit. You wouldn't know honest if you saw it. Because it was true, huh? I mean, that's what you would've done, isn't it?' I waited for his acknowledgement. He smiled, looked like he was waiting too. 'Isn't it? You would probably have kicked him in the head and all.'

His smile was wry. 'Probably. Once.'

The laugh that came out of me grated in the air. I glanced away, all prickly at the gills. 'I would never kick anyone anyway. I was just saying. I know you wouldn't too.' I pushed at my food with my fork. 'I'm not so sure if I like these prawn things.'

'Langoustine. I thought you'd love them. You've always loved prawns and these are the most lux you're ever going to get.'

'They're a bit in my face. A bit real.' Pursing my lips, I glared up at him. 'I'm wondering why you came to see me actually. Did you come all the way to Wales on the ferry especially?'

'I did, yes.'

'To make me feel stupid?'

'I don't think you're stupid. And what's to wonder? You're the star in a play. I miss you. I don't get to see you—now you never come visit me. And you don't do family Christmases, eh.'

I sniffed. 'I feel like you're up to something.'

'You are a one. I'm not *up* to anything. But there are a couple of things I'd like to talk to you about.'

'I knew it. Like what? Did the mother send you here?'

'No, she didn't. This has got nothing to do with her. Even though, I tell you, she's pretty sad she hardly sees you. But let's not get into that— that's between the two of you. Let's just take our time, relax a little, shall we? Get to know each other a bit more, from where we are; from here, this now.'

'Oh yeah, like now I'm really relaxed.'

'Why are you so angry, love?'

'I'm not angry.'

He gazed at me, his eyes like windows into somewhere good. 'No?'

Feeling myself grow hot, I glanced down, pincered a langoustine between finger and thumb, sank my teeth into it as if I were punishing it. The bite was resistant yet yielding, seemed to answer a need in me. My mouth salivated, sucked it in, its fragrant sweet body releasing its juices as I chewed. It was strange, the feel of his tender presence melted something inside of me, no choice, like I was butter in a hot pan.

'I guess I'm just like this langoustine,' I murmured, meeting his gaze. 'A bit real and in your face—but actually I just want to be appreciated.'

He chuckled. 'And you are. Always.'

'They're delicious.'

He nodded, took one up to his mouth. We ate in silence for a while, eyeing each other, kind of grinning a bit. A sense of ease grew between us, this lovely feeling of recognition condensed into the simple action of tasting the luscious flavours. It was really nice not to have to say anything, just know we were having a shared experience.

The waitress came and took away our plates, arranged new cutlery on the white tablecloth. She topped up our sparkling water, his glowing red wine, and asked me if I wanted another beer, which I did.

As she meandered away through the tables, he leaned forward on his elbows. 'Remember how I taught you to feel your inner energy field when you were little? Reckon you can do that now?'

'Why?'

'Because I want you to be present.'

'For what? I don't do that anymore. What do you want to tell me? Just say it.'

'Come on, humour me. Close your eyes. Start with your hands. Bet you can feel the tingling?'

My hands just seem to start up on their own, like they had been waiting for this instruction forever. I couldn't help smiling. 'You pig. I always knew you were a magician.'

'It's nice, right? But it's not me—it's there all the time, you only have to tune in, become aware. It's life's essential energy, eh—you know that. So close your eyes. Now, let it spread up your arms. Your feet. Your lips, nose. Your shoulders. You got it, right?'

The smile in his voice buzzed through the inner vibrations of my body. I could feel the energy of life inside of me: my life, his life, the life of the room, like every cell was awake with it. There was something lovely growing beyond, a kind of peace maybe.

'You feel the silence beneath it too, huh?' he asked. 'The stillness?'

'All like it's reaching out into everything.'

'Fantastic. You've always had this easy connectivity to the Eternal Being—hey, to big Love, eh? You remember? So stay in touch with it. It's going to keep you focussed, less reactive.'

I opened my eyes. 'Less reactive?'

He made a motion with his hand, touched his solar plexus. 'Stay with yourself.'

'No.' I let all the tingling drop back into obscurity, took a big slug on my beer straight from the bottle. 'That's a ridiculous thing to say. You're actually annoying me. Always telling me what to do and how I should be. I'm not that little kid anymore. You can control.'

'Ok, so just let the annoyance be—it will move through you. Observe it. Why not let the inner body keep you present?'

'I don't want to bloody observe it.'

'If you push against it, it will gain strength, steal from your true energy—it already has, eh? Observing it will let it dissipate on its own.'

I felt my teeth clench, eyes hard. 'You don't get it, do you? I don't have a problem with being annoyed. I *like* being annoyed. And you're annoying, that's a fact. Just tell me what you want to tell me and stop trying to be a bloody guru.'

His smile was empathetic. He nodded. 'It's about your sister.'

My guts flinched as the laugh came out of my nose. 'I don't want to know.'

'She's working with me.'

'At the stables?'

'Yes.'

'The *bitch*.' I shook my head, stomach twisting. 'That was always *my* place. I knew she wanted to take over my life. She always di—she hated me even before—before I loved Sw—don't you remember she coined me a slag—huh? She wouldn't see it any other way. And you're just accepting that? Where does she live? She doesn't live with you?'

'She does.'

I couldn't believe it, I felt like I wanted to burst into tears. 'How could you?'

'It's not personal,' he said.

'Is that why you came here, to rub my face in it, punish me for all that time ago?' He just gazed at me. My tears ballooned, made light refract on the edges of my raw pink lids. Everything shone and bleared.

I felt how he made a whole lot of space, holding me in his misted grey eyes. 'I would never seek to punish you. You never did anything wrong.'

'But I did, didn't I? Even though it was right, see. I lost him. I lost you. And all my other family too.'

'I'm here. I've never been anywhere else. All your family loves you, want nothing more than to heal. But you're carrying this wound like a trophy. Why are you clinging? The past is gone, it's just a story now—if you only let yourself see that, my lovely. Your ego mind is doing its best

132

to keep recharging the suffering. You're doing this thousands of times with something that doesn't exist anymore, extending the pain into years, my love.'

'I don't really get that it doesn't exist. I *want* it to exist. You think I want to forget him? That time? It was beyond anything I've ever known—how can you diminish it down to calling it a story? I didn't make it up. I *lived* it.'

'You lived it. You keep living it. I'm sorry it hurts so much still. And I don't mean to demean your experience. Of course it happened.' He nodded, his face reflecting my hurt, while at the same time exuding an infinite kindness, a radiance, as if a light was switched on inside of him. He made it impossible not to listen to the gap of silence, made my mind go quiet-as. 'What do I mean by a story, eh? I mean it's not here and now. I mean your mind keeps building and adding to it. It's keeping you identified with an *idea* of yourself, almost like a character in a play—do you see? It's the story of you, your lack-based ego self, not your pure essence, the consciousness of life itself—I know you get this—it's limiting you in *this* now—the one moment we've all got, eh? Look, the ego isn't bad, it thinks it's protecting you—some kind of development of evolution, I'm realising, of the human survival instinct but—'

'—what, now you're getting into your own messed up notions of human evolution? You're—'

'—*but* it's keeping you from You.'

'I don't care.'

'I tell you, my lovely, I'm very sorry it happened the way it did—but it was always going to hurt. Every *thing* does in the end. Unless you cultivate Awareness. Your relationships, your career, all external matter is going to hurt because you're going to lose every *thing*. The world will do that to you. It just does. It's the nature of life in its form state: change and ending. As long as you search for your happiness in the world outside of you, you will never find it—even when you get what you want, you'll find it isn't what you thought you were chasing after—it won't make you happy. Do you see? To believe that is a kind of prison. I know you get it.'

'But it will make me happy. And this moment is full of all my past and present moments, isn't it? It's all alive in me. You can't say it isn't.'

He smiled, raised his eyebrows. 'Yes. Sort of. And that's wonderful.'

'And if being "me"—my Self or whatever—means wiping away all my past and future—like being an actual person *actually*…well, that's stupid. I think your attitude is negative—*lose* everything. What kind of an idiot are you?'

'Look, if you let yourself just *be*, in this one moment, without past, without future, without the constant noise of the mind, that's freedom. You discover the one Life that pervades the entire Universe, a vastness which you are not simply a part of—see? A vastness which *is* you. We become the Intelligence beyond the small-self mind—*free* of the ego mind, see?—which we are not—and the body—which we are not—yes, free of *person*, you said it—"You die to yourself", as Jesus sai—'

'—now you're preaching Jesus? Fuck's sake. I thought you were a fucking Budd—'

'—or do you remember how the Zen master Dogan put it? "To forget the self is to be enlightened by the ten thousand things."'

'Arrghh. I'm not asking to be enlightened. I don't want all that. I don't even understand it. You're invading my space—I'm not asking for this.'

'Yes, too many words, you're right—if you try and understand it, you'll talk yourself out of it in a second. But the words act as indicators—'

'—but I *am* asking you to tell me where he is. Then maybe I can find my own version of peace with this. See him, find out. You know where he is, don't you?'

'You really want to see him after all these years? A man of, what, thirty-eight, thirty-nine?'

'I do, yes.'

'I cannot help you.'

'But you know?'

'You were a kid,' he said.

'So? And now I'm a grown-up. So tell me where he is. What you're doing is immoral. You never even let me say goodbye to him. I get why you had to do that then, but I'm old enough to choose for myself now.

You don't know what we had.'

'In a few short weeks?'

'From the moment I ever saw him—I can't—I can't explain—there's something beyond material, see—like, maybe two people are meant to be together for reasons beyond what we know.'

'He isn't your answer. You need to let it go.'

'That's easy to say, isn't it?' I felt as if I were drowning, clutching for breath under water and he couldn't see it. He was going to let me die. 'I don't know how to let it go. It's like I climbed inside of him and I'm lost and I don't know how to get out. And I don't want to anyway. I *know* he has this too. And whatever I do, whoever I'm with, I'm never whole and no one else can complete me.'

'But that's a fantasy, a construct of your mind. No one can complete you. Only you can complete yourself—through your bigger Self. By your realisation you are not separate. In fact you are *already* complete, you are already *realised*, everyone is, you simply need to recognise that.'

'You should go do some lectures.'

He chuckled. 'That much of a bore, huh?' He held me in his gaze and I knew what he was doing, knew he was opening the space of emptiness, wanting me to open up into it with him.

'Bugger you,' I said. 'Why must you be such a weirdo?'

I almost wanted him to get cross but he just seemed to light up some more, like he found all of life delighting. 'Resistance…' he said.

'*Rude.*'

'Aren't we all weirdos, eh? All uniquely different—yes, weird—but also essentially the same, of the same essential Energy.'

'You're the one that's resistant. You're still infringing on my— what?—spiritual free will or whatever. I'm not asking for your teaching, see.'

He nodded, all like he knew what I was saying was true. 'What if you come and work with the horses again? The foal you imprinted, Angel's Neck, remember him? He's seven now, full in his prime, and such a magnificent creature. He's a huge success, a winner. I'm sure you know. He's yours to keep in training. I always see you in him.'

My heart cracked, spewed the suffocating muck I was keeping at bay up into my throat. 'I loved that foal. I still think about him, see him in my head. But I see a baby, *my* baby. Angel's Neck. Do you know what that name means?'

He sucked on his lips, popped them. 'Perhaps you make that matter too much.'

'Yes. In your book I do.'

He bowed his head in a resolute kind of a way, lowered his eyes, then met mine openly again, all saying, 'Look, maybe it's time you hear this: I lost him too—if that's the way we want to see it—he was my friend, in a profound and singular way. He disappointed the hell out of me back then. And he *knows* this spiritual shit; I shared it with him like no one else—'

'—see then? He *is*—I shared it with him too—'

'—but I had to recognise he wasn't healthy—he broke my trust—he broke essential boundaries—and I had to let him go.'

'Well I won't—hey, in your language: how do you know we don't have karma together? That's what I'm saying. Maybe it's you who is having a messed-up perspective these days—you're stuck on the age thing when maybe this is beyond that. Okay, so I was too young then— according to perceived social norms and notions—I accept that—but I'm not now…if something makes you feel good, and it's not hurting anyone else, isn't that the energy of Love? Isn't it that big Self guiding me to him?'

'But it doesn't make you feel good.'

'But it did. And it would again—I'm sure of it. Life brought us together for a reason.'

He stared at me, his lips kind of pursed. 'I don't actually know where he is, love, I really don't. Just come to Ireland for a bit, eh, my sweet? Spend some time. I'll help you. And your sister is ready to make amends.'

'Fuck her. And what about my career? Now you want me to give it up? After you said I was so brilliant? What planet are you on?'

'I'm not suggesting you give up acting, not at all. Just come for a while—between jobs. It was you that said it was *your* place just now. Why not do both?'

The hard energy from my heart rose up, surged into my head. It was like I could hear it, integrated contradictory rhythms all asking for a piece of me. I could have stood and shouted, flipped the table with a jerk of my hands, but I just stared into the whiteness of the tablecloth, which seemed to jump and vibrate, and I knew that on some other dimension or whatever, I could put my hand right through it. My voice came very small when I said, 'I can't go back, not ever, you have to understand.'

He remained silent. I was shocked by the sudden desire to seek solace in his arms, feel myself enveloped in the simple love he had always provided when I was little. I stared into the tingling white.

'I'm sorry,' he said. 'I'm very, very sorry. But perhaps, one day, you'll be able to grow from all this. I know you will. Maybe *that* is your karma—what Life is asking you to do.'

I raised my eyes to his. 'Isn't that rather derisive?'

'No. I talk to you from...' I saw how he wasn't searching for words, not anything, was just letting me feel for myself the vastness he was, so I might go there with him, know it within me.

'From what?' A spur of hate pricked through me. 'Where? You're confusing me.'

He smiled. 'You think too much. You need to be more thoughtless.'

I shook my head. 'No. "I think therefore I am". You want me to be an idiot.'

'You have a very clever mind.'

'Not really.'

'My sweet, your pain is your biggest teacher. You'll find out, I promise. When you are ready.'

'Condescending again,' I said.

I saw, behind him, the waitress in her short white apron carrying two large plates, her intention directed upon us. I sat back, raised my chin to indicate to him and he turned, his bald head bouncing light from its surface. He smiled when he turned back to me.

'This is going to be good. I hope you're still up for it?'

I shrugged, my mouth already beginning to salivate.

Our steaks were delivered before us, dark streaks burned into them from the grill, the smell almost tortuous. The pomme frites were skinny, crispy, stood up in jars, all spiky, like bad yellow haircuts. He raised his glass to my stumpy-necked bottle.

'To you. To all you are in this moment.'

'You're very cringy,' I said.

I had a chocolate mousse for pudding, its smooth rich texture like silk on my tongue, while he chose a tart tatin, gave me half too, thinnest glazed apple slices on thinner crisped pastry, sweet and tangy at once. We supped a dessert wine, its thick musky flavour hitting high notes on my palette. Like flowers, I told him. We roamed through bits of our lives, shared moments from my childhood, his too, and all kinds of times we'd had alone and with others. I teased him we were sticking ourselves in the past; he was a hypocrite. He just nodded, all like he agreed and loved just everything. He ordered cheese and oatcakes, grapes. More wine. It felt like we had been eating for a year.

'Always the hedonist,' I told him.

'Not so always these days.' He gave me a look, eyes glinting. 'You sound like your mum.'

'Fuck off.'

'Those are her exact words.'

'Ah,' I said. 'See? Imprinting.'

He laughed, just breath. 'Good one. Yup, conditioning. We're all imprinted, that's for sure.' He smeared a melted lump of camembert onto his forefinger, straight from the wooden board. 'And we sure know how to create—whoever thought to make cheese? And so many kinds, the different yeast cultures? So many discoveries.'

As he sucked on his finger, I realised I had been reading the words on his hands all evening without really taking them in, so familiar they were. How many times had I read his fingers? How many times had I sat on his lap when I was small and traced them, asked him again and again how he made them, about the sharp compass, the blood and ink, my mother chastising him? How I loved their ragged blue letters.

'Hey,' I said. 'Why do you still have "hate" on your hand? If all your life is love? Why not get it removed?'

He made a fist, looked down at H A T E, face alight. 'Because it reminds me. Just as this does,' he said, aiming L O V E at me.

'Reminds you what?'

'Of the journey. Of life's shadow—which shows us the light, eh? The transmutation of pain into joy—without the suffering I might never have gotten here. Aha, and you know, I get it now: Consciousness can only *truly* know its Self by knowing what it is *not*. Perhaps that's why we live so much contrast…love and hate—anger, eh?—fear—sadness and joy…'

I blinked hard as my eyes stung with the sign of new tears. I nodded, and my voice came thready. 'That's rather beautiful. However much I hate it.'

His L O V E fingers reached across the table. 'Give me your hand. I've got something to tell you.'

'Not again,' I said, eyes sending glittery smiles at him. I snorted. 'Don't tell me you're dying.'

He took my hand, squeezed it. His mirror-shined head went to one side. 'You're a very clever girl.'

'What?'

He nodded gently. 'This body is dying. It's got maybe a year, maybe less, they say. But I say maybe more.'

'Oh no. No, no, no. I was joking. I was only joking.'

He was smiling. 'It's alright. Impermanence, remember? Everything dies in the form world. But I've never been so clear. It's my moment of flowering—and it is just *beyond*. No clinging, no wanting. No judging good or bad. I know myself for what I truly am. The actual joy of Being. I *feel* myself as all and everything; know you and I are one and the same, simply unique expressions—experiences, see?—of the one sublime Creator. I'm resting into this knowing. And I know, really *know* now, I am enough. Why do you think I'm pushing you to open to all this stuff, infringing on your readiness, your free will, as you so eloquently put it?'

My fingers were bunched into my lips, pressing hard, as if stopping a scream from coming out. Tears streamed down my face, branching into tributaries, blurred into a veil of salted water over the world. Everything hard and wet. It was so shocking to see how happy he was. I felt my shoulders begin to jolt. He stood, came around the table and held my head into his body.

'I don't want to lose you,' I said.

'You won't.'

139

'But you'll be gone.'

'And you'll learn I'm not. That I'm always with you. That we are, for truth, the One Life—all unique waves upon—actually *of*, yes?—the one infinite ocean. We are timeless. But all this is just words, labels. Don't get stuck on the words. The only way you can know your Self is by *wanting* it—more than anything—and letting the realisation happen.'

'But what's the matter with you? What have you got?'

'It's just the body. I am that which was never born and can never die. As are you, sweet girl.'

As I pushed through the hard slanting rain, I saw how the lines of it broke against the slur of water all washing across the paving slabs. Cars passed, great surges rushing in my ears, wavelets reaching, arcing, smashing into my bare calves, skin repelling the water, retaining the wet. I squinted up from the churning violence, found everything glistening, colours vivid and clean. The sky had that surreal quality, an intense luminosity within the grey. It kind of broke my heart how beautiful it all was. Arrested me. I stopped. Looked about. Seeing the world with fresh new eyes, as if I was just born into it, just like my uncle told me it could be in any moment. I saw I was awake. It felt glorious, life sparking up through all my grief and confusion.

My hair was plastered to my head, fat raindrops falling into my eyes. Who needs tears? I thought, though I knew them well enough. *You have to get to the theatre*, came the voice in my head, those clever thoughts that sought to own me, take me from my essence, make me a me, an ego, my uncle called it, small self, whatever, a me so strong it thought its thoughts, its mind, was itself, its body was itself, and cared only to escape the moment, fill the now with distractions and plans and worries. Why did my mind hate the now so much?

But I had to get to the theatre, it was true. This thought was guiding me, keeping me responsible. Thought had a function when you made it your friend. Hadn't he said that too? It was a necessary tool in the world of form. I had to get to the theatre. I was late for the warm-up. And Vera always wanted to do a speed-run. A shard of anger cut the energy. Life was so annoying. How could you get to be present, be all your stillness and essence, when the moment you found it you had to run around all over the place constantly doing things? I felt the growl of it all rush up from my guts and I began to run. He was going to die. I couldn't stand he was going to die, whatever he said. He was leaving me. He was all the family I had.

My feet slapped the sliding dancing sheet of water as they took me flying up the street. So many times I had trodden these streets of my stinking home town, bus-ing it the few miles from my village, circling the market on Saturdays, but never had I trodden this route to the theatre as a performer there. My damn parents were coming tonight and I was going to have to go out with them afterwards to some restaurant. Treating me they were, they said. Treating themselves, more like. I had refused to stay with them, opting for a grotty B and B, where I had my own room now Vera and Toby had made some kind of commitment to each other. I could've saved the money on the room, gained an extra bit of pocket money, as when you arranged your own accommodation the theatre company gave you your allocated lodging expenses, but fuck that, even though I was here for a week, one of our longest runs on the tour, I wasn't going to stay at home for anything.

As I reached the theatre, called Royal at that, I slowed, pausing to look up at the grand façade, the rain-sheened brickwork, the gilt and red lettering. The foyer was already bubbling with brightly dressed audience, ticket lines, chatter echoing up. There came the bloom of pride in my breast, a burgeoning excitement, me all wondering who might come and see me, like maybe my English teacher or my Art teacher or some old friend.

And then I saw him, a shadowy figure coming forward, smiling, those beguiling dimples like slashes in his flushed cheeks. A sort of bashful shyness grassed him up as we reached each other, and I knew for once, after all this time, when I couldn't care less, I had the upper hand.

'Robin Remick,' I said, feeling his thirteen-year-old kisses on my thirteen-year-old lips in a way that surprised me. 'Well, what do you

141

know?'

'I saw you were going to be here. On the poster.'

'Didn't waste any time, did you?' I leaned forward, took his sodden shoulder in my hand and kissed first one cheek, then moved toward the other, saying, 'Two.' Him quite awkward, unsure of where to put his face, his eyes, his mouth. 'It's the way we do it in London, you know. French styli.' And then, just to tease him, I added, 'Three.' Moved in for a third. His cheeks were crisp with cold, his olive skin soft and moist. 'A baby's bum,' I said.

'What?'

'Your skin.'

'You what?'

I gave him a look, like he was tiresome. 'Never mind.' I knew I was cruel and it did something weird to my heart, hurt it maybe. But I felt vindicated, felt I was punishing him for that younger Jane Graham. Even though I'd barely thought about her, or Robin Remick even, nor cared, since Ireland and *him*. 'Been waiting long?'

He looked down, shrugged. 'You know...'

'You're pretty wet.'

'You too.'

We stared into each other's eyes, a whole mess of teenage defiance, ardour and cool spooling up into my throat in a way that didn't make sense to me.

'You look good,' he said. 'Exactly the same. Only more beautiful.'

'Wow. Is this really you? You don't say things like that.'

'I thought I'd never see you again. I saw you on that video. And adverts. And in the magazines.'

'Ah, so that's why you're here.'

'No,' he said, his voice clear. 'I thought about you regardless of all that. All that just made it worse.'

I stood gazing at him, strange coils of arousal unravelling in my flesh. 'So what do you do with yourself these days?'

'Do? You mean my job?'

I nodded.

'I'm a scaffolder.'

142

'Oh.'

'It pays well. I'm fit as.'

'That's good. Listen, I've got to go in.'

'Can I see you later?'

'Are you coming to the show?' He shook his head. 'You want a ticket? I'll get you a comp if you like. But not tonight. My bloody parents are coming.'

'Can I see you after?'

'Got to go out with the fuckers.'

'So you still don't get on?' He sounded surprised. 'I heard you ran away.' I stared at him, anger playing in my throat. 'How about meeting me after that then?' he said. 'We could go out—they've turned that old roller-skating rink we used to go to into a club.'

I laughed. 'You're kidding?'

'No, it's quite good actually.'

'That I'd want to go to a disco in this dump.'

'Oh. Well we can go for a drive then.'

'At midnight?'

'Sure, why not? Or go to mine. I've got an okay flat.'

'Why would we go to yours? You want to play catch the peanut?'

He cleared his throat, scratched his ear, fiddled with his floppy rain-soaked hair. I saw one of his cheeks had a bright roundish scar in it, still pink, right where his dimple was.

'Fine,' he said. 'Forget it.'

'Okay.' I made to leave but he caught a hold of my arm.

'I mean it, I want to see you. I'm really sorry about—*you know*—I was an areshole.'

I eyed his scar, felt a strange tug to touch it, something tender in all the hard. 'It doesn't matter. It was a long time ago, Robin. A lifetime ago.'

'I've really regretted it.'

'What?'

'Treating you like shit.'

I winced, smiled. 'Honestly, it doesn't matter. We were thirteen.'

'And fourteen. And fifteen.'

143

'Whatever.'

'I've always wanted you to know, since you left, that I always liked you—right from the off, right from when I first saw you—I mean like, really *liked* you—maybe too much—right from when I moved here from Newcastle. But I was too young and I didn't know what to do with it.'

'That's very sweet.'

'And that's sarcastic. I guess your big life in London, being a model and an actress and everything makes you think you're better than me.'

'Wow. Harsh words,' I said, but felt the blush of truth in them. 'I just got over you, is all. You didn't matter since when I was fourteen. That's the truth.'

'What, so you're saying you didn't give a shit since you went with that old guy in Ireland? Even though we went together after him and everything.'

'We never *went* together. I went with him; I never went with you.'

'Oh, so what did we do then?'

'Played around. And you started that. Way before.'

'So you're trying to get me back?'

'Okay, this isn't going anywhere. And he wasn't old, for a start. You shouldn't listen to gossip. And I really do have to get backstage now. We're on in half an hour. They're going to kill me for being this late.'

'Thirty-two is pretty old,' he said. 'Even now. Especially when you're fourteen.'

'Fuck off, Robin. What kind of a judgement is th

   holding the small hard peanut between finger and thumb, i'm laughing like i'm dumb-as, him laughing too, all kinds of mixed-up feelings rising, swelling, listing in my heart.  body throbbing, head, thoughts, throbbing.  my eyes slide over the mess of red-skinned nuts scattered on his mother's white carpet, meet those of the reclining bo

   okay, i say, taking aim at his opened estuary.  one, two, *three!*  i used to want to kiss that full soft mouth.  now i don't know what i'm doing here.  all i know is i want to obliterate *him*, go back to how things were before.  but i can't.  head throbbing, thoughts throbbing.  i throw the nut.  nut soaring, arcing.  he dives, all like *before*, all like a seal and he catches it, takes another dive, grabbing for me, and i'm all yelping, a fellow seal. we are wrapped and rolling, tumbling, laughter still and kisses. then serious, bodies overtaking sense. some sort of vital need. pressing into each other, moaning, my thoughts at last dissolved into tingling, tugging urge. doesn't matter who it is. *li*

my top all up, we never get so far as nudity, us sweet little teenagers all in his mother's house, but my boobs are spilled and fussed over. our carnal love, up til now quite innocent, shifts its gears: i take his penis in my hand; he fingers me. he moves down my body and i can tell it's the first time he's done this, the way he comes at me all tentative, unsure, a slow investigation with tongue and lip. i know he's trying to prove himself. i push up my hips, clasp hard on his shoulders, sway myself back and forth, trying to show him. the ache in me wanting to screa

fingers, i say. use your fingers. i want to tell him to go fas

and what he does is, he blows on me. i moan, it's nice. for a moment; a sort of anticipation. but he blows on me some more. and some more. and i'm going cold, everything switching off. then he blows *up* me. or tries to. and i want to laugh at him, tell him he's a fucking idiot. i have no empathy for his unknowing. everything ruined. i pull away, sit up. he flounders, startled, embarrassed, i see it. his mouth is shiny. i liked when *his* mouth was shin

did-did you do everything with him? he asks, all kind of sheepi

pulling up my knickers, heart low as the setting sun, blue as black, i say, of course i di

'Look at him,' I said to Vera, raising my voice over the smoochy groove. 'He's doing exactly what he used to do when we were young, deliberately playing me with another girl.' She followed my gaze, stared over, right as his hands groped down the blonde chick's hips. 'For fuck's sake,' I said. 'He'll be kissing her in a minute.'

White light ricocheted off the giant mirrored disco ball, all the luminous broken pieces sliding and skating over a rippling crush of heads. Chunks of it slipped across Robin Remick's face, appeared to want to enter his mouth, swerved off downwards, outwards, touching the girl, connecting them.

I glared at Vera. She sucked on her beer bottle. I saw how her throat opened to the flow of liquid. She smacked her lips together, said, 'Ahhhh,' all like some kind of a cartoon.

'He makes me sick,' I said.

'Why do you care? I thought you said he was a prick.'

'He is. Look.' I watched him swaying right up against her, the two of them making the small town slow-turn on the spot. There was a gripping at my chest, something cold and harsh. 'God, I hate this place. It's exactly the same. Everyone all the same.'

She touched my elbow. 'I'm getting the feeling you still like him.'

'What, Robin? Don't be stupid.'

'He's obviously crazy for you.'

'Oh yeah, sure looks like it. He persuades us to come here—after hanging out with me for three days, driving me about, telling me I'm his eternal love or some such bullshit—like trying to get into my pants no less, more like—*confusing* me, and now look—pathetic. People never fucking change.'

'And he's getting just the reaction he wants. He's not so dumb. Maybe a dick, but not dumb.'

Staring into Vera's eyes, I realised mine were biting. 'God, I'm so stupid. I'm acting like I was twelve, thirteen again. Like it all really mattered. But he's not the *one*. It's ridiculous, letting him get to me. As if I cared. He's meant nothing to me all these years.'

She held in a smile, shrugged. 'Well, maybe that's changed.'

'No,' I said. 'I don't want it to.'

'You've finished it with Sunil, so you can do what you like.'

'But I don't care about Robin Remick.'

She smiled. The slow song made the merge into a faster track. My back to the dance floor I felt the energy shift, couples coming apart, and people were shuffling in gentle streams around us, some moving away, others getting to it.

146

'Let's go,' I said suddenly. 'Please. Can we?'

She gazed at me, nodded, but I could see she didn't really want to. She sipped her beer, popped her lips. 'I'll go and get Toby.'

I reached for her forearm. 'Hey, you know what, it's fine. You stay. Honestly. I'll see you later.' I thrust my part-drunk bottle into her spare hand, registered her look of surprise and spun away, not giving her a chance to answer.

My mouth grim, I shoved my body crossways through the throng. I couldn't bear to look at the herd, the hairdos and makeup, the cheap fashion, all that bloody fruit-flavoured lipgloss from those dinky roll-on vials. Like I used to wear myself, fucking idiot. Cherry. Berry. I'm a sweetie for you to suck on. Just the sound of the lilting Suffolk accents was enough to turn my stomach. I felt I was going to burst, was desperate for cool clear air, all gulping at it as the wide white bouncer levered the door open for me.

The streets glimmered in their coat of rain, bright spots glinting sharp against the streams forming in my eyes. I felt the warmth of my insides track down my cheeks, felt my shoulders begin to shake. What, oh what, was I doing? Four days at home and I was turning into a lunatic.

An image of my uncle steamrollered into me. Him all awake and aware and—*flowering*, he'd said. Flowering? I saw a flower lasts such a short time. Did we flower only when death loomed close? Flowering seemed a threat. One's petals could only fall. I took to running, feet thumping on the tarmac forecourt of the club, myself at thirteen, fifteen, twenty-one, roller-disco at my back, glitter-ball slicing speeding shards of memory into my live flesh. There came behind me the bright slap of footsteps. And yelling. I darted under the railway bridge, all its dry filthy paving stones echoing, never to know the wet sheen beyond. I knew it was him and I slowed, stopped. My panting breath all bounced around the brick archway, came back doubl

wrapping

our mess of arms and legs, we tug each other skin-close. his bed creaks. crappy headboard banging against the wall with every grasp, roll, heave. it feels like a skirmish, the kissing is hard and heartless, too much tongue, like we are starving, like i am trying to push him away my feet

147

kick at the tangle of dark blue bed sheet he takes his mouth over my
throat deposits butterfly kisses the like of which had set me off way back
when when he had first done it when i was just a kid had ignited
unknown beatings exquisite pulsings and pangs almost terrified me with
their force i throw back my head give him my neck feels pleasant
melting shivers scud down my nerve-endings into my cunt cunt it's a
nice word a beautiful sacred word sunil's voice snakes into the shivers he
is sucking and nipping at my breasts fingers skirting their edges near my
armpits those secret places and my body arches upwards calling him to it
even as my mind trips elsewhere past sunil to where it likes best to go to
*him* my *him* thick dark stubble scratching at my skin his furry belly
brushing he moves on downward my hands pressing into his muscular
shoulders soon to clasp to wrench his hot mouth enveloping his fingers
wet inside me crying out crying my clenched eyelids cannot hold in the
salty hot spills i scratch him he deserves it the cunt i hate you don't you
kn

he climbs
up my long slim body bends over me i won't let him enter me you're
crying he says did i hurt you are you alri

no i'm not crying it's not crying i'm
just turned o

[you couldn't hurt me if you tried *li* ]
why don't you want to he says am i still not
what not good enough for y

i need some time i say i didn't expect thi
but you like it he sa
i nod my eyes telling him i don't know
any more i don't know anything what i like or don't like and i hate
everything someh

you know i love you he whispers i
always did but i didn't know what to do with it the feeling was so strong
overwhelming we were so young i'm just so sorry i hurt y

you didn't hurt me you couldn't hurt
me anym

[i'm too busy hurting myse ]

148

{came back doubl}ed, my sigh vaulting all around the brick railway arch, his footsteps echoing with it as a song as he came to me. I felt myself slump when I should have been standing tall, defying him. I stared at the stained dry paving slabs, watched dusty debris and grass bits pick up, skim about the shadowy surface. A white crumpled paper bag, a bakery tumbleweed, skated over my trainer, made off and out into the free yonder.

Robin Remick, hands in jeans' pockets, stood before me. I felt him looking at me, slithered my eyes up from his hidden fists, up one densely muscled arm, saw how he tensed, the bicep lean, strong, pale on the inside. I met his gaze.

'What's the scar? On your cheek?'

He shrugged one shoulder. 'Scaffolding pole. It was a mare.'

'I like it.'

'Might it make you want to kiss me?'

'Might.'

'Then it was worth it. Best day of my life.'

We chuckled, something sweet arising, sweet, innocent, good. He reached toward me, took my face in his hands, tucked stray hairs behind my ear and across the top of my head.

'What were you doing with that blonde girl?'

He dropped his hands, lugged a breath, body sinewy under cornflower-blue t-shirt. His pale-brown eyes were troubled, brows knitted. He pulled down his mouth. 'Couldn't say.'

'Well, you have to say. You were doing what you always did to me, don't you see that?'

'Yup.'

'So this is ridiculous.'

'It's only because you wouldn't show me how you felt. I was cut up.'

'But that's not what I used to do. And you used to do it then.'

'But that was then. We're not kids anymore.'

'But we're acting that way—like kids.'

He smiled. 'We don't have to. Are you coming back to mine? Like no

My body shifted in the bed, drew me awake, rolled me onto my back, eyes meeting the mottled light on the white ceiling. I listened to the oceanic hum of traffic on the Cromwell Road, his breath beside me gentle yet heavy. I turned my head, gazed into his slumbering face. I sighed, stared up again, watching the play of day in the box of my bedroom. What was I doing?

He had taken three days off work, in unity with my own break, driven me back to London in his immaculate car, the very night our run in my home town had finished. We had arrived at gone-two in the morning, laid our bones, in all their sensuality, on my lumpy mattress, springs digging into us. We seemed to have become a couple, my early teenage fantasy, without even talking about it. We slept together, kissed, were sexual, but still I never let it go all the way; I never yet *went* with him, didn't know if it was possible, if I could, like I wanted to keep it that way forever.

As my sights scudded down the wall, I was hit by a thought, all jostling his shoulder. 'Oh my god. Robin. Your car.'

He opened his eyes, squeezed his lids together, yawned. Unstirred by my urgency. He smiled, reached his hand to touch my hip bone. 'I was dreaming I was with you—and here you are. I must be dreaming, right?'

Mirth rippled through me. 'Your car…'

'You what?'

I snuggled into him, him pulling me in, all kissing my head. Hot mouth, hot body. Stinky breath, we both. I let myself drift a little, melt into the warmth and the ease.

'I think we're in trouble,' I finally mumbled. 'We forgot about your car. What time is it?'

'What are you going on about?' I felt him tilt his wrist, his head, to look at his watch. 'It's ten thirty-eight.'

'Oh,' I said into the curve of his neck. 'I hope you're feeling rich.'

'Very. You?'

'You've probably got a ticket. You ought to move it to a metre.'

We tore into our clothes, both of us spilling with laughter, him saying, 'It's not funny. It's not funny,' all the time. And when we reached the street, his car was gone.

'Towed,' I said.

The two of us traipsed back up my six flights of stairs and I called the council, gave them the number plate, found it had been taken to a car pound on Park Lane. So we relaxed, sat at my round wooden table, had coffee and toast, giggling and harping like delinquent teenagers.

It was crazy sunny out, crisp, the air and sky clear-as. I took him up the grand promenade of Queen's Gate and into Kensington Gardens. We held hands and it was nice. Something was met in me, walking under the trees, on the open grass, the growl of London there but not there, distant, peripheral, reassuring. People strolled, ran, pushed buggies, called to their children, dogs unleashed.

My eyes played over the blades of grass shining in the breeze, saw the supple easiness with which they bent underfoot, unbroken, unbruised, with a capacity to spring back, keep growing toward the light.

Passing the small manmade lake, water all glittery, I saw myself a child, four maybe, running nude along the river path, my mum at my back, my clothes, my shoes in her hands. It was an image from a black-and-white photograph and my face was intense, concentrated, but infused with the simple joy of life and movement. My mother had a huge smile; my dad behind the camera. I felt the rush of that childish energy within my own grown-up limbs, felt the balmy air of then gliding over the chub I no longer had, all whistling in my hair.

'Robin,' I said at last, squeezing his fingers. 'You know this can't work.'

'No, I don't know that.'

'You know I really like you much more than I could ever have thought. You're—'

'—is this your Dear John moment?'

I stopped, looked at him, he at me. I wanted to tell him it wasn't but it would have been a lie. I sucked on my lips, nodded, felt a sting to my eye.

He was shaking his head. 'But things are going so well. I mean, we get on, we're having fun—it's lovely. Why?'

'We're just so different. We have very different lives.'

'What's wrong with different? And I'm willing to change my life, move here, whatever. I'll do anything. You know, I used to work in a portraiture place—I could become a photographer.'

I saw what I was saying was founded on nothing, I sounded like some horrible snob. I shook my head. 'I don't know. I just—I want it to end like this—happy, a choice. I'm sorry. This was my fantasy, being with you, when I was twelve-thirteen. It's a fantasy. Not real. I can't live it now; it's not right. But something is sated here.'

'For you,' he said. And his hurt was naked on his face. 'What about me. My choice?'

'I know.'

As I stood in the underground car pound, the chill creeping into my shoulders, watching him drive away, a part of me wanted to chase after him, but most of me was clear. I realised, on a level, there hadn't been much of a choice for me either; it had had to be this way. I ran my forefinger under one eye then the other, collected the wetness there, erased it on the hem of my skirt. The hole in my being seemed to open up. I hurried up the concrete stairwell, feet slapping, echoing, and emerged into the bright day, strands of dark hair dancing around my face like elastic whiskers, full of their own life, nothing to do with me. More tears sprung, the terrible tenderness of my heart all like a flower that needs water. I would lay myself on the damp grass, let the sun caress my skin.

Making my way back toward the park gates, I saw a couple of red telephone boxes and I remembered I didn't have to be alone just now, there were friends to call, friends to see, hug, laugh with—cry with, if I had to. I kept the door ajar with my foot, in an attempt to release the pee fumes I could almost see rising from the filthy floor, dialled a number. It rang quite a long time but I knew to wait.

'Hello?'

'Hello? Eliot? It's me.'

Wild red poppies grew out of fissures where the bridge over the canal met the pavement, all long and hairy stemmed, kind of entering my bloodstream and expanding my heart—and when I saw how they billowed in the barely-there earth-traps along the wall line of the shop, all like flags marking my journey, my pulse went wavy-as, so I had to shoot my sights up into the grey August day, seek safety in the soft and lustrous sky.

Returning to Earth I glanced upon a couple of petals in the gutter, purpley bruise all bleeding into silken red, and I let the willow of my body reach for them, snip them up into warm fingers.

I entered the shop. It had a good smell, sort of lemony, not the mustiness these kind of places usually spawned from all that old furniture and junk. And after allowing my vision to drift in the hazy light, no one visible, I stepped toward a display case. As if that was what I was here for. Leaning into it, I found myself drawn to a soft-coloured bunch of porcelain roses, a little brooch floating on blue velvet in a sea of small objects. Some kind of sharp thorn tore at me through the glass from those ceramic blooms, hacked into my memory, all recharging the envy for my mother's gift to my sister on her eleventh birthday. I still couldn't help wishing she had given that brooch to me; it was me who had spotted it in the antiques market; me who liked it.

The sound of footsteps brought me back. I glanced askance to catch dark blue jeans rolling toward me, low on his hips, kind of hanging off almost, and then he was standing next to me and I was tapping the transparent surface, heart thrumming high in my ears. I looked into my shadowy replicated self all soaring above the flowers, grazed my eyes across the glass to grab a glimpse of him; saw him blurry, a spectre.

'The rose brooch,' I said. 'I had one just like it when I was little. Can I…?'

I dared to stare up at him. My heart fell away. It was as if I were dropping through the sky slow motion, falling back in time—but not, because he was young and he didn't look like him anyway; even though he definitely did. I felt myself astride two timelines, here-and-now and *then*; saw both had the same outcome, crashed me into a snow of tiny blue flowers.

He said something about the brooch being Victorian and his voice had that rasp to it, sent shivers down the back of my neck. I watched, hardly hearing words—watched his same square fingers open the display case with a small rusty key, tiny in his grip, a child's storybook key with an oval loop at the top. The hum of his voice kept cracking through me, in it so many echoes. He delivered the bouquet into my open palm and I stood gazing at it, not seeing it, feeling myself blushing, boiling, his pale eyes playing over and over inside my head as if on a film loop. I said, 'You remind me of someone.' And I raised my gaze. He had the same dilated pupils, exactly the same enigmatic blue their surround. His smile showed a tremor; I could tell he liked me.

'Yeah,' he said, 'I get that all the time.'

'Sure you do.'

'You like the brooch?'

I nodded, barely aware of it.

'You can have it.'

'What…?'

'You started it,' he said, all chuckling.

154

'Started what?'

He shrugged, looked shiny. 'You want the brooch? I'll wrap it for you.'

'Oh. No—I mean, yes, thank you, I'd love it.'

He led me to the back of the shop, where the till was, swaddled the cluster of handmade blossom in creamy tissue paper. I watched in an alert trance, everything magnified. His breath. My breath. The shape of his fingers, the way they moved. I knew them. My heart was caught in them, seemed to bump and pulse with every turn of them, a wondrous feeling all convincing me this was real, it was right, I was doing the right thing.

I laid the crumpled poppy petals on the counter, smoothed them out with my fingertips. They were love hearts. That dark at their tips was the bruised-up shadows of my craving, of how fucked up this all really was. I was laying myself naked, knowing he couldn't know it, but felt exposed.

'I guess that's the oldest line in the book,' I said. '"You remind me of someone." You definitely look like no one. But you know they say everyone has their double somewhere in the world. Not that you look like a double actually.'

He held me in his blue whorls. There came quite a rawness at my core, a sense of sunshine opening in my head in a way I hadn't felt for maybe years.

'How are you on a motorbike?' he asked. 'On the back?'

'Pillion, you mean?'

'Yeah, pillion. That'll be it.'

I nodded, throat tight. 'Yeah.'

'I can tell,' he said. He indicated the petals. 'You want to press those? I can find you a book.'

'Do you?' I said.

'What?'

'Want to press them?'

He looked me in the eye a long moment, then took to scanning the vast old library bookshelves to the side of the shop. Seeming to move all slo-mo, he drew an antique ladder along its metal runner and went up

155

quite high. 'Do you fancy going for a coffee?'

'I don't drink coffee.'

Laugh in his throat, he said, 'Tea? Lemonade? A pint?'

'You're living the high life, aren't you? Up there? I hate beer. And what about your shop?'

'I can close up the shop, no problem. Whisky? I'm feeling a wh
                screech of seagulls hi
isky? Hello? Offer's closing,' he said, and I realised he was staring at me from up the ladder. 'Where'd you go?'

I wondered if I ought to run away. Stop this. I said, 'Do you take milk in your tea?'

'You what?'

'Whisky, yes,' I s
                some crisps i ye
aid. 'Yes, whisky.'

'You sure now?'

'You sound all Irish, the way you say that.'

He eyed me, still with the smile, eyebrows raised. 'Well, there's a funny thing.'

'Are you?'

'Is it a problem?'

'No, I'm in lo—I lov—I love the Irish.'

'Oh, you love the Irish, huh? I am, yes. But not—not really. Maybe a bit. If I am, I've forgotten. My mother's Argentine.'

'Oh,' I said, not wanting to know about his mother. At all. Ever.

'Are *you*?' he asked. 'What with that dark hair and your gorgeous pale eyes?'

'In spirit I am.'

'A past life?'

I really should run. 'Bushmills.'

'Ah, yes, I gotcha. Good bit of Irish spirit. Let's do it—aha.' He extracted a book from the shelf. 'This is the one.'

He stepped down the ladder, his easy gait, the slim body a million miles from *his*. But even so, he was busting out of him, all coming at me, present-as. Moving to the counter, he set the book down. It was a hardback without its jacket, brown, worn, fat, with those thick ragged-edged pages, cut as they'd been read long ago, for the first time. My pulse came irregular, still way loud.

'Pick a number,' he said, checking the last page of the book. 'One to…three-hundred and thirty-seven.'

I felt the light of my own smile. 'Um—ninety-one.' He flicked through the sturdy pages, searching. I saw there were watercolours of flowers, and a large-spaced old-fashioned font. 'What is that book?'

'Ah,' he said. 'You're between two hares. Harebell and Hare's-tail Cottongrass. You're equidistance from the pictures. We're doing it by pictures, okay?' He faced the book toward me, flipping the pages for me to see, his big thumb and forefinger as bookmarks. The paintings were delicate and lovely as the plants they depicted. 'Take your pick,' he added, as he swivelled it back to himself, squinted at the print. 'Harebell—Latin name, Campanula Rotundiflora. Or Hare's-tail Cottongrass—Eriophorum Vaginatum.' He cleared his throat in an exaggerated kind of a way. 'I'm not making this up.'

We laughed together.

'Well, you are a bit of a hare,' he said. 'At least. Long and lissom. Most especially your ears.'

'I'll take the cotton wool on a stick. They look like they just shouldn't exist.'

He nodded once, almost a small bow. 'Good choice. Put the poppies in there.'

'What a perfect book. Wildflowers. You can't know how perfect it is—or maybe you can by some weird telepathy. How much?'

'To you, two quid.'

'I'll take it.'

He indicated the petals on the counter. 'Go on then.'

'One,' I said, putting it smack-bang on the image of the hare's-tail cottongrass, closing the book, pressing my bodyweight full into my palm. 'Plus one for you. Number?'

'This is getting a bit serious, isn't it? A bit fast?'

'What? Picking pages is fast? Who just gave me a brooch?'

Grinning, he said, 'It's all flowers. Okay, two-hundred and twenty-

157

two.'

'Nice.' I located the page. 'Oh, it's Rockrose—known as Common—but look,' I said, letting the pages flick by, 'you could have been Hoary or Spotted or White. Never mind. Your Latin name is Hellianthimum Nummalarium.' I smiled up at him. 'Me, I love any kind of rose—common is good. Who would want to be hoary? Or spotty? Or white?'

'Well, that's that then. Stick my poppy petal right there.'

The shop door groaned, a loud bell dinging, and I turned to see a family coming in, the little boy in the arms of the dad, mother wheeling the empty pushchair. He gave them a smile and a wave. 'Any queries, just ask,' he said. He leaned down on his elbows, kind of into my face, so I could feel his warm breath, smell the musky tang of it, as I arranged his petal on his page. My whole body kind of flinched, my own hare's-tail cottongrass tugging, all sweet and sharp at once.

'Hey, you do know I know you, right?' he rasped. 'I mean, for serious, that's why you made that quip I look familiar, huh?'

The scent of his body seemed to grow around me, too much like *him*, and I raised my eyes to his, nerves snagging. 'You do?'

'You don't know? For real?'

I shook my head, too slowly.

'I came to the play. After that Lily director of yours persuaded me to lend you all my furniture. I delivered it too. You were rehearsing.'

My head went tight, eyes pulling and I had to blink hard. I felt like he had a spotlight on me, could see all into me maybe. I felt found out. 'She didn't tell me—I mean, I didn't realise you came.'

'You were extremely good. Scary, if I'm honest. I mean scary good. Super real.'

'I didn't know you came.'

'You sure you haven't got that little knife about you?'

'Yeah,' I said, limply. 'I carry it all the time. I'm not really me at all. I'm just a bunch of all the characters I've played.'

He touched the edge of my little finger. I went electric. 'I'm glad you came to see me.'

'I didn't know I was coming,' I said. 'I was just passing—and Lily, you know, she'd told me it was a good shop and—'

158

'—excuse me,' the mother said. 'Can you give me a price on this armchair and the little walnut desk?'

He smiled. 'Sure.' To me, he said, 'Won't be a tick.'

'You know what,' I said. 'I think I'm going to go. We'll do coffee—whatever—another time. Is that alright?'

He looked taken aback. 'Sure,' he said.

'Give me your card. I'll call you.'

'Sure you will.'

I snipped one from the little wooden box I'd spied on the counter, waved it at him. 'Look, I've got it.'

'Won't be a mo,' he called to his customers.

I tucked the card into my new book, put it in my bag, took out my purse and drew out two soiled pound notes, handed them to him. 'I will, I mean it. I'm good at that. At calling.'

He nodded at my bag. 'We should wrap that book—you'll lose the petals.'

'I'll be careful.'

'Don't forget your brooch.' He reached for my hand, placed the tiny parcel he'd made for me there. He kept his hold on me, gazing at me, like he couldn't quite fathom me—but could. The heat of him seared into my fingers, travelled like mists into my body, caused me to tingle, and I couldn't help smiling.

'You're not so good at life, though, are you?' he said.

I drew back. 'What do you mean?'

'I mean, you're a brilliant actress—on the stage.' He grinned, just like *him*, with all that knowing. 'But I feel like you came here on purpose.'

I stared at him, unable to say a thing.

'Stay,' he said.

Riding pillion on his greasy black bike, all holding onto him, ensnared in the scent of him, at first I lived always in two dimensions at once. I rode with him. I rode with *him*. With every swerve of the black bike came the tilt of the yellow. It was like one of those crossfades you see in a film, one scene into another, two overlapping living images, only this bleed bled on for the whole movie and the movie never stopped. There was the dark side and the light; I wasn't sure which was which. I betrayed him. I betrayed *him*. Did London and Ireland at once—impossible possible— my body singing with present and past, terrible pleasures singeing through my every cell.

We rode all over London, made a thing of the parks. He wanted the royal ones in particular: Kensington Gardens, Hyde Park, Regent's Park and Primrose Hill. St. James's Park, Holland Park and Richmond, where we saw deer. I insisted we wander Hampstead Heath and we flew there on a microdot of acid, my eye intimately glimpsing countless people on the street as we passed them. I saw, felt, in shearing starkness, every detail of their existence; heard their heart, their thoughts, their breath, their very inner nature, in a split-second, as if they were inside of me, *were* me maybe; and it felt like maybe I had the answers to everything in all the confusion I was living.

It was something like four weeks in when we cruised all the way to Windsor Great Park, me getting freezing on the motorway in my tiny ribbed skirt; at the same time all hot on the Irish moors. As we came to the gateway to the estate, he drew to a halt, told me we weren't supposed to ride in but he'd never been stopped before, like was I up for it? Of course I was, I said.

'I've got us a bloody great picnic, champagne and all, and fancy flutes, in the top box,' he said. He grabbed my thigh, cupped my knee in his palm. 'You're icy.'

I shrugged. 'I'm cool.'

But as we motored toward the fairytale castle way off, all kind of skating down the lavish avenue built for kings and queens, a dirty taste kept growing on my breath, breathing right into my veins.

He swerved off of the tarmac, skipped us across the immaculately shorn grass, pitched us on the far side of the river of regimented trees running three-four deep down the whole boulevard. I looked out for blue flashing lights but none came, just like he'd told me.

Standing with his arms spread wide, all like it belonged to him, he said, 'What do you reckon? Pretty fucking the bollocks, huh?' He unzipped his jacket and my dearest book flipped out from where he'd placed it next to his heart, just plummeted to the grass, all splayed open and sad-as. A fast string of barbed wire went cutting through my veins as he snipped it up in his fingertips, slapped it against his thigh. He wittered on, bending the paperback all up into a roll, turning and turning it in his grip. I just couldn't hear him—until he veered into my face—and then I sort of came to, more than that even, I found myself responding to his terrific smile and wanting him so much I could just about die. I kissed him. I took the book from him, fitted it into the inside pocket of my leather jacket before slipping the black skin onto the ground.

He threw down a proper red tartan picnic rug, outspreading it, and I spread myself there, a long lacy grass stem stuck between my teeth. I watched him rip the gold foil top off of his bottle of champagne—an expensive one he thought to be my favourite because I'd gone and fibbed to him, just for the hell of it. Perrier Jouet, it was, with all its white anemones traced in gold relief on the green glass just about hidden under the silver cooler he'd put on it.

'Don't you think they've got CCTV?' I asked.

'Course. But, I don't know, maybe they look the other way. Maybe there's a biker on watch who thinks this is what the avenues are for. They haven't bothered me before.'

My voice came kind of hard, 'Done this with other girls, have you?' I was surprised at myself. I sat up, grinned. 'Pass me a glass then.' His fantastic square thumb nudged the cork from its home in the bottle mouth and I made a little scream, laughed as it blasted into the air. I caught the frothy fountain in my long-stemmed flute, then held out his. We clinked, sipped the cool bubbly liquid. 'Doesn't matter,' I said. 'About other girls.'

'There are no other girls.'

'Right.'

And he kissed me in a lush telling kind of a way, so I had to break off from the intensity, just throw myself back into the rug. The sky stretched itself out, filled up my sights, all spangling blue and glorious. I felt I could fall into it, even though it was above me, felt I was floating in water in a fast-moving stream. I closed my eyes against it, fel

       *shhhh* of the door into the carpet turn onto my back will
slither into my shorts and hare out of here on the yellow dirt bi

       but it's that grey-haired friend of my uncle leering scanning
our teenage heap my sister sits herself up face puffy and blear

          i clock the way he stares at me and i get the sense he *kno*
          alan my sister sa

          i pretend like i'm kind of asleep all feeling the wrench
  within him as he tears his eyes off me to look her wa

          um tea he says you want tea in be
{my eyes against it, fe}lt the tension all kind of hard in me.

His body flopped next to mine on the tartan rug, nude chested, and
my own body just about ejected me as it sprung to sitting. I necked my
champagne, dropped my glass into the grass, gazed down at his face, all
making comparisons that might have been a bad idea. As I caressed his
sparse chest, his boyish body, I tried not to remember the shag pile fur,
all that burliness I had so much liked. He opened his eyes, the pupils
gone smaller against the light, grabbed a hold of my hand, said, 'Come
'ere, you.'

I let myself fall into him, all nestled my face right up into his armpit. I
breathed him in, the scent of him filling me. I felt myself loosening, all
that tension uncoiling. 'You smell so good,' I said. 'I think it's my
favourite thing about you. I think I'm your body odour junkie.'

He held my head in a tight clutch, made me feel safe-as. 'Hey,' he
said. 'Funny thing. You know that inscription in your book? I just saw it
today when you were being a dot.'

My eyes came open, staring into the soft blur of his underarm hair.
My heart rose loud in my ears. 'Hmm? Inscript

       green of the gra
ion?'

'"Swan Neck." "To my little Angel Fa
       searing blue flowe
ce." You know, it's funny, a bit of a fluke, it looks a hell of a lot like
my dad's handwriting—from the postcards he used to send me when I
was a kid every now and then. I wonder where the old bastard is.'

'Yeh,' I said. 'I wonder.'

'Where did you get that book?'

'Some car boot sale I think.'

'So you weren't Angel Face? Doesn't it make you want to know who they were, though? "I'll always love you. Your blood runs in my veins." This long-necked man with a beautiful girl? It would be a good name for you: Angel Face.'

'Don't know about th

blood all glisteni

at,' I said.

He sighed and his voice was a rasp, 'You know…I don't think anything's ever hurt so much, him just stopping seeing me, not even wri

runni

running down the

ting me postcards anymore. I was ten, for fuck's sake. I could never see how a dad could just stop loving you. I guess I thought I must have been a pretty bad kid. I mean, why else would my dad decide to forget me?'

The snap of a twig all broke inside of m

unnin dow th hentra

e. '*No*,' I said. 'You were never bad. I know it. I know it.'

He sat up, rubbed his eyes with his fingertips, looked like that little boy he once was. The one I hadn't wanted to know about. 'I'm sorry, it's just…Christ, for real, do we ever get over these things?'

Sun all stabbing my eyes, whole branches gave way inside of me and I saw what a terri

knees i th gra

ble thing i was doing. I was really hurting him. If he knew. And I was hurting myself, just like my uncle talked abou

indig blu flowe of th spee

t. He sniffed. I swallow

cow parsley all up to m

ed. There was a hurting lump in my throat. I put my hand on his shoulder, felt the heat of it, the hard of it. 'Hey,' I said. 'Maybe there was a reaso—'

ow parsley al

'—yeah, like what reason? No reason lasts fifteen years. And my whole childhood—I mean, when it really matters, the bit I really remember. I guess I just have to come to terms with it. I'm an adult now so he's even less likely to bother, huh? I mean, who wants a twenty-four-year-old kid?'

'But you don't know.' I raised myself up on my elbow. 'Maybe he does want you and now *he* thinks it's too late. Maybe you'll always be his kid. What was your—um—your-your mother like—with him? Um—like, what went down between them?'

'My mother? It's not her fault. She was cool with him.'

'She was?'

'I think.'

'You think? Or you know? It's not to do with her fault or anything like that, that's not what I'm saying. But what if they didn't get on and, well, maybe he was a nightmare for her and she didn't want to see him. Or something. Maybe. I don't kno

a green beetle tryi

w'. I was gazing at him. And he gazed at me, his face all soft and tender, a slight smile coming into it. 'But what do I know?' I said.

'You are so sweet,' he said. 'You are.'

I smiled back at him, 'Not really,' took his hand, laced his fingers into mine as we eyed each other. The breeze blew, a gentle warmth caressing my face—and I felt underneath it the stillness of everything, the underlying, the unmanifest, out of which everything came. I didn't need to say anything, became aware of the space between us, feeling, for all the paradox of it, we were in that space together.

'Fuck it,' he said. 'I don't need him anymore, anyway.'

'Yeah.'

'But I am in the phone book in case he looks.'

'Me too,' I said.

'You too?'

'I'm in the phone book.'

He burst out laughing and I joined him.

'I only just went in it,' I said. 'I used to be ex-directory. So no one could find me.'

'Hey, that's a good idea. Let's both go ex-directory and hide out together.' He flung himself at me, pushed me onto my back, all staring into my eyes. His own blues glimmered, the pupils bigger than ever. 'How'd you get to be?'

He kissed me, soft lips, pressure harder, melting softness. I felt the life in my body, felt it tug and call to me, an ache deep inside all opening, freeing. Energy flowing. He kissed me and I kissed him. We kissed. I was simply here, with him, with myself, arms coiling around him, pulling him into me. I felt his hardness, wanting to meet it; it was his hardness and only his.

I realised the crossfade had stopped. I wasn't thinking. I was really right there, right in that now—and only that now. But the realisation made me think again. My heart went tigh

> running down the hentra
> running dow th
> runni

t, and then I stopped clinging, I stopped fighting, just surrendered—and everything just kind of fell away. I let the moment take me into the sensations of my inner body, and it felt like we were vibrating together at the same frequency. His hand slid up through my hair to cup the base of my head, stroked up and down my neck, came around to my cheek. We, kissing all the time, merging to one, yet a wonderful two, soft and hard, we both.

❦

We stamped the snow off of our boots, great clods of it falling all fresh and white onto the stone slab under cover of the exterior porch. The snow out there was thick-as; even on the busy Cromwell Road the traffic crawled over a white crunching surface. The trees wore glittering replicas along their every branch, spread bright inverse shadows across the bluest late-December sky.

As I went to put my key into the communal lock he got a hold of my scruff, turned me into him and pushed me up against the door, pressed himself into me. We kissed like we'd only just met, hot mouths, cold faces. We stared into each other.

'You're all flushed,' he said.

'It's your fault.'

'It's lovely.'

We fell to kissing again and his hand was going up my jacket, letting in a shooting edge. There came a footfall behind him and my visual focus went from our blurred lips all up against each other, to Mrs Ramsey in her felt hat, heading up the steps. She grinned at me, raised her eyebrows. I tapped his hip, trying not to laugh, and he turned.

'Hello Miss,' he said.

'Hello sonny. It's a lovely day for it.'

'It is.'

'Oh, how I'd like a bit of that.'

He reached toward the old bird. 'Can I help you with your bags?'

'Thank you. He's a Prince Charming, isn't he?' she said to me, as the lock clunked open.

'Don't know about that,' I said. 'But he's not bad.'

'They don't come like him every day, pet. You're a very lucky girl.'

I stepped aside, made a gesture for her to pass me, caught his eye. 'Yes.'

'You doing anything for New Year?' she chirped.

'Going to a party.'

'Lovely. Perhaps you two might pop in for a glass of sherry on your way out?' I nodded, all grinning. 'Or what say you to a proper glass of superior champagne?'

'Fantastic,' he said. He clipped his head in my direction. 'This one's got a passion for a bit of that.'

We saw her into her ground floor flat, him wheeling her blue trolley up to her kitchen counter, taking out her shopping, stocking her cupboards, as she took off her coat and got into her slippers, me putting stuff into the fridge. After promising to pop in for that champagne toast in a couple of days, we ascended to the sixth floor, entered my long skinny hallway, feet clacking on the recently sanded old boards. The answerphone was flashing in the living room and I hit the play button, threw myself down on the sofa.

'Hey there, Slim.' It was Eliot, all boom followed by a big pause.

'Hello,' I said into the recorded space.

'So what's happening? I think someone's having a birthday this week. I think, like, maybe it's today? Or is it tomorrow?' A loud chuckle, another big space, as if he were conversing with me. 'So: I'm coming over. With Stuart and Merl and Todd-baby. We've got cake. And we'll be there about four.'

'Like we said,' I said.

'And no messing,' he added. 'We all want to meet this guy of yours. It's been long enough.'

'Like we said,' I echoed. I raised my voice, projecting it down the corridor. 'You hear that?'

'Yep.'

'You ready?'

'Oh,' came Eliot's voice. 'And Jessie might come with little Jim.'

'Oh,' I said, as the message ended with a loud beep.

He appeared in the doorway bearing two steaming mugs. 'Never more.'

'What?'

'Ready. I think you broke the record for keeping me out of view.'

'Mrs Ramsey knows you.'

'Yeah, well, you had no choice with that one.'

'La-di-da.'

He grinned. 'You're lucky I'm not the offence-taking type.'

'I just want to keep you all to myself, that's all. It's a compliment.'

'A tall story.' I took my cup of black tea off him, patted the cushion for him to sit up close. 'A very beautiful tall story you are too,' he said. 'My hare.' He curled his arm around me and I tucked myself into him, slurped my tea, a veil of nerves casting itself in my stomach.

'Listen,' I said after a bit. 'I do actually have something I have to tell you. I should have told you ages ago. It could get kind of messy.'

'Ah,' he said.

'Don't you want to know?'

167

'I'm not sure.'

'Okay.'

We sat there in silence a while, and then I said, 'You're very patient.'

'I just know you're getting to it.'

'It's been a nagging worry,' I said.

'So spit. You're dragging out the pain.'

'But only because I felt bad for someone else.'

'Ah, yes,' he said, all like he knew what I was talking about.

'So you know, then?'

'Know what?'

'I don't know. You don't know or you do? I'm confused.'

'I have no idea what you're talking about. But now *I'm* starting to worry.'

I levered myself forward, shuffled to the edge of the sofa so I could pivot my body to face him, put my hand on his thigh. 'Don't worry. It's not so bad. For you. But it could be awkward—if she comes. I hadn't planned it and I haven't told her. Yet.'

'Who? Haven't told who what?'

'My friend. Jessie. I've mentioned her.' I sat looking at him, expecting him to cotton-on. He shook his head. 'Turns out you went out with her a long time ago. I mean like when she was fifteen-sixteen—and you were maybe a bit younger, I think. And she really liked you and now I'm with you and she doesn't know. And I'm worried she might be hurt. Maybe feel betrayed or something.'

'Jessie?' His mouth pulled down at the corners. 'I never went out with a Jessie.'

'You did.'

'No. Never a Jessie.'

'Just for a few days. But so long ago you must have forgotten then.'

'No.'

'Well, maybe you knew her by another name. I don't know. But the point is, she might be coming today—and she'll know you for sure. And you'll probably remember her then too.'

'I remember all the girls I went out with.'

'Well, then you'll recognise her, won't you?'

'What does she look like?'

'Blonde. Very pretty. Big brown eyes. Tall, full-bodied. But she might have been different then. She used to have dreads when she was like nineteen.'

'Never went out with anyone with dreads.'

'But anyway, I'm probably worrying for nothing. I don't expect she'd be bothered anymore. I just feel bad I haven't told her—I should have. She might be bothered, see. And I should have told you too, because it's weird otherwise, isn't it?'

He laughed. 'It doesn't bother me. But hang on, I don't get it. How would you know she went out with me if she hasn't met me?'

I sighed. 'Believe me.'

'Ah, by my name.'

I was all shaking my head. 'There was a photo. She's an artist, see—she—oh like *duh*, I'm confusing this with—what a dimwit—of course, she rememb—that's it—yes, of course. Your name.' I felt myself flushing hot and I got up, crossed to the window, the snow-covered cityscape all greeting me, handing me a fresh breath. 'God, it's so beautiful out there. It's like another country.'

I felt his energy behind me, where he stayed seated on the sofa. There was a sort of density and I could tell he'd vanished into his own mind, was trying to work things out. I turned and he looked up and we spoke at the same time.

'Okay,' I said.

'Now listen,' he said.

And we laughed.

'Listen to what?' I asked.

'You first, birthday girl. But listen, I just want the simple truth.'

'Okay, so there *was* a photo—a tiny photo—of you. She put on her work, a collage, before I knew you. And we talked about you. And she went out with you for just a few days and you finished it and she was sad, like she thought maybe you were someone special she lost.'

'But maybe it's not me in the photo? I mean, it could be someone who looks kind of like me. I just can't think who she is.'

'I know—but it definitely is you.'

'Ah. So when did you recognise me?'

'Right away when I saw you.'

'At the shop? Or at the theatre?' I paused, eyes flitting away and back to him. He raised his eyebrows. 'When I delivered the furniture, huh?'

'Yeh.'

He smiled and I saw the way a light went on inside him. 'I *knew* you'd seen me.'

'Yes.'

'And how come you remembered me so many years later? That's a bit amazing, isn't it?'

'Because I did. Because I have the collage. It turned out Stuart bought it for me right then, when she had her first exhibition, when I was fifteen.'

'For real? Now that *is* amazing. Some kind of fate, huh?' He rose, all glossy, and came across the room to me, took my hand. 'So you had a photo of me *before* you knew me?'

'It's tiny. Just your tiny, tiny face. On a whole big collage. It's because we talked about you I...you know, remembered you and...because I own the collage...and we're all unique, even though we're all similar...and we have this incredible capacity as humans, out of all the millions of people on the planet, don't we? To recognise a face we know.'

'A face you *knew*? So you liked me, you must have?' I bit my lip, nodded. 'And what did you say, that day you first came to my shop? "You remind me of someone." See how tall your stories are? I get it now: I reminded you—of me. Didn't I know you came to see me especially that day?'

A sort of warmth ran through my heart. But of course with it came dark underground streams, a kind of geopathic stress all seeming impossible to excise, like the very soil of me was polluted. My eyes filled with murky wet risen from those streams. He held both my shoulders, arm's length away, gazed at me, palest blue eyes echoes of what I didn't want to be there. I felt the urge to spill the larger truth, felt it all bubble and gurgle up to my throat in a kind of strangulation. I took a breath, wondered if I had the courage.

170

'I found you out, huh?' he said, smiling. 'You should see how beautiful you look with tears standing in your eyes.'

I had to glance away and the tears bloated and fell and I felt an acute inner trembling. 'I'm glad you know at last. I really needed to tell you. But it scared me.'

'I'm not scary.'

'I know but I just felt like some weird sort of stalker, I guess. I still kind of do. And I don't want to.'

'I don't mind even if you did stalk me.'

A vague laugh came through my nose. 'Yeah.'

He touched my cheek, so I looked at him. 'Is there something else you're not telling me?'

'Always.'

'Is there something you *want* to tell me?'

'Everything. I just…I can't…later, can I?'

'Hey,' he said, pulling me into his arms. 'It's alright. There's plenty of time.'

I hugged him tight. 'Is there?'

'You've done nothing wrong,' he said.

Breath coming back at me all hot from the crook of his *him*-scented neck, I said, barely audible, 'I think maybe I kind of love you.'

'You do?' He drew back, his eyes searching mine. 'Now that *is* worth the wait. Same. I'm fucking crazy in love with you. I've been wanting to tell you for ages.'

We kissed all soft and there came a rushing sensation in my chest, something wonderful and true, like a clean fresh ocean almost— *almost*—obliterating the dark. I clasped his hand, led him toward the sofa.

'Hey,' he said. 'My lover-girl. So where's this collage then?'

'The collage?'

'Yeah.' He frowned, all cheeky. 'Maybe you can hang it back on the wall now, huh?'

❧

The six of us sat around my round wooden table, Merl perched on Todd-baby's lap, Stuart all long-haired and loungy, while Eliot leaned over the rugged cake he'd made, removing the twenty-three smoking candy-coloured candles. Pearly wax drizzled over his fingertips, dripped stars onto the cake. His mountain of a body rose out of the small paint-spattered vinyl armchair I'd found in a skip, brought temporarily into the living room from the small painting studio I'd set up in my second bedroom. He made it look like a child's chair, and I couldn't help chuckling inside at the ludicrous beauty of him. Only Eliot would choose to sit in that chair when he could have taken a regular dining one; only Eliot would ram himself where he could hardly fit, make himself bigger, more imposing.

He took up the large knife, a sort of cleaver he'd brought along, planted it into the cake with one swift motion, followed by another, made a triangle, under which he tucked the blade, extracted the piece, passing it to me on a little flowered plate.

As I went to take it, he yanked it back, 'Hang on,' and forced himself out of the chair, which had begun to rise with him, all pushing down on the small oak arms. He strode across to where he'd left his bag on the floor. He took out a couple of wilting pink rose blooms, tore off the petals, directed a few across my slice and tossed the rest over the main cake, allowing them to flutter all around.

We all kind of breathed in. It was like watching a performance.

'Fucking beau-i-ful,' he said, mutterings of agreement all around. 'A gift from someone's front garden. They had a go at me. Nature's miracle, flowering for you in the snow, Slim.' Passing me my cake again, he added, 'I'm off the wheat. It's ground almonds. And chocolate. Dark, very dark chocolate.' He hacked his cleaver five times into the cake, appeared careless, but each piece was perfectly divvyed up. He placed them on plates with scatterings of pink petals. 'I've adapted the recipe, been perfecting it. Cut down the sugar by half. It's a dried whole juice I sourced from Brazil. We're talking sophisticated, deep. We should all cut out the wheat—it's too commercial, over-farmed. Acts like glue in your gut.'

I eyed his rather large stomach. 'How long you been off the wheat then? Last time I saw you, it was all croissants and pastries.'

'Addicted, I was. I told you. I couldn't control myself. Look at the state of me. But it's only been a week, eight days. It's been pretty challenging. I've been dreaming wheat—little wheat girls all over my sleep. All the time eating little wheat women. It's a nightmare.'

'Sounds like fun,' I said.

'No, it's not.'

I nodded. 'Cold turkey. I'm soz.'

''Mare,' said Merl. 'We know all about it, don't we Todd-baby, Stu? Living with the lunatic.'

Todd-baby, eyes closed, looked blissed out, his mouth working. 'Your best one, Eliot baby. You got the balance perfect.'

'Aw Todd-baby,' Eliot boomed. 'You're supposed to wait.'

Todd-baby opened his eyes, face frozen. 'Shit man, you're so controlling.'

'You didn't even get your fork,' Eliot said. He gathered up the dessert forks he'd brought with him, all left in a heap on the table, handed us each one.

My boyfriend shot up to standing, scraping his chair on the boards. 'Just a mo,' he said, as he took off down the corridor.

'What's his deal?' asked Eliot.

I shrugged, smiling. 'He's nice, isn't he?'

'Cute,' said Eliot.

'Very fucking,' said Todd-baby.

'Nice,' said Merl.

'Into you, baby,' said Todd-baby.

'Really nice,' said Merl.

'Can you stop saying "nice"?' I said. 'You make him sound bloody boring.'

Merl grinned, nodded, splaying his hands. 'He's super nice.'

'Lovely,' said Todd-baby.

'I really like him,' I said. '*Really* like him.'

'Me too,' said Merl.

'You've hardly met him,' said Eliot.

173

'But I can tell straight away. I've got good intuition. You know that, huh, Todd-baby? I knew you were nice the moment I saw you—and look where that's got me.'

'Yeah,' said Eliot. 'He *is* very cool. I can tell too.'

I met Stuart's eye, and we smiled tight-lipped, all containing our secret. I felt myself flush, winked at him through a smear of guilt. 'Like?'

'Of course,' he said. 'He better treat you right, this one.'

'Yeah, or Stu will blast him into space like that little dog the Soviets disembodied in the Fifties,' roared Eliot. 'No return trip.'

'Disembodied?' Todd-baby said.

'Well, he died, didn't he?'

'Stuart wouldn't hurt a fly,' said Merl.

'Wrote a song about that dog, didn't you?' Eliot said. 'Ostensibly.'

Stuart nodded, wry. 'You're a twisted fuck, Eliot.'

My boyfriend exited from the kitchen doorway, dashed, beaming, back down the corridor, a clutch of champagne flutes like huge glass fingers fanned from one hand, a misted gold-topped bottle gripped in the other. It was my now (real and proper) favourite Perrier Jouet, with all those white anemones. His glass fingers made a tinkling music.

Merl and Todd-baby struck up noises of appreciation along with me, but when he offered a glass to Eliot, the big man said, 'Aw man, sorry, I can't.'

'It's okay,' he said. 'I know.' And he reached behind himself, yanking from his jeans' back pocket another glass bottle. 'Perrier. Without the Jouet. But plenty of play in the bubbles.'

Eliot nodded, smiling. 'Very cool. He's a smooth fucker, isn't he?'

He snapped open the lid, poured Eliot a glass, broke open the champagne. He toasted me and we all clinked and supped, finally about to try the cake all together, Eliot counting, 'One, two, three and—hang on, *wait!* I've got to—' There came groans while he wrestled in his bag, drew out his polaroid camera, shifted to get us all in the frame while we waited with our forks full of cake to our mouths.

'Come *on*,' said Todd-baby.

Eliot, loaded fork in one hand, held the camera at arm's length, leaned into his own frame and clicked off a couple of shots. The polaroids spat themselves onto the table. 'Okay,' he said. 'One, two, three and—in.' Two more shots.

'*So* good,' said Todd-baby. 'Your best, baby.'

'This is amazing,' I said.

'Seminal,' said my boyfriend.

'He's made one every day this week. We're all going to grow fat.'

'Isn't that rather addicted?' I said. 'Eliot?'

'It was trials. For you. I'll stop now.'

'Promise?' I said.

'He'll never stop,' said Stuart.

The buzz of my intercom sounded and a flurry of nerves hit my chest.

'Aha,' said Eliot. 'Jessie. She made it. Excellent.'

'Jessie,' I said, glancing at my boyfriend. Eliot was prizing himself out of his tiny chair and I tried to stay him with my hand to his shoulder. 'I'll go. I'll meet her on the stairs, give her a hand with Jimmy.'

'No,' he said. 'You sit and enjoy your cake. I'm going. She's bringing something you mustn't see. It's all arranged.'

He thundered away down the corridor, spoke into the intercom, swung through my front door. I listened to his footsteps thudding on the carpet of the communal stairs. Merl said something, smiling, and I smiled back, pretended like I heard, shoved in a mouthful of cake. Todd-baby was laughing, my boyfriend joining in. I watched them as if they were from another planet, speaking Mars or something, my inner attention down the stairs with Eliot and Jessie, wondering how I might manage to get to her before she entered the flat, how I might get rid of Eliot, get him to take Jimmy maybe. I had trouble swallowing the cake, which had become burdensome and mealy. A hand waved into my face. Jolting into focus, I saw how everyone was looking at me expectantly, all big smiles.

'I've got the car,' Todd-baby said. 'I reckon we could do it in an hour and a half.'

'Come on,' Merl said. 'It'll be stunning.'

I stood up, my chair scraping the floor. I looked at Stuart. I could tell he knew what was going on in my head. 'Gotta have a French yes.'

'You what?'

'Oui,' my boyfriend said.

'Wow,' said Merl. 'Creative flow.'

'Flow's the word,' agreed Todd-baby. 'I think we can take that as the next level yes, yes? Baby?'

Stuart nodded vigorously, eyes wide, indicating I join him. 'You love the sea; it's going to be stunning. Snowy beach.'

'Oh. Marvellous. Yes.' Turning my head, I saw Jessie was sliding through my front doorway, her body at an angle, as she manoeuvred a large square canvas into my hallway. 'Jessie,' I cried, all taking off toward her.

Eliot loomed forward from the shadows behind, little Jim floating on one arm. 'Wait,' he bellowed. He held out his hand. I heard the throng of laughter behind me. 'Come and get her, someone. Blindfold her. Take her away.'

'Jessie,' I said, eyeballing her.

'Darlface.'

'I wanted to speak with you.'

'Of course,' she said. 'We will. Just don't look right now, will you? It's not wrapped.'

Jimmy had his arms splayed wide, was tilting toward me, piping my name repeatedly. 'Here,' said Eliot, nudging past Jessie. And Jimmy was falling into my arms. 'Now get.'

''appy birfday 'appy birfday…' The child was kissing my lips, very hard, mouth sweet and biscuity, legs and arms wrapped about me, pressing his being into me as if he might merge.

I craned around his face, trying to catch my friend's eye. 'Jessie?'

Her little boy clasped my cheeks. 'Me,' he said.

And I just kind of let go. I laughed, limp-as. 'You,' I said. 'I love you too, you little imp.' He kissed me again, all wet, scridging my lips into a pout in his sticky fingers.

As Jessie moved toward us, she indicated with her chin I precede her. I didn't move, stared into her doe-like eyes a full second, she returning with an intense connectivity. Her smile was soft and supple.

'What can it be?' I said.

'I wonder.'

'Big 'ainting,' said Jimmy.

'Shhhh,' I told him. 'You'll give it away.' I stood aside, let Jessie shimmy past us, watched as she took in our friends, greeting them. I saw her register him, her face flickering with surprised recognition. I saw how her upper teeth pressed into her lower lip, like she was about to say his name—a shadow of the past, our past, her past, that day in her gallery space at the squat, all imprinting as yet another layer of time into our now-reality—and then her lips were parting and forming simply her big toothy smile.

'Hello,' she said. 'What a *trip*.' She swivelled her eyes to mine, mouthed something only I might understand, then said, 'So this is your new boyfriend?'

'Yes,' I said, and introduced them.

'Jessie,' he said. 'But didn't you call yourself Jasper?'

She laughed, eyes widening. 'Shh. This lot don't know.'

'You guys know each other?' Eliot said.

My boyfriend was nodding. Jimmy slid himself out of my arms.

She shrugged. 'Just a bit. Way back.'

'Jasper?' Todd-baby said. 'Is there something we should know, baby? Us "this lot", your nearest and dearest?'

'What's in a name?' I said, voicing Jessie's mouthed words, her laugh ringing around me.

'So how do you two know each other, then?' came Eliot.

'You know,' said Jessie. 'Just from hanging out.'

'Teenagers,' my boyfriend said.

'Ah,' said Eliot, raising his eyebrows.

'No,' said Jessie. 'Not what you think.' To my boyfriend, she said, 'But I am glad to see you here. I'm glad for this 'ere girl, here. I always thought you were a good un.' She tilted the canvas, held carefully with its back to me, toward Merl, who was closest. 'Take a hold of this a mo, will you?' and she turned to me, arms out. 'Happy Birthday, dear thing.' As we hugged, she murmured, 'Wow, nuts. Crazy. How did *this* happen? It's surreal—and, really, I'm happy for you—and I'm sort of not surprised—though I can't believe it—but it's kind of *of course*, isn't it?

177

Kind of the next logical step, type thing. But I've got to know everything. Like, *is* he? Is he who we thought?'

'Yes. For sure. He is.'

'How the hell did you meet?'

Over her shoulder, I caught Stuart's eye, saw him attentive, felt like I was going to cry. 'But he doesn't know and you mustn't…'

The others, including him, were chattering and laughing in a shimmer of glasses and cake. She pulled back to look at me, awe-infused concern spreading across her lovely features. 'Darlface,' she said. 'Come'. And she seized my hand, lead me into the kitchen.

❦

He was waiting for me in the café, sitting all upright on a lounge seat, the vista of spray-splashed windows at his rear causing him to have bright edges and the burned-out look of a sun-bleached Victorian photo. He appeared enigmatic, an icon, all the more like *him.* I didn't want him to look like him or be anything to do with him anymore. I didn't want to think of him. But the more I didn't want to think of him, the more I couldn't stop. It was as if my thoughts were a magnet to themselves, kept producing babies.

I stood in the doorway, just stood there, the sharp fingers of cold coming off the April sea all cutting a gash at the back of my neck. I couldn't tell if he could see me, so corrupted was his image, until he raised his arm. I had to presume he was smiling. My hand made its response, flew up, pointed a finger heavenward, all Leonardo Da Vinci, the gesture appearing to ask him to wait, as if an idea had just occurred to me; more like some kind of appeal to the great beyond, to my bigger Self, a bringing to consciousness my quest for peace and purity. I turned, letting the heavy door chase my back as I landed back on the deck. I felt like a sea bird, steady on my feet despite the unstable ground. My steel-toed bovver boots where as good as webbed things.

I leaned into the guard rail, salt-crisp air flat into my face, stared screwy-eyed, into the churning water. I remembered how I had wanted to

178

enter it, way back when, had let it soak right through me, as if by doing so I might have achieved non-existence. A laugh came out of my nose, something unkind and self-mocking. I couldn't believe now I wanted to wash it all away, all the him and the me of then. It was kind of terrible after the years of clinging and craving. My eyes scudded up the thick mottled paintwork of the hull, found their way into the sky. It had been misty that day, as I was exiled, and I found relief now, in the blazing blue.

Warm hands placed themselves onto my hips, caused me to start. I relaxed as they slipped over my belly, arms coming up to hug my waist, the deep dense heat of him tight into my back. I pushed into him, head into the brace of his shoulder, his hot sigh grazing my ear.

'You're freezing,' he said. 'It's deceptive out here. And your tea's getting cold and all.'

I turned in his arms with my eyes shut, felt the brush of his breath before the soft press of his lips on mine. A whole lot of stuff surged up in my body, a kind of rush, like every cell was awake and receiving him, offering me to him, and my mind went blank and open, all filled with the big sound of the sea and the soft spit our mouths made together.

The wind cracked through us. My hair was inside our kiss. He reached up, sweeping it away, but it kept coming back and we were laughing, his hand then tugging my t-shirt out of my skirt and sliding all icy up my ribcage, finding my breast. The tingling inside of me intensified, radiated from the rude flower of me, and the kissing deepened, hot at its centre, arctic where our lips left trails of wet for the wind to pick on. We were pressing hard against each other, the feel of him bright and distinct against my pelvic bone. His hand took a hold of my bum cheek, up under my skirt, laced beneath my knickers, while my fingers groped into his low-slung jeans, found the edge of his boxer shorts' waistband, skimmed his standing-up cock. He groaned, pulled away.

'Okay,' he said. 'We gotta stop. Seriously, we'll get arrested.'

'You like being arrested.'

'By you—yes I do.' He pinched my chin, staring deep into me, all kind of serious. He made a sharp nod. And then he kissed me in a

179

resolute hard kind of a way.

Heading inside, I threw myself onto the dark blue lounge seat, the foam so solid my bones jolted. 'Cripes,' I said. 'What is this—punishment central?' I sat up, reached for my tea. It looked like grease was floating on its close-to-black surface. 'This looks disgusting.'

'Well it's been sat there for over half an hour. It's cold, right?'

I nodded. 'Scummy. Get me another, will you?'

He eyed me. 'You get it.'

'Please. I'm cold.' I sifted through our pile of things, located my denim jacket. He just sat there watching me. I took up my Chelsea bun, tugged with my teeth at its end-fold like I used to, gnawing at it, unravelling it into my mouth in one unceasing bite.

'What's going on?' he said at last.

'Nothing.'

'Sure. One minute we're into one another, the next you're acting like you can hardly stand me.'

I dropped my hand with the bun, let the whole thing fall into my lap, my eyes too. 'I was thinking about—your dad.'

'My *dad*?'

'Sometimes it feels like he's between us.'

'What? How? What do you mean?'

My eyes were welling up. 'I don't know…'

He came around the small table, arm all around me, crushed himself right up against me. 'I don't get where this is coming from.' I could feel him staring at me. 'Hey you?' He jostled me. 'Look at me.' My eyes rose to his, the blue of them like bits of pale sky. Just like *his*. His large pupils dilated even more as he gazed at me. 'Sweetheart…what, you think I'm damaged goods?'

'No.'

'My dad is a distant dream.'

'I know.'

'So, what? You're jealous of my loss? You think that's a threat to you?'

I smiled faint-as. 'No. I don't know.'

'You think the idea of him distracts me?'

Shaking my head, I said, 'I wouldn't want you not to think of him. You're making me sound sick.'

'There's plenty of room for both of you in this ol' heart of mine. However much I try to extradite him.'

'You sound like a song.' My eyes slid back down to the remains of my bun and I unwound it along its seams, exposing its black raisons, things like soulless eyes. 'I think I hate Chelsea buns.'

'But why did you think of him now?'

'Because I feel bad for you.'

'Bad for me?'

'He shouldn't have left you. I'm pretty pissed off with him for that.'

'Fuck,' he rasped. 'You're going to make me cry. Right here, on this fucking ferry.'

I touched his forearm, felt the soft sparse hairs there. 'Don't cry. I'll cry too.'

'Why now, sweetheart? All this? I haven't mentioned him in months.'

'But I know you think about him. Most days, right? Because I do too. And I wish we wouldn't.'

'So you *do* think he has some hold on me?'

'Well, he does, doesn't he? Of course he does. Because he has a hold on me too.'

His eyes were soft and wet. He shook his head, all gentle. 'You don't have to take it on. What about *your* parents?'

'Who cares about *my* parents?'

'Let's just forget him. Them. All of them. We don't need them.'

'Yes. Okay…but-but I really wish we could—I mean, actually, really *could* forget them. See, because I'll tell you…it's kind of this: I'm worried—I'm worried because we're going to the raci—the stables. You'll have associations. Because he was a trainer, right? And you were in that environment when you were small. And it's going to hurt.'

'I can handle it. Don't think I haven't thought about all that.'

'To be honest, I have them too…'

'What? Associations?'

'Yeah. To my youth and all the messed-up stuff of it that made me…you know…run away and all that. And you know I haven't been back there since…'

'Yeah, I know.' He increased the pressure of his hand on my thigh. 'But what was so messed up? You've never really said.'

'Oh…yeah. I so wish I could—you know, articulate this…this stuff. But it's way too complex right now. And what if it ruined—I mean, *changed* the way you see me and…'

'You're kidding. Nothing could change the way I see you. Whatever happened in the past is the past and doesn't matter. You know that. Come on, all your philosophy, Buddhism and everything, tells you that. Non-attachment? The now?'

I pressed my forefinger to the tip of his nose, my energy held as a tight little knot in my stomach. I made my voice all like a cartoon character. 'I'll tell you another time.'

'I want to know now. I want to know everything about you.'

'I know. I want you to.'

'So spit. Can't you? Always these secrets with you. That you seem to taunt me with.'

'It's not personal.' I blushed at the blatant untruth, looked into my lap at the undone bun there. 'Maybe it will come out in Ireland.' I scrunched up the moist pastry, crushing it into some kind of a ball, drew my lips into a smile, threw it up in the air, caught it. 'Yours,' I said, aiming it at him. 'Nick it.'

As he grabbed it mid-flight, it fell apart, and we laughed. 'You're such a bad actress.'

'What?'

'I can always tell when you're not really you.'

'Come here.' I took his face between my hands, stared into his blues—the other him I didn't want all showing himself to me there all over again. 'Close your eyes,' I said. I kissed his tender lids. I felt I could burst, so much I wanted to spill it all, break the triangle I couldn't stop living. 'How about we go do it in the loos?'

☙

182

The house was exactly the same. You could never have known ten years had gone by. Except now it seemed cool, the Seventies picture windows of the living room, *his* room, with their metal frames and views onto the landscape, stylish as hell. It went all perfectly with the vintage flares I had in my bag, had found on a fleamarket in Paris—a style from my childhood I had thought I would never revisit, had derided as I'd gotten into straights, then skinnies, taken in my trousers, all that coat hanger lying on the floor stuff. You never knew what life might bring back to you.

I had feared I was going to be all losing myself with this *return*, and I was surprised to find I was smiling with a genuine heart, my energy grounded. There was a welcome sense of containment in me as I let my eyes skim over the bungalow and its surrounding wildness. 'But it's beautiful,' I said.

'What did you expect?' said my uncle, feet biting into the gravel as he came to stand beside me.

'I used to think it was hideous.'

He showed a look of bemusement. 'I thought you loved it here, nature girl.'

'I thought the *house* was hideous.'

'Ah. Yes, time changes all, huh? So…are you ready to go in?'

I nodded, reached for his arm, whispered, 'It is a bit weird, though, isn't it? This? My finally coming here?'

'It is what it is.'

'Yeah right. Monsieur le guru. How about a simple yes?'

Laughing, he indicated my boyfriend, who had wandered a small distance to survey the heather-hazed land beyond the driveway. 'I'm so glad to see you happy with someone. I really like him, there's something profound about him. He feels good for you, my lovely.'

'He is.' I looked deep into my uncle's bright eyes, trying to detect if he saw the resemblance. 'You look so well.'

'I am.'

'Is that a hundred percent? Last time you said there was still a shadow or something.'

'Yes. Completely clear.'

'I still don't really get it. You didn't even have any treatment.'

'Yes, you do,' he said.

'I do?'

'It was everything we've talked about—before and since. I surrendered totally, just let go, and all fear left me. I really *let* my Self in, huh?'

'That's kind of whimsical, isn't it?'

'I realised I had a choice as to how I responded to the situation; I chose happiness and ease, acted as if the disease didn't exist.'

'Denial, you mean?'

He laughed. 'I didn't allow the conditions of my life to be the dominant effect on me, put it that way. And I *was* ready to go, huh? It wasn't a tactic—and I learned, therein lay my power.'

'You looked really bad, though, at one point. Skinny-as. And hardly had any energy.'

'And I put my focus elsewhere, didn't I? On appreciation of the beauty around me—for the simple pleasure of it. On the horses. You. On the very fact of my beating heart. That's big. To wake every morning with your heart beating. To take a breath. And then another. There was so much effortless wellness I could focus on.' He held me in his gaze and I found a sigh filling my chest cavity, my being. 'They call it a spontaneous remission. It's the label they give to anything they can't explain. I told them it was all about how I felt, the inner harmony. But they didn't really listen.'

'It *is* pretty radical. Imagine how things could change.'

'It's just their resistance. I had it myself, until…even with my spiritual practice. You remember, at first, I didn't expect to live? And I didn't *try* to get better. It's true, it *did* just happen.'

'I remember you saying you were—um—flowering.'

He nodded, the smile coming through his eyes. 'It was a wonderful feeling. Still is.'

'I hated it. All I could see then, was that a bloom had such a short life. Oh god…' I found myself moving in to hug him. 'I didn't know how I was going to carry on without you. You were the only one who understood anything.'

'We are blessed,' he said, breath into my hair. 'We only have to realise it.'

'Even though you made my life a living hell.'

'From the darkest roots of hell, you are able to rise up and touch your own heaven, the light within. Carl Jung said that—more or less.'

'I already had the heaven.'

'So you thought. But it was conditional.'

'La-di-da.' I looked down, kicked at the gravel. Saw *him* in a flash-frame all coming toward me, hair wild and silvery-as, all connected to me by invisible threads. 'You don't know anything.'

'Heaven is a continual inner unfolding, dear girl. If we can enter the state of allowing it.'

'You know what? Bugger you. All this unconditional stuff is not realistic. Maybe you should've just died after all.'

He threw his head back, sunlight bouncing off his bald head in a kind of golden halo, big laugh ringing out. 'Only you…' I watched him in thrilled terror, the taboo words I had spoken echoing through me as small grenades. 'You are a renegade angel,' he said.

'Angel?'

My boyfriend called out, 'You never told me how stunning it was here.' He was crunching our way. 'It's unbelievable. The land looks like velvet. I have this bizarrest feeling of coming home.'

'He's kind of a bit Irish,' I said, heart pulling. 'Or not. Huh?'

'I always liked to say I'd forgotten, because I didn't want to know, thought I was kind of clever, but now I'm getting to see it was true, I *had* forgotten—fundamentally—until now, when I'm hit with recognition.'

'Well, it doesn't surprise me,' said my uncle.

'What doesn't?' I said.

'He looks it, doesn't he?'

'What?'

'Irish. But then so do you. She's Irish in her blood somewhere, this one. Metaphorically.'

'Metaphysically,' he said, chuckling. 'This poem of a girl. What a pair we are. The Irish-not-Irish.'

'I'm not Irish,' I said.

My uncle was staring at him curiously. 'It's funny, you almost look familiar to me.'

'Fuck's sake, are you being funny?' I said.

He looked startled. 'No.'

I widened my eyes, swerved into him, all shielding my angst with a lairy grin. 'You do *live* in Ireland, surrounded by *Irish*-looking people. Course he looks familiar then.'

'Yes, of course.' He picked up my bag from down by my feet. 'Come on, let's get you settled. You must be tired, it's a long journey.'

'Yes,' I said.

We all three headed toward the front door. My boyfriend caught my eye, signalled a look of concern or something. I shook my head.

'I'm giving you my room,' my uncle told us. 'There's a nice bed so you'll be comfortable. You could have a rest before dinner.'

'But where will you sleep?'

'In the living room.'

'Oh. But that's—but what about that tiny room we used to stay in? Wouldn't that be better?'

'One of the stable boys has it. He's living here presently. It was your sister's room but—'

'—yeah well I wouldn't be here if *she* was here, would I? Hey, there aren't any photos, are there?'

'There are, of course.'

I flared my eyes at him, paused at the threshold, turned to see my boyfriend's attention involved in the landscape behind us. All hushed, I said, 'But not any *photos*? Of…? In the office or anything, like there used to be? No certificates or anything?'

'Of course not.'

Entering the bungalow, my eyes were struck dark for a moment and it was like I had swallowed a vitamin pill without any water, the lump of it scraping harsh inside my throat. My uncle led us into his bright bedroom. I squinted as if I was just being born, was attempting to fend off the shock of the world. I saw the newborn foal, all lying in the straw, pushed his name from my mind. *That* name. *His* name and my name come together in the golden foal. He was showing us the ensuite bathroom, my boyfriend saying all the right things, and I was mute, not really there anymore, just not ther

treading down the corridor passing the dimpled glass colours all distorting my nightie clings to my shins feet into the carpet i'm nudging open the door to his roo

{just not ther}e at all. I flinched as his arm came around me, and I turned and looked at him through all the haze, heard him speaking about the way we met in his shop and he was chuckling and the sound of him was like a cracked cup with rivers of gold running through it, gold running through the cracks, like that Japanese thing, so beautiful, made more beautiful than if it had never broken. The love just fell right out of me, wrecked-as, all my beautiful golden past transmuted to base metal, something ugly, heavy lead—and I was coughing up the rich stench of my own betrayal—coughing the stuck vitamin pill out into my palm, real violent, throat all grating, choking, eyes spilling. I pulled away from him, hand into my mouth.

'Sweetheart, are you okay?'

I was all gasping and spluttering, all slime coming out of me.

'Are you okay?'

'Yes. No. I just I have to—' he tried to take a hold of me as I fended him off '—please. Leave me alon—I'm going—I have to—I'm going to the loo.'

'You can use this one. We'll—'

'—it's okay,' my uncle said. 'Let her go.'

'Sweetness? Sweetheart?' I felt him chasing after me.

'*No*,' I spat, spit-stars catching in the light, all into his face. 'Please. I need to be—I just need to—I jus—*get* the fuck off of me, you hear? Just let me go. Can't you jus—'

'—get the fuck?—what?—what's the matter?'

'Just leave her a moment,' my uncle instructed, tone forceful. And turning my head as I stumbled down the corridor, I saw him grab a hold of his arm.

'What's going on? Sweetheart, wha—'

'—*give* her a bit of space. You can see she's asking for that.'

It felt like they were having some kind of tussle, a mash of

187

overlapping words, my own galloping footsteps and thudding heart causing the sense to be unintelligible, until, in a voice that sliced through the mess, my uncle said, 'It's a stress reaction to the past. You have to let her be. Just give her time, she—'

I pushed open the door to *his* room, crashing through the opening, slamming it shut with my back. Sliding down the glossy paintwork, I was full-on crying. I didn't know what I had expected or wanted even, but the slap of the truth, of his absence, of nothing recognisable in the space, no bed on the floor, no striped sheets, just nothing, came as a visceral pai

running down the hentra

n. Sweat fell inside the loose folds of my t-shirt. My tears were hot and thick. Throat burning. My hand over my mouth, all keeping the noise in, my ribs heaved, joltin

bites stings legs like pink sli

g, jolting, I was jagged, the door was pushing up my back.

'Sweetheart? Let me in. Please. Just open the door, I—'

'—*go* away. You have to—' my voice came viscous with dark spume, breath coming hard, 'I can't…'

'You have to talk to me. This is really freaking me out. I've never—I don't—'

And then screechy, like a gull '—just *later*, okay? Leave me alone. Just leave m

everything open blue speedwe

e—alone.'

'No, not okay.' He tried the door again. My body felt the sho

searing blue flowe

ve. Maybe I was yelling. I was fighting the door. 'You're hurting me. Please. Please *stop*.'

The door clicked shut as he released it. I let my weight fall…falling through space, falling into myself, my history, my cellular memory, all everythi

most natural thing headlamps eating up nature stolen what's got into you since you'll never see him agai

ng.

My breathing
came in judders;
time splayed out...disappeared…

Something snapped, dropped, some kind of giving way. Everything seemed to stop and I was just wide-open space like nothing at all existed, not me, not him, not him, not them. Up from my centre moved a spiralling relief, shuddering breaths breaking the rings—*no*, not breaking the rings, the rings were my life and it could *not* be broken—were the energy snaking up my spine, were my lifeforce sending ripples of calm up into my head, spreading into my limbs, all warm water, limbs all soft, just flopped, my spine spreading the ripples, I could see them, the infinity of them radiating ever outward on an endless glassy lake. I went quiet. My mind just quiet-as. As if I'd worn it all out. Excavated it as gluey sputum. Shining on my hands. My heart left my ears, descended back to where it belonged, a low baseline in my chest.

I became aware of his breath on the other side of the door, spiky as gooseberry thorns. I pushed myself onto my knees, shuffled to the door edge, cracked it open. He was slumped, legs drawn up, against the doorframe, all like he'd just collapsed there. He raised his head from the cradle of his arms.

'What the fuck?' he said, the darling rasp in his voice almost breaking the words apart. 'What went on here? This is fucked *up*.'

I drew a breath, parting my lips, couldn't speak.

'It's that same thing you're hiding from me, isn't it? The thing that made you scared to come back?'

I kind of shrugged. I nodded.

He shoved his face into mine, eyes bald with resentment, hissing, 'I just meet your uncle and next thing is I'm having some kind of a fight with him. I'm staying at his house, for fuck's sake. I'm his guest. This is—it's unbearable. I've never—I'm just…*fuck*.'

'I'm sorry…' My voice was a thread.

'Perhaps I shouldn't have come. Should I leave? Do *you* want to leave?'

'No.'

'You want *me* to leave?'

'No.'

'Are you going to talk to me about this? Because otherwise this is unacceptable. You've got me in a compromised position. Don't you trust me—or what?'

'It's not that.' I shuffled forward, laid my hand on his arm, cringed as he pulled away. 'I don't know how to tell you.'

'*He* knows, doesn't he? Your uncle. He knows.'

We stared at each other. I sighed, lips bitten shut.

'Was it your mum? Your dad? That made you run away?'

I shook my head.

'Was it to do with a man—a boy?'

'I—what makes you say that?'

'Because I'm not dumb. If it was anything else—I don't know—what?—a horse or a death or something, I figure you'd have told me.'

I dropped my gaze, let it blur into the carpet.

'Were you—raped or something?'

'No.'

'You weren't forced into something?'

'No.'

He let his body slouch against the doorjamb, finger and thumb hard into his eyes, just stayed like that for some kind of eternity. I could see he was stoppering an urge to cry. I stared at him, just stared, all sort of numb.

When he looked up, his features were slur-y. He held my gaze, breathed in then out. 'I told you it will be okay with me. Anything will be okay. I told you on the ferry. It was when you were a kid, right? I mean, fourteen. Right? When you were last here? How can I mind what you did when you were a kid?'

My voice was copying his cracks. 'I wasn't a kid.'

'Oh. It was another time?'

'Um…no…'

'I honestly wouldn't care if it was right before I met you. It's all in the past. Sweetheart?' He reached the crook of his finger under my chin, put pressure there to make me look up into his eyes like his like his like his… Bits of time quivered through me. He reached and wiped beneath my eyes with his knuckle. 'There's black…you look too luminous when you cry. You're all kind of swollen, flushed. Sweetheart…please don't keep me guessing any more. It's torture.'

I nodd

little nodding dog in the back of the car birdie against my legs called swan neck not like picass

never see him agai

and then i found yo

ed. 'I need to hug you,' I said. As I moved toward him, he pulled me into him and we half-lay against the wall, me curled into hi

he was a tiny little head in a sea of black gold thread wrapped around him what's in a name poppies like flags sta

m. A motion, a soft scrape of a footstep, drew my eyes to open. My uncle was stood in his bedroom doorway. With a look he asked me if I was alright and I answered the same way. I could tell he caught my lover's eye, gave him a single approving nod, then closed the bedroom door, himself within.

'Shall we go in there?' he said, indicating the living *his* room.

'No.' I twisted my head up from his chest to look at him, held his eye, pulled myself out of his hug to face him. I nodded. 'It *was* a man. He was older, much older. And everyone freaked out. I was in love with him, deeply, crazy in love. There was something between us, it was—and we were separated, torn apart, and it was the biggest agony I've ever known. We wanted to be together and we weren't allowed. We were in love with each other, see. Meant everything to each other. We *did* everything—I mean, you know, we made love, all of it—and it was more than making love, even, see. I can't even explain. It was beyond material, see— something like that. So you see, I *wasn't* a kid. Even though I was fourteen and they all thought I was. A kid. And I lost everything because of it. I lost my family because they wouldn't understand. I lost this place. And the horses. I thought I would never get over him, not really. I thought I could never find anyone to love like that again.'

'How much older?'

'A lot. Eighteen years. But then—then I found *you,* see.'

His hand was in mine, fingers interlaced, as we traversed the paddocks running along the river. I kept us on the upper slopes of the fields, biased away from that familiar aching ground, but I was aware of how the lazy water aimed to lure, all soft sheen and cloak of misty rain. I pointed out the rabbits nibbling the horse-shorn grass near the hedgerows above us.

'See the babies?' I said.

'They look like toys. Any hares here, my little—vaginaitum?'

I held his gaze. 'I never saw one but I think there must be, don't you?'

'I reckon,' he said. He tweaked my ear and we took to kissing, the heat of our mouths stirring other deeper heats, chilly lips accenting the disparity between our inner and outer worlds. It was an amazing feeling for me to be kissing him here in Ireland. And not to be running.

He broke off, the smack of our kiss in his lips as he turned his head to indicate. 'Shall we go down by the river? It looks stunning in this rain.' I laughed through my nose, punched his shoulder, head shaking. 'What? It looks like a rope of jewels. I'd like to see you wear it at your throat.'

'You want to drown me now? For my sins?'

He caught a hold of me, kind of laughing at me it felt. 'What sins? There are no sins. You never sinned.'

'It's just an expression.'

'An old patriarchal expression—and you're falling for it.'

'I was hardly serious.'

He sucked on his lips. 'Hmm. Debatable methinks.' Our eyes were tied together by invisible ropes. 'But hey, let me tell you about the bear gods sometime. From when man was innocent. None of this bearded bloke in the sky shit, telling you you're bad. It's a beautiful myth—one of the earliest—and one of my favourites.'

I nodded. I could hardly believe how striking he was. 'You know you have tiny little droplets in your lashes?'

'I do?' He made a breathy smile. 'Hey, so do you. I love how you see the detail; how you show me. And how your eyes are the colour of the river. Silvery. Life is a jewel, huh? If we let it.'

'He said you were profound.'

'Who?'

'My uncle. Right when he first met you.'

'Where'd he get that idea?'

I shrugged, drew a cheeky smile. 'I have no idea. Wishful thinking?'

'Oi.'

'Oh, so now you agree with him?'

'Come on, enough.' He tugged me by the hand, the weight of him pulling through to my toes, propelling me into him, and then he was turning, taking us hurtling down the incline. The two of us yelled out into the grey. The grass beneath our feet was slidey, all kind of like sensual juices lubricating our run.

'Watch out,' I yelled, as we approached the bottom. 'Electric fence.'

'Fuck.'

We were trying to stop but the momentum was in the ground and the fence came looming. I veered to the left, pulling on his hand and the two of us skidded sideways, almost falling, legs working like mice in a cartoon, all exhilarated fear, running ourselves alongside the dreaded fence with less than an arms' breadth to spare. We came to a standstill, panting and hanging over our knees, all breathy laughter, eyes eating each other up. And he bulldozed into me, grabbing me, twisting his body so he took the impact of our fall, all rolling me over onto my back, one swift movement, the mass of him pressing along my length in the sodden grass. My legs split open and around him. His hands were up my t-shirt and they were down my pants and I was undoing his belt, kicking off my wellies, toes manoeuvring his jeans down his thighs as his hips shifted, all accommodating the undress. The intensity between us contracted the world to a tight compass of him and me, slippy grass beneath, wet cold, wet warm, eyes locked. I was open. Open inside and out. Open. Like nothing else existed. Coming...and staying...licking life.

We lay side by side, tops all up, baring breasts and chests, wads of jeans and flares down by our ankles, legs, cock, cunt, singing out to the elements. Of which we were, we two. He still had his boots on. We broke into laughter, eyeing each other, struck by the comedy of it come through all the passion.

193

Taking hold of my hand, he said, 'You know this is much more than sex to me?'

'Really? You're kidding?'

He went serious. 'My feelings for you are…I mean, I've never felt like this before. About anyone. And being here, the recognition of the land in my deepest recesses…the truth of you, this thing, your dark secret, finally revealed…' He sighed. 'It's the sweetest thing, has allowed me a meeting with…and I mean this in the most profound, innocent way…with my inner godliness…with clarity. It's like I've gone on a mythical quest, the Shamanic journey I've fantasised about for years. And I'm finally clean.'

I gazed into his blues, felt the swell of heat up my body, dirty tears standing up in my own eyes. I swung my body to drape his, head tucked into his throat, the physical restraint at my ankles a strange perfection, gratifying even, a reflection of the prison that still held me. A prison made from a thing of beauty. I wondered if he could take the next layer of truth, the real one. He reached his hand to clasp my neck, the back of my head, in the way that made me feel safe, as if it was the most loving gesture possible.

'There is no "finally" anything, you know,' I rasped. 'This life is a constantly unfolding revelation, an on-going journey, right? Cleansing has to be…on-going, huh? How else can we grow? There's always more we want—more clarity, more peace, more harmony, love—more *realisation*, huh?—there has to be, or else it would all be finished. Wouldn't it? Doesn't that keep us—maybe the Universe itself even, huh? Which we are a part of, huh?—keep us forever expanding? We have to clarify, to realise our—um, kind of transcendent wants—our truest nature, again and again and again.'

'Are you crying?' He touched his throat, fingertips confirming the wet.

'I'm   I'm just happy.' Muck stuck in my craw. 'I feel that way about you too—kind of never more me.' I omitted the "since *him*" that sprung to my mind. 'And really, it's wondrous, it is, but…but maybe it scares me a bit. Because of the past.'

'We won't be torn apart. We're adults. No one can separate us and

I'm not going anywhere.'

'Yes.' I shivered right through my whole body, like a tremor that might turn into an earthquake. 'You smell so good. Maybe you should wear deodorant.'

'Come on.' He projected a light pressure into my neck and lower back, drew his arms into a tight hug round my middle. He kissed the top of my head. 'Let's dress.'

We came apart, each tending to the pulling down and the pulling up of our own clothing. It felt as intimate as the sex. We were soaked through but neither of us commented on it, like that unsaidness was intimate too. We smiled at each other. I focussed my attention, made an actual choice, and allowed the look of him, just him, here and now, the feel of him, to fill me up; no room for more anymore. The breath I pulled gave only a fraction of the relief I hoped for.

I pointed at the two strands of thin electric wire. 'I'll go first. Be sure not to touch it.'

We slithered beneath and, me in front, we beat a track through the drifts of cow parsley and nettles which formed a divide between fence line and river. All the spring growth was already waist high, rampant with life, and the musky aroma of the starry white flowers came stirred into the air. I snapped off a thick hollow stem, held it up to my face, then to his.

'I used to think maybe I smelled like cow parsley.'

'You do. Only better. You smell like the whole of summer.'

We came out onto the hentrack running along the water. The compacted mud of it was sticky. I steadied my mind, turned, gave him a peck. 'They say there's otter here. But I never saw them.'

⚘

ow comes the imprinting he says all bending over the newborn foal drying it with a brown towel my heart rises up at the sight i watch as the little creature tries to get up he tells me to stroke all over its face up its nostrils and even into its mo

Walking hand in hand, we closed in on the main stable doorway, a yarn of snarled nerves outspread in my chest. So many years it had been. What would it be like to see my foal all grown? My feet grazed the concrete, fingers entwining tight-as with his, and we stood there, we two, at the wide-open mouth.

'Is this okay for you?' I whispered.

'It's surreal.'

'*So* real, huh?'

'Yes. In your face real.'

'Too real?'

'I don't know.'

'It's bringing stuff back for you, isn't it?' I said.

'The smell…'

'See, I knew it would.'

He made a sort of stifled sound. 'We used to come here—I mean, not *here*, but you know what I mean—where he was training.'

'In Ireland?'

'No. We never lived in Ireland; I thought you knew. In Devon.'

'I do. Of course. Know that you didn't live here. You lived in Devon though? He—you never said.'

'When I was little. He left when I was six, didn't he, and my mum moved us to Maidenhead.' He turned to look at me. 'I really think we should go visit her when we get back. She's desperate to meet you. I think she's getting offended. Will you do that for me?'

I averted my eyes, felt the murky wet. 'This smell is the most comforting thing in the world to me. It's kind of electric. I forgot how much I love it.'

He gagged a bit on a breath. 'I'm not sure how I feel about it.'

'I know.'

'I just completely forgot it. And now all this-this stuff…is—it's crowding in.'

'That's what smell does.' I cupped my hand at his jawline, fixed upon his glittery eyes. 'You loved your dad, didn't you? I'm sorry.'

His pupils contracted more maybe than I'd ever seen. 'I guess I still do.'

Me too, I wa

angel's neck

moves beneath me at last, his palomino coat as pale-gold.  he responds to my slightest signal, *before* i signal it feels, as if we are connected on a cellular level.  beyond physical maybe.  the white fence of the training track flickers, his thundering gallop al

fingers over his velvet nose inside his mouth it is almost religious this newborn creature so dea

{Me too, I wa}nted to say.

Heading into the stable's cavernous maw, we were greeted by the scrape of metal shoes, the intensified scent of hay and musk, by whinnying. Even as I wondered where my horse would be, I saw him, some way down, looking out from his stall, all curious—my heart went leaping. But I hid it. We ambled from one beast to another, patting and petting. I noted how he began to relax as each one made its communication with him. And I saw his natural handling of them break through from some core knowing.

'I just want to…' I said, as I left him with Ma Jolie, quick-stepped to reclaim Angel's Neck alone. His brown eyes met mine, lashes blinking slow-as. He puffed hot air through his nostrils, thick lips rolling a raspberry. I copied him. I kissed the pink streak on his black nose.

'My Angel's Neck,' I whispered. 'My little golden angel grown so big. My baby. Do you remember me, bo

all laid out on his side in the glittering straw his little tail whisking back and forth you're a natural he tells me i knew you would b

we're galloping

past my boyfriend and my uncle, white mane knotted like a rope of pearls up the ridge of my angel's neck.  my sights are trained between his ears, into the sprinting track, my legs crouched, taught, haunches all up from the saddle.  the men wave high arms in my periphery.  elation sings in my bod

{do you remember me bo}y?'

Coming up behind me, he murmured, 'This is amazing. And who is this magnificent fellow?' He wrapped his arms round me and I felt him lean to take a look at the nameplate on the stall door. 'Angel's Neck,' he said aloud. He made a sound through his nose. I felt it against my throat. 'Excellent name.' A kiss followed his bre

electric spangles rippling like water across his fresh yello

{bre}ath. I turned in his arms, let myself be kissed. My horse nudged me with his head, thrust me harder into my lover's embrace.

He let go of me, went to stroke him, said, 'Angel's Neck…? Angel's Neck…?' I watched. Waiting. 'The name reminds me of something. I can't think what. Angel's Neck?' The horse nuzzled his offered palm, then raised his head, sniffing at him with an alarming inter

we're racing round the track for the third lap.  angel's neck and i are at one, no question, liquid energy pulsing our veins, his blood running through mine, mine through his, and i know for sure he knows me and we belong together through time and memory and into the new.  tears spring out of my eyes, whisk off into the win

{with an alarming int}erest.

'He's the one I imprinted,' I said. 'You probably heard the name when I told you.'

His mouth pulled down. 'Imprinted?'

'You don't remember?'

'I don't think you've told me. I don't know what that means in this context.'

'Really? I thought I told you about it. Okay so, what it is is

i signal with the gentlest pull on the bit.  we slow to a canter, to a trot, to a walk. the froth on his neck, his flanks is white as sea foam, just as salty.  we are greeted by cheers and clapping as we near the men at the exit from the tra

you've still got it, my uncle ca

i can see why you ride the motorbike so easily, he sa

'You ride a bike?' My uncle looked at him, looked at me.

'She rides with me—pillion.' He gave me a wink. 'She's a natural. She knows how to *blend.*'

'I love him,' I said. 'He remembers me for sure.'

'You want to take him for his cool down?' my uncle asked.

'Of course. I'll meet you back at the stabl

an amazing pure feeling the vulnerable newborn animal giving over in my hands he is docile-as all lying there with his little tail flappi

Kissing my horse's nose, I said, 'This is the horse I'm going to ride. He's sort of mine, see.'

'Because of the imprinting?'

'Yes. But I've never been up on him.'

'It must have been an amazing feeling, that intimate contact with a newborn creature. New life embodied. The spirit yet unblemished.'

'Yeh...isn't that how animals remain, unblemished? Don't you think?'

'What, closer to god energy or whatever? To spirit?'

I nodded, not really knowing. 'I mean, like, they don't get all caught up with worry and ☐onfus, like we do. They seem to stay unconditional, huh? Happy whatever the circumstance, easily making the best of things.'

'Sure, but these racehorses are heavily trained to behave in certain ways.'

'They are. Yet joy remains their set-point. They're still unconditional. You can feel how they love the racing. See, they don't have a mind driving them crazy and not accepting a situation, right? They don't work against it, like with resistance, type-thing—except if they're scared—and then that's natural survival instinct.' We smiled at each other. 'And now I'm going to go get changed and I'm going to race and you just watch how much joy this horse will express as he runs with me on his back.'

He nodded, paused. 'Why don't you want to meet my mother?'

'I do.'

'No, you don't. It's been nine months and you change the subject every time I bring her up.'

'Do I

as i come out of my horse's stall, all exhilarated, sweaty and angel-scented, i see him waiting for me in the main doorway to the building. he's alone. he comes toward me as i move toward him.  he takes a hold of my ha

you really are something, he sa

i just can't believe it's been so long since i rode at all, i
say.  eight years, can you beli

you'd never know.  you look like you did it yesterd

hey, you should get up on a horse tomorrow.  why
don't you?  you used to, didn't you, way back then?  when you were
small?  i can see you have a core connection.  you could ride ma jol

we'll see, he says. i'm not sure i could deal
with it someho

We walked out into the sunlight.

'I'm hungry-as,' I said. 'Ravenous.'

'All that energy spent on riding your Angel's Neck, huh?'

'For sure,' I told him.

He was rubbing his chin, forefinger looping over his lips. 'Hmm…I
just love that name. It's somehow so familiar. Angel's Neck…? But I
just can't work out what it's ringing for me…'

*Episode Seven: white hyacinths*


e are
tonning it were tonning it down the motorway two as one no longer we
two separate me all pressed up against his back he is was shaking i can
feel it and his stomach was is tight clenching small jerks maybe he is
crying i wasn't i can't cry any more but my heart hurt with the love of
him of him it hurt with the hurt i had do

and then i found yo

yo

swan nec

dilated pupils slithers of palest blu

jolting
jagging skidding fast so fast and every detail slow like moving through
water the world the green of the fields one blurred stream now broken
into millions of blades trillions i see them all divided each one different
yet interconnecte

one slow slur of green bod
lunging plungi
bike jarring away from beneath away from betwe

                                        arms ripped from arou
                                          my legs torn fro
                          this body catapulting flying every bla

          angel fa

          swa

                                    and tasselled stems like lac
                                      pathetic sticks in plasti
          *action!* Saying words that are not me is a character all
emotion spilling cut print perfect what a performa
                    audience clapping whoopi me in the midd   uncle shiny hea
                    same square fingers bumpi
                    knees crushi  th  searing blue flowers o  th  spee
                    rising up like his c
                    silvery ma   all golden haze of arm-hai
                    white bumps make joined up writin
                    runni
                    boy crushing his hips into mine   all tight budded mouth on
mi  i'm sayi  fuck fu
                    see mum watch me run alo   the wall   run alo    the path i'm
big i ca
                    barefoo   shoes held loose in her fingers laughin
                     y sister punches me  i'm cryi
                    steppi  into falli   all on my chubby toes al
                    tight tunnel journey into ligh
                    whaaaaa
                                                            no thing
but *every*thing and all elation bursting bliss love is all love only Love
pure energy of of meeting of the bright one body all One an
        Hammering down the motorway, the beauty of the unfolding day felt
to emanate from us, for sure like we were the centre of the Universe,
everything manifesting out of our forward thrust, the moment all making
itself simply because we were there to reap it. Everything was lambent-as
in the landscape, the horizon drawn by the clearest azure sky. I let out a
fairground whoop, my arms tightening around him, the sound all muffled
up in my helmet. The visor fogged from the intensity of my breath. I felt

him laughing, his gloved hand squashing into the padding of my own. He yelled and I made out the words, 'You and me.' And yelled them back.

We were encased, the both of us, in motorbike leathers, combinations of white and red, and black and chocolate-brown, each with a full helmet. Our pants had kind of bibs and braces, so they came up high and no crack of wind could penetrate. The strands of my hair were the one part of me left free to the elements. I felt its whipping rhythm against my shoulder blades, as if I had wings, was the instigator of our momentum.

The feeling of coming off the motorway was always delicious; the slowing velocity sort of velvety, a relief in the muscles, followed by the brilliance of our two bodies leaning with the bike, the swerving as one into space as we sashayed the bends in the road.

We soon hit the traffic filtering toward the racetrack, and he decelerated, the feel of the gear-change clicking through my body. I squeezed him with my thighs, pulsing them a couple of times. We took to overtaking the cars in two and threes, swerving out past the broken central line when there were breaks in the oncoming vehicles. The heat built inside my leather suit. I felt my skin spring with a sheen and I cracked my visor, allowing the warm air to brush my face.

On reaching the wide flat fields which served as a car park for the July schedule, I tightened my grip, bracing myself for the uneven ground. It was our third summer frequenting Newmarket, among other racetracks, since that first trip to Ireland, these familiar playgrounds now a shared delight. We were directed by a parking monitor in a day-glo jerkin to an area in which many bikes were parked and we pulled up alongside a shiny white machine with blue lightning bolts flashing its flanks. The sweat trickled down my spine as gentle fingers.

My body slipped itself off the back, digits undoing and yanking off my helmet in one movement; him all intuiting the ground through his feet and the tyres, inching forward, perfecting the position of his greasy black bike in the knarly grass. When he cut the engine, the quietness was heaven.

He doffed his helmet, all shaking his head like a dog coming out of the water, patted the bulbous tank. 'Come here.'

My leather bum rested into the metal, the heat spiralling through me, and I shrugged off my jacket, chucked it on the ground. We kissed. The engine ticked as it cooled, all like the tension of the ride was running out of our bodies. He loosened my hair, fingers caught in its wind-made tangles, extracted them—*ow!*—to unzip his own sheathing, unzipped my trousers. He pulled down my braces, parted the bodice of my leathers and began driving them over my hips.

I kissed him with a little shove in my lips, the warmth of the sun and his hands feeling nice against my damp skin. 'I got it,' I said, all propelling myself off of the gas tank, peeling my sticky pants downwards, fingers working to keep my knickers up at the same time. Leathers round my ankles, I drew down the flared skirt of my indigo-blue dress from where it was bunched up around my hips, let it fan out over my legs. I dumped myself in the grass alongside the bike, took off my boots and tossed the trousers. 'Phew. So hot.'

He watched the whole thing, then took to removing his own leathers, folded up our gear and squashed it into the top box, throwing me my snakeskin kitten heels.

We made our way across the field, wielded our tickets, headed to the pre-parade ring. My heart soared at the sight of the thoroughbred horses, all rippling muscle, gleaming coats, the finest possible balance of strength and high-strung sensitivity. Resting our arms over the white fencing, I felt his smile coming through the contact of his elbow against mine, felt the pent-up energy of the horses all controlled by the handlers in the way they leaned into their animals' thick necks, clasping the reins right up under their chins, just like I was doing it myself. A few horses bore jockeys already on their backs, thin legs bent up in the high stirrups of the tiny racing saddles, bi-coloured silks fluttering as their boy-like bodies dipped back and forth to that racehorse gait. The echoing tannoy thrilled through me; the banter of punters and bookies in the distance; the horses' puffing breaths, clack and scrape of shoed hooves.

'God, I wish I could get in there with the handlers,' I said. I swung my body below the rail as if I was about to dip in. Swung myself back, catching his eye, the two of us feeling the sex we made together.

'You always do—wish that.'

'But it would be fun, wouldn't it?'

'Yeh. I'd love to see you up on one, to be honest. In those pink-and-yellow harlequin silks I got you.'

'You always say that.'

He pointed at a dun coming round the ring a few horses away. 'On that monolith. Number eleven. I reckon you'd be a good fit.'

We eyed it as it passed. I nodded. 'Good choice. Really good form.'

'You going to bet on him?'

'No. But you are.'

I pointed at a straining chestnut. 'See that one? All that white froth where his tack rubs against his chest, his flanks? He's expending too much energy.'

'Like you, when you're about to go on stage.'

'Like what?'

'You're saying he's nervous, right?'

'Yeh. But his nerves are not creative. That fellow's not going to win. See how he's tugging? His nostrils all flared? They can hardly hold him back. He's for sure young. Inexperienced. But keen-as, huh?' My eyes slid over each thoroughbred. '*That* one,' I said. 'Number five. Look at his springy stride. He's my winner. I'm going to put a tenner on him to win. Maybe you should too.'

'I'm going for my dun. Fiver each-way.'

'Each-way? Coward.'

'I'm going to imagine it's you up on him.'

'No you're not. You can't. That's cheating. I'll be up on my fellow.'

'Come on,' he said. 'Let's go lay our bets. And get a paper. You're a bit disorganised, aren't you, sweetheart? Don't even know what our beasts are called.'

'Ah but I just recognised my trainer. That's Martin Forest—know him?—he's really been coming through lately.'

'So who's the cheat around here? Springy stride, my foot.'

'He does have a springy stride. I said, *just* recognised, you pleb. So are you sure you're not going to change your mind and bet with me?'

'Probably rubbish odds if he's such a cert. I'll take my chances, follow my intuition thanks.'

I pursed-up my smile and raised my eyebrows, behind the tease feeling proud of his commitment to his hunch, the instinct he had developed with the horses. He shoved me and I shoved him back and we linked hands and made our way down to the grandstand to check out the odds at a few different bookmakers. We grabbed a racecard and together took delight in my horse being called Silent Spring, him calling me a psychic, all big-upping me.

'But In Or beats all known naming,' he said of his own horse. 'Super fucking clever. I'm telling you, mine's the one. Plus much better odds, like I told you. You sure you don't wanna…?'

I shook my head. 'I'll stick to my guns. I know a winner when I see one.'

We crushed into a spot right up against the rail by the winning post, peering through our binoculars to watch the horses manhandled into the starting stalls, a sort of razor-sharp ache spread into them. The chestnut was skittish, shy of the pen, even when they tried to back him in, and he had to be lead away, was not allowed to run. He gave me a look, told me I should be a trainer myself, forget Martin Forest.

The tension was cuttable before the shrill sound of the bell. But in the very moment the gates sprang open, there came inside of me a fantastic hush, a stilling—my blood next moment roaring as the beasts launched out, energy uncoiled, all leaping legs, at once in full motion. I was electric, hairs on end, the rhythm of Silent Spring in my body as he tore past us on the first straight, a good horse-length in the lead. And then the thunder of many hooves entering me through the kicked-up turf.

We craned against the fence, all yelling and frantic arm gestures, connected to the pack of horses as they raced into the distance and turned along the far curve of the track. Silent Spring maintained his lead. In Or was gaining on third place. And then they were hurtling along the final straight toward us, our yells intensifying. I could feel the wind in the silks I wasn't wearing, feel the high in my chest, legs loose and tight at once, surrendered to the tug and thrust. In Or was coming in second. We were screaming for them. And his horse was gaining, gaining on my horse and they were neck and neck and they were flying past us, over the finish line and we couldn't tell, we couldn't tell which one had won.

We leaped into the air, arms all up, crashed back down and into each other, arms around, a cacophony of noise drowning out, joining with, our triumph. And then we were arguing, all laughing and jostling. We went running up the stands, our energies released. Waiting, we surveyed the glittering track, taking in the activities of the groundsmen as they prepared for the next race, all towing the starting gates back into position, checking the condition of the track. I leaned my body into him and the kiss we shared was super-charged.

'I want you,' I said into his mouth.

The tannoy crackled. 'The winner for the 12:30 race this afternoon has now been determined…'

'Will you still want me when I've won?' he said.

'*I've* won you mean.'

'Shhh.'

'Shhh.'

'…and our winner is…*number 11!* In Or…and what a champion! What a result from this youngster, this superlative outsider…'

He was jumping up and down, cheering like crazy, his betting ticket pincered between finger and thumb. I stood, trying to look cross, and then he was spinning me round in his arms, yelling he beat me and I was echoing him, all delight.

'Told you I've won,' I said. 'I couldn't lose. You're bloody brilliant, that's what. You've pipped the expert. It's in your blood, boy. I always knew it was.'

'I've got a good teacher.'

'And some.'

'Come on, let's pick up my winnings. Ten to one—that's a hundred smackeroos.'

'A hundred? It's fifty.'

He made a slow show-off blink. 'I put it on to win in the end. None of this cowardly each-way stuff over here.'

'You cheeky blighter.' I kissed him, tore up my ticket and dropped it like snow over his crown. 'I'm going to the loo. Meet you at the pre-parade ring for our next rollicking froli

*uh!* i am

everythi  i am in everythi  so big there are no edges no confines just this beautiful expanding beyond all known sublime  I AM  just jo

{next rollicking froli}cking,' I told him.

I hared it across the tarmac, weaving in and out of the crowd, legs all sun-blessed, revelling in the way the thick cotton fabric of my tulip skirt held its structure even as I ran, gave the feeling of an unbroken space within, no constriction, so I felt some kind of secret nakedness right the way u

bounding about the fields after my sister in my red daisy-flowered knickers i'm her dog her dog *oh!* unstoppable wildness in the furrows of the undulating crop fields the hum of the golden wheat all native black-eyed poppi

two red poppy petals smoothing them out with tender fing

flip the pages of the book find the petals all dry and pressed and translucent so delicate love hearts and in the same wildflower tome other blooms we together collected and pressed as marks of our days sweet celandine daisies foxgloves dog roses we searched but hadn't found any harestail cottongrass ye

{right the way u}p my thighs.

The loo queue threaded outside and it was a slow shuffle before I got to release my pee, hovering above the toilet seat, my skirt an indigo-blue speedwell all radiating out of me. I didn't let myself think of what this last meant to me; but it did give me joy. As I ran my hands under the cold water at the tap, I gazed into myself, saw something lovely issuing from within, was filled with such a rush of pure love, pulled-as into something beyond me—and then I caught the eye of a woman waiting behind me, in the mirror. I blushed, side-stepping her as I dashed out, water dripping off my fingers as happy tears.

I kind of cantered back toward the pre-parade ring, the feel in my body taking me back to the ecstasy of bouncing around on my hands and knees, all barki

*good dog* she says patting my head *silky girl* i lick her hand her cheek roll onto my back arms and legs all up whimper for her to pet my bel

head-butting her leg i play at beggi

enough now she sa

i whine i nuzzle pant all smiling tongue hanging ou

*ok then come on* and we head for the kitchen where she takes out a tube of doggie chocolate treats fishes one out and feeds m

{all barki}ng for her to stroke me. How I'd hung on to being that dog, right up to aged eleven, right until the day I first saw Robin Remick. Then never again. No blurred transition from childish games to grown-up ones; one day I was a dog, next I was a girl. And three years later, kind of a woman; kind of.

Reaching the pre-parade ring I caught sight of him from behind, his tall slim frame pressed up against the white rail as if he were jammed in a crowd. I liked the way his dark blue jeans hung off of his bum a bit, sort of low on the hip, held up by an aged brown leather belt. I liked the waffle-knit long-sleeved t-shirts he wore, original American thermals from New York, the way he pushed the sleeves up to his elbow. I snuck up behind him, slipped my hands up over his eyes, breathed a laugh. I expected him to return, to turn in my arms maybe. But he barely moved, as if he didn't register me. I dropped my hands, leaned round beyond the fence line to get to see his face.

He met my look, said, all hoarse, 'Sweetheart…'

'Are you alright?'

He nodded, shook his head. 'I don't know.' He indicated out into the ring with his chin. 'Look.'

I followed his gaze, scanning over the horses. 'What?'

'It's him. He's here.'

'Who's here?'

'Him.'

I shook my head. 'Who?'

'My-my dad.'

'Your *da*—your *dad*—' I spun my sights all about us, bile rising in my throat '—here?—wha—what, where?'

'He's here…'

'I don't see—I don't see him. Where?'

'Over there. See?' He was gazing, dazed-as, into the ring. 'He's leading that dun horse—the one wearing the red blanket. Another dun. You-you think he'll win too? He's bound to, isn't he? He's bound to win.'

'I don't—I can't…'

'No, you can't see him, he's on the other side of the horse. See his legs there? Black jeans.'

'That's him? That's your dad? You're sure?' I was clinging to the rail so hard it hurt.

'I'm sure.'

'But you haven't seen him in over twenty years. You—'

'—I remember him. Only now he's old. You'll see.' His fingers crept around my wrist, gripped it in a vice. 'He's old, sweetheart. What am I going to do? Oh god, look, now you can see him. See him?'

My throat clogged right up at the sight of him, my voice coming as a thread. 'He's not…he's not old…' I watched him heading toward us round the ring.

'In the light brown bomber jacket.'

'Yes…I know…you…you walk kind of like him too. Wow, crazy, I never—*oh!*—' everything was going wavy inside of me, all kind of slowing down and abstract '—that's a gaucho jacket, not a bomber.'

'Gaucho jacket.'

'Argentina, see.'

'Argentina.'

'Your mum. You.'

'My mum.'

His shoulder was rammed into the muscular neck of the horse, a mare, body weight into her, and I saw he was muttering words to her and I knew pretty much what he was saying, hearing his steadying Irish brogue in my hea

       all mashing chips into my laughi

d. I could see how the horse was listening to him, all loving him for sure.

'He's old,' he said again, voice a cracked blue eggshell.

'He isn't. He hardly looks any—you just—you-your—your memory of him is from when he was twenty or something, yes? Younger than you are now, see.'

'Twenty-two.'

'What?'

'I last saw him when he was twenty-two. I was six.'

He was sure-as fitter-looking than before, his belly flatter, his skin burned dark, so he looked almost glamorous. His hair wasn't even any greyer, just shone with those beautiful glints of silvery lights, all like his body had been preserving itself for this moment. I tore my sights away from him, from the blue flash of his eyes, whipped my head to meet those same blues of his son. I saw they weren't the same anymore. 'I love you. I think we should go.'

'Go?' He stared at me, startled, scared-looking. 'But—'

'—*now*—come on.' I tried to pull him with me but he wrenched me back.

'But this is my dad. Are you mad?'

'I know. And he left you, didn't he, the fucker?'

'But you always say—'

'—I just think we should take—let's get some distance—give you some sp

        everything ope

ace, yes?—spa—'

'—*space*? For what? I've had years of fucking sp

        eyes open heart ope

ace—'

'—I'm all—' my voice gurgled in my throat '—op

        cun

en—I mean, I-I—can't—' I was trying like crazy to stop my springing tears '—I ca

        self op

n't—I can't—we can find him later. Come on.'

'No way.'

'We need to pro

        all on top of m

tect you, see—'

'—it's my dad, sweetheart. My *dad*. Why would I lose sight of him for a second?' He was staring into me, thrown-as.

'I-I—you've lost sight of him, see.'

He flung my wrist, real violent, raised his voice. 'No, I haven't.'

'Ages ago. He left—he left you.' The quiet tears fell down my cheeks. Snot was making my voice thick.

'I never lost sight—I never di—I've always wanted—and now he's here. Right now. What's the matter with you?'

'I don't—I don't—I don't want you to be hurt.'

'I'm already hu—

       body wrapped round hi

—rt.'

'I mean, wrecked, see—disappointed, I—' He lurched his eyes back into the ring. I got the feeling he was going to call out. I grabbed his shoulder. 'Don't. He's about to run a race. This is public. Please.' My eyes on the other, I felt something in my boyfriend give way. His shoulder went saggy beneath my grip. I glanced at him, saw his face contorted into the shape of grief. I glanced back at his dad. Back at him. At his dad. I saw how there was no blur anymore. Saw each as only himself. 'I have to go,' I said.

He smashed his fist into his eye as a tear spilled the lip of his lid. 'I'm staying.'

And I just stood there, heart a trapped bird in my throat. He was almost parallel with us. Intent on the horse. And then, as if pulled by a string, my energy maybe, definitely, his head twisted around and he was staring at us, at me, his eyes stepping right inside of me, all the way in. I saw the stunned expression, some kind of leap inside of him, felt the connection deep in my own body, a horrible rushing, a pulsing, right into that centre where he'd long ago opened me—and there was an appalling wetness, sweat all over.

I watched him pull himself back, eyes untangling, head turning away on his short thick neck, all directing his focus into his horse. His solid body passed us, showed us his back. I followed his bandy cowboy legs.

'Argentina,' I murmured. 'That's where…'

'I think he was just looking at *you*. I don't think he saw me. I don't think he saw me at all.'

'…that must be where he's living all this time.'

'How can he—maybe he's seen you in one of your films—do you

think? He recognised you, I'm sure. He looked totally—totally struck by you.' I tore my eyes from his dad to meet his bleared gaze. 'He didn't even see me, sweetheart. He doesn't know I exist.'

The bird in my throat flapped its wings, manic-as, and my voice came scratchy. 'But he knows you exist. He knows he has a son. I know that.'

'He was just interested in yo—'

'—*not* interested in me. Yes, he just saw an actress he recognised, you're right. He just didn't see you because…there-there *wasn't time*, see. And he was distracted by—that's it, like you sai—by some idea of fame. I mean, I'm not even famous but he…'

'He thought you were gorgeous.'

I shook my head, my body throbbing, so hot. My eyes reached through him, past him, sought the stocky form of his dad. I felt him following my stare.

'This is fucked,' he said.

'It is.'

We watched as his jockey came alongside him and he gave him a leg-up, without a pause in pace. We watched as he rounded the bend in the enclosure and went pretty much from view, obscured by the dun mare and his red-and-gold harlequined rider.

'Hey, sweetness, you're crying.' He sounded surprised.

'Am I?' We moved as one into a hug, kind of clinging to each other. 'I love you,' I said.

'You're trembling.'

'It's okay. It will be okay.'

'What shall we do?'

I forced my thoughts. 'Let's—um—go and watch the race, shall we?'

'Watch the race? I can't do that.'

'Yes, let's bet on his horse.'

'I need to speak to him. I need to find out.'

'I know. Look, they're leaving the enclosure. You have to let him be, until after. You don't know how he'll react—this will be like a massive shock for him, huh?' We stayed in a loose hug, watched him take the trail to the track with the other horses. I told myself I wasn't pulled by him, wasn't with hi

213

unnin dow th hentra

m on that trail.

'After the race, okay? You can go and find him. You might have to wait a while, mind, let him take care of his horse. If he gets a place, he'll have to parade round the winners ring too.'

'Aren't you going to come? I want you to come.'

'I don't know. It might be better on your own. I think it will be. You need the intimacy.'

'I want you to come.'

'Let's see. Come on, let's bet on his horse. Number seven it is.' I extracted the racecard from his jeans' back pocket, located the horse. 'Her name is Darling. What a terrible name.'

⚜

We put a bet on his horse and watched the race from high up on the concrete steps, and it was like we were contained in a kind of cold circle, sort of isolated from everything beyond us. Darling won. Pretty good odds too. But we didn't cheer or smile or anything. Our eyes made contact a moment after she crossed the finish line—and we held each other in the silent gaze of muddied understanding. In some ways I felt we were closer than ever before, as if the boundaries of our skin just disappeared, our circulatory systems linked through our pounding hands; yet I'd never felt more distant, more alien. I was a charlatan. My stomach was a stone.

We watched as he ran forward to where his horse had been reined in by his golden-boy jockey, watched as they conversed, watched as he led the mare off the track and toward the winner's ring. I wondered what he was feeling, knowing I was here. I had the sense of him inside of me and really I knew he was tightly wound, like a spring, like the horses before the race. I knew he was excited. I almost hated him for it.

With the bare minimum communication, little more than slurs, we began the descent to collect our winnings. He grabbed my arm. 'Let's not cash it in,' he said, returning the ticket to his pocket. 'I want to…I don't want…'

I nodded, eyes flitting away. 'Yeh.'

'Let's—' he began to head in a different direction '—are you coming?' I shook my head. He stopped, staring at me, mouth open, all like a gormless child. After an interminable gap, he said, 'Just to the winner's ring.'

'I'm not ready to meet—I think you should meet him on your own. Me being there will confuse matters, see. After all that earlier. And I don't think you should go to the winner's ring. I think you should wait.'

'Well, if you're not there he won't even notice me, will he?'

'He will. Of course he will. If I'm not there.'

'You being with me might help.'

'I don't think so.'

'You can act as a buffer.'

'I don't think so.'

'As an introduction, I'm thinking.'

'I'm thinking he'll want to discover you on his own. He'll hardly need to be distracted by some silly actress. You're going to blow his mind. He's been waiting to—wanting to see you forever.'

'You're not silly.' He stepped back toward me, brushed my cheek with the back of his fingers. His eyes were moist and he expressed a tender smile, something slight yet budding inside. 'You always speak like you know him. It's the sweetest thing.' I wanted to look away but I forced my burning eyes to stay. 'Alright. I'll go it alone. And I'll wait till he's back with his crew. Shall we get a drink?'

I trailed him up the steps toward the bar, everything tight. And in the grip of this constriction came a crazy knowing, something releasing, speeding, reaching out. I *knew* he was coming, my head all turning itself so I saw him tripping around the crowd, up the rake, eyes fixed on me.

My heart seemed to halt, stillness spreading out in me, beyond me, but not like the hushed exhilaration at the opening of the starting gates; this was as grimy as it gets; it was a cellular reaction where attraction and repulsion came as best buddies, took charge of my body, stoppered my breath, bathed me in a silky sheen. I stood all hypnotized in the reaching silence—then sound crashed in, heart as a tilting motor, breath short and hard to grasp.

'Angel Fa—' he was calling '—Angel Face.'

The breeze came up under my blue speedwell dress, blew on my damp thighs. I watched as each step brought him nearer. I couldn't take my eyes off of him. And then he was reaching out for me and I was stumbling backwards, kitten heels ramming into the riser of the step behind, and I was falling backwards and he was catching me, drawing me into him. I was limp and I was dying, but he was holding me and I was an elastic b

        pinging against his tooth

and. I was pulled taut, and I was alive, like all hell was running through m

        *phalange phalange* same square fingers breath in my face

        harestail cotton grass stay

e.

'I can't believe it,' he was muttering, cracking me right open with his crackling voice all into my throat. 'I've never forgotten you, not for a second. I've wanted to—every day I've—' His hair was all in my face and in my mouth, the scent of him a soft sh

        same scent junki

awl. ' I've seen you in magazines, in movies, you—'

'—Dad? *Dad.* It's me, Dad. Dad.'

I felt the shock shoot through his body, could feel him looking up at his son above him on the raked steps and he tightened his noose on me, hurting me with the way he held onto me. I staggered, realising I was going down again, his weight all pressing into me, but he caught a hold of himself, propelled us upward, levering us somehow and releasing his hold on me as he sprung back and almost danced down, then up, a couple of steps. His face was rabid, about terrified it seemed. '*Chri*—what the fuck—Christ…'

'It's me, Dad—'

'—it's your boy—'

'—Dad. It's me.'

'He's my—' I turned, stepped to the son, raising my palms, words just stumbling out of me '—can you believe this? He recognised me, you were right. I was falling over and he caught me, see, and—'

'—you two *know* each other?' He was skimming us, one to the other. 'I don't—'

'—but Dad…here I am…it's me…it's me…'

I wound my arm around his waist, guts a cat's cradle. 'He's—this is my boyfriend, see.'

'Your boyfriend?'

'Don't you know me? Dad…'

'We saw you in the pre-parade ring—he told me who you are, see— he told me—'

'—wait, your *boyfriend*?'

'Wake up, man. Don't you get it? Who cares about me? I'm just an actress you've seen in a movie. This is your son. Your *boy*.'

'Your boyfr—'

'—*your boy*—'

'—it's me, Dad, it's me—'

'—oh *fuck*—' I stared as he filled right up with tears that came splashing down his rugged, pock-marked, beautiful ugly, almost ugly face. He shoved his fingers into his eyes, dropped his head. His hand was trembling, hairs on his fingers all like seaweed sending old messages '— my boy…oh god, my *boy*, I—' He threw his other arm out, the flat of his hand toward us. I saw his palm was grazed, fresh bright blood '—just- just give me a moment. Just a moment. I'm sorry, this is all—it-i

> flecks of my red in the gree
>
> o  th  gra
>
> and th  seari   blue fl

t's…*Christ*, it's…very fucking…'

I didn't dare look at his boy, though I wanted to. My whole body was on fire, was vibrating fast-as, like I was going to break apart into sub-atomic particles. There was no perceived stream of thought, just this incoherent noise and sort of mixed up ima

> blue speedwe
>
> two red poppy petals all smoo
>
> stings like handwriti

ges.

217

I felt judders coming through the son's breath and then his ribs were heaving as he worked hard to restrict his escalating emotion. He sank down to sitting, me going with him. I wrapped my arms around him, drawing him into the haven of me.

'It's alright. It's okay.'

'Dad…' his voice was

a hairline crack

a cracked cup

into my chest. 'He doesn't know me…he doesn't want me…it's only you he wants…'

'No, that's not possible, see. I'm just—he jus—'

'—no, no, *son! Listen*, I do wan—*Christ*…' He plunged to the other side of him, laid his hand between his shoulder blades, tears splashing down that face of his. '…I just—I can't believe this. Look at you—you're grown up…you look just the same…oh *Christ*—but of course I-I want—*fuck*, listen to me, I'm sorry—I didn't—I just—just couldn't compu—I mean, I just couldn't—I couldn't take you in wi—with *her*—I mean, this is *very* fucking confusi—like too fucking impossible. It's blowing my head off. *You* with *her*—I thought I'd never see you agai—and now you two together, I—son, look at me—' but he shoved his head deeper into my fold '—oh god, I *never* stopped loving you—you cannot know how much I-I've *wanted*—I've missed—*beyond* missed—you cannot know how that's hurt. I just—listen, I didn't know how to approach you, how to deal—I was *pathetic*, so fucking pathetic, I'm sorry, so sorry. There is no excuse. Please tell me we can…'

I pulled back, looking at the two of them, just not being able to marry the reality. I expected him to look at me, over his son's quaking hung down head, for his eyes to want me, and I was ready only because I had to be. I had no idea what I was going to do, only hoped I could signal to him not to give us away.

He craned his un-swan neck instead, to thrust his face into his beautiful son's field of vision, hand hugging the back of his neck. 'Look at me, son. I've never stopped thinking about you. I thought you wouldn't—wouldn't want to know me…after…'

And with a jolting action, which excluded me, they were clutched in a tight embrace. 'Dad... Dad...' I saw how his face cried in a dry agonised kind of a way, soundless, whilst his dad filled the void with a strange deep yowl, sort of smothered even as it escaped. I wasn't sure my heart could take it.

I stood, became aware of people looking on. I scanned several faces, everything kind of blurry, observed how they quickly looked elsewhere, shuffled, began to break away. I wanted to shout at them all. My eyes slid down to the racetrack below. A clutch of rippling horses and riders were heading toward the starting stalls, all bright colours fluttering like animated cartoon characters. Looking at them kind of hurt and I funnelled my gaze up into the infinite blue of the sky, found there a soothing grace, let myself be held in it for something I wished could be forever.

When I turned back, they were both looking at me, sat side by side. The son slid his arm from around his father's back and I saw how his face wore a look of evolving comprehension. I watched as a horrible shock dispersed into his skin, the redness of his raw emotion draining away into a ghastly white. I felt the reflection of him in my own body, renewed fright leaping into me, and I flung myself down beside him, tried to take his hands, a flurry of words, of sorries and pleases, ringing only in my mind, weird-as shushes all coming off of my breath.

'You—' his voice was drowned out by the buzzing tannoy, but I knew what he said; I read his lips, his heart.

I nodded, kind of reeling inside. I never looked at the other.

He said it again, and then we just stared at each other, all dying flames in our eyes, the tug of the crowd around us as they were drawn down the steps toward the track.

And when the announcement ceased, he repeated, barely audible, 'You know each other.'

'Yes,' I said.

'I get it now.'

'You do.'

'It was him.'

'Yes.'

He turned to his dad. 'It was *you*. My dad. All along.'

'What was?'

With a twisted mouth he said to me, '*He* was the reason you wanted me.'

The starters' bell rang out and there came a rush of sound, of excited yelling voices all intermingling into some kind of white noise.

'No. At the beginning—only at—'

'—"*You remind me of someone?*" Shit, I've got to get out of here.' He jolted up to his feet, took several steps downwards, sights spiralling away toward the galloping thoroughbreds, then jerked his head back to hiss at me, his face sopping wet, '"*He knows you exist?!*" Did you talk about me? Then? When you were fourteen? What kind of sick game have you been playing? "*You sound Irish*". Irish this, Irish that. All because of *this* prick.'

I wanted to stand, go to him, but I couldn't. It was like I was screwed down to the step. I was aware of his dad sitting pretty damn close to me, could feel a demand radiating from him. It was him who answered. 'We talked of you, yes. I told her how I felt.'

'So you knew about me?' His stare never left me. 'Sweetheart?' I drew forth a shadow of a nod, eyes throbbing. 'And Jessie's photogra— you *knew*. You knew who I was all along. Does *she* know? Oh fuck, it doesn't matter. I've been living a lie all this time—five fucking years. What did you think you were doing?'

I felt his dad flinch at my side. 'Five—?'

'—shut up,' I whispered, eyes slanted toward him but into the ground. 'This is *not* about you anymore. This is about him, your son, who I love now, don't you see? You never got in touch with him; you never got in touch with me either. You never tried to find us, either of us.'

'*Us?*' said my boyfriend. '*Us?* This is fucked.'

'Yeh, it's fucked,' I told him. 'But it's real and my love for you is real and if it hadn't been for—' I flipped my head to meet his dad's eyes, was startled-as by the black of his pupils stripping away all sign of the blue.

'I loved you,' he said.

My throat was tight as a virgin's cunt. 'You don't know what love is. All those years I carried—'

'—I still do.'

'How can you say that, right in front of your son?' My body was starting to convulse, stupid tears running hot down my face.

'Because love is a stream that never stops.' He reached his hand and slid his fingers down a ribbon of my hair. 'What we had was the most singularly joyful love I have ever known. It was probably the truest I've ever been with another. And I never should have let myself. You were too young and I never should have. I was wrong. I never came to find you out of respect.' He rose, reached for his son who let him take him by the shoulders. 'I'm sorry. I was weak. I was a shit dad. But I never stopped loving you. I never will. Stay with this girl. Don't let this ruin it. Let this free you both. Love her and never stop.' And then he was walking awa

e are

tonning it down the motorway were tonning it we two separate he is was shaking i can feel it and his stomach was is tight clenching small jerks maybe he is crying wasn't i can't *can't* cry any more but my heart hurt with the love of him of him it hurt with the hurt i had do

and then i found yo

yo

swan nec

dilated pupils slithers of palest blu

jolting

skidding fast so fast and every detail slow the green of the fields one blurred stream now broken into millions of trillions of blades i see them all separate each one different yet interconnecte

one slow slur of green bod

lungin

bike jarring away from beneath away from betwe

arms ripped from arou

my legs torn fro

this body catapulting flying every bla

angel fa

swan ne

his bo

*oh!*

221

*oh,* i *am* that green bod
     *whoa!*   searing light—so bright,  all white
### silence
at once a full-on ecstatic hum;like every sound that ever was is—
                —*hey but joy!*everythi tha  hur
                    doesn't  hur    .     anymore.
inabright instant nothing matters, whole personality and all ,  all it meant
to be a separate self called me ,  with a past and a future  ,delight, it's
finished  .   no more pai .  .

   huh but?am me but not me  .,

  i am   —what?—a pure positive energy  ,  *yes!* a true uncondition  .
  my *god*

 no matter ;nomatter where iam now.   *and*everything  matters,  really
matters ,like see it's all connected.this is so natural. i am in everybody
.and everything  .  i am *not* everybody —AM I?—,well i *feel* everybody .
i *know* everybody . i am flying as every bird .and joyfully solid ,   slow
, as every tree , dancing     as every flower and every blade of grass .
and yet I AM nowhere , without dimension ,a sort of no thing in the
everything.  I AM that **silence**. there is no dea
                 just life
                   and more Life
                     what you doing, pet?
             it is my granny . i don't see her as a form like i used to but
 i know it is her , just feel it is her. she has that exact same low-down
dirty laugh  .   butshedoesn't have a voice , is a part of the
     hum .i can't say what i see her as ;i can't say i see
       without my voice i say ,  gran
  at the exact same time i hear my mum, she is all crying
.   and my dad is holding his hand over his face , glasses smeared-as .
         *oh look !*  it's me in a white bed  . there's a big
fat plastercast on my left leg. tubes all coming out of me. but i'm over
 here; i'm not in that
   —body—
    I AM
     the love from my gran is total  , the most beautiful love.  and all  i

am is just held in  Love . iamthatLove.

   you're home ,you scallywag, she sings,  but it's not your time , pet,
it's not really your time at all. hey ladida  —you got here , didn't you?—
so now you have a choice.  see?because you are partway  .you can
   stay *or* you can goback

                                                *huh?!* go back *?!*

                                                    why  *?!*

      ?   why would i want to goback to all that tricky life and pai  ?
         look at the mess of me , it's going to hur   some
                                     more
aha  !  she says   .   but c'mon ,  You know why : you, in the physical,
you're leading the dance, you're at the helm, yes?   ,
                        you get to create ,to—
   —*ah* !  i trill, all cutting her up in a harmony of hum :  ?why don't *you*
go back?
      she hoots    .   because this "i" that was, she doesn't have a body to go
back to, my silly pudding.   besides, I AM back. here isback
         *.and* there is back

                              at theexactsametime i feel my sister and i
see her getting on a massive jumbo jet  ,  i feel how gutted she is ,feel
her tears    all like they're streaming down the cheeks   i don't have
like i must be inside of her. i feel just  pure
                        Love for her
   *hey!*  and my uncle is driving .     all steady in himself

            .

            my mum and dad are talking to someone    … the doctor.he
is saying she may not come round ,  his voice very grave.    i feel his
gravity like i'm all in him . but without attachment to any of it ,see. .i see
like i'm all looking from inside of him  .he tells them about her brain
scan , it doesn't look good.without the ventilator she wouldn't be
breathing. the reflexes aren't functioning.
                  i feel amazing  ! !    i tell them. but they don't hear.
they are veryvery stressed   but i just can't ,i *can't* feel stress with them,
i only know this glorious love space ,this pure
   energy ,and i keep calling them to come    come play with

                                223

me .   you are bigSelf too

    I AM That .

    oh stuart—,i see you,allcrying

    eliot

    jessie merl todd-baby

            iloveyouallsocompletely

you must choose, hums my gran ,along with a whole mess of other
voices i can't see   .there's a kid from my primary school who drowned
.i forgot all about her ,she was my best friend when i was

               six

           orsomething,

we wouldgoback if we were you .gowith this realisation of who
you truly are   .go make the life youshe*we* really want for you;be your
unique expression .explore: discover your influence: you humans create
 your own experience,   see   .

   see ?  says the kid ,  jessica nolan,that's who she wasiswas

              asks ,do you get it        ? ?

gran warbles  :  in your physical body   in your physical universe
,you are a powerful creator, see—via every thought and perception, you
get to choose ;itisall a dream you get to play, pet.    you agreed to see
yourself separate; you agreed to perceive your small-self beliefs as true ;
you get what you believe,  see? you just have to train yourself—see?

  teachthat wayward mind of yours.to see the truth again ; to look upon
  the world with Love ; this is its true and only value  —

   you knew this ,when you agreed to go into your

        body

          into your physical laws—

      ilaugh    .i blurt    —but everything i ever wanted  ,  complete
and total freedom, thislove without conditions is here
  is here    i AM it all now—

     —take it!

      —take it  !

        —*nick* it, pudding! go for it   !

   take this opportunity.   the hum grows and intensifies and me too i'm
all hummingit , it's just busting out through the voice i don't have:  go

live with the joys of seeming matter manifest —*with* this knowledge, huh?—it is an uncommon, a *wild* moment in a finite human lifetime ,to goback with this

remembering —a meeting with the non-physical ,with your
Eternal nature and Being

i break off, say: i don't want to leave you.   this . IS ALL so blissful and perfection

aha !you won't be leaving us ; this you do now know, dear one .

*oh blimey ,i do! wow!*     i say   : *i   see !*—you will come with me …*of course!* bewithme always;there  IS  no separation;it is an

*oh!*

that's what it means: illusion

yes! comes the hum: all is One ! the field of infinite Awareness *is* you,you physical humans.   the One Life runs through you.   {and you…and you ; every you ,hums the hum…}One sees and feels and hears and tastes and touches *through* youall   how else to—

*ah !*  i say.*yes!* experience a world    of diversity ;  a multipliciy ?!   *ha!* what,expandtheUniversal consciousness, huh !?all like what is happening inside of  me outside of inside of me here—now !  *oh i see!*                                             I

AM

theCreator,

both dreamer and the dreamed ;all humans are dreaming the world .glory be: *illusion!*

*ah yes!* gran sings. you *do* see, pet ;this is Reality ; you got it, little scallywag.    words cannot teach. in hereness youare remembering

oh gran-notgran…i know   i know

i do so know it all   oh Infinite Source
: of which i am:

:i went with joy  and  excitement ,entered the apparent manifest world and yes,  *crazy-nuts-as!*  iagreedto forget , to believe the limitations of my senses ,to chart pain, resistance   —buts still: *why  ?*

the hum fills me up again and me too,

225

i am that hum all speaking to myself: youcame youwent to know
contrast to know yourSelf through what you are *not* ; how else
  to?!experience your true nature ?to feel the sacred heart
      of existence? yea: in ever new and evolving ways —to gain
    billions of unique perspectives, huh .? to realise ourSelf through
    living the spice—see how You have simply the One experience
                              here *?!*

      *oh yes!!* i trill : yes,and *oh! light needs to know darkto know*
*light*, right? white needs black. love needs its opposite— shadow ;fear
            — toknow— to experience— *oh!*to be the expression of—
IAM love

                        oh *weeeeeeee!*

   yes ! i-they say. youare remembering OneSelf. who youwe truly
are. in the vast part non-physical,the infinite indivisible, all projected
into physical—soyou stay*and*you go. and when *you* are in your
vibratory physicalworld, You are shining your love uponandthrough
yourself . as One too ,we shine our love the love of Love is
holding you in grace.so why not take the fullness of who you are, —*nick*
it, pet*!*— take this awakening,your connection to the Source of life —*go*
*open the eyes of the blind, little pudding; you've always been ace at*
*rebelling against the system hey?!*— the only Reality is your extension
of Love; go feel your Inner Being in your human form , be both at once.
no either or .no dea or alive
      just life and

                        more

Life

*ah! oi, pet!*   *!* hop it now—or never*!*

youhavetodecidenow  , hums the hum. you cannot come any further —or it will be final

    you is travelling deeper into the non-physical  state, puddipie

               .               any further from your body and You will lose kinship ,your cells will cease consciousness  their connection to Source energy —this You ,all us— and then you cannot return into that life and the you that isyou still,the youweLOVEsomuch,  you—as untamed young woman in her bed—will cease to live.you will have togoback as a newborn in     a newform

            {*you are a transmitter and receiver*  }

        either way is theway  .you never get it wrong and younever get it

                                 done

           {*your feelings are your guidance syst*  }

A warm flood raced through my blood and into my limbs, all elastic pulsing energy flying my eyes open, lungs trying to draw an in-breath out of time with the ventilator. The spring of joy was like a racehorse in my heart, even as thorns wrenched at my throat. I remembered the plastic tube I had seen stuck in my mouth; didn't mind the pain one bit.

'Oh my god, my—' my mum swerved into my face, all wide eyes spilling delicious warm wet on my skin. 'Darling? Can you—can you hear me? Do you understand?'

She was so clear. And beautiful. I could see actual life throbbing through her skin, see it dancing in her black hair. The light behind her made something of a halo around her, all sort of trembling and spangly. I drew my mouth into a hurting smile, a sound wheezing from my hurting throat. I said yes with my eyes.

'Oh my love. My little lovey. You're here. You're alright. It's going to be alright. Don't worry, my lovey, everything's alright. Oh…'

Her hands clutched my cheeks, so painful. And she kissed me, lots of pecking kisses all over my face. I was laughing inside and she seemed to know. Her kisses were joy bumps, felt as if never before had I known what it was to be touched. Her scent vaporised up my nostrils, sweet warm honey—and *yes!*—pancakes.

The air being forced in and out of my lungs was just about suffocating me, disallowing my own natural rhythm. I reached my fingers up to the tube, emitted another wheeze.

'Oh, but of course, of course, I'm sorry, my lovey, let me get—Terry! Terry?—she's—our baby, she's—'

There was all this commotion and I closed my eyes because they ached. I was suddenly tired, realised I ached all over, and I started to drift.

'Sweetheart?' my dad's voice reached in.

I cracked my eyes a slither. He was leaning over me, looked wiped out. I put my hand on his, where is rested on my belly, felt his fundamental nature. He started weeping, body all convulsing.

My uncle came, stood at the end of my bed, the smile on him bright as sunshine. Beside him stood my sister and Stuart. Each of them had these shimmering auras of light around them, all rainbow colours flaring and shifting, kind of like fire, and I understood this had to be the fine line between this reality and the other; the line where energy was translated into physical form maybe, all through my senses; I saw I'd always known this fine line without actually realising it, had known it right in my body and into my being. It was no longer hidden. Life was manifesting out of the infinite void, the underlying bliss, the energy of stillness, of silence beneath and beyond. And I was decoding it. Everyone was.

The doctor loomed in, came around to the other side of my bed. I remembered how grave he'd felt when I was sort of in him, and I flickered my eyes as he stared at me. He asked me to open them, to look at him, asked me to follow the end of his pen, which had a little white light on it, all like a speck of the beautiful light I had left behind, all showing me the song was inside of me. Still. And always. I eyed him as he studied the data on the monitors, bright undulating lines in green and red that marked the wonders of the workings of my body. Every cell has its own consciousness, I thought, and is connected to my supreme energy, is capable of true wellbeing. He looked at the print-out spitting from a machine. Every cell is communicating with my big Self.

I made a grating sound from my throat, touched the tube.

He nodded once, brisk, turned to my parents. 'Her brain functioning looks entirely normal. Her reflexes are working. I've never seen—this is quite unusual. I'm going to switch off the ventilator.' To me, he said, kind of loud and slow, all like I might be thick or foreign or something, 'I'm going to switch the ventilator off. Do you understand? And then once we're sure, we can remove the oxygen supply. I need to monitor your reactions first. This may be uncomfortable. Are you ready?'

I gazed into his eyes, the colour of spring leaves, made a small nod which caused me to gag. He looked confused, concerned; as me, I realised the wonder of physical sensation; saw how in the other realm, this simply was not. My eyes smarted as I tried not to cough.

'Her body seems to have over-ridden the drugs—' he said, clipped-as

'—I've never—' All clamping my forehead beneath his palm, he told me, 'Don't move.' He hesitated, fingers on a small black switch, flicked it—and relief hit as my lungs rose up and then down of their own accord. He watched me for several minutes. My mum and dad watched me. My uncle, my sister, Stuart. And I felt my inner being watching, holding, loving me. I felt myself liquid.

'Okay,' he said, with that nod. And to my mum, 'Hold her head still. I'm going to get the nurse.'

❧

As the sound of a rowdy crowd came bouncing down the corridor and right through the walls, I eased myself to sitting, all using my fists into the mattress. A laugh came up and out of me as the rabble gained in volume. And then the door was flying open. My friends poured through, Stuart at their helm, faces breaking with smiles, a mass of merged hellos and affection chiming out as the sweetest music. They seemed to jump down my visual cortex, enter me, super in-focus, outlined each in a thick band of fizzing light.

'Sorry we're late—' Stuart began.

But was drowned out by a chorus of jokey protest.

Jessie darted from the group, arms ringing around me, warm mouth nuzzling into my neck. 'Oh darling, darlface, it's so good to see you, to feel you.' She drew back to meet my eye. 'Are you alright? Really? I mean, *really*?'

I nodded, saw she was spilling tears, wiped at them with my fingertips. I was aware of how amazing it was to have fingers; in awe of the lustrous feel of her skin and the tears, the lioness colour of her eyes. 'You are beautiful,' I told her. My sights spun out to take in the cluster of wondrous people around my bed, noticed they'd gone all sombre. 'It's okay everyone. Look at me. I'm fine, so fine—I've been restored, see? Never been so fine.'

'You're covered in fucking bruises and bandages and shit,' boomed Eliot. 'There's a fucking great lump of plaster on your leg. You look a mess—a right royal fucking mess—'

'—give our girl a break,' Merl said, a kick in his slipper-soft brogue. 'She's just come out of a coma.'

'You don't say? And she looks it too. You look fucking terrible, Slim, a mess—'

'—*El*iot,' said Jessie. 'Stop it.'

'I haven't given the punch line yet.'

'Well, leave it, you pug. No one wants to be punched.'

He plunged toward me, a softness in his face, his gorse thorns nothing but foam rubber, all leached gold. 'Like you couldn't get a more beau-i-ful mess. Like look at the raw beau-i-ful life beneath the surface.' Jessie was driven back by the force of his forward thrust, and he took me by the shoulders, wet eyes piercing mine. 'I love this girl like no other. We all do. One of a kind. One of a kind. Who else can say they died and came back? Did you go to heaven, did you? Died and went to heaven and came back. Fucking prodigal, that's what. You put us through it, that's for sure. I could just about kill you for it.' He yanked me into a bear hug, my bum lifting up off the bed.

'Ow, oh, ow.'

'You're hurting her,' yelled Merl and Jessie in unison.

'It doesn't matter,' I said, all laughing.

'Grrrrr,' went Eliot, actually jiggling me in his arms.

'Ow.'

'Blimey,' said Todd-baby. 'I've never seen anyone so glad to be in pain.'

'I told you she's gone all elastic,' said Stuart as he squeezed in beneath Eliot, wrapped his arms around the both of us, face up against mine so I was a squashed head between the two of theirs. 'Hey sis.'

'Get a shot of this,' Eliot yelled.

'Ow.' My lifesprung ecstasy was splitting my face.

'Seriously lost it,' said Todd-baby.

'Oi,' said Merl. 'Look at her, she's blissed out on a near-death experience, eh.'

'On the drugs, more like. Huh, baby?'

'No drugs,' I piped.

'Are you getting the shot, or what? Polaroid's in my bag.'

'No drugs?' said Todd-baby. 'Baby's missing the chance of a lifetime.'

'She likes the pain,' said Eliot. 'Life, isn't it, Slimster? Shoot it, someone, or I'll kill you all.'

Laughing still, with tears plopping out, I watched Jessie dive toward Eliot's leather holdall where he'd dropped it on the floor. She extracted the camera, did the maestro's bidding, catching the black polaroid as it spewed from the machine.

'Two more,' said Eliot. 'Side shot. And me and Stu, us face on, Slim sandwich.'

'It's wearing a little thin,' chimed Todd-baby, as Jessie darted around the bed. 'Lost the moment, I think, Eliot baby. Gotta let go. Put the poor girl down, she's crying her eyes out.'

'She loves it.' Eliot shook me some more.

'Ow, ow.'

'Don't you, Slim?'

'I do, I do.' I heard the whirring of the polaroids as they disgorged. 'I do.'

'See? Life,' said Eliot, as he lowered me with enormous tenderness back into the bed. He stood, looked at everyone, beamed as if he'd just birthed me. 'Heavenly.'

Todd-baby and Merl came, one each side of the bed, bent over me, offering kisses, little snatches of shared sentences, all sweet-breathed and gentleness, as if they were one consciousness, so connected they were.

'Where's Jimmy?' I asked.

'Aha! Jimmy?!' Jessie called, her sights flung toward the door. 'Now.'

'Ta-da.' Jimmy stepped into the doorway, a cake on a plate held in his hands. We laughed and gasped, all like he was an actor in a pantomime. The polaroid camera flashed and whirred in Eliot's grasp. There was a ridiculous mound of rose petals, pink and white, piled on top, and as Jimmy moved some flew off, spiralling, glittery, to the floor. 'I made you a cake,' he said. 'With Eliot. Didn't we, Eliot? We made you a cake, a new cake, a lemon cake where we boiled the lemons—'

'—*organic* lemons—'

'—*organic* lemons, yes, see, three of them, big ones, boiled them for whole two hours and then jooshed them up with a whizzy stick thing and we put in two-hundred-and-fifty grams of ground almonds *exactly*—yes, alright Eliot, *organic* almonds—everything organic, see, everyone, yes?—and we put less eggs than the recipe said, just four eggs, and Eliot's special sugar stuff from Brazil, and we cooked it gas mark five for fifty-eight minutes but it said in the book fifty-five minutes or even an hour but we like it a bit more cooked and a bit more moister—so. But not like the wet time when we did forty-five minutes, see. That was eurghh. It was pongy! And we tried it three times and this one's going to be perfection. Four on the floor. We're so glad you're alive.'

Everyone clapped and Jimmy cracked the cutest smile, gliding across the room, rose petals tumbling about him. His aura was bright and spangly. He delivered the cake to my lap.

'Eliot isn't going to get fat again,' he said. 'We've got candles.'

'We figure it's your birthday, Slim. Right, Jimbo?' said Eliot.

The little boy nodded, face grave. 'I cried when no one knew what would happen to you. Everyone was crying. So now you are born on two days ago. Your new-born birthday. We didn't know what to do if you didn't get born again.'

'You want a hug, Jimmy, my darling one?' I reached my arms out. 'I'd really like a hug.'

As he scrambled up the bed, Merl leaned in and grabbed the cake, leaving a spill of petals into which Jimmy planted himself. 'I love you,' he said, little arms around my neck. 'Will you marry me?'

'Yes.'

'Good.' He scridged my cheeks, so my lips puckered up, made a soggy kiss on them. 'Eliot said I have to ask.' He shifted his body, riffled in my lap and held up a clutch of crushed petals, showing them to me close up. The scent was exquisite. And then they were all bouncing off my face. 'From my garden. Can you come back to my house?'

We were all delighting in the swell of elation. I felt it like sweet popping Space Dust on my tongue. 'I will in a while, when I can walk about a bit. I'm going to have to be on crutches.'

He patted my cast. 'Can I write on your plaster?'

'Of course.'

'Great idea, Jimbo,' boomed Eliot.

'Cos Gareth Jacobs broke his arm and he let us write things on it. Is your leg broken, isn't it?'

'It is.'

He nodded, serious. 'Does it hurt?'

'Yes, but I don't mind, see.'

'Oh. Yes. Hurting goes away. Everyone, we can all write her a message on her plaster and when they cut it off, she can keep it. Can I draw a picture?'

'Let's all draw pictures,' said Eliot. 'Flowers.'

'I want to draw me and you,' Jimmy told me.

'Let's all draw me and you,' said Eliot.

'No,' said Jimmy, rubbernecking his giant friend. 'Just me.'

'Whatever you say, boss. I'll draw a camera, actually.'

Jimmy gave him an approving nod, eyeballed me, all smiling. He spread his palms, 'Your sister's here too.' He clapped his hands together, 'Come on everybody. Let's have cake.'

'Cool thinking, Jimbo.' Eliot lunged for his bag, plucking it up with a couple of fingers despite its evident load. The clatter of plates and cutlery played in the air, the sound akin to some outlandish birdsong.

I looked around at Stuart. 'Where?'

'She was on the blue seat,' chirped Jimmy. 'Waiting. I was on the red one. But she went outside for a smoke. She said she couldn't handle this.'

'A smoke? She doesn't smoke.'

Stuart nodded. 'Has for years.'

'I've got a doobie,' said Todd-baby, brandishing a single-skinned skinny spliff.

'A doobie?'

'Pure grass, baby.'

'He's been in lala land,' said Eliot, as he laid small pastel-coloured plates on the end of my bed. 'Doing some pop diva's hair for a crapola video.'

'A pretty wicked video actually, baby. He's just jealous because he didn't get the job.'

'They stole my idea though. I pitched it and they stole it.'

'True,' said Todd-baby. 'Undeniable. Got a light, Merl baby?'

'And watered it down—' Eliot boomed '—hey, man, you can't smoke in here—they ripped the guts out of it. Like they do.' He pulled a rolled-up tea towel from his holdall, wielded it like a gun-slinger, and in a slick move flicked it to reveal a large sharp knife.

The spliff was pinched between Todd-baby's tightened lips. 'Eliot wasn't willing to compromise, huh?'

'Stop talking about me like I'm not here, man.'

'He did his best to make them hate him.' He raised a brass lighter, clicking open the lid, igniting the flame with a sharp stink of gas.

'Todd-baby, man, I'm telling you, that's not cool. Not around me. Not around her. And not in a hospital ward. No—I wasn't fucking willing to piss on my own parade. Their loss.'

'Eliot,' I said, smiling. 'It's alright. Whatever. Who cares what Todd-baby or anyone else does? It's a private room. Just don't let the bugger get to you.'

'He knows it triggers me.'

'You would've been the first to do this in your day,' Todd-baby said, taking a deep draw.

'You're deliberately provoking me, man.'

They eyeballed each other across my bed and we all went silent, watching them. Todd-baby blushed up, his eyes going all kind of dewy. He took the doobie from between his lips. I saw how his lip-skin stuck to the paper, went with it a split second before ripping away, leaving a darkened little crusty line. He tamped out the tip against the shining body of the lighter. 'Shit, Eliot baby,' he said. 'You're right.' He looked at me. 'Sorry, baby. Don't know what—I guess this is more stressful than I realised.' He held his flattened hand over his eyes, all sniffing as tears fell. 'It's so good to see you. I've been so fucking freaked out, baby. I'm sorry guys…I'm sorry…'

We all chorused in about just how okay it all was. Eliot laid the knife on the smooth white sheet, down by my feet, rumbled, 'I'm such a

238

fucking egoist.'

'I love you, baby,' Todd-baby told him, all from his thickened throat.

'I love you too, man.' And they headed for each other and hugged at the foot of my bed.

'Shall I cut the cake?' Jessie asked. 'With Jimmy?'

'Yeah, good call,' said Eliot hoarse-as. 'Jimbo, cut the cake, little dude.'

'First the candles,' trilled Jimmy, pulling a small crushed box from his jeans' pocket.

'Yes, the candles,' Jessie said at the exact same time as Merl, the two of them catching each other's eye and chuckling. 'Jinx.'

'Bum.' Jimmy was crestfallen. 'They're all crumbled up. Look, I broke them.'

'Cool,' I said. 'Even better. They go with my leg. It's a theme, see. Here, pass them here, I'll sort it.' I poured them into the mess of rose petals left in my lap and began picking through them, felt a keen prick of pleasure at their delicate nature and silky form. The white wicks held the broken bits together like joints. 'Let's bandage them.' I unravelled a strip of bandage from my arm as Jimmy craned forward to see the wound.

'Ooh, all your skin is scraped off. Scabby.'

'Friction burns,' said Merl.

'What's that?'

'It's where her clothes dragged against the skin when she crashed, eh?' Merl looked at me. I shrugged. 'And it rips the skin off with such speed it's like burning it. That's why racers wear really tight leathers,' he said. 'A second skin. So it doesn't happen if they have an accident.'

'Does it hurt?'

I nodded, grinning.

'Weirdo,' said Todd-baby.

Jessie, Merl and Stuart joined me in ripping the bandage into skinny strips and we wrapped a candle each, keeping a decent head of wax on them so they could burn. Here, gone, I thought. Where did they go when they burned away, candles? Eliot snapped a medley of polaroids, wowing it up all big, while Todd-baby docked himself next to me, just kind of leaning his shoulder against mine, all sort of blissy.

239

As Jimmy stuck each rescued candle into a dinky holder and poked it through the surface of the yellow cake, he hummed Happy Birthday under his breath.

I caught hold of Stuart's hand. 'Will you go and find her? She should be here for this. I want her to know there isn't a problem. Everything from before, it's finished, over—it doesn't matter. I just want to see her and love her, it's that simple.'

'Sure thing, sis.' He grinned, scooted out of the room.

'Shall we order tea?' Eliot said.

'It's not a hotel,' Merl said. 'I think we have to go down to the cafeteria. I'll go. Who's going to come and help?'

'Me,' said Jimmy.

'Yup,' said Jessie.

Todd-baby stood also, rubbing his forehead. 'I need to pee.'

I watched the four of them exit, enjoying the silent glowing light each was wrapped in, then turned my attention to Eliot, who was all in my face, right up close to me on my bed.

'I want to do a shoot with you all fucked up like this.'

'Of course you do. It's kind of a perfect representation for you, isn't it?'

'Like what? My pain, you mean?'

I laughed, shaking my head. 'There's only one of you too, for sure. You *know* you keep sabotaging yourself, yet you keep sabotaging yourself. Right? Keep creating more pain.'

'I know. It's a pathology.'

'Yeah, but it's not a pathology; seems like you just keep agreeing with it and giving it your blessing, have decided to limit yourself somehow.'

He looked like he was trying to retreat deep into his body. 'Hmmm…'

'See, I think…like maybe you could try looking at things with a bit more ease. Positivity, see?'

'Sounds like hard work. Positive thinking is bullshit anyway. Sabotaging myself is way easier. It's what I know. And maybe I like it, twisted fucker that I am.'

240

I shook my head, grinning. 'Nah, but you wanted that job and it was yours. See, our thinking influences—yeh, see, you just let your old habits—your famous self-proclaimed resistance, huh?—you let that drive what you wanted away, huh? I wish you could see how fantastic you are—really let yourself fly, like love yourself.'

'Aw bullshit, I do. I love myself.'

'You make out like you do but you're constantly getting in your own way, like playing it all arrogant when underneath it—what?'

'Scared shitless. Still fucking ten.'

I reached my hand to cup his shoulder, the strange glory of pain, the physical life of it, racing through my battered muscles. I suppressed a wince, made him look at me. I found myself nodding, whispering, 'She's with you all the time, you know.'

His eyes went kind of hooded. 'Who, Slim? What are you saying? I hope you're not—'

'—*ten*,' I said. 'Yes, I am.'

'This is fucking with my head. Out of order. If you weren't in the state you're in I'd be walking out of here.'

'I know. That's why I'm saying it now. I just want to crack the mirage.'

'It's not your business.'

'I know. I have no right.' There was a long silence, in which he took to picking at his fingernails. 'I wouldn't say this to you if I thought you couldn't hear it, huh?' I told him, gentle-as.

'Shit,' he muttered. 'No one else could say such a thing to me, you know that? Shit. I still miss her, Slim. Am I really defined by my mother fucking off and leaving me?'

'I guess that's up to you. Brutal, but true.'

'Look who's talking.'

'I know. I did it too, for a long time. I clung and clung. And it hurt me. I hurt myself. But look—maybe she didn't "fuck off and leave you"—maybe she's *never* left you…because she is the One Love energy, see? And so are you—if you let it—and you're linked in Love forever. Bob Marley really knew what he was talking about, huh?'

He raised his eyes, the blue of them just about molten. 'Are you saying you actually *really* went to some other place? And what? saw my fucking dead mother there? There isn't such a thing as heaven, we know that's all bollocks.'

I shook my head. 'I didn't see her—well, maybe I did—I don't know. I just know she's with you. And you're right, there is no heaven—*out there*—because see, I'm getting to realise heaven has to be on this Earth—and it's right inside of us. More than that: it *is* us; you are That. Perhaps we can reach ascension without dying, Eliot. A peace state. I'm sure of it. But we have to want it. Like nothing else. And we have to believe. Even when we don't believe type-thing.' I chuckled. 'It's a bitch, but I came back to tell you.'

'Well, so who did you see, then? In your coma dreams? That gives you the right to be so sure?'

'Eliot, you are a funny one. You do know I've just had the most profound experience of my life, right? This is everything we've always talked about, only big-upped ad infinitum.'

'Aw, fuck it, Slim. I'm just very fuck-off envious, is all—I wish *I* could get to die and come back with the knowledge. That's what you've got, isn't it: the knowledge? like a London cabbie?'

'Well, maybe you don't have to die to wake up and remember yourSelf.'

'How would you know? It sure looks easier.'

I stared at him, and he stared back, all intensity. And then we broke into laughter. 'Jessie's right—you're a pug.'

'You saying I'm ugly?'

'Hardly. You're one of my best friends; a part of me in a way I really know about now. You're kind of another me type-thing; and I am another you.'

'Sounds ugly.'

'I'm saying…I don't know…you're a dog with a bone—that won't let go—but won't actually gnaw away at it either—like you're determined to see your old self-limiting, distorted perspectives—like, from your old conditioning, see. Yet you've got it all—' I broke off, feeling a presence in the doorway, looked round to find my sister standing there with a big bouquet of white hyacinths, all like a little lost bride. 'Hi,' I said. 'Oh

242

wow. You're here.'

'I haven't got long,' she said.

'Aren't you coming in?' boomed Eliot.

I gave him a look. 'Wanna go see what's happening with the tea?'

He raised his eyebrows. 'If you say so.'

'I do. Delay them a little, will you? And grab Todd-baby—who's no doubt stoned out of his tree by now, in the gents—take him along.'

He got up, began to turn away, then whipped back and grabbed me up in his arms, all kissing my head. The pain spiralled through my body, spangles erupting behind my closed lids. Letting me go, he caught sight of some expression of this, said, '*That's* the look I want to shoot. Just that—ecstatic pain. There's got to be a realisation—a record, huh?—of such terrible beauty. The bridge between two worlds.'

I watched him go, my sister all shrinking into the doorframe as he bombed past her, her eyes into the floor. I saw how she wanted to run away.

'Sis,' I said. 'It's okay…my god, it's good to see you, it really is.'

'Yeh.'

'Are you going to come in?'

'I should've come alone. I don't know why I listened to Stuart.'

'I've bought us a bit of time.'

'I heard.'

I indicated the vacated edge of the bed. 'Will you…?' She made a nod, face serious. Stood there. 'Close the door, sweetling. Come in.' She did so, then leaned against it. Seemed reluctant to take the few steps across the room to me.

I let the silence lay, just held her in my gaze, and quite suddenly she burst into tears, eyes nailed to the linoleum, face reddening, a gush of incomprehensible words spilling out. I watched her, my mind hushed, felt as if I were a magic carpet sort of rolling out into a gentle emptiness.

'Hey,' I said, words coming of their own accord. 'Hey, it's alright. Everything is working out.'

'You have no idea,' she wailed.

'But I'm here. I'm okay. Better than okay.'

She stopped crying so abruptly it didn't seem real, took a manky

243

tissue from her pocket, scraped it across her eyes and cheeks, blew her nose. 'You really do have *no* idea.' She drew a mammoth breath and marched over, her body all kind of stiff yet sleek. I saw how she had become quite beautiful, her awkward angles disappeared.

'You look amazing. It's like I'm seeing you for the first time since I was fifteen,' I said.

'Well, you've only seen me a few times since then anyway.'

'And just about ignored you, I know. I'm sorry. But now is now and no point in regrets, huh? How about we just let it all go? Be now and forward?'

'Just like that?' she said.

'Just like that.'

'Oh god,' she muttered. 'This is too much. I can't really…' She pretty much dumped the flowers into my lap. 'I don't know if I can…'

I shook my head, all tender feelings souping in my gut. 'There's plenty of time.'

'But they're coming in a minute, your crazy friends. And Stuart.'

'I mean, there's time forever. No rush. We don't have to do it all *now* now. Now is forever always, huh?'

'You're determined to make me feel like your kid sister. Why must you always be so *clever*? And telling me what to do?'

'I don't mean to. I…I just want to show you all the past and everything is—well, passed. I want us to…find our way together somehow.'

She dropped her gaze, nodded, biting her lips. 'But what if we can't?'

'Why wouldn't—I mean, we have the choice.'

'There you go again.'

'You know, I saw you…when I was—I saw you getting on a plane. I felt you, so much grie—'

'—you what? What do you mean, you *saw* me, *felt* me? You just shut up with all your—will you? I mean, what the fuck?'

As she looked up from clenched fists, just flicked her eyes at me really, I held my lips together. She stalked over to the window, stood looking out with her back to me, her aura bleeding into the grey and light of the sky, so I couldn't see it. I got the sense she was crying again and her hand went up all violent, sweeping across her face. I cast my gaze into the pure-white bouquet, each flowerhead a cluster of tightly-packed miniature blooms; they made me think of cow parsley. They made me think of *him*. And him. But I swept the thoughts away. I saw there was a little card tucked amongst them and, glancing at her, I plucked it out, read in her handwriting: *I love you.*

She cleared her throat, and without turning to look at me, said, 'There was something I came to—I wanted to talk to you—but I can't.'

'That's okay.'

'It's not okay. Please don't be saying things like you know everything.'

'I won't say anything.'

She turned, saw I had the little card, a look of shame scudding into her eyes. 'Oh god, I'm…I'm sorry…'

'It's okay.'

'Stop saying it's okay.'

I nodded.

'Look,' she said. 'I have to go.'

I nodded.

'I'm sorry,' she said, bleaty-as. And just fled from the room.

---

The new sofabed they'd bought for me was quite the island, a small dishevelled landscape in which I was lounged with their young tortoiseshell cat purring away in my lap. My mind lay quiet, followed simply her vibrating inner motor, until she sat up, her weight coming through her front paws. She gazed right into me. Her pink tongue flicked out.

'What is it, little one? You want your dinner?'

Her eyes, all golden filaments, narrowed.

'Soon,' I said. 'You'll have to go ask our mama.' I stroked my fingertips through the duckdown of her chest, cupped my hand over her face. She pressed her head there and I felt the exquisite prick of her wet nose, my sights all drifting to the sun-drenched drapes, those green-and-pink curtains I had once felt so persecuted by. The cat tugged her head from my hold, tension coming through her, attention to the door. There came a gentle rap. 'Hello?' I said.

My uncle's face poked into the room, bald head a beacon. 'It's me.'

'Course it is.' Pan leaped away, tail all up, ears back as she hot-footed it around him, slipping through the gap in the doorway before he pushed it to.

We chuckled together. 'Always the animals and you in love,' he said. 'And how is the patient today?'

'Patient.'

'You don't say.' He made a dive-bomb sound as he threw his body into the upholstered sofa back, swung his legs up, let them slap down next to my fat plastercast. 'So?' he said.

'So—what?'

'So *what*?'

I held in a laugh. 'What?'

'You're really asking me: *what*?' We looked at each other, all energy shining in our tethered gaze. The light coming from him had a spread wider than most anyone else's, was vivid, danced in my peripheral vision.

'What's to tell?' I said. 'I can see your aura.'

He fell kind of serious. 'You died, sweetheart. You know that? The parents want me to tell you. The emergency services resuscitated you. It was lucky they got there on time.'

'I didn't know that, no—or maybe I did. I don't know.'

'Without the life support, they said you wouldn't have survived. They were concerned you may  have brain damage. It's a bloody miracle you made it.'

'Well, it just wasn't my time, huh?' I held a pursed smile. 'That's what. Ya get me?'

'That's evident. And a great relief…'

'No but, I mean, it *could've* been my time. If I'd wanted it to be, see.'

'What—hang on—you're telling me you had a choice? I *knew* there was something went on—you had an actual *conscious* choice?'

I shrugged, still smiling. 'I guess…'

'Why are you being vague?'

I shrugged some more. 'I don't know.'

'You don't want to tell your ol' uncle what in the hell went on for you over those three days?'

'I do. It's just difficult. To put into words. It was all wordless, see. Just something like an all-encompassing hum and—'

'—what, like the primordial OM?'

I blew a smile through my nose. 'Yeah, something like that…wow…' my eyes felt spangly. 'Wow, I hadn't…but see, it was somehow also our field of Silence, all at the same time. I think I was in a kind of in-between space—because I was still in my body in some way too. Had to be, huh?'

'Um—fuck, that's out there, it's—but *hang on*—your continuum of consciousness took you into—what? another realm? that you remember?'

I nodded. 'Yeh. And I could translate the wordless into words somehow—from these infinite voices blended into one—all into my kinds of words too, see—full-on wild, it was—like, all the lingo I know from you and my small self-personality type-thing. So it made sense to my little me, huh? I've realised life isn't what it seems. It isn't what I thought it was.'

'This is—this is phenomenal.'

I raised my eyes to his, all kind of light-feeling. 'I know what you meant now, when you would tell me everything is an illusion—I mean I *think* I do. Like, life is maybe a kind of a glorious passing dream our Source energy is having, and the only reality is the Eternal state—yes?— Awareness itself. Hey, do you think there's a kind of agreement we all have: to see and experience this world, this perceived reality, like we do? Like we kind of translate it from vibrations type-thing—from frequencies or sub-atomic particles or whatever? They said something…just as I was pulled back into my body. That must be it, huh?'

'They; this is blowing my brains out. Um, I don't know…I never thought of it like that. To me, the illusion concept has always been more about how the ego mind invents stories and holds onto them and cements us into the limiting ideas in the world of form, prevents us realising our Selves, eh? Something we are called to eventually see through. Can you say a bit more?'

'I can't really—but yeah, that too. For sure that too. Maybe it will come clearer over time. But I'm getting to realise death *has* to be an illusion too, then, see.'

'Yeah, well, makes sense—you continued in consciousness, actually experienced…*fuck* me…'

I nodded, feeling the echoes of it all expanding in my chest. 'It was pure bliss, that's what—just exactly unconditional love. Everything was Love—capital "L"—just like you told me. And I felt myself a part of everything…I mean really, *every*thing—the grass and the trees and the sky—which I knew as all a part of Consiousness, you get me?—and you too—*all* of you, the family, my friends—even the doctor.'

'You-you felt yourself as the Infinite Self?'

'I think that might be what it was.' I looked down into my lap, followed the contours of my raspberry-pink skirt where it rippled over my thighs, the cast. Quiet-as, I said, 'I think I might know what being unconditional truly means now.'

'I'll say; no "think" about it, my lovely.' He breathed deep-as. 'You were *in* us all…it's a confirmation of everything…' He was just about crying.

'I know. Nuts, huh?'

He paused, drew a breath. 'My lovely?' He squeezed my hand, got me to look at him. 'Listen, I'm well into it, this unconditional state of yours, but just for a moment—to come back to this form life of ours—I mean, don't you want to kno—'

'—hey, I'm *not* so sure that sister of yours will be unconditional though—' I jabbed his ribs way too hard '—about your shoes up on the bed, huh? She aint just died and been to heaven, huh? You're risking it, methinks.'

He held his ribs, laughed, didn't shift his feet, and I could see what he was thinking. I wondered along with him why I hadn't let him say. And we sat in silence again for some minutes.

Pan came in, pushing her face to widen the crack in the door, body all slinky as she wound around it. I saw a thick band of cerise-pink light outlining her—the colour exactly like the Eighties crop-top I used to wear when I was a teenager. She jumped onto the bed, made herself into a ball in my lap, her pink light blending with my pink skirt—all so I got to see the non-physical blending with the physical, it looked like—and my heart made a little jolting hop. She got up again, feet taking her in the other direction, rolled herself onto her back, paws up, head to one side, staring into my eyes. I buried my hand in her silken belly. Whispered sweet nothings to her.

'I'm blown away,' he said.

'Me too. But somehow not. I don't know. It was just so natural. Like—of course.'

'Like you knew it all along…'

All nodding, I said, 'Hey, remember that day you told me you were dying, in that fancy-pants restaurant in Wales? you said: "I am that which was never born and will never die"; pretty much that, yes?'

He was nodding in return, spilling a kind of happy delirium. 'I did. I did.'

'Looks like you spoke the ultimate truth.' I raised an imaginary glass. 'Here's to your big-Self-small-self bollocksia, monsieur.'

He showed me his glass in echo. 'To Life,' he said.

'And more life,' I said. 'Because: death-not-death…if it was real.'

'Oh, it was real alright—as real as it gets.'

He took my hand and we sat side by side in simple communion for some while, our two breaths merging into one, like being in step when you walked. 'Wow,' he said. 'I'm having my own bliss experience right now…this is making me very fucking hungry.'

'Me too.'

'Shall I get us something? Toast?'

'Chocolate,' I said. 'And that funny rye bread stuff you like. With manchego. And avocado. Your lashings of olive oil.'

He saluted me. 'Yes, captain.' And just sat there, all eyeing me.

I prepared myself, elbowed him. 'Well…spit then.'

He cleared his throat. 'Yes. I can't leave this, my sweet—it's too weird, even for me. You haven't asked about…' He gave me a significant look, letting his top teeth press into his lower lip, just holding the unsaid name.

I stared at his mouth, shook my head. 'Maybe I don't need to ask.'

'You *can* ask, you know—just how far do you take this letting go?'

I shrugged, smiled, felt a sting to my eyes. 'I'm just doing what feels, I don't know—easiest—I mean happiest type-thing.'

'Still, it's a little odd.' He frowned. 'Even to me, at this point. Kind of extreme. You do know he's alive, right? You know that?'

'I—yes.' Tears started to sprout out of my eyes. 'Stuart said something. Eliot too. But…I don't know, I just couldn't go there for some reason. Like I wasn't ready maybe. And they were kind of angry. And I didn't want that.'

'Well, I want you to know I hold nothing against him. You know, he was completely unscathed. I mean, just a tiny limp, like a sprain. He came to see you…he was devastated.'

'He was? But why didn't he come back? Is he at the flat?'

'I checked. When he didn't reappear. He's gone away. The old lady downstairs told me.'

'Away? Did you check the shop?'

He nodded. 'There was a girl there. She said she was taking care of things but she didn't know where he went.'

'Oh.' My lips were trembling.

'My lovely...' He leaned over and drew me into his arms, my body all awkward, anchored as it was by the cast. Shudders fell into my chest, the tears coming hot and heavy. He let me cry, just holding me, and it felt fucking great, so full of life and relief and allowing…until the gale subsided of its own accord, and he lowered me back into the pillows. I realised I'd been holding back some kind of fear, refusing it, but making it stronger, all like when a judo master used your strength against you if you gave it to him, was able to beat you with your own force. The pain in my leg seemed to subside too.

'What you resist, persists,' he said, articulating what I was trying to work out in my mind. 'You give power to what you push away—or what you *think* you're pushing away, eh?' He smoothed my hair from my face, wiped my cheeks, snipped at my nose with the cuff of his long-sleeved t-shirt as I stared into his eyes, feeling all like a newborn, so open and full of trust. 'Feelings have to be felt, my lovely. So you might re-align yourself to that very place you went. They are your messengers, your guide, you might say. Better, yes?' I nodded. 'You did choose to come back, eh, to have this human experience? So keep on letting it in, why don'cha? Love what is.'

'Magician,' I said, just for the cheek of it.

And he smiled and smiled at me—all so I knew he knew I knew I was doing it all myself. But then he fell serious-as. 'What happened there?' he said. 'Between you? It wasn't just a fluke, the accident, was it? He indicated as much to me. I think he felt to blame. But he wouldn't tell me anything.'

'Where did he go?'

He shook his head, lips bitten. 'I don't know.'

Into my chest, I said, barely audible, 'We saw...'

'What?'

'*Him.*'

I felt his jarring energy. '*Him*?'

'Yes...*him*. Swan Neck. At the races. You do know...? I mean, you *do* realise...?'

'What? Know what?'

'Now he knows everything.'

'But he knew anyway. We went through all that years ago.'

I lifted my eyes, gazed into his, felt a strange sad smile come into my face. 'You really never realised? I thought it was so obvious. He's his son.'

I smashed a green mark across the canvas, just one thick line coming all broken, streaking out of the trashed-up bristles of my brush, and straight away you could see how it was all one and many at the same time. I stood looking at it, brush loose in my hand. I stood a long time. The blur of green cut a run across the field of starry blue flowers I had been perfecting for some weeks, gave the sense of velocity, of something out of control, yet kind of in control, because there was a choice involved. Pearls of green fell from the brush, plap plap plap, onto the floor. And then I was yanking up the leg of my pants, planting my bared knee into the wet paint, pressing hard with a rocking motion. As it dropped, my leg drew a downward smear from the circular swirl of my knee print. I placed the brush across the open tub of grass-ish green—an emerald pigment all mixed into white water-based house paint, my colour making style, see—and took up a smaller brush, prising open the lids of two of my indigo-blue hues.

Letting the paint of the first soak way into the tip, I wiped off the excess against the leg of my khaki overalls, swept two alive flashes into

252

the circular swirl, then one with the lighter hue. I inserted several glints of red. There came a sweet expanding sensation in my chest as I dunked the green brush and let it fly again—one-two-*three!*—across the ground of flowers, all cracking and splitting the image, but making you see the flowers in a more focused aware kind of a way.

I sat before the painting in my vinyl armchair, sat a long time, looking at what had come out of me; feeling myself in it, a part of it, un-separate. I was aware of the paint drying, of the late November light falling in the room. A blackbird played its flute outside, sounded like it was all inside of me too. And as it descended, I relished the space between light and dark, when everything went almost colourless; a vivid world almost not there.

I went to the kitchen without turning on the lights, made myself a cup of nettle tea, the green of it, almost black anyway, all ebony-black in the shadowy now. I didn't turn on the heating yet, and still in my baggy painting jumper, army boilersuit tied at the waist by its arms, I scudded down the long skinny corridor, guided by the golden tint of city-bright leaking into my windows. I went and stood, all hugging my cup in fingerless gloves, gazing down at the floodlit Natural History Museum and the many people still milling in the gardens and at the entrance, wrapped up in winter garb.

At the sound of the key in the lock, I turned smiling, said, 'Don't turn on the light.'

He laughed, said, 'Awesome.' And threw his knapsack right by the door, lolloped over, put his arm around my shoulders, all drawing me into him. 'A good day, then?'

'Yeh.'

'Can I see it?'

'Yeh, in a bit.' I indicated with my chin. 'Just look at the life shining from everything, everyone. You can see it just emanating, all tender somehow.'

'*You* can see it.' He took my tea and slurped on it. 'Yeah, my day was pretty good too, sis.'

I chuckled. 'Oh, so how's you then?'

'Pretty good an' all. The meeting with the record company was—for real, superb.'

'I knew it would be.' I sipped the tea from his hold on the cup, felt all childlike as it dribbled down my chin. 'You going to do more recording tonight? I'm done in there—so it's all yours.'

'Yeah…I want you to do that out-of-tune humming thing again for me.'

'Are you still saying I can't sing?'

'I'm saying I love it.'

'That I don't have a musical bone in my body?'

'And I want more of it. It's very…innocent…and almost taboo in context. You can't manufacture such off-key tone—you either have it or you don't.'

'You teased the fuck out of me when we were teenagers, huh?'

'It's quite moving, sis. And unexpected. And it really works. So, will you?'

'Yes, of course.'

'They're booking me into the recording studio next week. It's going to take a couple of months, we reckon, in all. I've told them I want a little more time before, but they're kind of pressuring me. Impatient. All this stuff about timing with a second album.'

'Did they listen to your demos?'

He nodded, velvety-as. 'For serious, all kind of tripping out they were. Even if I say so myself.'

'Well, I think you're ready too. You always want a little more time, don't you? But I reckon you don't want to overwork things. Part of your talent is the raw thing you do.'

He nodded, attention going within himself, a frown coming, then met my eyes with a livewire energy. 'Hey, I'm thinking it would be awesome to do a single recording on each song, huh, just one take, all like the old days? Just have everyone pure and in the moment, really alive and connected. Wouldn't that be great? With the sound of the room, the space and all.'

I nudged him, raised my eyebrows at him. 'In the moment, eh?'

'Yeah, yeah…how'd you get to be so funny?'

We stayed fixed to each other's eyes, sunshine all spilling out. 'So…?

Have you talked to them about it?'

'I didn't quite realise,' he said, his wild long hair all glinty blacks as he shook his head. 'It's really only just come to me, when you said about my raw thing. I kind of knew it, but hadn't articulated it to myself…'

'I think it's the perfect idea.'

'Okay, so I'll call Larry and get him to set up another meet in the next few days, tomorrow if they can. They're a bit bloody controlling, mind, probably won't want me to.'

Risking annoying him, I said, 'If that's what you put out, that's what you'll likely get back, huh, my darl? Better to put your attention on what want; not what you *don't* want, huh? Ya get me?'

He lit right up, all in the zone. 'Yeh, I get it. You get—you actually *grow*, huh?—yeah, you grow what you think about, it's true, I'm seeing it for myself these days. You line your energy up with what you want— and it's like a fricken superpower.'

'Hark on him,' I said, all as if to someone else.

He swigged my tea, drained the cup. And next thing, he was grabbing me by the hand, pulling me down the corridor and into our studio, doing an impersonation of the raspy little hum I had unintentionally come up with for him.

'You see?' he said. 'I can't do it. It's un-copyable.'

'I can.' I hummed his melody and inside my own head I couldn't hear it the way it came out. 'Sounds well in tune to me.'

'Arghh,' he said, face screwing up like he was handling physical pain. 'It's positively angelic. It about breaks my heart. In the best way.' He was turning on the power to his recording equipment, flicking switches. 'Yes!' he trilled, glancing at me. 'I got it—*that's* what I'm calling the song: Positively Angelic. There you go, who was to know having the worst voice *ever* would turn out as perfection? Come on, get over here.'

꧁ꕥ꧂

The buzzer sounded, throaty-as, and Stuart and I gave each other a look, all sort of spirally energy merging. He went to answer it while I continued to lay the table. I heard him call out, picturing him leaning over the mahogany handrail of the communal stairwell, heard their voices chiming in response and before long, made out the thudding of their footsteps on the wadded carpet. They greeted him outside the flat, all heavily puffing breaths, and then came the clack of shoes on our wooden boards. I turned, headed down the corridor to meet them.

'My little love,' my mum said, panting still. 'What a lot of stairs. No wonder you couldn't…until you… Oh, but you look *so* well.' She hugged me, checking out my flat over my shoulder: 'What a lovely place, so much sunlight blazing into the living room. That *is* the living room, yes? Shall we go in?'

'For sure.'

'Shall we leave our coats here?' She indicated the loaded coat hanger on the wall. 'What a lot of—won't they fall off?'

Stuart proffered his hand. 'Here, let me. There's a technique.'

'Thank you, my lovey. Well, you are looking well, the both of you. A bit too well.'

'You said,' he said.

'Well I'm saying again. And I expect I'll say…again and again. You young people constantly amaze me.'

'Yeah, cos you're so old now, these days, Mater.'

'The nerve of you.'

'You said it.' He kind of chucked her chin. I felt a small swell of wonder, something infused with a gnats of envy. 'You should watch what you say, you know. Power of thought and all that.'

She laughed all girlish, took a hold of his hand, said something about his pluck, led him off down the narrow hall. As they freed space, my dad sloped toward me, tall slim frame bowed, greased hair falling over his face. 'One hundred and two.' His breath was entirely settled.

'Wow, you don't look it,' I said 'Impressive.'

'Stairs, you funny—keeps you fit, I expect. Good therapy for that leg of yours.'

'Which is completely better—isn't that great? I told you I wouldn't have a limp, whatever they said.'

'Already? Isn't that rather fast?'

'Yeh, they call it an anomaly; I call it…something to do with allowing—um, peace and wellbeing and all that, see.'

He sort of hugged me, patting my back a bit too hard, the way he did. 'Good girl.'

'So are you going to give us a grand tour?' my mum called from the living room, as if Stuart wasn't right next to her. 'I've got to use the loo first.'

Stuart and I pointed. 'Door at the end,' we said in unison, catching each other's eye.

I clocked how she looked at the closed bedroom door as she hit the hallway and how her head craned to peer briefly into the visible slither of studio as she went on down the corridor. 'Ooo,' she said.

Stuart swung into me, whispered, 'Lucky I cleaned it,' and the two of us just about withheld our mirth, vibing into the whole conversations we'd had, me not feeling it was necessary to put on a show, him insisting we give them the best possible window into our living arrangements.

My dad just stood there, so I said, 'You look fit yourself. Still with the cycling?'

'Yes. Keeps me busy.'

My laughter bubbled. 'Come on—you love it. And why not? You're allowed.'

I was surprised when he laughed right back, saying, 'I do, love. I really do. Well, it *is* good to be here.'

The three of us were still all kind of laughing and saying easy little nothings when my mum rode up, her face splitting a grin. 'What's so funny?'

'Kind of nothing,' I said.

'Little squirts of life,' said Stuart.

'His new song,' I said.

And my dad went, 'Riding through the glen.'

'Lovely and clean,' said my mum. 'Exemplary.' And me and Stuart went sinking into each other, my dad wiping at his eyes, my mum joining in. 'I really don't know what's funny.'

'This *is* nice,' said my dad.

'Shall we eat, then?' Stuart said. 'Are you hungry? We've made a

257

roast.'

'A roast. Yes, I can smell it. How lovely. Smells wonderful.'

'Stuart's the cook, mostly,' I said. 'But I made Eliot's almond and chocolate cake for afters.'

'Eliot?' said my mum. 'Now, is he the big wild one? With the booming voice?'

'Yes.'

'Terrified me,' said my dad.

Stuart and I laughed, me saying, 'You *do* know Stuart went to that boarding school with him? Before he went to the home and came to us?'

'With *him*?' my mum said. 'But isn't he rather older?'

'He was then,' said Stuart.

'And he made friends with you, a little boy? Isn't that rather odd?'

'Ma,' said Stuart. 'He's an awesome friend. He was then and he is now. He took care of me back then, when I had no one.'

'And Stuart made him feel understood, didn't you Stuart? Something like that. They saw themselves in each other—that's what Eliot told me.'

'I love him,' said Stuart.

'*We* love him.'

'Oh. Lovely.'

'Terrified me,' said my dad.

'So…the tour? Before we eat?'

'I don't see a similarity at all,' my dad said. 'Couldn't be more different…'

'Shall we start with the studio?' I said.

'…your physique, everything. His whole countenance. And I mean, does he *sing*?'

'Like a lark,' said Stuart.

'Like a lion,' I said.

'Your dad hasn't seen the living room yet,' my mum said. 'And I stole a quick peek at the kitchen. Very nice, my lovies. Very clean.'

'A lion, yes,' my dad went on. 'I can see that. I don't know about his making cake. I just can't imagine him doing a thing like that. I can't imagine him cracking an egg. You're the lark, Stu, my lad, you're the lark.'

'Maybe *you* kind of are,' I said. 'I'm not sure I've ever heard you say so much.'

'You want to see the living room first, Terry?'

'That's alright, dear,' he said. 'I'll get to it. Yes, do let's see this studio of yours, love.'

'Ours,' said Stuart.

'Of course, Stu, that's what I meant. The both of yours.'

We led them into the studio, me explaining about the boon of the northern light for painting, and how lucky we were to be backed onto the French lycée. I showed them the huge expanse the playground provided out the window, the relative privacy, while Stuart got to waxing about the oftentimes hum of the schoolyard and how he'd recorded the chatter, the laughter and screams, for one of his tracks.

They stood looking at my couple of paintings on the wall, the blue speedwell one and a new one I'd started only yesterday. 'So that's flowers,' said my dad, leaning in to get a close-up look. 'Very well done. You just painted over them though...what a shame. What's this red? And what's this other one? Some kind of birds?'

'Seagulls,' my mother said. 'Beautiful, my lovey. Such life about them. Are you going to keep them soft-focus like this, just part-formed? Or will you get more literal?'

I glanced at Stuart, my heart threading to his. 'I didn't know you knew about painting.'

'Oh yes, I used to love going to the galleries. And I did like painting myself, as a girl.'

'You did? I never knew.'

'Ah, there's a lot you don't know.'

'Wicked,' said Stuart. 'Did you sing too?'

'A bit. I was in the choir, you know. But come on, do let me in on your intentions, seeing as I'm lucky enough to be seeing it at this early stage.'

'Yes...I'm wanting them to be more of a feeling, an energy,' I said. 'Like you say, part-formed. Rather than exact. As if in the moment of manifestation, part here, part...there...you know...'

She nodded, absorbed in my images. 'Yes...well, that's what I'm getting. Visceral life coming through. And yet one can know exactly what they are. Marvellous to see this in process.' She turned her attention to the first painting, moved her hand in rhythm with the speeding green blurs. 'I rather like them, these paint marks. You capture some unsayable force of nature, of movement. They seem to be splitting, I mean, breaking up, but at the same time it's one force, one impetus.'

'Exactly,' I said. 'Just totally exactly.'

She stood almost trance-like, all transfixed by the painting, turned, eyeballed me. In a low voice, she said, 'It's your crash, isn't it? Is it?' I saw how her face had turned pink, saw she was welling up, a tear slipping unheeded down her cheek. 'I can't believe how you can make something so terrible look so beautiful, love.' She pinched her nostrils between finger and thumb, turned back to the work, her shoulders working to hold in her surge of emotion.

'Maybe it wasn't terrible,' I said gently. 'And maybe this painting is lots of things at once, other things…too. Another thing…that made an impact.'

'Yes. Yes, I understand. The many layers of—what did you say, Stuart? little squirts? *big* squirts maybe, in this case—yes, big squirts of life. Encapsulated. You're really very good at this. I'm very impressed. You have an instinct for it and—' And then she was bawling, sort of held in and releasing at the same time, a freedom in her that struck me as beautiful and fragile and present in a way we none of us were used to. 'Impact,' she murmured. 'Oh god, yes…impact…'

We others were silent, moved with her each in our own way, yet letting her be. She came and hugged me, and Stuart came and hugged us both. My dad stood nodding, his face flushed, quite youthful-looking.

'And what about your acting?' he said, as we broke apart. 'She's really very good at that too. Aren't you, love? And I do enjoy watching you. Proud, it makes me feel. You used to tell us it was your life.'

'I don't know,' I said. 'It's not my life anymore. I mean, nothing is, see, except…discovering an ever-deepening inner—um, awareness type-thing and—'

'—but haven't they come back to you on that Hollywood movie?'

'They re-cast it in the end. They had to. They couldn't wait for my leg. They've shot it. It's fine; I don't mind, honestly.'

'And the director definitely wants to work with her,' Stuart said. 'He fucking loves her.'

'Stuart,' my mum said, giving him a faux sharp look.

'Soz.'

I snickered, my dad my echo.

'Well if your painting makes you happy and you can support yourself, that's wonderful,' she said to me. 'You *can* support yourself?'

I nodded. 'I'm kind of loaded, I had such a run of it. What with the film I made before. And that big commercial too.'

'Her film's coming out in January,' Stuart said.

'It is?'

'And the commercial deal went worldwide. Including America. Massive.'

'I didn't know that. Did we, Terry? We saw it on the telly, of course.'

'Very nice,' my dad said.

'I could buy another flat with the buy-out,' I said. 'If I wanted. And Stuart's doing incredible.'

'My new deal is pretty out there.'

'Gosh,' said my mum. 'Who'd have thought? All this art and success coming out of our little household. Isn't it wonderful?' She crossed the room, went and stood by Stuart's home-spun mini recording studio, just looked at all the equipment with a glowing smile, all like it was his actual work.

My dad joined her. 'Very good.'

'Wonderful.' She was still sniffing.

Stuart said, 'Hungry?'

'Rather,' said my dad, all like a posh English school boy.

'What-oh,' I said.

'You know,' came my mother, looking at me all starry. 'If you hadn't nearly—erm—well—how *awful*—but if you hadn't nearly *died*, lovey…I get the feeling we wouldn't all be here like this. Together. Laughing. We probably wouldn't have come here at all. You wouldn't have let us, would you? I can't believe I can think this, but it seems it *was* a—a good thing, you know, I mean the result of—I mean, I understand what you've

261

been saying now, lovey—it seemed like a madness at first, and after all the terrible stress—I mean, it was terrible but…' She sighed.

'Yes,' I said. 'Thank you.'

She looked at Stuart. 'Are you going to play us something, love?'

'In a bit. I'm starving.'

'He's been cleaning all morning,' I said.

'Shh,' he said.

'He always was a good kid,' my mum said. 'You always were, Stuart.' As we headed back into the hallway, she said, 'Oh, do let's see the bedrooms first, shall we? Finish the tour?'

'This way,' Stuart said, and swung the bedroom door open, sunlight splashing onto us. 'There's only one bedroom.'

'Only one?'

'Yes.'

We clustered at the threshold. Stuart and I shared a look and I knew what he was telling me and shook my head.

'It used to be my second bedroom, my painting studio, when I lived here wi—before the crash—but we had to make my old bedroom into the studio to make room for both of us to work. And because I'm working bigger now. It's just too small in here. And the light, you know…And we wanted to keep the living room clear and the bedroom clear, separate the spaces for clarity of focus and reflection and relaxing and that.'

'But what? You both sleep in here? In that one bed?'

I nodded. 'We've always done it. I mean, when we were teenagers and we…you know—when we lived in the squat—we shared a bed. There's nothing to it, honestly.'

'Well, it's a bit weird, isn't it, however arty you are. Two grown adults sharing a bed. I mean, sister and brother. And that bloody squat.'

My dad split off, disappeared into the living room.

'We're not *doing* anything, if that's what you mean.'

She looked at us, one to the other. 'I suppose not. Couldn't one of you sleep on a sofa bed? That one we got you at home is very comfortable. Probably more comfortable than that old bed, by the looks of it.'

I laughed. 'We like a lumpy mattress.'

'Playing the bohemians, still? Despite owning your own flat and having all this money, huh? Why don't you rent a studio elsewhere?'

Stuart put his arm about her and she tensed, I saw how he felt it, red bleeding into his face. 'We decided to be honest with you, Mater. I wanted to tell you I slept on the sofa. But we're not into lying in any way at all. I knew you might freak out.'

She cleared her throat. 'I'm not freaking out.'

'Well, be freaked out then.'

'Yes, well, it is a bit of a shock. It's not exactly what you do, is it? I mean, it's not normal.'

I shrugged, smiling. 'What's normal? Who cares about normal anymore?'

She swivelled, taking the several steps to the coat hanger, tugged at a sleeve. A rain of coats fell at her feet but she didn't seem to notice, just brandished the old black leather biking jacket as if it was contaminated. 'And who's is this? It's *his*, isn't it? That ex-boyfriend of yours who nearly killed you and just disappeared like quicksilver, the little bastard. This is *not* good. To have this here. What are you doing, my girl?'

My body seemed to radiate out of itself, get really big and beyond me, then snap back, all contracted to a frenzied buzz of energy in my bones and in my ears.

Stuart said, 'You just said what a good thing it was, how we wouldn't be this close if it hadn't hap—'

'—*no*, this is horrendous, it's disturbing. This attachment to a man who clearly doesn't care. Of course it wasn't a good thing.'

'But you said you guys wouldn't even be here if he hadn't—and they—'

'—*oh*, so I've just got to accept that my daughter has a dysfunctional attachment to some murdering cowboy she—'

'—she does not—it's not like tha—'

'—she *clearly* has a man problem. It's obsession happening all over agai—'

'—shit, Mater, why are you—'

'—it's *alright*, bro,' I cut in.

'No,' he said. 'It's not.'

'*Alright*?' she said. 'Are you out of your mind, my girl?'

263

In one swift movement, he slid across to her, grabbed a hold of her shoulders in a way I would never dare. She made a kind of whimper as he thrust his face into hers. He held her eyes in silence for some kind of an age, and then, with astonishing gentleness, he told her, 'Mater, you've got to let it go. You have to let her be who she is this time. You have to let her be free.'

Her face kind of fell out of focus. She shrugged him off and stepped over the mess of coats, the jacket all leading her, like it was a dog tugging on a lead. Raising her gaze to mine, she said, 'Yes. Yes, of course. I don't know what…here, take it.' I did so. 'I don't know what…I'm just very worried…I think you should think about therapy…I think you're carrying trauma…'

'It's alright…' I said.

'I think we underestimate the power of our trauma. Will you at least think about talking to someone?'

'Yes, okay.'

'You and that renegade brother of mine, you act as if you've been on some kind of *God* odyssey. I mean, *really*, you're like a couple of freakish born agains…'

My dad appeared in the living room doorway. 'So shall we eat?'

We all of us looked at him like he was nuts.

And then he said, 'Quite a time of it, huh? But what a lot of love.'

Emitting some kind of a cockeyed giggle, I shot a look at Stuart, glanced at my mum.

'Are you alright, love?' she said to him.

'Well, it *is* all love, isn't it?' he said.

᪥

His tugging breath came loud, all in harmony with my own—we two, hurtling into the watery sunshine, December's gasp gnawing into our cheeks, ploughing right into our lungs. My hips danced up on springy legs, weight pressing into him, me leaning over his blonde-maned neck in a kind of joyous arc. Everything was fly-by in my periphery, all smeared browns into blurred whizz of green, white fence lines flickering like frames in a silent movie—me rushing inside, outside, blood rushing, hair rushing, riding hat just about keeping me capped inside my body. I felt my heart as a blooming rose; in it contained the world, the Universe, my past and future, every him—and him—and *him*—every shooting birthing moment of my life. Condensed into now.

I rode my Angel's Neck back to the yard on long stirrups, all laidback in the saddle, body rocking to his loose and easy gait, was met by Sam, my sister's golden Greek god of yore turned into just a guy, his blessèd hair all threadbare. He didn't have any spots anymore and he was married with a little kid and a baby on the way, had become my uncle's barn manager.

'Hey you,' he said in greeting, Cork accent soft and splendid. 'Good ride, yeh? Shall I call one of the lads to take him?'

'Don't worry, I'll take care of him myself.'

'Did your uncle tell you we've confirmed yet another stud booking this morning? Aurora, coming in February, from California. Real amazing. They're keeping her under lights at the moment.'

'He sure did. Awesome. Come on, Angel,' I said to the horse, barely needing to signal. 'What a champion you are.'

An image bled over my now reality, him just born, that dear little body laid in the glittering straw all damp from his mother's womb, my hands running over his entirety, desensitising him, all except at that essential point of contact with his flanks. Petite Feuille was still going strong at twenty-three. I realised I never knew who had sired my Angel's Neck—apart from a swan.

He was retired from racing, of course, was now fourteen, had been the biggest success in his day, and there was high demand for him at stud. The mare coming from California was prestigious and Sam was buzzed for sure. I jumped down from my darling at the entrance to the stables, led him to his stall, where he drank a good draft of water before I rubbed him down. As my hand skimmed over his shoulder I got the feeling of a slight tightness, remembering I'd had the sense of it when we'd begun to run. The feeling had dissolved within seconds, transformed to fluidity and all the humming we'd shared, but now I realised it wanted a bit of attention.

When I emerged back into daylight, I sought out Sam, told him about it. 'I'll get Jerry to take a look,' he said. 'You've always had quite the instinct for these things.'

'It's nothing serious. It's more of an alignment thing, really. I think he might just need a bit of a lean in his workouts. It'd make him run better. He'll be more comfortable. Just a slight habit in the muscles he's picked up from somebody.'

'His optimum health is tantamount.'

I grinned. 'Yeah, what with his racy vocation these days, huh?'

He laughed. 'Hey, you wanna grab a pint in a bit, before I push off home to the family? Be good to catch up.'

'Sure. But mine will be a single malt.'

He chuckled. 'Not cider then?'

'I recall it was you that was into the cider.'

'True…you didn't really want to come that time, did you?'

We held each other's gaze. I said, 'Sam, it was a long time ago.'

'For sure it was.'

'But you know it was my sister who liked you really…'

He smiled, all to himself mostly, all sort of inside, and I felt a resonance of sadness within him. 'Yeah…that sister of yours. She kind of ruled me for a while there—when she was living here those couple of years.'

'Oh, so you mean…you…you two…before you were with your wife?'

He nodded. 'She was *some* filly. Something wild in her I could never get to grips with. She got to me there for sure.'

I felt I'd gone kind of crimped inside, stumped by this idea of my sister, by the realisation I didn't know her at all. Wild? I thought. When was she ever wild? I felt like she'd pocketed my turf, a shard of anger gripping, beginning to run—when *whew!* I saw what an arse I was being—laughed out loud at myself with a whole lot of affection in it, all like Jessie was laughing along with me. My heart rushed with a sense of forgiving myself—and Sam—yes, and my sister too—and the whole situation—and my small little ego-self for sure gave way. I saw with

266

stunning clarity this reaction, this self, wasn't even really me; the supreme thread of my life force giving me to think instead how amazing this was, this great surprise, my sister's story—which wasn't really her either. And I saw Sam was a whole lot more than just a guy too.

He was beet. 'Not that I'm bothered. Anymore. Of course.'

'Oh. I'm not laughing at you, honestly I'm not. I just—I just never knew my sister had any wildness in her. At all. She was always such a proper kind of a girl, all good, you know, when we were young. I didn't even realise I had boxed her into a bunch of ideas. So thank you for saying.'

'Well, I wouldn't want to let her down. Perhaps I shouldn't have said anything. Just don't be telling her I said so, will you? I mean, I'm sure she never gives me a second thought but…sure, she was quite the starry filly.'

We sat cross-legged, eyes closed, each in our own space of allowing, at the same time aware of a connectivity the sharing of the meditation accented; our two breaths, which at first had been separate, were now indistinguishable. An expansive field of silence opened up in my body, coming kind of light, and I felt how I fell inward, which was somehow *outward*, way beyond the boundaries of my form. I got to feel this body was a gateway to the all I AM. Light shifted and played in constant motion behind my lids. The still point opening and growing larger. I felt myself both the motion *and* the still. The energy of my inner body buzzed and vibrated; my outer body felt weightless, almost not there.

A wordless voice entered the silence, my own voice, yet not mine. It told me I was on the right path, I could never leave my path—because my path *was* me. It was a pathless path; I was already there. And it told me, Things may not be as they seem—stay open, accept, allow all that comes—you will get what your life is asking for. You can never get it wrong. It is perfection in its unfolding…

My breath deepened, layers of resistance I hardly knew existed melting away, and then I was falling further into the bright void: no body, no thought, just simple harmonious Awareness; joyful surrendering to forever expansiveness, the never-ending outer bounds, the not-aloneness, the remembering of who I really am, true Being; there were stars, the milky way, super novae, swirling galaxies.

It might have been an hour, could have been minutes, when I whistled back into bodily sensation, triggered by the sound of my uncle beginning to move. His clothes whispered, a joint clicked. He drew a breath of his own making. I could feel the sweetness within him, as I felt that same within me.

We linked our gaze, silently expressing the rapture of the unified field, then he nodded and we rose from our stout cushions, left the room together to go down the corridor and into the outside.

The air was biting in the shadow of the house. Seeking a scarf of tender sunshine to wrap about ourselves, we stood some time, ingesting the falling-away vista of heathland in its winter glory, all sort of silvery greens and the dusky heather blurring the contours of the hills, so they seemed to be wearing furs. The sunshine painted its fringes of gold into my eyelashes, lit up my vision.

I saw him then, that first day we had arrived together in Ireland, he was right there, standing in the gravel, staring out, was turning, saying, *what a magnificent view*; and right on his tail came his shadow, all getting off of his yellow dirt bike, cowboy legs crunching toward me. I tried to push him away. I tried to push *him* away. But all they did was keep on coming, as if with more insistence. Another slew of silent wet fell from inside me, heat of me coming down my cheeks, turning cold on my bitten skin. I had to just let the whole thing be; it was all I could do. Let the expression through me in kindness. Be true to something that in this moment of love hurt.

I gave way to a sigh, felt my uncle looking at me. He smiled, drew me into him and I followed his lead, focused myself up into the navy-blue sky. There were wispy bands of clouds, all like egg whites straight off a whisk, ephemeral, in movement, shapes morphing and disappearing and manifesting again. The air grew colder, our sunshine wrap falling away before we knew it. The feel of the cold had its own wonder—when you let it. We shivered and chuckled, emitting our first vocal hums, continued to stand arm in arm as the sun descended, sending into the clouds bright epiphanies of gold and pink, this reflecting into the furry landscape, so the world was gilded transcendent-as.

❦

Standing on the quayside, murky water lapping against the metal hulls of boats like buildings so huge you could hardly believe they were floating, we gripped our collars up around our throats, eyes slitted into the wind, all watching a colourful stream of passengers disembarking the newly docked ferry. We sought his form among them—the flow becoming a trickle, then no one, then the uniformed staff beginning to filter onto the shore. More than once, my uncle suggested he wasn't coming, perhaps it was time we left…? But I shook my head, puckered my smile.

'He'll be here. He said he would. I know he's here.'

The layered grey sky weighed heavy on the scene, all eating everything up, sensual and compelling, like some kind of a Turner painting, unworldly luminosity calling upon your heart. He stamped his feet. 'It's very fucking freezing. I hope he's going to pay for the damage.'

'He'll pay. He likes to pay.'

'I'm talking about my toes here.'

'Yeah…' I studied him, my eyes sparky. 'Where's your faith?'

'Ha. In my pocket.'

'Well, put it back in your soul.'

'My soul? *Ar-se-hole*,' he said, raising his eyebrows at me. '…is what your friend just might be.'

'Yes. Very up his street. You're going to get on, alright. It's going to be love, for sure. Just pocket your toes, then, and give him the frozen little jimmies when he appears.' I got a whiff of him then, turned to catch him disgorging the ferry with a small young woman in uniform tucked under his arm. 'There he is, the bugger. I told you. Check him out, he's picked up one of the staff already.' I waved. 'Eliot!'

My friend's smile just about ripped his face apart, all big noise erupting out of him as he picked up the woman like she was a fluffy ginger dog, tore toward us, her all laughing and bouncing against his bag. She looked like she was drunk and I had a moment when I thought he might have fallen foul of himself, realised they were just high on each other and I wondered what they'd been doing that had created such a delay…knowing exactly what they'd been doing, that they'd been under the influence of the dense sky, in whose body I quite felt a wish to requite myself too.

My uncle pipped me, said, 'Waiting for a mate with a new crush, having it away in some dingy cabin, is not my idea of a polite reunion.' Eliot placed his hook-up neatly onto her clicky heels, grabbed a hold of my uncle and the two of them shared a massive slappy kind of a hug, a great deal of laughter emanating from them.

'You're like ice,' boomed Eliot warmly. 'Wonderful to see you again, man.'

'Great to have you here. We would've left ages ago if it was up to me.'

'Slim,' he said, stooping to encompass me in his large frame. 'Another freezing mortal. Were you seriously early or something?'

'Hell yes. Like, what else would we do?'

He jabbed his thumb over his shoulder at me, said to my uncle, 'Who *is* this chick?'

My uncle indicated his shaggy dog. 'Who is *this* chick?'

'Oh yeah…meet Amber. Isn't she the bollocks?'

The young woman laughed. 'He's a riot.'

'So?' said my uncle. 'Talking of seriously *late*…shall we get going?'

Eliot turned to his diminutive redhead, 'It was good while it lasted.'

'Very,' she said.

'You want my number?'

She shrugged, still with the big grin. 'Why not?'

'Why not?' he boomed.

'Sure.'

'But you're not going to call. I get it. Let's not go there.' He bent, picked her up and flattened her against him like a cloth doll. 'I like your

270

style—you're a bit fucking on it—we're not a project and would probably—*definitely, for sure*—hate each other in any other context.' He put her down and she grinned up at him. He tapped her bum. 'Go on, then. I like to see a woman walk away.'

She tapped his bum back, said, 'Arsehole.'

'Spot on,' said my uncle.

And off she waggled, never looking back.

'God, I'm a sucker for a girl in uniform,' Eliot told us.

'This is news to me,' I said.

'I like the way you can't tell anything about her, can't make any judgments via her dress, like she could be just about anybody.'

'I don't bide with that,' I said. 'Longer than a few seconds.'

'You mean, *a*bide.'

'Sounds kinky to me,' my uncle said.

'Or I suppose you could say "bide",' Eliot continued, 'in a free-base kind of a way.'

'Ah,' I said. 'I knew that girl was a kind of a drug for you.'

Eliot eyeballed me, his breath stoppered. 'Oh man. Oh Slim. God, am I that fucked?'

'You? Fucked? But of course. Isn't that what just happened?'

He slid his hand over his face, rubbed it vigorous-as. 'Am I still seeking solace? Obliteration? Fuck, do I still hate myself that much?'

'Eliot,' I said, all gentle. 'I'm not criticising you. I shouldn't have put it that way. It's just when you said—'

'—"free-base", I know. Bit of a wanger, I know.'

'Hey,' said my uncle. 'You were just having a good time with someone, what's wrong with that?'

'Quick fix,' he said.

'So you got a little high. You didn't hurt anyone; you didn't hurt yourself. I wouldn't consider that akin to losing your sobriety.'

'I'm the one who made the clanger,' I said.

'Unless…' my uncle said. 'Unless you're a sex addict?'

'Blimey,' I said. 'This is all a bit thick and fast. Hardly in Ireland and it's all kicking off already.'

Eliot eyeballed my uncle. 'I love this man. Nothing's too fast for me.

Straight in with the arrow.' He slapped at his heart, acting up the spike there, flashed a vast grin, shook his head. 'But nah.'

'Anyone but Eliot would be doing an about-turn and scarpering back to the boat,' I said.

'A *love* addict?'

'Whoa…I dunno. I mean, like, aren't we all? Love addicts?'

'And what did you mean, you like to watch a woman walk away?' my uncle said. 'You like to watch their ass? Or you like the pain?'

'What do *you* think?'

'I'm reckoning on the pain; another form of distraction, of obliteration. Replace one pain with another, something of that nature?'

'You obviously have no idea what you're talking about,' Eliot said, smiling.

'You're doing very fucking well, kiddo.' My uncle moved to embrace him. And they stood a while just holding each other. When he stepped back, he said, 'Let's get out of here, shall we? I hate to say it, but I think you owe me a few little piggies.'

We piled into his fancy black Range Rover, me hopping into the back, and as we journeyed back to the house, they continued to traverse the cliffs and gulleys of the subject of addiction.

'But I reckon we're all addicted to all kinds of stuff,' Eliot was saying. 'It's just that some are worse for you than others. Some are allowed. Everyone's addicted.'

'To some degree,' my uncle said. 'Although a conscious movement toward awakening softens all that.'

'But couldn't you get, like, spiritually addicted? I mean addicted to perceived spiritual needs? You know, beat yourself up when you ain't a saint?'

My uncle chuckled. 'You could.'

'I reckon taking heroine was my closest thing to getting spiritual—to this 'ere girl's sojourn into heaven,' Eliot said. 'I mean, resistance would just fall away, my body feeling as if it barely existed, me just held— *totally* held—in a bright sort of ecstasy, like nothing mattered any more except the moment. Even the moment didn't matter.'

'Interesting, but hate to say, it doesn't quite wash,' my uncle said.

'Because the moment—the Now, yeh?—is all we really have, no? So if the moment itself doesn't matter...*you* don't matter. Hey, how about each moment *is* matter?—a *condensation* of matter into the illusion of time—our unique translation of energy into matter, ya get me?—in our human form? So that's how we create our reality?'

'Wow, rad—I love it. You're the dude, man.'

'And wouldn't you say taking drugs is actually a losing of yourself? Rather than a coming to your Self?'

'If that was full-on me, I'd say I'm very fucking brilliant—how about I was the moment manifest, eh? Kind of like you were saying, only I was *so* the moment it didn't even register, sort of thing.'

'Nice. You're on to something—but the whole thing was conditional, I'm thinking. You see, the drug created the condition in which to experienced your bliss.'

'Yeah, true dat,' said Eliot. 'Dude.'

'And you didn't gain awareness—of your eternal Self, I take it?'

'Nah. It's an escape, I reckon. It was an avoid-dance.'

'Or hang on—you did, but didn't realise it, eh? Maybe it was an indication of your capacity, your unconscious always-connection. Because of course you *are* that fucking brilliant. But in that other realm, our little lovely here, came to absolute conscious Awareness.'

'Yeah, so how do I get to feel anything like that...?'

A misty rain had begun to fall and the headlights of oncoming cars fractured against the windscreen, all sort of dreamlike, made my eyes go squinty. I felt the whooshing heating breezing around my throat, the ease of the warmth right through me. Their voices became abstracted, gave unto that lovely feeling of being a kid all letting the grown-ups' conversation wash over me—

—someone jiggled my shoulder. I opened my eyes to look into those of my uncle. 'We're here, sweetheart.'

'Oh,' I rasped. 'I was dreaming.' And I had to remember where *here* was and it came to me he wasn't here—and *he* wasn't here—and I felt the slump in that.

My cheek flat against the leather of the seat, I stared up at the million tiny stars all spattered on the windscreen like winking greenfly. I groped to sitting, my uncle opening the car door for me, reaching his hand in to assist my exit. I felt the rush of cold damp air. I slid myself out, feet hitting the crunch of gravel. We smiled at each other, all gentle and sweet.

Eliot's voice boomed out. 'Wait.' There came simultaneously the high sing of a metal zip.

'He's getting his camera—Eliot, you missed it,' I said.

There was the glorious click and whirr of the polaroid. 'I never miss a beat.'

'You should've got her asleep,' my uncle told him. 'That was the picture.'

'Yeah…I've got scores of those. One of my pet collections. You've never seen anyone quite so beau-i-ful than when this one's in slumber. Except maybe when she was all bashed up and just come back from the dead. Hey, Slim?'

'From your perspective, yeh,' I said.

'We did a wicked shoot,' Eliot said.

'I saw it,' my uncle said. 'I got the magazine. It was very fucking out-there, what with that cast and the freshly healing skin. That was a *lot* of fucked up skin. I loved the way you captured the messages of love on the cast too, huh? I loved the close-ups of her. And the raw sense of a person—*more* than a person, you could say, eh?—*that*, in contrast to the slick fashion.'

'But I didn't quite net what I saw when I first saw her at the hospital. Hey, Slim?'

'She'd shifted, more like,' my uncle said. 'You missed it.'

'Oi!' Eliot punched him on the shoulder and my uncle yelped, spun round, grabbed a hold of him, got into ramming his head into Eliot's chest.

'My camera. Slim! My camera.'

I loomed in to snatch the camera from Eliot's outstretched arm, vaulted back away from the fray, watched them skidding about in the gravel—found myself wowed by my uncle's splashy strength and directed focus. Although my friend was the bigger and younger man he couldn't compete with that kind of rigour and pretty soon found himself wrestled to the ground, all begging for mercy.

'Give. Give,' he yelled—but went for my uncle's ankle, the trickster—the moment he was freed.

Another flurry of fighting ensued, ending with my uncle sitting astride Eliot's chest, pinning his arms beneath his knees.

'Enough?' he asked. Eliot nodded, groaned, melodramatic-as. 'Okay—well, first let's get a photo of *this*, shall we?'

My friend made a show of protest but I knew he was loving it all. I snapped a shot, caught the shiny black square as the camera coughed up, took to flapping it back and forth, went and fanned their flushed faces with it, and my uncle dragged Eliot up to his feet.

'Seminal,' Eliot said. 'I'm inspired to new heights.'

We went on to a feast of a dinner, my uncle having bagged a couple of pheasants which he'd left slow-cooking the whole afternoon in red wine from the Lutry's vineyard in France. He had said Eliot would be cool with it because the alcohol burned off, just tenderised and gave taste, but I had called my friend to make sure, gotten the okay. We ate roasted red-skinned potatoes dug up fresh from the garden, along with home-grown carrots and whole broccoli heads, and a salad of bitter winter leaves.

'Wow,' said Eliot, 'he's kind of like Jessie, isn't he, growing all this himself?'

'Gardener,' my uncle said, out the corner of his busting mouth. 'I've got a bloody great gardener.'

'So ferociously middle class.'

'Bourgeoisie,' my uncle corrected. 'I'm a wanna-be.' He took a big glug of the wine he was drinking.

'You're an are-be,' I said. 'By now. And let's not pretend, Eliot, *you* didn't come from some posh beginnings. With your fancy schools and the Bentley and your Harley Street entourage.'

'Me, I was upper class,' he said. 'My mother was an actual Lady. Didn't know that, did you, Miss Slim? My little secret. I reckon that's why my old man married her, for the status, the fucker.'

'What, so you're a renegade Lord?' my uncle said.

'Covert. Not really.'

'But you inherited the title?'

He shrugged, pulled his mouth down. 'I don't give it any attention, any credence. Anyway, that's not how it works.'

'But maybe you should.'

'I didn't actually—'

'—we could do with your calibre, your honesty, in the arena. You'd get to play part of the peerage, right? Imagine *you* in the House of Lords.'

'Why?' I interjected. 'Aren't you being snobby? You still have a draw for some kind of elite. For all your spiritual beliefs.'

My uncle threw his head back, laughing. 'You're the one who came back and told me everything is spiritual. You woke me to the spiritual in the material. To pure Being running through everyone—even the perceived elite and the baddies, huh? Anyway, I'm talking about Eliot smashing it up a bit.'

'You loved it—you *wanted* it already—way before I gave you that notion.'

'I didn't say I didn't. But you freed me from a last modicum of guilty ego on that one, my lovely. Really, imagine Eliot rocking the system in the House of Lords—it's quite the fucking idea.'

'I don't have guilt about it my beginnings,' Eliot said. 'I just don't care.'

'Ah, but do you see—you can *only* not care because you have it. That is the privilege, sir.'

'It's meaningless. Anyhow, my mother didn't inherit the Estate—because she was female. Her younger brother got it. So I'm not actually titled myself. I'm just saying my old man liked her title by association—especially in the gossip pages of the glossies.'

'Ah,' my uncle said. 'The ins and outs of the aristocracy. Not a fair game.'

'Fine by me.'

'I hear that. Respect…' My uncle nodded, chewing on a pheasant bone. 'Just out of idle interest, does this brother of hers have any boys?'

Eliot breathed an almost-laugh, shook his head. 'No, actually. You're like a dog with a bone, man.'

'He's a man with a bone, man,' I said.

My uncle tapped his bone against his nose. 'Yeah, so when he goes…you inherit, *right*? I knew there was something. Your mother gave you that much.'

My friend nodded, sort of sank into himself, shoved a large potato into his mouth, seemed to swallow it whole, shoved in another.

I cupped my hand over the back of his fist, said to my uncle, 'It's a bit of a tender subject.'

'The peerage? Inheritance?'

'No. Just…let's be kind and change it, right?'

My uncle wiped at his oily lower face with a burgundy cloth napkin, then wrung his greasy fingers in it, holding Eliot in his gaze. I saw how his face went all clear, eyes like pools. My mind came overlaid with moments gone yet suddenly starkly present, that time again, in the restaurant in Wales, when I was battling with him and with myself and he had told me he was going to die. And I felt such a rush of love for him, wanted to cry in the sweet bliss of it, wanted my friend to receive his uncanny gift of light. Eliot looked up and I saw him register the gaze, saw a small shock bolt through him, saw his well of tears show its lustre on the surface of his eyes. He kind of nodded, all allowing the love to flow to him. He split his face with a smile.

❦

My uncle banged the side of his bell with his cloth-wrapped mallet so the burnished brass bowl sang out, marked our transition from the meditative state, which we now realised as a kind of sojourn into conscious Oneness, a wordless aligning with the ever-flowing energy of Self to self. It had become my daily practise, knowing now the quietened mind allows this flowing in an absolute sense, so I could effortlessly feel the fullness of all who I am and swim in the waters of my potential. It is a kind of ultimate receiving. Makes ground for what is positively brewing to come. Really, for peace to become the known space of being. The bell sang three times and we waited til the last tone disappeared before rising.

My uncle did a little bow, hands pressed together to his heart, his forehead. Eliot mirrored him.

We filtered into the kitchen, got into coffee and toast cut from Eliot's homemade wheat-free brick all crunchy with sunflower seeds. We spoke very little, kind of basking in appreciation of our life's blood, of one another, of the honey and tahini glistening on the matt surface of our toast, the contrasting tastes and textures.

A short while later, my uncle dropped us at the footpath leading down to the river through the fields, himself racing straight to the yard in his Range Rover. Everything was laced with raindrops, all kind of dazzling, the toes of my friend's leather boots darkening as they soaked up the wet. 'Oh man,' he said, as the river came into view. 'Just look at the water. It's like a band of light.'

'Yes.' All kinds of thoughts came and went. I let them, they were so fast; but I didn't cling to one. 'This river has seen everything.'

Eliot increased his speed, I could feel his delight as he crashed onto the muddy hentrack, all like he was going to dive right into the silvery belt. I joined him at the river's edge and we stood, allowing ourselves to be hypnotised for a while by the surface reflections endlessly breaking and coming together, all wobbly upon the underlying currents.

'Isn't it incredible?' he said. 'Water? Just think, all water is linked across the whole world—one body, ya get me?—forming itself in millions, *billions*, of waterways. What with the cycle of evaporation—cloud formation, rain, the earth spinning, right?—water perpetually re-enters another part of its body. And *we* are seventy percent water. Excreting. Ingesting. Huh—you could say we *are* the body of water—we're all linked by water—we're linked to each other by the water in our cells.'

Relishing my friend, I said, 'And look how our breaths are full of miniscule water beads all hanging in this vaporous air.' I puffed with direct force. 'Even our breath contains water, evaporating all over the place.'

He gazed at me. 'That would make a great shot.'

'They look like foggy speech balloons, all like in a comic strip.'

'Illusory words...*beyond* words...' He made a low whistle, eyes going into the river, grew a silent smile, muttered, almost to himself, 'A river-man, that's me. Going with the flowing…yeah, man…' He gave me his sense of pleasure in himself, eyes almost crying. 'The river—nature—knows, right? Brilliant. Your "path of least resistance" larkola, yeh?' He gave me a nudge, a kind of shove in it designed to set me off balance, so I might fall in maybe, and my body had to use the intelligence of its toes—without me even thinking to direct it—just like that, all on its own, I noticed, tickled, as I got to remember how *I* wasn't the body, even though the tendency was to forget and think I was. 'Talking of flow, I want to make my whole life into an art piece. I'm just formulating how to do that, like, how to really do that.'

'I think it already is, huh?'

'Yeah…but I mean I want to document it—on a whole 'nother level. Conscious living. Get it? I'm reckoning on some kind of permanent installation—you know, an invitation to observe this life in flux—any time; like anyone can just enter my space and live it with me.'

'Actually enter your space?'

'Yeah, join me at any moment. Whatever I'm doing—doesn't matter.'

'So not just when you're at your art? Like, when you're eating your breakfast?'

'Yeah…sleeping, fucking, dancing, taking a shit, whatever.'

'No limits?'

He shook his head. 'All good. No edit.'

'You do know you're going to get called an arrogant fuck? If you do that? You know that? Don't you?'

'Course. Isn't that part of it? Saying, Here I am: love me; hate me; shit on me; whatever—because I'm saying, This is my life—and what's the difference between life and art? I'm saying, Life *is* art. The original creation. I want every moment to be shot. On video. For fucking ever.'

I sucked on my smile, heart radiating pure to him. 'It's kind of brilliant.'

'It is, isn't it?'

'And you'll give your endless stream of deifying assistants something to get their teeth into too. That's full-time filming. They'll have to make seamless changeovers and that. Night shoots; your door always open.'

'Yeah. More purpose, right? These young guys are vitality itself, always there for me, up for anything—they're well into it. They're a part of my life support.'

'And you theirs. Some of your old protégé are getting bigger than you these days.'

'Yeah, well, that's because they play the game, those guys.'

'Fashion smashion. But *you're* the artist,' I said. 'Maybe you should put a time limit on it, this project? A year or something?'

'Are you kidding? It's got to be life: *For* life. *A* life. It's always on-going, every breath, yeh? Now. Now. Now. This is about tapping into the force of *now*. If I stop, it's "lived", not "life" anymore. It's got to be hooked on the flow, like the river here, never ceasing until I—ha, until I re-emerge into my—what d'ya call it?—yeh, that spirit state shit. Thinking about it, it's got to carry on *after* I make it there—because *I'm* carrying on, right? You can't see me but I'm still energy, yeh? Like, Eternal and that. Fuck, sometimes I can hardly wait to kick the bucket, huh…'

'You fantastic nut job, Eliot—yeh, and then what, just a recorded space? A white space? Nature? Your studio? Something you-not-you?'

'Yes—and *fuck*, maybe we erase the video as we record it, so there's only forward momentum, like the river, no looking back. And who the hell would want to look back at the next fifty years of my life, anyway?'

'Good point.'

'But then everything that ever existed—in my life, in your life, in the whole human race life—doesn't it all still exist as some kind of left-over—I dunno—pulsation?—resonance? It *has* to if energy never dies, surely? Which means every thought and action must have some sort of continuum, can be tapped into even *after* you cash in your chips—like as what *was*? Fucking radical. Your past residue, huh? As opposed to that pure unconditional spirit-type state you say you return to? So then the residue is—what? Your thoughts?' His mouth pulled down, made an upside-down smile, I could see his mind dancing. His head bobbed. 'Yeh, makes sense—how thought is accessible through the subconscious and the collective mind. The zeitgeist. People making the same discoveries at the same time or some such. Why people see ghosts and shit. So why keep it on a recorded format when I can be tapped into via thought?'

'And impossible to store such a massive ever-growing body of work.'

'In a warehouse.' He eyeballed me, full of knowing. 'As archives, accessible to the public at all times. With monitors; a kind of library. You rent the videos, too, like a video hire shop. *And* have some kind of permanent gallery space.' He nodded, chewing on his lip.

'But you're not going to store it if you erase it.'

'Can you stop with the upstream thoughts, Slim?'

'I'm just saying what you just said—you're thinking to erase it…'

'Nah…this internet thing is going to get big, I reckon. Huge. You know that band—rubbish—you know, what's-their-name?—they just did a live performance via the world wide web?—had it playing in the actual moment, for anyone who had the technology to tune in. I fucking watched their shit arses, live on my computer at home—just for the hell of it. Phenomenal technology. Imagine, as this thing grows, Slim, I can literally show my footage as it records—like a river, yes, a stream of life—and maybe I can store it virtually *as well*. It's bound to happen. In addition to the physical archive.'

'So you want to store it then? After all?'

'Why not? This is all in flux, in conception. It's all possible.'

'You're beyond a nut job, Eliot. What's all this positivity, huh? You must have gotten yourself mixed up with someone else, huh? Like your Self maybe?'

'And maybe by the time I get to pop my clogs and, you know—by the way,' he said, aiming his eyes at the sky, 'I know what I just said, but I'm not in any hurry—apart from if I get to do what Slim here did, by the way, and get a taster, I wouldn't say no to *that*—' to me, he continued '—by the time I transform into my spirit state, yeh, there might be a way of recording my on-going energy. Yeah, fuck it, that's what I'm going to do too, explore, yes, *develop*—with some spiritual scientist dude maybe—some American, has to be—West Coast for sure—yes, develop a way to do that.'

'I actually think you should keep the life recordings.' The flowing water caught my eye. 'Or maybe you shouldn't. It's the braver way. And actually truly then reflects life. It's the ultimate non-attachment—erase your work as you make it—that was that moment, that was that moment. Now it's gone, now it's gone. What a lesson—no looking back—no stories, no identifying. All now and forward momentum, like you say.'

'Or is it the ultimate ego at work, to make it and wipe it out simultaneously? I mean, why make it if only to bin it? What am I saying by doing that?'

I eyed him. 'You're the one who's got to know that. It sounds pretty powerful to me.'

He shrugged. 'Seems like there's more ego in keeping it. Keeps me identifying with this person me, doesn't it? But what the fuck.' He nodded, his thoughts for a moment drifting, before making sparky eyes at me. 'I've got the boys researching funding and there's already some interest from a couple of big curators—no name dropping here.'

'I thought you were still in conception?'

'I am. But. You know.'

'Eliot's gotta put it out there—he wastes no time—I get ya, man. I'm liking the idea you keep it, to be honest. Because it *is* art.'

'And listen to this—on another tip—I'm wanting to set up a commune. Remember how I used to always say it, like: "comm-unity"? When we were squatting? With unity—all One—right? I've always believed in that. I've realised now where I was coming from; what I wanted to create saying that shit. I've been thinking of South of France but being here…I'm wondering…this land feels so spiritual and core somehow. I'm going to look into it, visit some places maybe, check out if I could buy some land. Slim, I want you to be a part of it, the commune. Are you up for looking around with me?'

'What? And then we'll all be a part of your art? Getting filmed at living?'

'Wow, yeah. I like it,' he said, all nodding in a self-satisfied kind of a way.

We were cosied up on the sofa together like a couple of stringy cats, the both of us all kind of dreamy, hypnotised-as by the fat January snowflakes, an infinity of crystal flowers swirling beyond the big windows—for sure seeming to materialise out of the infinite void.

'You think they're luminous from within?' Stuart asked, his velvet breath skimming the top of my head.

'Definitely.'

'Coming and going. Each one unique with a lifespan.' He hummed a few notes into my hair, then began singing to a sweet melody he invented in the moment. 'Coming and going. Each one unique with a lifespan. Is there really a god?' He hummed a riff, continued, 'It is we, you told me, you showed me, it is me. I am One, I am you, you are me. Living in a snowflake, in a blade of grass, in the eyes of your lost lover…'

'That's lovely,' I said, as I raised my head from his chest, sights all into him.

'…luminous from within…'

I stood, stretched my arms way up, embroidered a gusty yawn, padded to the window and gazed out at the view of the yellow-and-dove-blue museum in its snowdome. Stuart went quiet. I could feel him all eyeballing me.

After a minute or so, he murmured, 'You're thinking of him, aren't you?'

'A little bit. Not really. Better not to.'

'But you are.'

I let my forehead press into the cold windowpane. 'Seems that's what you wanted...' My voice thickened in tone as it refracted off of the glass.

'It's the snow makes me think of him, that fantastic day we all met him. It was your birthday, remember?'

'Course. Just about everything could make me think of him. If I let it.'

There was quite a silence and then I heard a small click of saliva, his lips parting or something; then another pause, in which the nape of my neck went prickly.

'Sometimes,' he growled. 'I get to agree with what Mater said that time. I mean, I know I shouldn't say this and all, but it is a bit bloody shit, his just disappearing after nearly killing you. Not even a word to you. Even I can't hardly stand it. He was so cool. He loved you. I just don't get it.'

I turned, tension in my chest, but smiling a little. 'Stuart. Stop it, will you? You know I'm not into talking about this or criticising him or anything. You know that.'

'I know—but sometimes I feel I'm fostering your denial.'

I breathed a laugh. 'Foster, ha. Good one.'

'I didn't mean anything by that.'

'But it was cute.'

'I'm not into suppressionism, is all, lil' sis. Nor deflection. Actually.'

'You really are ganging up with the mother ship, huh?' My voice came kind of hard. 'You'll be wanting me to go to therapy next, yes?'

'As if,' he said.

'Right,' I said.

'Well, it could be a good idea.'

I took my eyes back out to the snow-blurred museum, tried to slow down the wave, the anger at him, the anger at myself. Tears rose up out of the wadded layers and I turned, kind of skidded across the room, just plonked myself into his lap. He received me with a thumping breath. 'I'm not denying or suppressing anything, you idiot. I'm choosing not to put my attention there, that's all, because if I do, I'll miss him, see. I'll feel the not-hereness of him—and then what kind of a frequency do you think I'll be spewing? And getting back? "Just keep on coming, this grief that's all hurting me". I'll just feel worse. More feeling of lack. More sense of his absence. Don't you think I did that for enough years already?'

He expelled a rush of air through his nose, mouth pulled in. 'You're kidding yourself. You should let your feelings out, sis.'

'I know you're not into this, so let's not even talk about it. Just believe me when I say I know what I'm doing and it's the best thing I can do. It's called quietening the mind, giving the love to myself. Accepting what is. Being here right *now*.'

'And what's wrong with the grief? You do miss him.'

'Stop pushing. I do that grief thing when I need to. What do you want?'

'You're spewing out that vibe, I feel it, whatever you say. I feel it a lot.'

'You're projecting it.'

'Not that he deserves it. I just can't believe it—I thought he was such a cool, genuine guy.'

'He is. What happened was no normal situation.'

'You're not kidding, y-you were in a fucking coma and he walked away.'

'Stop it,' I said, levering myself off of him and into the half-hug of the inner curve of the sofa. 'I'm not saying any more. No more justification, no more defence or—*nothing*.'

We eyed each other. A guffaw sounded in his throat. 'I *am* a bastard, huh?' he said.

'Yes.'

'And you're a—what are you?'

'Everything you hate. A fucking part of—a spirit in a human body—in a human experience. Just like you, you twat.'

'Arrogant, more like.'

'We all are. More than we think. Energy—vibrational energy—in this vibrational Universe. Transmitters. Receivers. It's up to us.'

'Bor-*ing*.'

'We *are* the Universe, if you really want to know.'

'Duh.'

'And anyway, nearly dying or actually dying *actually*—but not dying—becau—'

'—there is no dea—'

'—yes, *alright*—was the best thing that ever happened to me.'

'So you keep affirming: "Just life and more life."'

'Stuart, you actually are a pig.'

'Careful now, you're being judgmental.'

'La-di-da. I love you too. Got what you wanted, huh? Person à la carte.'

He opened his mouth to say something, then shut it again and I heard a small tick in his throat. We sat a while, just breathing, both staring out at the whirling snow. I became aware of his hands moving and I glanced down, saw he was pushing back his cuticles with slow fingertips.

'Know what?' he said. 'You're not being fair, I reckon. I am into it to some degree—you know that—but I just think being human is more complex than your non-physical buddies know—or remember, if you like—because these days, in their pure *spook* state, they have their own limited perspective.'

'Oh?' I said.

'For them, it looks easy-fucking-peasy to choose how you feel, to be non-reactive, to find your best fucking feeling place and all that horse shit. Okay, so maybe they *were* human once—so *what?*—cos they're not actually physical now, are they? And so, by my reckoning, they've forgotten just what it's like to *really* have a body, and a wilful, bullish mind, to feel bad or carry pain or whatever—they forgot all that the moment they died or transitioned or whatever the fuck. They know it only conceptually now, right? And that's the easy bit. So sometimes you—*they* piss me off.'

'Huh,' I said. 'I'd never thought of it that way. I suppose they—we have to forget, or sounds like we'd never come back but—'

'—as a teacher of this shit, I really think you should take that on.'

'I'm not a teach—'

'—and *really*: "You can be, do or have anything you want"? Okay, well then: I want to fly. I want to teleport myself in an instant anywhere I choose. But it's just not possible, is it?'

'I don't know. How about the laws of physics are maybe as powerful as all the frequencies and vibrations and stuff of our physical world? They have to be, because they make our world stable, huh? Hey, and don't we, too, have our own limited perspective? We, too, have forgotten. Our Infinite Being. We chose to. Like they told—like I was saying…' I gave him a light kind of shove with my toes. 'Hey, what if the flying you do in your dreams is the flying? And how is it that people can walk on burning coals and not get hurt? It *has* to be a state of mind, belief. It's documented all over the place. There's even some story my uncle told me, about some old Indian sage being seen in two places at once. Look, probably some things resonate with you and some don't— and your lessons or whatever will be in alignment with where you are at right now. But sounds to me like it interests you, that stuff…which means there is resonance…and maybe the uncertainty is a kind of a resistance, huh? Hey, maybe your human mind is thinking too literally about this—isn't it really energetic?'

'Ah shit...' He sighed. 'It's easy for you, isn't it? You just got enlightenment in a bottle, drank of the potion of Infinite Intelligence or whatever, some fricken elixir that dissolved the illusions. The rest of us have to keep working at it. Know what? maybe that *is* why you came back, though, don't you think?—to teach—like show us, yeh? Otherwise we'd all be in a right mess, grieving all over the place, instead of getting to learn shit and that…'

I laughed, all gentle-as. 'Hmm…I think they said for me to really live it and that way others will—something like that…but hey, don't you think we're all teachers for each other, like every minute of every day?'

'I'm talking about you. You teach; just by being you.'

I manoeuvred myself into his field of vision. 'It is easier for me, true. I saw the light. Literally. Was in it. But you know, enlightenment or awakening or whatever…the peace state…it is an on-going practice. It's not just done and it's done—I still experience anger, pain, the contrast of what I want, what I don't want, who I am, who I'm not—I feel resistance. Otherwise, I suppose, why be here? I still fall out of harmony with the whole of me. I forget to be in the moment…so I can get to properly realise who I really am more deeply each time, I suppose, huh? Truth is, feelings show me when I'm out of alignment with my true nature—so however uncomfortable they are, if I recognise their purpose, they are a gift, huh? So thank you, meester teacher-mine.'

'Yeah…you saint. I don't know. But maybe you dreamed the whole thing—how about that?'

'Well maybe I did. But how can you explain I knew verbatim the conversation my doctor had with the parents—when they were in another room a couple of floors down even?'

'Yeah, I dunno, I—oh fuck, I'm sorry. Maybe I'm just scared of what I don't know. Like, what's *real*?'

'It's okay.'

'I think we're all just a bit envious of your near-death experience, to

287

be honest. I wouldn't mind a bit of that.'

'Yeah...' I sighed. 'I'm the lucky one. I got to meet some kind of ultimate knowing. I think. Or maybe I am making it all up. And maybe it doesn't matter if it's real or not. Because what *is* reality? All I know is that it resonates as real. And it's given me the knowledge of something much greater than this small body me. Which has to be Reality. But hey!—whatever—just think: he's having to journey some horrendous self blame for the crash—can you imagine? Plus all confusion and hurt, too, for the realisation about me and…fuck's sake, *him*—his-his dad. You know about that more than anyone. I mean, that was huge. I'm still getting over it myself. It had to be the shock of it caused the accident. He was a wreck—we should never have gotten back on the bike.'

'Shit, and he doesn't realise what you found was—*alright* bliss, yeh? Teach? In the coma. He just saw you lying there, all plugged into a machine with tubes coming out of you, them all saying you weren't likely to make it—and if you did, you'd probably be a vegetable. *Shit*. He doesn't know. We have to find him and tell him.'

I began to laugh. 'Stuart. You're brilliant. Just let the whole thing be, okay?'

'Not so sure about that, you know, sis.'

'No?'

'Does he even *know* you're alive?'

'I don't know.' I gazed at his flickering face. 'So what do *you* feel is the way?'

'For truth, I'd like to go and find him, bash his brains out, just about kill him for being such a dick 'ed—tell him how much I love him, how much I hate him, how much you love him, that he's an idiot because you're totally awesome, always have been, and he's got you in the blink of an eye. I'd like to tell him to get over himself, that's what.'

'And give him a near-death experience?' I said.

'Ha. No, me and Eliot are the ones want that.' He was all nodding, I could see his mind working. 'I think *you* should go and find *him*—that's the path. There's more resistance in "letting it be", aka: working not to think of him. And denying your emotion. If you ask me.'

'Oh,' I said.

'Listen, shall we go out? Change the energy here? My head's fricken fried. There's a band I want to see playing at The Mean Fiddler. We're talking of getting them to come on my US tour, as the opening act.'

'I'm hungry.'

'Of course. We'll go eat first. That Italian you like. My treat.' He nodded, widened his eyes. 'I want you to come on tour too, you know.'

'Just for the one track, humming?'

'And for the fun. We're supposed to have fun—isn't that what they told you, your nightmare buddies? That much I can handle. How about it? Will you?'

*Episode Nine: Blue Speedwell*

The motorbike beneath me purred like a lion, soft and hard at once, buzzing between my legs, transmitting a million echoes of the past. The vibrations roared into my hands, up my arms, connected to the river of my spine, for sure making love with themselves in my body. I felt my subtle inner nature mirrored by the visceral, and I felt as if I was being called—*this way, this way*—into a state of joyful connectivity to my greater flow. I bigtime got the sense this non-physical energy playing through me *was* me, was experiencing life through this body.

All the landscape was polarised, the contrast of colours and shapes exaggerated by the tinted visor of my helmet, me flying between endless fields of cultivated vegetables, seas of green leaves all springing from dark soil. The road ran straight, cutting through the countryside with the precision of a cheese wire. It created an ease, a sort of kick-back, so my attention floated without strain, the muscles of my body feeling to shimmer above the frame of the bike. I saw how the crops were irrigated by ditches lacing the highway, sparkling lines of water teeing off and between the rows, like strands of diamonds. And I felt connected to him, hearing the echo of his words that day when he had caught sight of the misty river below us, *it should be at your throat*. My eyes stung at the realisation of the love in his words—regret at my then reaction all spinning through me. I directed my thoughts into a sort of blank page and

*see* him as an eagle soaring way up high riding warm currents of air i feel the sing in his soul something beautiful clarity a cosmic perspective some aerial meeting with himself and the world belo

Hitting the small town I had planned for, I meandered through the streets until I spotted a pleasant-looking restaurant with huge pots spilling salmon-pink geraniums. I slowed on the uneven road surface, pulled into a gap between cars. The heat came magnified and I slid the zip of my brand-new bike jacket partway down, realised the sweat inside my leathers. I slipped off my helmet, shook out my hair, squinted up at the liquid sky.

Inside, the restaurant was cool and shadowy, white plastic ceiling fans wafting my hair into my face. I ate *lomo*, fillet steak, the tender flesh of it burned to a curious chewy frazzle on the huge grill, the *parrilla*, which was outside, along with *patatas frittas* and some kind of tepid boiled green leaves. The waiter didn't speak a word of English, something I'd noticed was commonplace here. Before I left, I took out my map, checked the remainder of my journey, noted in my head the directions I would take through the town, all the way to the eventual turn-off to my destination.

A short distance up that last tarmacked bit of road, my way was barred by a metal gate. I dismounted, swung the gate all the way back, looped the rope over a post, wheeled my vehicle through the hole, all enclosing myself within a new boundary. The track became dry tamped earth and gravel-filled potholes; grass, daisies, buttercups grew abundantly down the middle—and the tiny blue flowers I knew too well licked around the edge of my boot, all searing sapphires tugging at me where they shouldn't. Sighing, I raised my eyes to take in the immediate landscape. Huge eucalyptus trees rose along the long driveway, great swathes of peeling bark hanging off them in dappled colours like partially discarded clothing. A field of thigh-high tasselled grasses spread itself to my right, all kind of yellowy and ephemeral, beyond it, way in the distance, blurred lines of white fencing. To my left lay a thick hedge. The track made a bend, turned between fields, disappeared into trees. The sky was bigger than anything.

I tore off my helmet, stuck it into the top box, a part of me wanting to strip off my leathers, know the warm wind against my bare legs once more. As I rode solo and slowly, I had the sense of my thighs wrapping him, my arms about his soft belly, hands sneaking a feel of his furriness.

The track was longer than I expected, and generally raggier, the fields containing many cows, no horses; then involved another gate, immediately after which I bumped through a lazy stream and up a shallow incline, a kind of residual riverbank of smooth parched earth.

On reaching the top of the hillock, a wide vista opened up to me. It was as if I had entered an emerald, the sun glinting on an infinite spread of shorn green blades. I stopped, let my feet hit the ground. 'What a glory,' I said out to the landscape, bike buzzing through me. 'It had to be, didn't it? It had to be.' The sun came and laid its rays into my lashes, made halos of golden mist, so gold leaf seemed to be gilding the landsc

and he comes toward me all leading the two-day-old palomino foal on a hemp-rope halter he says *he'll know you like his own* his fingers brushing mine as he hands me the rope same square fingers giving me the porcelain brooch his eyes *his* eyes bore into me you know who i am he says doesn't say i say don't say i know you yes i've taken a journey of love to find you in ways you can't imagine we smile into each other and his look goes haggard *my dad* my da  he says love is a river that never sto

{gold leaf seemed to be gilding the landsc}ape. The lightness of tears glanced down my cheeks.

I sat a while astride the thrumming bike—then coasted through the pastures, awe striking me at the sight of the many splendid thoroughbreds grazing, all swishing their tails. I greeted each one with smiles and nods as they looked up at me. I wondered if I would see Darling, aware of the nearing buildings, concrete structures, architecturally pristine, and the training track to the left, with its white railings. There were people dotted here and there about their work.

Someone began toward me from the yard, her arm raised to catch my attention. I slowed to a halt beside her.

She wore beige peddle-pushers and an open-necked shirt, must have been around thirty-five, kind of pretty and blonde, with that long-faced horsey look, made me think of an old school friend. She spoke in Spanish, fast, so I couldn't understand, and I attempted to make a response above the motorbike hum.

'Excuse, so sorry, me Española es…I can barely speak a word. Do you speak any English?'

She laughed. 'I *am* English.'

'Ah. Of course.'

'Can I help you? I don't think we're expecting anybody.'

'Um. Yeh. I'm not expected.'

She paused, gazed at me. 'Do I know you?'

'No.'

'You look familiar.'

I shrugged, decided to fib, even as I felt the pang of it in my gut. 'I get that a lot.' And actually it wasn't such a lie; I did get it a lot. Because of my acting. But usually people realised who I was and I saw she didn't and I wanted to keep it that way for as long as possible.

'No,' she said. 'I'm sure I've seen you. On the scene, I suppose. Are you looking for a job?'

I averted my eyes, my lips holding onto themselves then letting go with a popping sound. 'Yup.'

'I guess you heard about our strong UK connection here, huh? Quite a few of us. But you don't have to be English to work here. At all. We have mostly Argentines. Do you want to come to the office and I'll take down your details? We do have some openings—I suppose you're aware?'

'Sure.'

'Ok, well, pull your bike up over there.' She pointed through the open double gates to a large parking area. 'I'll wait for you.'

I did her bidding, then tagged along beside her across the main forecourt, passing the huge stables building before entering a wooded area. The sweat trickled in rivulets inside my leathers. 'This is an impressive facility,' I said. 'I've never seen one like it. It looks spanking new.'

'It is. It was completed only eight years ago. The original estancia is way out the back; our boss trainer gets to live there. Lucky guy. But he's the best. I guess you kno—'

'—yeah yeah. I know. Awesome.'

'So you *are* experienced at working at a racing stable, yes?'

'Um, yes, sort of.'

'Sort of?'

'Well, my uncle runs one in—and I've spent a lot of time there—and at the place he ran before, which was right near my home when I was growing up. Do you always invite random visitors in?'

She laughed. 'Not always. So you've worked at a racing stable? Or just hung out at your uncle's? Maybe that's where I've seen you. Who's is his stable?'

'Oh—no, I mean—yes. I've worked there alright.' My eyes fluttered and my mouth pulled in on itself again. I realised I was self-conscious, became aware of the tug in my solar plexus, made a breathy laugh, offered friendly humour to myself. I gave myself an inner nudge, said in my head, Who am I? Felt instantly a small rush of relief.

'You alright?' she said.

I met her eye. 'Very.'

'You're going to get dehydrated in that suit, by the looks of you. You've got to watch it in this heat. We English aren't used to it. Let's get you some water. You might want to take your jacket off.'

'Great. Thank you.'

'And so?'

'So?'

'Your experience?'

'Ah yes...so: I worked with the horses intensely I helped with the training, as well as all the rudiments of grooming and mucking out. I like to rub down the horses myself after working with them anyway.'

'Training? That's a big deal. How?'

We reached the office building. It was massive, a double-story modernist build with a lot of glass, all amongst silver birches, strong

294

shards of sunlight reaching in.

'Wow,' I said. 'That must be the most glamorous stables' office building I've ever seen.'

She smiled. 'There's a lot goes on in here. Office is an understatement.' She slid open the wide door, ushered me into an expansive open plan space with minimalist sofas, chairs and side-tables, also a large marble oval dining table, and a generous kitchen. There were maybe five or six people there.

'This is swish,' I said, making a semi-whistle.

She closed the door. 'And air-conditioning is essential with these massive windows at this time of year.'

I nodded, felt the instant chill as a relief on my wet skin. 'How long have you been here?'

'From the beginning—of this new era—you know, the modernisation and everything. They poached me from Huffington-Smythes. Know it? I'll just grab us some water. Hang on here.' She went into the kitchen, filled two tumblers from a free-standing cooler. I gazed up at the high ceiling, slipped off my jacket so the nippy gusts of air came and played at my armpits, wove into the fabric of my damp men's vest. As she ambled back I got the feeling she was looking at me in a focused manner. She gave me my water, jerked her head, 'Come this way—my office is up in the gods.'

Turning, I was wow-ed by the concrete steps, which appeared to float, almost magical, defying gravity. I refrained from cooing. 'So eight years, right? You've been here? Did the facility used to be elsewhere?'

'Yeah.' She paused, turning to stare at me. 'Listen, I'm sure I recognise you. But it's not from a UK stable, I don't think. Or maybe it is? Or a meet? It's doing my head in. What is you uncle's outfit?'

'They're French owners. Lutry. Know them?'

'Gosh, of course.' She nodded, and I could see she was impressed, ruminating. 'They're major league.'

I was waiting for her to tell me *he* used to work there, many moons and suns and heather bells ago. I said, 'The facility's based in—'

'—Ireland,' she piped. 'Yes, I know. They have Jelly Roll and Homer's Ride, big runners at the moment—but of course you know.

295

Both sired by Angel's Neck, huh? I've been wanting to send a mare to him for a while now. Can't quite get the go-ahead, it's driving me— *anyway*...' She kind of chuckled as she turned, continued up the stairway.

'Angel's Neck is special to me, actually,' I said. 'He's kind of mine— I mean, I did the imprinting when he was a foal, see—when he was just born, you know?'

Her face thrilled. 'You didn't?'

'Right when he was damp from the womb and all—too dear, all kind of curly—his fur, you know?'

'But how old were you? You don't look more than twenty now.'

'I'm twenty-eight. I was fourteen.'

'Gosh, well that is a privilege.' We entered her office, an airy space overlooking the back. A path ran through the silver birches, glimpses of long low buildings showing through. She saw me looking, said, 'That's where some of our staff live. The original estancia's just behind those dwellings. See the brick wall? You can just make it out behind them. That's the boundary wall. It has its own private grounds.' She stood regarding me as if she was waiting for me to ask the question I had been avoiding. I couldn't believe she didn't just offer the information; but on the other hand, she had to know I knew.

'So in what capacity do you train?'

'I ride.'

'*Ride*? So you're a professional trainer?'

'No.'

'But that doesn't happen, does it? I mean, how...?'

'Yeah, well, because of my uncle, you know. Growing up in it. I get up on the young ones in the barn. Sometimes I've helped break them in. And I train on the practice track too—but mostly without other riders. You know, safety, because it's not my profession or whatever. They say I have the knack.'

She gazed at me askance, pursing her smiling lips over a frown. 'But you *must* kno—'

'—yeah, yeah, I *do* know him, of course. I *did*. A bit. You know, I was young. But I worked with him quite a bit.'

296

'Trained with him?'

'Yup. He taught me a lot…' I mirrored her wowed expression. 'I did the imprinting with him.'

The excitement flushed her up. 'Oh, well, he's going to want to see you, isn't he? Why didn't you say?'

'I'm saying.'

'But I mean, *before*?'

'I was trying not to…um…bias you.'

'God, I knew there was something about you. You have this way—' she laughed '—have you been imprinting *me*? You have the knack on humans too, it would seem. I nearly told you all our business and stuff. Listen, I'm going to call him, let him know you're here.' She was making for the phone on her desk.

'No, don't,' I said. I bit my lip as she looked at me all bright-eyed. 'I'd like to surprise him. Shall we?'

❧

The setup was in a bar in the local town, right near the restaurant I'd stopped at on my way over. She'd made out like she was wanting to pick his brains about some guy she liked who worked at the stables. She needed it to be elsewhere, she told him, so there was no chance her crush would walk in on them. She told me she actually did want to speak with him about just this and she was a terrible liar and if she didn't speak some truth she couldn't have arranged things. She said she wished she could be there to see his face when he saw me, and I knew she was hinting, so I just laughed and played like I didn't get her inference.

The place was brutally basic, all white plastic chairs and tables, strip lighting and those cheap white ceiling fans that seemed to proliferate in the region. There must have been forty-fifty people, men mostly, producing a low rumble of chatter and a fog of cigarette smoke. A regular clinking came from the pool table, all with its own crowd of younger locals hanging about the game.

I spotted a couple of free bar stools, hopped up on one, putting my bag on the other. The bar was made of plastic wood. I went for their only Irish single malt, one I didn't know, no ice, had to hand-signal my communication to the non-English-speaking barman. I kind of liked the way pretty much no one spoke my language, loved the fact I couldn't understand the drone around me. It made it seem romantic, gave me a chance to imagine these guys in profound conversation, all that psychological angst Eliot had told me the Argentines were famed for.

Time seemed to open up, just about stand still, as I sat not letting myself wonder what I was doing here, the nagging echo of a longing playing itself somewhere in my background. I let my eyes rove the bristled faces of middle-aged men, their sun-drenched skin yellowed in the lurid light, sweat-sheened, almost otherworldly, and my mind ran to him with his cowboy-stained chin and windswept tangle of hair, sunlight all seeming to radiate from him. That fuzz of arm-hair making a halo around him, like the auras I saw all the time now, around everyone. I found enjoyment in thinking about him and the words came again, Did I love him? still? after all? was I making a circle? There felt to be an absurdity in this as his son slipped himself between us, the mental-emotional video of him spooling into my inner vision, more real, more solid and substantial. I saw his younger face looming into mine, slivers of blue rimming his expanded black pupils, felt his fingers slide into my hair, grasp my neck. I closed my eyes and his kiss came soft and vivid, so I believed it; felt somewhere, somewhere right now, he too, in this moment, was entangled in this kiss in his own experience. He felt so near I got to wonder if he was maybe at the stables, had sought out his dad.

I scrolled my sights across the garish mess of the room, hit upon the door as it swung open, let in a couple of twenty-something females who looked like they'd come from a picnic at a makeup counter. I thought of the roller-disco in my home town; Robin Remick, Sunil, Shirty and others, sparking up from the electrical storage facilities of my human brain uninvited—and I saw how I had access to everything I'd ever lived, everything waiting for associative connections to bring them forth; for their little forays back into being. Yet if you chopped me open, you wouldn't find any of it, only flesh and bone. It seemed like it must all be held in the ether, in some kind of vibration, I supposed, to be downloaded when triggered by a resonant thought, choice or no choice. Keeping me thinking I was an identity.

I watched the two women weave through the bar, many an approving look, a salutation coming their way, a sort of lascivious ripple in their wake. I could almost smell their cheap perfume, and I sat perched on my stool, wishing them well like the weirdo mystic I seemed to have become. Laughing to myself, I necked the whiskey I'd been sipping, felt its rush, ordered another, passed my eyes back toward the door—and there he was, a few metres inside, just like that, looking around for someone I knew he wasn't going to find.

There came a wrench to my solar plexus. He said something and my eyes followed his to see the back of a girl's head, all shiny black hair—very like mine, I couldn't help thinking—as she threaded away towards the loos. I realised he must have come with someone, wondered what my friend at the stables would think of that? The draw on my guts increased. A part of me wanted to duck down below the bar, slink away, disappear, but I straightened my spine, stayed, stared.

His head at last made the pivot, his eyes hitting me. And I saw the realisation of me strike him. I saw how the recognition entered him on ever deepening levels, himself rooted, until with a jolt, he was pushing his way toward me, then halting, eyes wide on me, a swell of panic washing over his ragged face as he twisted to look behind him. I couldn't help smiling, the love I had for him kind of rising up in my throat. However almost ugly he was, I found him beautiful, took delight in observing his familiar gait, the eternal inelegance of it, and his swan neck. I saw in him his son and I loved him even more.

He came at me. His expression didn't crack, but of course his voice did. 'Angel Face. Angel Fa—what the fuck?'

I slid down from the stool, went to touch him but he recoiled. 'I just had to—I wanted—'

'—did Antonia put you up to this?'

'No. I mean, I asked her, is all, so I could surprise you and—'

'—*surprise*? What the fuck are you *doing* here? After Newmarket and you and my—*oh Christ*—you and my…' His thumbs went into his eyes, face screwed up, then his pale-blue shards lanced at me. '*Listen*, you've got to get out of here. You—your—you really don't want this next moment to happen. I'm sorry, but you have to go—immediately.'

'You can't even say hello to me? Get through something with me? I've come all this way.'

His eyes darted about. 'Is he here? Is *he* here too?'

I gazed at him, felt the tension in my chest, let my eyes close as I gathered forth some inner stilling, returning to some sense of myself. 'No…I thought he might be here.'

'Here?'

'Yes.'

'You're not together? You don't know where he is?'

I shook my head, smiled weak-as. 'It's a long story. A lot went down after we—after we saw you. I suppose that's why I've come. To help me place everything maybe. I don't know actually. I just had to come. I didn't want to leave it after—after—after… And we never had a proper goodbye or anything really—*ever*. Did we?'

His hand scoured his clenched face. He slung his head round to look behind him, came back to hold me in his gaping pupils, motionless now and intense as anything. 'Please don't get me wrong, I want to see you. But not here. I need you to go. Immediately. There's things you don't know and I-I want to speak with you—somewhere private.' He looked behind himself again.

My head was shaking. I felt my mouth twist, my forehead come together. 'Okay, so let's go somewhere else.'

'I need you to leave. Now.'

'But how will we—'

'—*call* me,' he rasped, wrenching something from the breast pocket of his denim jacket. A snow of cards fell to the floor, and he stooped, snipped one into his fingers, held it out to me. 'In fifteen minutes. Go find somewhere and call me.'

'This is…do you realise how strange this is?'

'Yeh and believe me, it's way out of the ordinary for me too. I wish you'd let me know you were here, then all this—just get out of here, will you?'

'Was that your girlfriend I saw, going to the loos? Is that it?'

'You saw her?'

'Sort of, yes.'

His face appeared manic, head all nodding. 'I've got a very jealous girlfriend. That's it. You got it. Now go.'

'Okay. I don't want to cause any trouble.' I began to move past him, stopped, touched his shoulder, felt an energy blow through me. 'I don't mind about a girlfriend. I wouldn't expect—I mean, of course you—and that's not what I'm here for, you know. You know I lo—'

He nodded sharply, wouldn't look at me. '—I *mean* it, Angel Face.'

'Okay.'

The room had become full-on populated and I found my way barred by bodies. Muttering 'Excuse me', possibly in Spanish, maybe more English, I turned myself this way then that, looped my way to the exit. The heat coming from inside of me was hotter than the air, which was hot, and I felt the sweat bead on my forehead, break and run, the breeze from the ceiling fans emphasising the bodily streams. I told myself my eyes stung from the thick atmosphere of cigarette smoke. But I knew they were making tears.

As I reached the door, I looked back, and she was with him and it was as if my face was slapped repeatedly and greenfly were and I am tearing downhill without breaks and pitching into nettles and everything muddy came clear I understood everything so many nuances of things I hadn't understood she was with him standing right there at the bar the jumbo jet she was smiling and she kissed him and *she* was my sis—

—I ran down the street, way off my head, trainers all bouncing off of the paving stones, everything abstracted, exaggerated, forms coming in and out focus, my own form feeling to ricochet out from itself as if it couldn't keep a hold of its atoms or thoughts or anything, the mind-momentum just channelling through the movement all on its own as a mental-as incomprehensible kind of a chatter and—*oh but stunning! wow!* beneath it all there sustained a transcendent kind of clarity, a joy even, in which I was aware of everything, just kind of knew so many everythings, as if it was all beaming to me as some sort of transmission: I knew the sublime Being of me felt differently, just couldn't agree, felt only love, the unconditional, and it was this chasm between my self and my Self, in perception, in my misperception, which was creating the hurting. Even as fury stabbed at my bigger energy for not joining me, I knew—yes, remembered, from being in that place myself—it couldn't, just *didn't* see the world that way—yet the ire just wouldn't stop going for it, bigtime escalating with the realisation this crazy inner spirit, my fucking Sublime Being or whatever, was actually *loving* her, loving *them*, seeing the whole of them—some whole knowing this self-limited little me just wasn't willing or able to entertain.

This body just kept running. And my human mind was finding words, going mad at the betrayal; I couldn't stop it; nor wanted to. I hated her. I hated him. She'd lied to me, blamed me. And all the time wanted what was mine. I couldn't believe her treachery. The way she'd hated me when it all came out, how she'd let it loose into our school and relished the slagging I had had to live with. My ruined reputation. The names. How long had she coveted him? From the beginning? Or only after she'd discovered how I loved him? Fuck, she had to have sought him out. When? How long? 'You bitch,' I yelled into the frazzled night. 'You lying, nasty fucking—you're *disgusting…*'

I pulled on the brakes, skidded to a heart-thumping breath-wrenched standstill. My throat felt raw and torn, the hot air like razors, tears as acid, muscles, everything, ripping. I bent double, clutched my knees, coughing and spluttering—then stood abruptly upright, began pacing to and fro along one side of a triangular green, stark-as aware of a jacaranda tree in fragrant pale-purple bloom, its beauty exploding above me in great arching splitting lines. I saw I was going to paint it and couldn't believe I could think such a thing at such a time.

'Fucking bitch,' I ranted on. 'How could you? All that guilting and blaming me for years, and all the time—god, I *knew*, I just *knew* you liked him right off—but of course I didn't belie—you were so convincing. And what the fuck—' I yelled to him '—"*Get out of here?*" "*You're not going to want this moment?*" What kind of a—the two of you, both—I can't believe it— this is totally fucked up. I want to kill you—I totally fucking want to murder you both—I—'

My head tilted, my consciousness taking in, deliberately logging, the

302

loaded mauve branches set against a dark starry sky. The streetlamps, few and far between, barely impacted the great light-speckled blackness up above, just seemed to emphasise the glory of the tree, glamorise it, so it looked hyper-real and too fertile. I opened my throat and let out a roar, no words. And another. Was stunned as some sort of mad satisfaction filtered into my heart—and without knowing why came a nuts-as influx of hope, a kind of dense realisation I might finally be—*what?*—free? relief coming hot that the truth was out, yes, *all* the truths were now ousted—mine—his—and hers. I yelled again, up through the insane beauty of the branches, the lushness of the full bursting blossom yielding a sort of sexual ecstasy. I was struck with bright echoes of my early awakenings with *him*—through my body and his together—saw now, how this had been a profound connection to the whole of me, a rude awakening to the Conscious Awareness my uncle had always gone on about, and which I now knew as truth. I understood we had set me on a path, a path of pain in seeking joy, pain because my focus had been on the missing, the craving, how I didn't want things, rather than the on-going love. Appreciation for him kicked me in the guts, came as pure Love, initiated a spiralling appreciation for my uncle, my mum, my dad and yes, for my sister, the bitch.

Beautiful tears sprung as gratitude broke within me for this very moment, for the aching emotion out of which it was manifest, for the showing me how unbearable being split-off from who I really was felt. And it broke for him whom I hoped I would find again: this beautiful him who had killed me on his bike and given me the doorway into Real Life, beyond real life, into a new awareness I might be capable of anything. Anything was possible. I would find my love—my love—my love again.

The crack between my self and my Self had diminished to something hairline, viscerally so, and I felt myself springing back into fullness on a flesh-coloured elastic band. I felt how I came into the untamed expansion jammy big Me had experienced through all of this—felt the very moment this merged with my human body and *pop!* like a firework, spreading bright wondrous sparks inside of me.

I actually started to laugh. I saw I had been called back to the whole of me—*this way, this way*—and my sensitivity, yes, the crazy-seeming developed practice of caring about how I felt, had triggered me to follow. So there, Stuart! I had screamed myself from devastation into blame, then sort of upward it felt, into rage, revenge, hope, belief and knowing. Joy and—*fuck it, yes!*—unconditional Love. It was like I'd danced some kind of theatrical tango, each turn and step and tone nearer to this moment of absolute attuning with my bigger Me.

I swung my body downward, planted myself on the curbstone, saw with sudden clarity what a hypocritical reaction I had played into. A new wave of relief swelled in my heart. And the laughter spread itself into my limbs: hadn't I gone and done pretty much exactly the same thing? Seeking out his son and making him my own?

I sat a while, letting my mind go quiet, aware of the gorgeous field of stillness beneath the form of things, this non-judgemental space of Eternal Energy from which every action sprang, was allowed, had a purpose even. A gentle breeze came and kissed my damp skin, lifted the dark fronds of my hair, cupped my shoulder. I heard its whisper in the jacaranda flowers, looked up to see the petals billowing softly, perceived how they stilled when the wind disappeared. I asked, could I see the vibration we were supposed to made of, can my focus change, can my visual instrument tune into another level? So I could actually *see* another dimension. Feed my knowing of the layers of perception. And gazing at the pale-purple flowers I became aware of their gentle aura growing brighter, appearing to crumble into a mass of vibrating particle and wave forms, which almost looked like a thick kind of water, a kind of connecting—*oh! a field!*—a joined-up fluid-like field—*yes!*—which felt to connect me into the flowers, the pavement, into the air, everything, on and on, into infinity…

I thought about how we'd been told at school you could put your hand through a table, anything, if only it vibrated at a different frequency. It was vibrational energy that made this physical world possible. This really was a vibrational universe. It kind of blew my head off still.

I stood. Felt the shimmer of the world, of my physical body in it. The knowing coming viscerally I was some kind of a transmitter and receiver, a translator, so good at it, I didn't even know I was doing it every moment of every day, interpreting with my five senses—and transmitting and attracting back the essence of what I put out emotionally—actually manifesting my life, via my thoughts and feelings and perceptions. And my choices. It made a sort of sense to me why we were here, how we were catalysts for Universal Love and the essence of joy. How the great I AM energy expanded, moment to moment, through its physical systems, the Me through the me; and vice versa; how the limitless expansion made us eternal. It just added up to a kind of delicious wordless knowing.

The townscape about me looked different, more alive, like everything was singing with me, for me, because of me. I took a diagonal route across the road toward a restaurant with tables and chairs outside, realised people were watching me, whilst all sort of looking away at the same time. I saw they'd just witnessed what would have appeared as total madness. But no one looked afraid. Smiling, I spread my hands, shoulders held in a shrug, heading toward my—*aha!*—not-so-incidental audience. I caught one eye and then another, was surprised as my smile was full-on returned, and then someone began clapping, and then everyone was clapping, including a waiter who came to the door. It was an amazing feeling, this open quality coming off of strangers in a strange land after a very very strange happening.

'English?' a young guy asked me, nodding.

'You guessed it,' I said.

'You are actress,' he said. 'I know you. From film, *Present Laughter*, Noel Coward production. I just see last week. In Buenos Aires. You make important character in this movie. Very talent.' I laughed through my nose, nodded. Someone at another table asked him something in Spanish and he replied, everyone listening and grinning, someone else saying a couple of things, looking from him to me. 'I tell them you are famouse.'

'Not really.'

He looked like he agreed. 'No one has seen this movie. I too am actor.'

The girl with him piped. 'You were make practice, we think? What you call?'

'Make rehearse,' he said.

'You could call it that.'

'We are great privilege,' he said.

'Don't tell anyone,' I said.

'Oh, we tell everyone, of course.' The laugh burst from me and again he turned to the others, translated, received a buzz of agreement. 'They say they will go and see you in the movie. Make big—how do you say?—office box hit. They want you to make very grande famouse.'

'Thank you.' I pointed inside. 'You think there's a phone in there I could use?'

He rose quickly, his white plastic chair taking a backward flip, clackering behind him. The waiter ran forward, picked it up, and the guy fired a rapid instruction to him so he stepped aside, let my friend lead me into the place, his stance all proud and important—and I just had to love him more by the moment. As I crossed the threshold, I smiled back at his girlfriend who stuck her thumb up, looked pleased.

He led me through the throng of patrons to the bar area, saying, 'Maybe you would like see this play I am act in? We have first night in tomorrow.'

'Great. I'd love to—if I'm still here. I'm not sure what my plans are yet.'

'You make stay. I like. It is in Spanish but I think you enjoy tremendouse. Very importanto Argentine writer.' He said the unfamiliar name as he leaned on the bar, beckoned the woman there. They had a short interaction during which she produced a heavy green dial-phone from below the bar, offering it to me with smiles.

'There's not a payphone?' I asked.

'Not for you,' he said.

I took out the card, said to him, 'Listen, this is a mobile phone, so it will cost quite a bit I think. Please can you tell her I'll pay for the call.'

He shot off my words in Spanish and the woman looked impressed, then asked him if it was to England and when I said no, it was a local friend, told him it was fine, just not to be too long. He stood watching me like he wasn't going anywhere, and I made a face, said, would he mind, it was a kind of private call, and he made big theatrical gestures, all wide eyes and knowing, made himself scarce.

I dialled the number, pressed my face to the wall, let my forehead seek its cool relief as it rang for quite some time.

'Hello?' His voice came with its divine split in it.

'Hi.'

'Where are you?'

'In some place down the street. But listen, I—'

'—tell me where you are. I'll come meet you.'

Gentle-as, I said, 'And what about my sister?'

'Eh? What?'

'I know you heard what I said.'

'I—what?—you saw…? You saw her?'

'Yes, I did.'

'*Christ*—fuck…I-I don't know what to say. Are you okay? Angel Face?'

'You don't have to be saying anything—but I think you should stop calling me Angel Face, huh.'

'Oh…'

'I mean it's kind of nice but…' a sigh came out of me.

'Are you okay?'

'Yeah, I am. Are you?'

'I'm a bit—a bit—a bit shell-shocked—to say the least.'

'Are you outside the bar? Is she still around?'

'You always know, don't you? You haven't changed.'

'Oh, I've changed.'

'I didn't mean it like that. I mean you're—you—your fundamental nature. And like, you always had a sixth sense.'

'And I mean it in a good way too.'

There was a long pause in which both of us breathed deep-as, all kind of linked, so you couldn't deny we were still connected.

'Listen,' I said. 'I can't stay on this phone. They won't take my money. I think I should come and meet you. Both.'

'I'm not sure—'

'—well, I am. This needs facing head on. No more hiding.'

'For sure, I get you, but I think I should prepare her first. She's going to freak. She should meet you tomorrow. Why don't we arrange that?'

'Do you love her?'

'You what?'

'Do you?'

'Well, I—of course. But—'

'—so let's do the best by her—best by all of us—keep nothing from her. I know she'd rather be included from the beginning—once she's over the initial shock. Why don't you get her, and I'll speak to her first.'

'Christ,' he rasped. 'Hang on.'

I heard the rush of noise enter the receiver as he returned to the bar, heard a crackling swish as he walked, pictured the phone held down by his slim hips. There was music blaring out in the background as well as the rumble of chatter. He said something, I couldn't make it out, and then I heard her breath into the receiver.

'Hello?' She sounded like she didn't know who she was speaking to.

'Hello sis? It's me. Didn't he—'

Her voice came sort of shouty '—it's *who*?'

I raised my own to be sure she heard me. 'Me. Your sister.'

I heard her sharp intake of breath. 'You—how did you get this number? Why are you—what do you want?'

'Listen, it's okay—I mean, it was a fucking big shock but—I don't know—it's kind of nuts but—I know it's freaky but I want to see you and—'

'—how did you find out? What are you up to?'

'Don't you know, I'm—'

'—yes, of course I know. I know all about it—so you can hardly say anything, can you?'

'Okay but… Are you up for meeting? I could come back there now. Or it might be better to find somewhere quieter?'

'Come back here?'

'You *don't* know,' I said.

'I do.'

'Listen, I'm here. Maybe half a mile away—less. He didn't tell you?'

'He tells me everything.'

'Well, so look…I'll be with you in a few minutes.'

I hung up the phone, drew some money out of my wallet, waved it about at the proprietor, grabbing her attention. She came over and we conversed each in our own language about her taking the cash until she pushed my hand away so firmly, and with such a smile, that I thanked her and accepted her generosity. As I left the restaurant, my friends outside made big grins and the guy sprung up, his chair enthusiastically taking its fall. He gave me a flier for his play.

'See here,' he said. 'I make our telephone. We want invite you at our house.'

'Thank you. Very kind. I'll call you tomorrow, yes?'

'We like very much,' his girlfriend said.

I looked around at everyone outside. 'Thank you all. You're all so lovely.' She translated for me and as I walked away I received a chorus of Argentine goodbyes, along with words I knew to be appreciation.

I paused to gaze into the jacaranda, felt myself a part of it, then took off up the street. I let my head go empty, pretty much, my senses all translating the slide-by world in deep recognition of the moment. As I approached the bar I realised they were outside, standing with a definite space between them, on the opposite side of the road. I waved and they both raised their hands in response. They stepped toward me, each with a version of a grim expression.

'Hey,' he said.

'Hey,' my sister echoed.

I felt how my eyes spun over them. My heart had gone tight. Even though I didn't want it to. I just kind of allowed the whole thing, didn't try and fight off all the arising confused feelings. And I stayed in contact with the field of peace that lay inside of my body, the still of Me beneath all the chaos, somehow trusting the intensifying shadows would bring present a brighter light. 'Hey…you two. It's okay, you know. This is okay.'

My sister's face swelled with tears she worked to hold back. 'No it isn't. I don't want to see you. Just go.'

'Oh,' I said.

We stood wordless, in an isosceles triangle, he at the furthest distance.

'It was a big shock,' I said.

'Yeah, you can full-on hate me now,' she murmured, barely audible.

'How great that must be for you, huh?'

I shook my head. 'I don't. At all. I did for a moment—but of course I'll always love you. That's the truth.'

'Oh shut up. I fucking hate you—just shut up. You think you're such a fucking guru. You're not uncle Gordie, you know. What are you doing here anyway? Spying?'

'Are you going to give us a hug?' I said.

'No', she said. But she was reaching for me, all snot and mucus blubbing out of her in a suppressed wail, and we were holding each other real tight, and her body was spasming.

I felt his presence closing in on us, opened my eyes to find him reaching for the back of her neck, felt within my own body, my physical memory, the stunning beauty of his touch there; felt her response, the initial tensing, the fear, and then the ripples of relief in the opening gates of her emotion. His black hole pupils drew my eyes, held me, blue and sunshine reflected in the parings of palest colour at their rims—and then my breath went jagged-as, all kind of stolen, as something opened up, right into the silent heart of me, like every flower I'd ever known was blooming, and I thought maybe I was dying, right there and then. Beautiful-as. I swear I could see the cosmos in him, all glittering sparks in the dark centres of his eyes—and I felt an interface with the whole I AM consciousness, like I was falling into the absolute truth of me—and him too—of we, he and me—of my sister and all everyone—as if in this moment he shone the Oneness of humanity and the whole fucking Universe right through him for me to know. Again. I saw how time didn't exist, the moment exploding every-which-way so the Eternal Now stood still, Silent; was *always*; and I was That. I watched in slow motion as a slither of a tear ripped down his cheek—coming back to the awareness she was emptying her secretions in a rush of broiling breath on the bare skin of my shoulder, all kinds of murmurings, self-flagellation, sorries, and blame at me flushing out in the wet. And I understood I was *living*. She gripped me tight then pulled away, himself stumbling backwards and off, she striking my chest with the flat of her hand, eyes boring into me in the familiar way she had done for years.

'I hated you—I hate you—you always got everything you wanted and

I—I—I just had to stand there and be your ugly big sister who no one ever wanted and you rubbed it—you were horrible—*I* was horrible—oh god, I wanted you to die and then you nearly did and—'

I just let the stream run its course, knowing the release of it was a release of years of resistance, and I was pretty damn sure we could somehow find our way together, even if it took us a million years—and that maybe everything really was, really *was*, working out for all of us. I had brought her to him; him to her. He had brought his son to me. You had to say that was working out in a kind of a way. Didn't you? And whether I had my him or not, whether I ever would again, having him in my life had been incredible, had given me a love and a knowing I could never without him have reached.

I felt tremendous ease in that moment, even with all my mixed-up desires—whatever they were—even with the echoes of hurting. I felt myself as the continuum of the Oneness, of some sort of simple isness just letting life be.

My sister heaved herself out of my arms, used her sleeve to mop up the shining muck she'd produced. She wiped beneath her eyes with her knuckles, said, 'I guess there's a whole lot of black streaked down my face?'

I nodded. 'It's a good look. Very Hollywood.'

She cracked a one-tone laugh, looked shy, eyes all skating about. 'I think we should all go back to—to the house. Shall we? Have you got a place to stay?'

I shook my head. 'Never got that far.'

'Come stay at our—at the estansia.'

'Really?'

'Of course.'

'It's not a bit fast for you?'

'I don't know. Is it a bit fast for you?'

'Ha,' I said. 'Good one. Maybe it is…'

'I think it's a good idea.' She looked at him. 'Don't you?'

He let his expression show his uncertainty. 'Sure…'

'It might be asking too much—just now,' I said. 'Maybe tomorrow?'

She nodded, kind of grave. 'Well, I want you to come back. Or just to leave the country. Basically.'

We gathered into their car, she driving, me in the back, spoke a little of the racing stables and then fell into silence mostly. She pointed out the odd landmark. We arrived in the private grounds of the old estancia within twenty minutes.

It was a beautiful setting, a generous expanse of grass with specimen trees here and there, enclosed by woods. 'Mulberries,' she said all smiley, her voice dull. There was a swimming pool to one side, with its own changing and shower rooms. The house itself was red brick, stylish and romantic-looking, covered in wisteria and clematis not presently flowering. The scent of gardenia filled the hot air.

Inside it was naturally cool, with tiled floors, while the original dark wood beams ran gorgeous seams about the walls and ceilings. The long hallway was papered with scenic designs she told me she'd gone to great pains, a few years before, to source, so as to reproduce the pattern on the once water-damaged walls. She took me into the guest room, pointed out the rose-covered paper with matching curtains and quilt, while he disappeared.

'It's funny,' she said, tone kind of harsh. 'It's as if I made this room for you. It was always you that loved roses, huh? Yet I never, never could've imagined you'd be here.'

I sat on the double bed, let my body flop backwards, arms spread above my head. I gazed at the chandelier, thought of the squat, felt a pang.

'You alright?' she said.

Tears were building behind my closed lids. I felt them slither out, run down my temples. My voice was a wisp. 'How long…?'

'Um—coming on three years.'

'Oh. I thought it was longer.'

'Why?'

'Just—I don't know.'

'Because of doing up the house?'

'I guess…'

'Yeah, well, I did it almost as soon as we were—we were…you know. There had been a flood, like I said. The roof was leaky. And the need just happened to coincide with—um—with my coming here—he was staying in one of the ranchitas, you see. Antonia was trying to get him to let her sort it out but he…so it seemed like a good idea for me to do it. They couldn't believe how much it fell into ruin in just a few months, like almost out of nowhere, they said. It was much more than the water damage by the time we came to do it. Are you hungry? Do you want to eat?'

I levered myself onto my elbows. 'Yup, I'm actually ravenous. I have an idea why that happens…'

'What?'

'The house.'

'The house?'

'Falling into ruin.'

'Oh. Things just rot when they're abandoned, don't they.'

'But so quickly. In just a few months. When it's stood perfectly all these years, see? It seems to me it started to fall apart type-thing, because it wasn't held in anyone's attention—like, it literally started to de-manifest because…' I forced enthusiasm into my voice. 'Wild, huh? It's what you can do with thoughts and that…when you don't focus on…yeah…'

'Yeah,' she said. 'I don't know what you're talking about. It just wasn't maintained. Me too, I'm hungry. I thought we were going to eat out. Come on.'

The realisation just coming, I screwed up one eye, said, 'I left my bike in town. With my stuff in the topbox. I totally forgot about it.'

'You came on a motorbike? After…? Are you insane?'

'Isn't that a superfluous question?'

Standing in the doorway, she gazed at me a long moment, a whole mix of stuff flitting over her face. 'This is fucked up. Crazy. All of this.'

'It is. But what's crazy? You're happy, right?'

'I don't know. Some of the time.' She sighed. 'But it's been eating me up. Him too…he never says, but I know it.'

'Of course…it's only human, isn't it?'

'Yeah, right, okay. Enough already…' She gave me a look, face all kind of pointy, so familiar.

I felt myself blush. I let a few moments pass. 'Look, I-I'm wondering…'

'What?'

'I don't know…but…'

'Go on, say it.'

I blew a heavy kind of a breath. 'I'm confused, see. I mean, doesn't—doesn't he know about the accident? It was right after we saw him at Newmarket. On our way back. *Because* we saw him, huh? He told you, right? You do know who my—you know who I was with?'

'Yes. I didn't until then. Obviously. No one did—did they.' She cast her eyes to her bitten-down fingernails, put one between her teeth, tore off a slither and chewed on it. I heard it snap. 'Nope…I didn't. I didn't tell him about the accident.'

'You didn't?'

'I know.'

'Cripes.'

'I know.'

'Fuck.'

'I know. I told you I hate myself. Not only did I get to be here, with him, taking your place, your happiness, knowing I would be hurting you, but…I'm a fucking liar to him too. He's going to hate me too, when he finds out. I mean, you were nearly killed—he would have wanted to see you. And his kid might have been hurt—and when he finds out he just pissed the hell off out of your life, he'll want you back. I deserve it.'

'What *did* you tell him?'

'I told him it was Dad who was hurt.'

'Shit.'

'I know.' We stared at each other in a weird kind of understanding. Then she said, 'I thought I was pregnant, you know. This morning showed me I'm not.'

'What?'

'Which means your boyfriend would have been my baby's brother. That's pretty messed up. I mean, if he was…I mean, like, if he was still your boyfriend. Which he isn't, is he?'

'Wow,' I said flatly.

314

'Otherwise, what? Your Swan Neck would have been a dad *and* an uncle at the same time, huh?'

'That's a bit rough. I didn't come here to get him back.'

'So why did you come then?'

I stared into her. 'I'm not actually sure. But are you intending to hurt me some more, basically ramming it at me you sleep with him? That you nearly had a kid with him? How low can you go?'

She pursed her lips, pushing them out, sucked them back in so they disappeared, face all saying: "see?" After a long moment, she said, 'Well, obviously it wasn't meant to be—I mean, the timing and everything—it's so uncanny—like my body knew you were here. And it *should* be why you came.'

'You sound like you want…'

'Does it matter? What I want?'

'I just had to see him, see. Like, to end it—I don't know—we never got to say goodbye, did we? And it's not as if I knew about you, huh?'

'Do you know how hard I've had to work never to be in the Press with him? I never go to the meets. He thinks I hate them.'

'Do mum and dad know?'

She flinched, a sort of smile, something desperate showing through. 'God, no.'

'They told me you live in Spain.'

'They think I live in Spain. I couldn't say here, could I? They were sure to tell you and what if you got to know, like through Uncle Gordie or the papers or something—what if you found out he was here?'

'Does our fucking uncle know?'

'About us? No! He thinks I'm in Spain too—but I expect he knows *he's* here these last few years. It's a big stable.'

'Well, he never would tell me where he was. I begged him enough, years ago. But isn't it weird I never saw him in the papers?'

She shrugged. 'Not really. He was out of this game for years.'

'I guess I never thought to look. How dumb of me.' I felt a tightness in my face, in my mouth. I couldn't control the sharp points of anger prickling inside my chest. 'So they all think you're in Spain. You built quite a—how could you live all these lies?'

315

'I don't know. Because I had to.'

'But how did *you* find him?'

'Oh.' She showed surprise. 'I didn't look for him. It was just one of those things.'

'But our uncle knew where he was, you say. And you were working with him and—'

'—it was chance. Uncle Gordie never talked about him—ever. I left his stables and went travelling, that's all. I went all over the place. For almost a couple of years. I was pretty lost. And when I came to Argentina, I needed some money so I came here, because I heard they had an English bunch and could get you working papers… and that's how we met again.'

'So you didn't seek him out?'

'Why would I? I thought I hated him, along with you.'

'But then, how could you—'

'—we just fell for each other. It just happened.'

'Ow.'

My sights scoured the repeat pattern of pink-and-creamy roses on the bedspread as if looking for a fault, a change in rhythm, so I might free myself somehow, from the prison of pain I was making. 'Talk about upstream,' I said, of myself.

'I'm sorry?' she said.

'Nothing.'

'You know, I really *am* sorry. I never meant for this to happen.'

My throat went thick, voice a splinter. 'I can't blame you. I did my own version, didn't I? With his estranged son, huh? who I knew about from way back then—if that wasn't fucked up, what was? If you want to look at it that way.'

'I've been wondering. How that happened?'

'It was horrible, I can tell you. I even tried to tell him quite a few times. But I never could. I was scared of losing him. And then I did. Of course. It had to happen with all that energy, that fear I was giving out. I even pictured it. You know, I love him. It's him I love now, see.'

'Yeah…'

I couldn't look at her. 'I'm getting this feeling he's in South America somewhere, Peru maybe. With the Shaman.'

She bluffed a breathy laugh. 'Mum told me about the biker jacket.'

'They're going to freak out. When this all comes out.'

'She told me about Dad too. What he said.' I met her eye in a sudden surprise and she sort of guffawed, all sort of anxious and like a little girl. 'He really said that, huh? "It's all love?"'

'He really did. And he's right.' I took a breath, let it out slowly. 'I'll be honest. I'm realising I did kind of come to see if I still had feelings for…for him. Some buried part of me thought the whole thing might be bringing me back to him. At last.'

'And you do, don't you? You're going to want him back?'

'I don't think so. But I'm still a bit processing it, you get me?'

She gave me a look, sharp, said, 'Yeh.'

I sighed. 'I did feel this would be too much.'

Her face went defiant. 'Well it isn't. Come on, really, let's eat.' She took the few paces toward me, stretched out her hand and yanked me up when I accepted. 'This is all a massive nightmare, isn't it?' She tugged a breath, projected it out. 'But it's a relief, somehow. All a bit phew. I'd rather this than the other. I never thought I'd think that. Even though I'm going to lose everything.'

'I know what you mean. Relief is a powerful…yeh…'

After some moments, she said, 'Yup. I can't believe I'm saying this either, but—oh I don't know—nothing. Or something. I don't know.' She laughed, all girlish again. 'Maybe you were right, what you said to me at the hospital—that things will be okay. That's what I want. Oh god, though, what a nightmare, huh?'

※

It was bizarre to wake in that rose-splashed bedroom and remember where I was, the situation sucking into me with such terrific speed I just had to surrender, let the wheels and weight rush over me, make welcome the fast tears my body made. I figured the reaction as an old loop, an outmoded habit reignited by his proximity, and I just let the feelings be there, in an unattached yet supportive sort of a way, have expression through me if they wanted to. I tuned into the pure Awareness I knew myself to be, consciously witnessing the whole thing. Yet still, I felt a powerful energy; I felt I wanted him.

No, I said to myself, whipping back the covers, swivelling as I sat up. I stretched, all attending to the glory of my physical form. Although totally ordinary, it still felt extraordinary to be in a body. I watched my hands splay into the air with a genuine kind of wonder, almost as if they weren't mine and didn't have any meaning even, other than the very essence of Being; it was like glimpsing through bigger eyes, a reminder of the temporary nature of physical life.

In the adjoining bathroom I brushed my teeth with the brand-new brush my sister had given me, relishing the tingle of my gums, then took a long draft of water, which I'd been told came from a deep bore-well. It tasted kind of salty. Everything felt idyllic. Again, I couldn't help feeling maybe I really did want this life, here in this house, with him…but I reminded myself I didn't. There followed an odd kind of gladness for the unimaginable chain of events which had led me here, all of it making up the life I was now, in this very moment—which would take me into the next moment and the next and the next. Into the best kind of a life I didn't know yet. Coming out of all the desire I had lived maybe; for love and for Love; from the act of Life all flowing through me, all of it beyond my control.

I slipped into my little skirt and men's ribbed army vest, padded down the shadowy hallway into the kitchen. Everything was quiet, just my own sounds accompanying me—the stickiness of my feet licking on and off the tiles, the whisper of my skirt. The clock on the wall said it was some time before five. I found my trainers by the back door, twisted my feet straight into them without undoing the laces.

Taking an apple, I let myself out, the soft warmth of the sun reaching for my bare shoulders, thrusting itself into my hair as I wandered down the pathway I knew led to the stables via a sun-bleached door in the boundary wall. The apple was sweet with a tang in it and very crispy, a lot of juice splashing into my mouth. I made childlike noises, relishing it, only realising I made them as they spilled into the air as sort of tiny roars. I made myself chuckle and it was nice.

I mooched through the woods, past the ranchitas and the flash office building, came out into the yard. No one was about yet, so I took myself into the stables, went from stall to stall all acquainting myself with the horses. I sipped on water I got from a cooler. It must have been close to an hour, at which point I was way near the back, before I heard someone at the entrance.

I waved, headed toward her. 'Hey. Speak English?'

She was a teenager, didn't look like me, but in a funny way reminded me of me, way back when. I realised it was the way she walked with an easy kind of knowing. 'Ola. You are new?'

'Sort of. I'm family of…boss trainer man.'

'Boss trainer man?'

I indicated the direction of the estancia. 'I'm staying at the big house. Listen, I'm really wanting to go for a ride. I didn't want to wake them. You think—'

As a movement came behind her, his voice smacked out '—let's get you set up then, shall we? It's a dream to get you up on one of these lads—actually, no—I've got a rocking filly I'm thinking for you. She's set to be a winner—jus-just like you, for sure. Pasala.' He came toward us and the girl muttered a question in Spanish. I checked to feel if there was any energy between them, relieved there was nothing. He answered her, and she went on up into the stables. 'Did-did you see her? Pasala?'

I nodded. 'I'm loving her vibe.'

He stood just gazing at me quite a bit too long, and when his voice came it was ruined as hell. Which was some kind of a twisted heaven. 'It's a new day, Angel Fa—um—did—did you sleep okay? How're you doing?'

I nodded. 'I'm good. You?'

'I-I'm still pretty fucking winded, to be sure—but I'm doing my best to view this as—*Christ*, I don't know, *is* it good thing? We're all dealing with it like adults, it would seem. On the surface. But I feel like a royal mess-up inside.'

'Yeah…'

'It was fucking mind-blowing to sit at a table with the both of you—

319

to be okay with it. Sort of okay. Not really okay. Not okay at all, to be honest. It wasn't—it wasn't eas—it was *hell*.' He was shaking his head, all kind of trembling. 'I can see how badly she feels, even though she's thinking she's hiding it. And good to talk—but I mea—Angel Fa—*fuck*—' a harsh dry sob came splintering through him, his fingers and thumb pressing into his temples, all obscuring his screwed-up eyes '—I don't know what the fuck I'm doi—to be honest, I just don't—I mean, what's going *on* here?—' his breath was ragged '—you—my Ang—it's you—*you* are my—' his fingers fell away, showing me his wet eyes '—I mean, what the—*who* the fuck have I been having a relationship with these few years? Really?'

Neck all electric, my own fingers flitted up like some delicate dusty bird, all trying to still him. 'Don't…'

He just grabbed at my hand, thrust it up against his mouth, pulling me almost into him, breath crackerling hot into my palm. 'Seeing you…feeling you…'

I went staggering backwards, fingers tearing away, 'Don't,' mashed them into my own lips so I couldn't make words. But tasting him.

He stood solid, let a vast pause go by, just staring all the way into me so I couldn't move—finally stating with a definite certainty: 'I felt it too.'

'What?' My voice was foggy through my fingers. 'Felt…?'

'When you were holding her—outside the bar—we were totally—I know what you felt.'

'You what…? I don't…?'

'I-I don't quite know how to verse it—but it felt like—crazy—like—I don't know, the Big Bang or something. Yes. Love in its fucking highest.'

'Oh…'

'And I for sure got the feeling all this was set in motion from the Big Bang itself—and we were always supposed to be here now. Just like this. You get me?'

His eyes wouldn't let me go, the softest kind of a smile entering his face, and the truth of his words stung me, all like the nettle-written words on my legs of long ago were just swelling right up again.

'Oh…'

'The stream,' he said. 'I told you, it never…'

'…stops,' I found myself saying, in a fractured-up whisper.

'You get me?'

I nodded—shook my head, muttered, 'No,' pressing my fingers harder into my lips.

'It's you I want, Angel Face. It always has been. You.'

'It's too late.'

'We could make it work.'

'It's changed. I don't need you anymore—do you see? For sure, when I first saw your boy…yeah, you know, he was kind of you to me. And I went to him, somehow going to you—'

'—yes—'

'—but it changed. Honestly and deeply, right into the heart and soul of me. I loved him. More than you, in the end. It was him I knew. And him I loved. Still love.'

'But I feel you—'

'—you're feeling the past. That's all. The past.'

Vehement-as, but still with the smile, he shook his head. 'You open me up all the way down. I know you feel it too. Just this: the way I can talk to you, be honest with you. The way I feel Life with you.'

'That was then.'

'It's now—I know you feel it, whatever you say. The resonance between us is clear as a bell—I feel I almost know your thoughts. Listen to me, I mean it, I want to do the journey with you. With you, I am another animal. I am an honest man.' I thought I was going to speak, but I just couldn't say anything, all like my throat had glue in it. 'I want to be with you. I love you.'

Our gaze stayed all tied up, the both of us dropping silent tears like we were looking in a mirror at ourselves. How many times I had done this: looked in a mirror and seen him? His pupils ached and gaped, and I felt I might fall in, the pale-blue pencil-line around the black vortex making a beautiful terrible song within me. He moved, was for sure going to take a hold of me. And I almost let him, but his scent overwhelmed me and I pulled away.

'No,' I croaked. 'This *isn't* honest. You've got to be kidding.'

'It's over with—' he told me '—with—it's over—you have to know that much at least. I've been trying to tell you. She—'

'—oh god…'

'She decided—and we've agreed—*she* wants it—and she wants me to tell you. She said she knows we should be together.'

'And what about your boy, huh? You should be loving him over me.'

He nodded, crumpled up his eyes, a kind of sharp breath issuing from him as his un-swan neck jolted several times. His blues came back to meet mine, pupils maybe smaller than I'd ever seen them, wet still coming out of his agonised expression. 'Maybe my boy was part of this bringing us back. However fucked up that sounds. Maybe he too will know this. I don't have the answers, but I'm willing to do the journey, like I said. With him too, somehow. I hope. If he'll let me.' He held my gaze, eyes going clear. 'This is where we get to choose; the stream of life has brought us here, to this moment, this choice—it can't be denied. Listen to me: I'll be here. Angel Face. And I'll be waiting.' He made a single sharp nod, cleared his throat. 'Okay. Come. I'll get you some gear.'

I stumbled out after him into the rapidly heating day, trailed him toward the concrete building. He felt to be solid, all like he had a hold of himself, a blunt sort of confidence emanating from him in the way I had always loved. I saw how the sun in the fuzz of his arm-hair made a golden halo, all extra-glowing within the silvery tone of his aura. And I realised I had *always* seen his aura.

He led me into a side room, where there were rails of training clothes, and somehow, in all the blur, I picked out stuff my size. He told me he'd wait in the kitchen, let me get changed. He got quite formal, asked, Did I want anything to eat before I got to it? No, I told him. And then he pointed me to the tack room, told me he'd let me be.

'Just one thing,' he said, as he turned to leave. 'I'm sorry, but I really need to know—what's going on there, with my boy? Where is he?' All I could do was stare at him in a dumbfounded kind of a way. 'Has he left you?'

There came from within me an unlikely steely manner. 'I've lost him, yes. I don't know where he is. But please, I really need to get up on Pasala, ride out on my own for a bit. *Now*. No more talk. I need…'

'…space.'

'Yes. Exactly. Just be with myself for a bit. And this horse. And the land.'

'Sure, sure. I know. I know.'

'And *then* I'm going to go.'

'Go?'

'I'll need a ride to pick up my bike from town.'

'Like, literally, leave?'

'Yes.'

'Where?'

'I don't know.' I held his eye. 'There's nowhere to go, see. And nothing to do. It's all here already. And that's where I'm at—in the best way.'

His smile came through his nose. 'You really are…' he said, all shaking his head. And I knew he knew exactly what I was talking about. 'I knew from the first moment I saw you.' After a long kind of a breath, he let go my eyes, nodded some more, lips pulling in. 'Okay.' And he walked away, off through the trees, with that walk of his I didn't want to know about.

All kind of trembly, as if I were a tiny be-tailed seed clinging onto a dandelion clock under heat of some someone's wishing breath, I fitted Pasala with a bridle and the crimson blanket and treeless training saddle I had picked out for us, hooked up the girth, all the time nattering away to her, trying to be gentle, my heart and voice pinging like some once-was knicker elastic under some someone's thumb. It was the filly that guided me. She took us out of the stables complex, stopping herself among the silver birches, clearly indicating I hike myself up onto her, which I duly did, keeping the stirrups long. As she rode me out of the yard her metal shoes scraped and clattered, and I got to feel the first hints of her rhythm beneath me, the twang of excitement, her pure energy all surging up from her muscles and moving into mine. My chest made a strangled sigh in some crazy kind of a relief.

This body falling into tempo with her gait, I found myself in a riding-

323

trot as we struck along the track, my legs working me up and down all on their own volition. We reached a white gate leading into free pasture, and she stopped again, took us through it as I opened and closed it still upon her back. Her energy escalated without my direction and she broke into a canter, then opened into a full-blown gallop, her dappled-grey flanks undulating, glistening, her breath self-regulated with a kind of rare effortlessness, and I understood why he had chosen her for me, felt an expansive appreciation for his innate knowledge of me—felt the love we shared—and there came a strange joy in the realisation I had spoken the truth: I didn't *need* him. I was free.

Throwing my attention into the moment, I found myself exalting at the ease with which myself and the horse blended, the way her energy spiralled up and into mine, so we felt to become one. I would have believed she had been sired by Angel's Neck if Antonia hadn't told me she had been trying to send a mare to him for years. And then my mind did this thing all on its own, without my trying: went quiet-as, the visceral experience of our physical reality supported by the deepest state of grace beneath the thunder of the horse's hooves.

Approaching a bank of trees, we slowed all the way to a walk, and the filly guided us to a small wooden bridge, took us across it. I found myself in one of those dancing fields of fern-like grasses, all silvery-gold, in which was strewn masses of wildflowers like shining jewels. There was all kinds of birdsong and a breeze softening the heat. The buzz of cicadas vibrating into my physical body. As we moved slowly through the wildness, I had an intense feeling of being inside of it, like I was every particle of landscape as well as myself, felt myself in the undulating grasses, in the reaching tree branches, in a bird flying in the sky I was, and the sense of joy in it all, embodied in me, was so sweet it almost hurt; and then I got to feel it was all inside of me, simply radiating out of me and back into me in a never-ending circle. I had a clear kind of knowing that everything was generating from me; that I was the centre of my world and the Universe; the world lived through me and because of me. Through you; because of you. It existed because I existed. I knew myself as in love with everything around me, just as everything around me was in love with me. My life was opening and opening, never done, my heart about bursting with the exquisite perfection of the dance, of the allowing and resisting and allowing again, an evolving interplay of contrast, light and shadow, of drama and ease and asking for love through it all, of receiving that love, of all potential, yes, of *realising* my natural state of relief and peace and wellbeing. Now. Only now. The ever expansion of a life (and more Life). All acting through me. No separation. I am flowing and I am flowing and I am flowing... just where?... *oh wow!* I saw I really wasn't in control; I saw I never had been...and I just let it all go. I said, Life, show me the way I have created...and I will f-l-o-w...

.

Printed in Great Britain
by Amazon

86456081R00192